PENGUIN BOOKS

The Watcher

Charles Maclean was born in 1946 and educated at Eton and Oxford. In the mid-seventies he researched and wrote *The Wolf Children*, a true story of two girls found living with wolves in the jungles of Bengal. It was published to wide acclaim in 1977. A founder of *The Ecologist* magazine, he has written a number of books on the landscape and culture of Scotland, including *Island on the Edge of the World* (1972), winner of the Scottish Arts Council Award, *Scottish Country* (1992) and *Romantic Scotland* (2000). His fiction includes *The Watcher* (1982), *The Silence* (1996) and *Home Before Dark* (2009). Married with four children, he lives in Argyll.

The Watcher

CHARLES MACLEAN

PENGUIN BOOKS

PENGUIN BOOKS

Published by the Penguin Group
Penguin Books Ltd, 80 Strand, London WC2R 0RL, England
Penguin Group (USA), Inc., 375 Hudson Street, New York, New York 10014, USA
Penguin Group (Canada), 90 Eglinton Avenue East, Suite 700, Toronto, Ontario,
Canada M4P 2Y3 (a division of Pearson Penguin Canada Inc.)
Penguin Ireland, 25 St Stephen's Green, Dublin 2, Ireland (a division of Penguin Books Ltd)
Penguin Group (Australia), 250 Camberwell Road, Camberwell, Victoria 3124, Australia
(a division of Pearson Australia Group Pty Ltd)
Penguin Books India Pvt Ltd, 11 Community Centre, Panchsheel Park,
New Delhi – 110 017, India
Penguin Group (NZ), 67 Apollo Drive, Rosedale, Auckland 0632, New Zealand
(a division of Pearson New Zealand Ltd)
Penguin Books (South Africa) (Pty) Ltd, 24 Sturdee Avenue, Rosebank,
Johannesburg 2196, South Africa

Penguin Books Ltd, Registered Offices: 80 Strand, London WC2R 0RL, England

www.penguin.com

First published in the USA by Simon & Schuster 1982
First published in Great Britain by Allen Lane 1983
Published in Penguin Books 1984
Reissued in this edition 2012

1

Copyright © Charles Maclean, 1982

The moral right of the author has been asserted

Printed in Great Britain by Clays Ltd, St Ives plc

A CIP catalogue record for this book is available from the British Library

ISBN: 978-0-241-95622-9

www.greenpenguin.co.uk

MIX
Paper from
responsible sources
FSC
www.fsc.org   FSC™ C018179

Penguin Books is committed to a sustainable
future for our business, our readers and our
planet. This book is made from paper certified
by the Forest Stewardship Council.

For Jamie

BOOK ONE

THE
SLEEP OF
REASON

ONE

'There was no warning of any kind. No discernible pattern of events leading up to the incident. No catalyst or precedent. No explanation to be had from delving into the subject's history. It was an isolated phenomenon – unaccountable, not to do with anything else.'

I wrote this down for Somerville's benefit four or five days after it happened. Just to put a stop to all those questions.

I wanted to prove to him that I could be objective about things too.

When Somerville had read the note through, he said, 'If one can only discover *where* to look, there is an explanation for everything, Mr Gregory.' Of course, he was bound to say something of the sort: it was what he was getting paid for.

I've had to revise everything – change my job, my name, my life – to accommodate what I now know. At the time, I knew nothing. There really was no warning.

Certainly a few details stand out in relief, but even with the advantage of hindsight I can't pretend that they add up to much. Everything that happened after I left my office that Friday afternoon was unremarkable. It was the end of another busy week, and I was looking forward to spending a couple of days at home with Anna and the dogs.

Saturday was Anna's birthday and I had a surprise for her.

Most Fridays I caught the 4.48 to Bedford. This meant leaving the office half an hour early – the prerogative of our senior executives, but I was prepared to take the risk of stepping on their toes. Anything to avoid the weekend crush on the 5.28 and having to sit on an upturned briefcase all the way.

Leaving early for the weekend did a lot for my prestige around the office. It was an old trick – assuming privilege rather than trying to earn it, and it rarely failed.

Also, I was good at my job.

On that Friday I almost missed my train. I was held up at the office and arrived at Grand Central with less than a minute to spare. Cutting it too fine; it wouldn't have been the first time . . .

I fought my way across the concourse, with my ticket between my teeth, an enormous package (the surprise) under one arm, two large packages under the other, my briefcase, a bottle of Veuve Cliquot, a shopping bag full of groceries and, of course, the statutory bunch of roses. I'd never felt more conspicuous – I've always disliked carrying things.

I was already resigned to the misery of the 5.28 when I noticed a fellow commuter scything his way through the crowd. He saw me and pointed frantically toward platform 5.

We only just made it.

I stood for a moment in the corridor trying to catch my breath. My friend looked beat. Pink-faced and gone to fat under his gray pinstripe, he was wheezing badly. He pushed his fingers through a hank of sandy hair that had fallen over his face.

'Boy, that was a close call!' he got out at last.

Although we'd sat opposite each other often enough, we'd never actually spoken before. Sensing that now we would feel uneasily obliged to make conversation for the rest of our working lives, I thanked him and started to move away.

'Take it easy,' he said. He was sweating like a pig.

Maybe it was the redness of his face or maybe it was the way the light struck him as the train pulled out of the station, but for an instant I got the impression that the beads of perspiration standing out on his forehead and the rivulet running down by his left ear over a large, soft jowl had turned to blood.

I quickly found a seat in the adjoining car.

The rest of the journey passed uneventfully. I did a little work so that I wouldn't have it hanging over me on the weekend. I wanted everything to be just right for Anna's birthday – down to the last detail.

I spent some time trying to decide in what order I wanted her to look at her presents. We'd open the champagne – just before she came to the surprise.

My only concern was that she might not appreciate it as fully as I hoped.

You see, I really loved my wife. Unlike almost every couple we knew, Anna and I still had something to talk about. We still enjoyed each other – after six years of marriage.

We'd never been happier.

Anna and the boys were waiting for me at the station. The sun in her eyes, she was squinting up at the windows of the slowing train. I have the memory of her face as she saw me step onto the platform. Pushing forward like an eager child, breathless with excitement, she threw her arms around my neck and gave me a long, tender kiss.

'My God,' I said, 'what did I do to deserve *this?*'

Claus and Caesar immediately started leaping all over us, barking their heads off. I tried to calm them while Anna made a silly, charming fuss about wanting to look at her presents there and then. In the confusion, the train nearly went off with my briefcase. I accused her of being foolish and irresponsible. She laughed and stuck out her tongue.

We piled everything into the back seat of the station wagon, the dogs climbed into their gated compartment, and Anna at the wheel, we set off for home, stopping to buy cigarettes in Bedford Village. We reached the house at exactly 6.30: I remember looking at my watch – partly out of habit, but also to see if I had time to take the dogs out for a decent walk before dinner. It was the last weekend in September and the evenings were drawing in.

After changing my shoes for a pair of rubber boots, I released the boys from the back of the car. They were overexcited at the prospect of a walk, racing around in circles, yapping playfully at my ankles.

Anna stood watching us. Without a word she turned away toward the house. I called her and she glanced back, but with resentment.

She was wearing a big Aran sweater over faded blue jeans, and her long blond hair, the color of white sand, caught the evening light. I went up to her and whispered in her ear how beautiful she looked, slipping a hand under her sweater. She snaked her arms around my waist, tugging at my shirt with knee-weakening urgency.

We pulled away laughing. I tried to persuade her to come on the walk; she insisted she had things to do in the kitchen. I set off with Claus and Caesar toward the open fields behind the house.

Soon we reached the mound at the end of the road that rises sharply at one point to an outcrop of stones overgrown with bushes and bracken. You can get quite a reasonable view of the surrounding countryside from there.

I closed my eyes and, stretching out my arms like a celebrant, took several deep breaths. If that didn't blow the junk out of my lungs, at least it was preferable to jogging around Central Park.

When we first got the boys, Anna had insisted we should live in the country as soon as we could afford to move. She felt it was cruel to keep large dogs – they were long-haired golden retrievers – in the city. I have to admit taking my time to come around to the idea. Living in New York, after all, had its advantages.

Looking back at our house, though, I felt a certain sense of achievement. It wasn't particularly large or handsome, and the barn was still awaiting the conversion we'd been talking about for the last three years. Even in the flattering September light it all looked a bit run-down. But it was ours.

The dogs had grown bored of hanging around. They ran ahead, out of control as usual.

Claus, or the 'senior partner', as we called him, had a few years' start on Caesar – in fact, they were father and son. At three Caesar was still a puppy or, at any rate, chose to behave like one. He was the troublemaker – always getting into scrapes, much to Claus's disapproval, though the senior partner usually ended up joining in, if only to assert his authority. Claus had a rather heavy, Germanic character. I often used to tease Anna about his pedigree, joking that the blood of the Hapsburgs coursed through his veins, when in fact he was from a kennel – a perfectly good kennel – outside Hackensack.

We were both devoted to the dogs. If there was a tendency to let them dominate our lives, I did my best to resist it – not always successfully. As a result, I took a sterner line with them than I might otherwise have done – a complete waste of time, of course, since both animals were thoroughly spoiled and refused to take me seriously.

On the way home, about half a mile from the house, Caesar picked up the scent of a rabbit. He went zigzagging off, tail in the air, nose skimming the ground, leaving Claus to bring up the rear. The sight of the senior partner going into his official, stiff-legged lope made me smile, as it always did, but after that I lost interest. In fact, I'd almost forgotten about the dogs when an agonized squeal went up from the woods, followed by loud barking.

At first I thought one of the boys had actually caught a rabbit. I plunged into the undergrowth, only to find Caesar rolling about just inside the fence, trying to extricate himself from a tangle of thorn. Claus, meanwhile, stood over his progeny, expressing his contempt for the younger dog's antics by stolidly barking at him.

The last thing I wanted was to upset Anna, and coming home with a hurt dog would have done it. I freed Caesar from the patch of thorn and examined him as well as I could in the light that was left. I was able to establish that he hadn't cut himself. He tried limping about for a while on three legs, to gain sympathy. When I saw that he was really all right, I gave both dogs a severe dressing down. They followed me home, I was pleased to note, with their tails dipped.

As I sat on the porch taking off my boots, they approached sheepishly and began licking my hands. This was so unlike them that I laughed out loud, and their tails started wagging furiously.

TWO

'But darling,' she protested, 'it was you who taught me how to cook.'

'I just paid for the lessons.'

'You wanted me to learn.'

'So, I'm only saying how good you are.'

'And to think I hardly knew how to boil an egg!' She gave me the benefit of her most ingenuous smile.

We were lying together on the sofa watching TV, stupefied by food and wine. I accused Anna, only half-jokingly, of trying to sabotage my waistline so as to spoil my chances with other women.

'I like other women to be attracted to you,' she said.

'Oh, you do? And am I supposed to want other men drooling over you?'

'Yes,' she hissed, digging her elbow into my back; 'unless you'd prefer me to get fat?'

'Don't!'

'Men are such hypocrites!' Anna laughed.

'I forgot to tell you, Caesar had a little accident out walking.'

She sat up, wide-eyed, and looked at me. I tried to backpedal, but it was too late. Nothing would satisfy her now short of the whole story. Afterward she insisted on giving the animal a thorough inspection so she could see for herself that he had come to no harm. Only then did she begin to relax.

I had never intended telling her. The incident was so trivial. But neither of us was capable of keeping anything from the other for very long.

About half past eleven I sent Anna up to bed. I needed the freedom of the living room to wrap her presents. We weren't going to celebrate until the following evening, but I had to get things organized well beforehand. You see, I believed the world revolved around the principle of efficiency, and even at home, much to Anna's amusement, I was a great one for order. I was also notoriously bad at wrapping presents.

After a long search for scissors and Scotch Tape – they were naturally not where they were supposed to be – I finally got all the paraphernalia together and set up a kind of operations center on the rug in front of the fire. Then I poured myself a stiff drink, before starting to bring the stuff in from the car. On my second trip, coming out of the garage with an armful of packages, I dropped the car keys somewhere in the driveway.

It was pitch dark. Groping around in the gravel, I realized I would probably have to go inside and get a flashlight. Just then Anna came into the upstairs bathroom through the connecting door to our bedroom and turned on the light. It was a good thing that she'd forgotten to draw the curtains: the light from the window fell directly on the driveway, and I found the keys right away. As I straightened up, preparing to go back in, Anna appeared in front of the window and, unaware that she was being observed, began to take her clothes off.

My first thought was practical: to have frosted glass put in all the bathrooms. I also intended to warn Anna against performing free striptease for any lucky trespassers – myself included. Although the house was set back from the road and well screened by trees, it was only a couple of miles from the village and the town boys often walked past it on a Saturday night. A few months before, we'd had an incident of sexual assault in Bedford which had never been cleared up. There was no sense in asking for trouble.

I have to admit here to something rather unsavory. As I watched Anna getting undressed, although I'd seen her naked a thousand times and in every possible circumstance (except this one), I began to feel the kind of desire that might be regarded as aberrant. Perhaps because she had no idea that anyone could see her, she was acting for once completely without inhibitions; and all her most intimate gestures, the small, unconscious ways of the body that I knew and loved better than any other, seemed unfamiliar. The person in our upstairs bathroom might have been a stranger.

I was an alien pair of eyes. She was unknown, forbidden territory, inviting exploration.

Like some Peeping Tom scarcely able to believe his luck, I concentrated my whole gaze on that bathroom window, determined to miss nothing. Anna matter-of-factly removed her bra. Then she drew the curtains. I stood there a minute or two longer, expecting I don't know what.

I began to work on the fantasy that the girl up in the bathroom really was a stranger. I started back toward the house, treading carefully to avoid crunching the gravel. By the porch I stopped to light a cigarette.

It took me less time than I had thought to wrap her presents. Using expensive gold wrapping paper from Bendel's, I stuck everything down with Scotch Tape and purely as decoration tied a black velvet ribbon around each gift. Then I cleared the table behind the sofa and laid out all the presents around a cut-glass vase, filled with the dozen red roses I'd bought in the city. I'd put the champagne to cool in the refrigerator along with a four-ounce jar of caviar from Poll's, carefully hidden behind the lettuce at the back of the salad drawer. Everything was set now. When Anna came down in the morning she would see this munificent display – it looked like Christmas in September – but she would not be allowed to touch a thing until half an hour before dinner. The suspense was meant to kill her.

The only present I did not wrap was the surprise. I left the box in its original brown paper and simply shoved it under the table. It was four by two and a half and nearly a foot deep: too big to cover in gold – and anyway, I wanted it to look different.

I fixed myself a weak Scotch-and-water and sat down, trying to think up something to write on the birthday card. It was one of those elaborate Victorian efforts, with a picture of two haughty-looking Irish setters – the closest I could find to golden retrievers – being petted by a little girl in lace and ribbons. I thought Anna would be amused by the poem inside, which began: 'I love my dogs, oh, how dearly!'

I wanted to add a witty postcript, but my imagination failed me. I decided to sleep on it.

Last thing, I took the boys out and walked them around the

garden at the back of the house. The light was still on in our bed-room. I looked at my watch. Anna was an hour into her twenty-ninth year. Picturing her half-asleep, propped against the pillows with her white-blond hair brushed out over her shoulders, waiting for me to come up, I suddenly felt ashamed of myself. The joke I had intended playing on her seemed unkind – and in the worst taste.

After locking up and turning out the downstairs lights, I said good night to Caesar and Claus through the wooden gate at the bottom of the stairs, which confined them to the ground floor. I went up to Anna. She gave me a sleepy smile as I bent down to kiss her Happy Birthday. I undressed quickly and slipped between the sheets. She looked so demure and innocent. After a couple of false starts she reached over and, putting her arms around my neck, whispered something in my ear.

I asked her to repeat it, but she just laughed.

'Did you manage to get everything done?'

'But what was it you said before?'

Again she answered the question with one of her own. 'Darling, don't you think we ought to get a blind or something for the bath-room window?'

'A blind? You mean you knew I was out there the whole time?'

'Of course,' she said. 'Why do you think I left the curtains open?'

'You little whore! I don't believe it ... Then why did you go and close them?'

'Because I wanted you up here, you idiot.'

I slid my hands around her neck. 'You nearly got more than you bargained for.'

'Oh, really?'

'I was going to play a nasty little trick on you.' Very gently I pressed my thumbs into the softest part of her throat.

'Imagine the whole house suddenly plunged into darkness,' I began in a sepulchral voice that was meant to be an imitation of Vincent Price. 'You hear strange noises from one of the down-stairs rooms. Nothing to worry about. It's only your husband look-ing for the fuse box. You call his name.

'At the sound of your voice the noises stop. A deathly silence envelops the house. Where are the dogs? You call them. Nothing.

The cold hand of fear clutches at your heart. It begins to dawn on you that something has happened, something not at all nice.

'That's when you hear the footsteps on the stairs . . .'

'But I'd have known it was you all along,' Anna interrupted.

'In the dark? I'd have torn the bedclothes back, ripped your –'

'Darling' – she looked up at me – 'why don't you just show me what you were going to do?'

THREE

It was raining when I came down at a quarter of seven to let the dogs out. I'd awakened from force of habit with a nagging sense of obligation, a feeling that I had something important to do. I even put on a suit. Then I remembered it was Saturday and I didn't have a train to catch.

I opened the back door and Claus and Caesar ran out, oblivious of the rain. It was an odd, murky sort of morning. I hardly recognized the view from my own doorstep. The modest swell of Guard Hill Road seemed like an enormous wave rising above the dark screen of trees at the end of the garden, threatening to engulf the house. The air was misty and cold, and everything smelled of mildew.

I began to prepare Anna's breakfast. Even the breakfast tray felt damp and sticky. I made tea, covered the pot and let it stand while I fixed myself a cup of instant coffee.

At five after seven I took Anna up her breakfast.

Careful not to disturb her, I put the tray down on the bedside table and left a single rose beside it, which I'd taken from the vase in the living room. She was sleeping soundly, her face buried in the crook of an arm. Asleep she looked like a child – trusting. Very gently I closed the bedroom door and locked it from the outside. Then, almost forgetting, I went into the bathroom and bolted the door on the inside. Then I went out the other door and back downstairs.

The smell of mildew had found its way into the kitchen. Although I'd shut the back door after letting the dogs out, the room felt colder than before and peculiarly damp. I picked up the cup of Nescafé that I'd left sitting on the side of the stove, took a sip and nearly spat it out, the coffee was so cold.

Looking around, I saw that the walls, the floor, the ceiling and all the surfaces in the kitchen were covered with a fine film of moisture. I ran my fingers along the top of the Welsh dresser – soaking wet! I checked the ceiling for leaks, but there was nothing to suggest the water was coming from any particular place. It was everywhere, as if the whole room had broken out in a clammy sweat.

It was time to feed the dogs.

I took two cans of Alpo from the cupboard under the sink. From the shelf over the stove I took the twin blue plastic bowls marked CAESAR and CLAUS, which Anna had given the boys for Christmas last year. Opening the cans at both ends with the wall opener, I gave them a little shake; the cylinders of dog food flopped out solidly into the bowls. I mushed them up a little, adding a handful of dog biscuits and a cup of water to each bowl, till I had the right consistency. I put the bowls down a foot apart on the rubber mat in front of the stove. Then I washed my hands under the tap. The water ran icy cold, but now I hardly noticed.

My every movement was swift and precise; I made sure to make as little noise as possible. I knelt down behind the sofa in the living room and pulled out the surprise from under the table without disturbing the flower arrangement or any of the presents. The package weighed next to nothing, but instead of carrying it, I dragged it along the carpet, then across the hall and into the kitchen, where I parked it in the middle of the floor. I took a knife from the drawer in the kitchen table and removed the string and brown paper.

There it stood: a plain cardboard box, stark white against the terra-cotta tiles. I opened it and pushed the lid back.

The box was empty.

Until that moment I think I had genuinely believed the box contained a present for Anna. And yet – I can't explain it – I was not in the least surprised to find it empty. I couldn't recall what it was that should have been inside; or where I'd gotten it, or when. All I knew for sure was that it should have contained *something* and it didn't.

I can only repeat and go on repeating that all I had consciously planned was the joyful celebration of my wife's birthday.

Somehow I understood that I had to put a lining in the box, though it wasn't clear yet to what purpose. I found some bin liners and laid them in it lengthwise and overlapping each other until the bottom was well covered in thin layers of black plastic. After a minute or two I saw that tiny drops of moisture were beginning to collect on the inside; this gave me a sense of urgency, as if I knew the die was finally cast.

Pulling on my boots and a pair of yellow rubber household gloves, I unhooked Anna's apron from the back of the door – one of those striped butcher's aprons with a humorous 'THE BOSS' motif across the front – and slipped it over my suit. Then I started going through the cutlery drawers.

The electric carving knife still had the price tag on it. It was one of the few laborsaving gadgets we never used. I switched it on to test the batteries. It came buzzing to life in my hand. I tried the fine cutting edge on a piece of Anna's homemade bread. It was quick and efficient. It would serve better than any ordinary blade. I turned it off and left it lying on the table with the handle pointing toward the stove.

Not wanting to wake Anna, instead of the usual yell I gave a soft, low-pitched whistle to call the dogs in from the garden. They came almost at once, trotting around the corner of the barn with their ears pricked up and their pretty, plumelike tails waving from side to side. Seeing me standing just inside the back door, they broke into a run. As always, when it was feeding time, the senior partner led the way, with Caesar chivying at his side, respecting – if somewhat grudgingly – his father's right to be first. Their long golden coats were dark with the rain. Before I would let them in I gave them a moment to shake themselves. Then I opened the door wide and they pushed past me into the kitchen. The smell of mildew rose in my nostrils – stronger than before.

They didn't even bother to inspect the unfamiliar white box in the middle of the floor; they were so hungry, they made straight for their bowls. Heads down, tails wagging, wholly concentrated on their food, they paid no attention to me whatsoever. Their indifference suited my purpose. I picked up the carving knife and, holding it behind my back, switched on the blade.

It was Claus who cocked an ear at the unexpected sound. He looked up briefly, but my presence close behind him must have been reassuring. He shook himself and went right back to his food. I leaned forward and found myself stroking his curly wet coat as he ate. The knife I kept out of sight. Then, moving my left hand up onto his neck, I took a firm grip of a fold of loose skin and pulled it tight. Still he kept on eating. Until the moment the electric carver came up under his throat, he kept on eating.

At the first touch of the blade I felt a tremendous jolt pass through his body. But after that he didn't struggle – at least, not as much as I'd expected him to. He just stood there while I sawed the knife up through his neck, almost to the vertebrae. The blood spurted and came gushing down his chin into the bowl. Undigested food fell out of the wound in his throat; his breath rasped through the severed windpipe. He made one lunge; he must have thought he could still run; but I held him between my knees, feeling the strength ebb from him. I waited until his eyes glazed over and his body sagged against my legs; then I pulled him across to the white cardboard box and heaved him into it.

The senior partner lay there on a bed of plastic bin liners, limbs still twitching and jerking. He looked as if he were enjoying a rabbiting dream. Except that there was not a whimper out of him, only the harsh rattle of air escaping from the hole in his throat. But then he tried to sit up, his head lolling at an impossible angle. He almost got clear of the box ...

He fell back at last in a welter of blood and lay still.

All this time I'd been keeping a close watch on Caesar, who'd finished eating soon after I cut Claus's throat. His only reaction so far had been to sniff cautiously at the blood in his father's bowl. I called him to me, the knife once more hidden behind my back. He cowered, his tail between his legs, behaving as he did when he'd done something wrong and knew he was about to be punished. I moved toward him, stretching out my free hand in its sticky yellow glove, calling his name.

At the critical moment, I slipped in a pool of Claus's blood and almost lost my balance. The sudden movement scared Caesar. He ran backward and forward, backward and forward across the kitchen, making a sound I had never heard from him before. He began to shit everywhere. I stood very still, waiting for him to calm down, talking to him all the while in a gentle, soothing voice: 'There, Caesar, good dog, take it easy, boy, take it easy.'

In the end, he came to me – or rather, he came close enough for me to catch him.

... I slid his body into the white box alongside his father's. There was just enough room for the two of them. I watched the blood from their wounds collect around them till they appeared to be drowning in the stuff. They looked sadly diminished lying there, insignificant and somehow artificial – like a couple of blond wigs in a basin of dye. Only an eye that wouldn't close and Caesar's young white teeth, exposed by a clumsy slash of the electric knife, and their lifeless paws sticking up at awkward angles; only the smell of wet dog, of fresh blood, of death, of dog shit, mildew ...

And then, driven by some savage compulsion, I did things that I cannot bring myself to put down. Afterward I went over to the sink and threw up.

I stripped off apron, gloves, boots – all terribly spattered with blood – and dumped them into the garbage pail. Underneath the apron, my suit was clean.

I closed the white coffin and dragged it back out into the living room. This time it felt heavy enough. It left a trail of bloody skid marks all along the way. I pulled it up in front of the table where the presents were piled. On the lid of the box, using a forefinger I'd dipped in the dogs' blood, I carefully inscribed the phrase 'OUT OF THEIR MISERY', and on the side, at one end – as it were, the bows – the word 'MAGMEL'.

I stood back to admire my work. Too many smudges – the blood hadn't taken on the shiny white cardboard. I'd have to use something else.

It was the picture of the little girl hugging her setters that caught my eye. Anna's birthday card lay on the table – still unsigned. I read through the poem inside.

> I love my dogs, oh, how dearly,
> Words but faintly can express,
> This fond heart beats too sincerely,
> E'er that I should love them less!
> No! My fancy never ranges;
> Hopes like mine can never soar;

If the love I cherish changes,
It will be to love them more.

I had to laugh. It was grotesque ... Anna would never understand, but then, it had nothing to do with her. I took out my gold
pencil and drew a line through the whole poem; then, as an after-
thought, I encircled the word 'love' wherever it occurred.

I signed the card: *Martin Gregory*. I stood there for a moment
staring at my signature as if it had written itself in letters of fire;
then I put the card back on the table in front of the eleven roses.

The sound of Anna's sleepy voice calling to me from upstairs
caught me off guard. She hadn't discovered yet that she was locked
in. There was no time to lose. I took a last look around. Everything
in its place – the flowers, the presents, the surprise (blood was
oozing from a soggy red corner of the cardboard box onto the
carpet) – and a place for everything.

I had done my duty.

I looked at my watch. It was 7.45 precisely. If I hurried I could
just make the 8.03 to Grand Central. Very gently I eased the front
door open and walked over to the garage, keeping the gravel quiet
under my shoes.

It must have been the humidity or something. The car refused
to start. The sound of the engine brought Anna to the bedroom
window. She flung up the sash and leaned out into the damp, bird-
less morning, wearing nothing but a thin nightdress. I remember
thinking, She'll catch cold ...

'Where are you going at a quarter to eight on a Saturday morning?' she shouted, laughing, full of birthday spirit.

She threw the rose at me that I'd left on her breakfast tray. It
fell just short of the car, scattering a few red petals in the driveway.
Leaning forward, I smiled up at her through the windshield of the
station wagon and held a finger up to my lips – as if to say, It's
a secret.

FOUR

Darkness was coming down, storm clouds rolling in over an immense black lake where the south of the city should have been, its lights sinking one by one beneath the oily surface. I had to get through to the other side – if there was another side. I could hear the din of panic as the waters rose. The air was thick with dust and fumes; those streets that were still dry were barricaded by fire. And everywhere hung the stench of decay. A hot wind blew, stiffening my neck with some shrieking virus. Flies and rats clung in terror to the underside of things. Any moment now the storm would break and the earth would open up.

I could hardly see to find my way. Wading across the torrents of scum that coursed through the main arteries of the city, I kept falling over things – human debris: the floating dead were being sucked toward the center. Jostling with these waterlogged zombies, I wanted to run, but I was one against the flow.

All the time it was getting darker. I couldn't understand why so many people were on the streets. They bristled together like iron filings caught in magnetic flux. Dressed for a summer's day, they seemed unaware of the approaching cataclysm. I tried to warn them, but they acted as if I were invisible.

I knew that we had to find shelter, before it all started coming down.

... I remember a man with slits for eyes, a hand at my elbow, guiding me up some steps, through a glass door covered in worn stickers. An exchange took place in a foreign language. Then the blur of a departing face and I was alone again. Gradually the darkness retreated.

'Single room with bath for two nights sixty dollars in advance if you would care to sign here please.'

The receptionist swiveled the register. 'Joe will help with your bags.'

'I'm afraid I have no luggage.' The sound of my own voice startled me.

'That's all right, sir.' The girl's moon face beamed. Her singsong had a soothing effect.

My hand shook a little as I picked up the pen and began to write. The name *Anna Gregory* stared up at me from the page. I let out a groan. The receptionist asked me if anything was wrong. Immediately my suspicions were aroused. She was being too solicitous. I glanced down at my hands. There was a trace of blood under my right index fingernail.

Suddenly I became convinced that there was blood on my face, my guilt plain for all the world to see. A mirror hung on the wall behind me. I had to force myself not to look around. Waves of darkness came up again in front of my eyes.

I tried to reassure myself. This hotel seemed fine, dingy as it was – a sanctuary. The girl was just being friendly.

Scratching out *Anna Gregory*, I filled in my own name with a fictitious address and turned the register back around. The moon-faced receptionist was smiling as before. There was no need for any explanation. I wrote out a check, and without comment, she handed me the key to room 9.

I was losing ground again. The girl's directions were swamped by a roaring in my ears. I set off along a corridor that seemed to grow darker and narrower at every turn. The walls bulged out at me, pressing in on the middle. I had to push them apart with my hands. A sensation spread like an electrical fire through the circuits of my body. The whole fabric of skin, nerve, muscle and bone was rotted away. I had no strength left. I groped my way, feeling the shapes of numbers on the doors.

15, 13, 11, 9 . . .

Fumbling with the key, I get the door open at last and pitch forward into the room, down into everlasting night, riding the spiral to the edge of the drop.

When I came to, it was almost dark. I was lying just inside the vestibule of my room with one foot against the door. I had no idea where I was. The room was nondescript. I could make out the name of the hotel on the key ring, but it meant nothing to me. I had a headache and severe stomach cramps, and I felt feverish. But I was lucid.

I remember locking the door, drawing the curtains and turning out the lights before retreating to the bed. I was preparing myself for a siege. I sat there in the dark and waited, as if somehow I knew what to expect.

The details arrived in no particular order. It was like one of those electronic games. Random images flashed up on a screen, and I had to make a selection. It was easy for me; I couldn't make a mistake. You see, at first I didn't understand that I was part of the game. Then I began to realize that they were *my* hands mixing up the dog food; that it was *my* back bent over the white cardboard box; that the blood-spattered rubber boots were *mine*. I felt a sudden surge of panic. I tried to block out the images, but the picture on the screen wouldn't fade. Nor would the light in my eyes switch off. The images were there forever.

Afterward I broke down and wept. In a way it was a relief. There then followed a long period when I can remember nothing but terrible physical pain. Just to withstand it required all my energy and will.

When the pain finally eased, I found it impossible to accept that I had killed the dogs. An act of such senseless, perverse brutality wasn't part of anything I could yet recognize in myself. I tried to take refuge in the idea that I'd had a fit or a brainstorm of some kind, but I knew that was not the case. And the more I resisted accepting responsibility for my actions, the more troubled I became.

I kept seeing Anna in her dressing gown and slippers hurrying down the stairs, opening the door of the living room and running toward the white, bloodstained box.

I was concerned about her, yet it never occurred to me to do anything. I wouldn't have been able even to lift the telephone. I sat huddled in a corner of the bed, overcome by agonies of remorse.

Later that night, or the following morning, I dreamed that I was on trial. Although at the outset I had pleaded guilty, I suddenly realized that I had been wrongly advised. I stood up and boldly denied that I had committed any crime at all. This provoked uproarious laughter throughout the courtroom. Even the judge could not restrain a guffaw.

Realizing how serious my position was, I made a long impassioned plea, which ended with the words:

'After all, people have done worse things than put their pets to sleep.'

Silence.

An ominous muttering.

I knew that I'd failed to convince the court. In despair I turned to plead with the jurors and saw for the first time that all twelve of them ...

I woke with the apprehension that something terrible was about to happen. I sat straight up in bed and turned on the light. The memory of what I'd done came flooding in again, and the immediate threat seemed to pass. But there had been a change.

Apart from specific remorse, I now began to be tormented by a more general and overwhelming sense of guilt. I didn't know what I was guilty of, only that my 'crime' was so heinous as to be beyond redemption. The burden of it was literally insupportable. It was as if I were being slowly crushed by an enormous, invisible weight.

I don't know how long the attack lasted. It came on very suddenly, the first onslaught knocking me to the floor. I lay at the foot of the bed winded and badly frightened. Tears started from my eyes, and I was fighting for air. The weight sat on my chest. Blood and mucus and saliva leaked from my nose and mouth. I felt that I was going to suffocate in my own juices. I vomited; violent spasms convulsed my body; my limbs bucked and twisted in futile protest. The weight kept coming down. I thought it would never stop.

And then the pressure began to ease. It left me in the end as suddenly and inexplicably as it had come. I lay in a pool of my own exudate, trembling from head to foot – a stunned fish on a riverbank gasping for its element.

For two days and two nights I remained in that room with the curtains drawn, the door locked and a sign up to keep the hotel maids away. I had no sense of time passing, no memory of being hungry or thirsty or wanting a cigarette or even of going to the john. As far as I can remember, I never moved from the bed. Some of the time I slept, but mostly I just lay there.

*

I didn't recognize the sound at first, its harshness belonged to another world. This time two rings. The interval between was unfamiliar, but the jarring notes insisted. Somebody knew I was here. I must have been followed ... I followed the sound to the extension on the bedside table.

I reached for the receiver.

'Hello, ah, Room Nine? Desk speaking. Checkout time is noon. It's already quarter of twelve.'

'I'm sorry' – I tried to clear my throat – 'I don't understand.'

'Guests must vacate their rooms by noon or pay for another night. Sir, you wish to extend your visit?'

I wasn't ready for this; the decision seemed momentous. 'What day is it?'

'Monday, sir.' I could hear the girl trying to suppress a giggle.

'I'll be staying another night.'

I cut her off, slamming down the phone.

Monday! I realized how much time I'd wasted – just lying there.

Without thinking I picked up the telephone, waited impatiently for an outside line and dialed home.

'Can I help you?'

It was a woman's voice, not one I recognized. I hesitated, trying to guess the situation.

'Hello?'

The voice was crisp, neither friendly nor unfriendly – official. It meant the dogs had been found.

'Hello, can I help? Hello!'

I couldn't bring myself to answer.

A hand covered the mouthpiece while she spoke to someone there.

And I hung up.

FIVE

NAME OF INTERVIEWER	R. M. Somerville
DATE OF CONSULTATION	Wednesday 4 October
NAME OF PATIENT	Mr Martin Gregory
AGE 33 OCCUPATION	Computer Sales Executive

A. REFERRAL

Urgent call from Dr Heyworth, a very competent G.P. who has referred a number of patients to me in the past, asking me to see one of his patients – a seriously ill man whom a psychiatrist at Lenox Hill wanted to hospitalize. The psychiatrist, Marcelle Hartman, is not known to me personally, though I have good reports of her.

The patient, however, seemed to take strong exception to the psychiatrist and after submitting to a Rorschach, refused to have anything more to do with her. It was then that Dr Heyworth called me up. He is an old friend of the patient's wife and asked me as a special favor to see him right away.

I agreed, of course, but insisted on a letter from the psychiatrist and on seeing the Rorschach report, which arrived the following day. In her letter Hartman appeared to be relieved that someone else was taking over the case.

BI. APPEARANCE AND MANNER OF PATIENT

Tall, well-built, air of confidence. Strong profile, rather distant blue eyes, hair close-cropped – an intelligent face. Neatly but not scrupulously dressed – i.e., suit but no tie. Hands mostly hidden during interview.

Under stress, but controlling it reasonably well. Patient appears tired but otherwise looks to be in good health. A little drawn around the eyes. Complained to Dr Heyworth of various aches and pains; these are mostly gone now. According to Dr H., patient has a curious bruise, very large, spreading over the chest and rib cage. Claims to have no idea what caused it. Possibly self-inflicted.

His story coincides with the G.P.'s on all main points. It was presented coherently, though with some reluctance. Distaste for what he calls 'scab-picking' – i.e., psychiatry. Occasional outburst. Some rigidity. Aggressive insistence on his being regarded as 'perfectly normal'.

B2. COMPLAINTS

Incident described triggered acute depression lasting a couple of days. Patient claims to be recovered, though shattered by what happened and the effect it has had, or is likely to have, on his marriage, work, life, etc. Also worried by the possibility of a recurrence – i.e., that he might do something similar or worse.

Five days ago, on his wife's 28th birthday, after locking her into the bedroom, patient cut the throats of their two golden retrievers and left the carcasses in a large container on the living-room floor as a 'present' for her. He then caught the train to New York and took a room in a hotel where he remained for the next 48 hours. During this period no one knew his whereabouts. He made no attempt to contact his wife nor, it seems, anyone else, until about noon on Monday, when he called Dr H. on the telephone, urgently asking to see him.

By then the G.P. was already familiar with half of the story. On Saturday morning he had received a hysterical, very confused and alarming cry for help from the patient's wife. Although he is a busy man with a large practice, he cancelled all his appointments and drove out to Bedford to see her, since it was clear she was not up to coming into the city.

Heyworth, it must be said, has known the patient's wife since she was a young girl living in her native Vienna, where he worked for several years as an intern in a Red Cross hospital. When her father died in 1968, shortly after the family emigrated here from Austria, he began to take a paternal interest in her welfare. In time of crisis it was only natural for the patient's wife to turn to the doctor for help. Apart from her husband and a sister who lives in California, he is her closest 'relative' in this country.

The patient contacted Dr Heyworth in the hope that he might be able to tell him how his wife was. Although deeply concerned about her, he felt, and still feels, too horrified by what he'd done to get in touch with her – even to talk to her on the telephone. It is accepted that they both truly love each other. They were also devoted to the dogs.

Dr H., who has a high regard for the patient, did his best to reassure him about his wife. He remains, however, in a state of some anxiety about her. After examining him and finding nothing physically wrong (apart from the mysterious bruising), Dr H. persuaded him to allow the initial psychiatric investigation which led to his referral.

C. Factual Material

Patient comes from old New England family – several generations of educational-book publishers. Father inherited family business, but after the war chose to stay on in the Philippines helping to advise the new government. Early part of patient's childhood spent out there. On their return to Boston, the father went back into business with his younger brother who had been managing the firm in his absence. Patient attended the Noble and Greenough School in Massachusetts, where he was considered 'a bit of a rebel', but did well enough to get into Brown. At college, by his own admission, he did very little work and only just scraped by with a 'gentleman's C'.

Upon graduation the patient went to work in the family business. Sometime in the early seventies, he succumbed to the malaise of the times and quit his job. He set off around the world following the 'dropout trail', and spent a year or so wandering through Europe, Afghanistan, India and the Far East. Ending up in California, he decided to remake his life there and settle down. He dusted off his engineering degree and joined a small electronics firm in San Diego. When the business was taken over by a multinational corporation, he was offered a place in its computer division. After three years he was promoted and sent back East. Since then he has risen steadily and has good prospects of being made branch manager of the New York Office (Communications) later this year.

It is, in broad terms, a success story, though the patient is still regarded by some of his family – particularly his two elder brothers who now run the family firm – as being 'not quite serious'. They seem to mistrust and perhaps resent his venturing into a wider, more sophisticated world than theirs. Patient readily admits to no longer having much in common with any of them. Still sees his parents occasionally, who are now retired and living in a villa on one of the Florida Keys. Gets on well with his father, who also had a reputation for being something of a 'wild one' in his day. Patient's mother a sensible, loving and evidently long-suffering woman.

Soon after his return to New York, patient rediscovered affinity with an attractive Austrian girl he had been in love with before going off around the world. Ignoring mild family resistance, because she was a foreigner, he married her. Past experience of women considerable, but this was his first and only love. The marriage has been happy from the start. The couple are prospering and live well on his salary. No children through choice, as they are still very much involved in each other and do not feel ready to start a family.

D. PATIENT'S CONCEPTION OF HIMSELF

Ambitious, efficient, reliable. Affectionate, kind, but not overly demonstrative. A loner since childhood, has found companionship and contentment in marriage. Cares about his comforts; believes charity starts at home. Reads less than he used to. Believes in God, not in any organized religion. Distraught over what has happened, but determined to get to the bottom of it. Insists that he's 'a very ordinary sort of person'.

E. DOCTOR–PATIENT RELATIONSHIP

I. *How patient treated doctor* – reluctant to discuss 'personal matters', which he insists have no bearing on what happened. Obviously prejudiced against the idea that a psychiatrist might be able to help. But a heartfelt desire to solve the 'mystery'. Since patient has agreed to a second interview, the fear of recurrence, which I carefully did not dispel, may be edging his chair toward mine.

2. *How doctor treated patient* – kept a fairly low profile in order not to frighten him off at this point, especially after his experience with Hartman. Playing it very cautiously – i.e., not probing too much, nor appearing in any way critical. Hinted only that he might be able to use me as a litmus paper for his own experiments in the search for an explanation. This seems to be the safest approach. Made no therapeutic interventions nor gave any diagnostic interpretations. Decided not to mention the possibility of using hypnosis – though may suggest it after next session. It already seems clear that short of long-term therapy, hypnosis is going to be the only way to unlock what is undoubtedly an interesting case.

N.B. Must remember to ask the patient or Dr Heyworth what was written in the note he left his wife.

F. SUMMARY

To be completed after second session.

SIX

It extended diagonally from just below the collarbone to the base of the rib cage: a black-and-blue-and-mauve sash edged with a ribbon of mottled yellow. On either side of the bruise and reaching down across the abdomen almost to the groin, the skin was traversed by the tiny crimson threads of countless ruptured blood vessels.

I caught Heyworth's slight intake of breath as I removed my shirt.

'How exactly did this happen?'

'I don't know . . . really, I never even noticed it until this morning.'

'How is that possible?'

'I didn't take my clothes off.'

'Were you in some sort of accident?' He eyed me suspiciously. 'Somebody beat you up?'

'Not that I remember.'

He unhooked the stethoscope from his ears.

'Nothing broken, no abrasions, no swelling.' His crabbed old fingers moved slowly across my chest, expertly feeling their way. 'Extensive purpura – I've not seen anything quite like it before.'

'What is purpura?'

'Extravasated blood. Blood forced from its normal channels into the surrounding tissue. Does it hurt when I do this?'

He pressed gently against the wall of my abdomen.

'Only when I laugh.'

He gave a sigh. 'I can't make you tell me, Martin, but it might help, you know.'

'Look, it's got nothing to do with anything.'

Even if I'd tried to explain how I got the bruise, he would never have believed me. Heyworth was the down-to-earth type, sober, meticulous – he wasn't going to listen to some wild story about my being pinned to the floor by an invisible weight in a seedy hotel room on Forty-fifth Street.

35

'I want to know about Anna. That's why I'm here, Bill. Not because of a lousy little bruise. You haven't said a thing.'

'Haven't I?' He shot me a quick, disapproving glance over the top of his glasses. 'I apologize, if that's the case.'

With his forehead creased back and the familiar shock of grizzled hair standing up over his long, sagging face, he looked tired and almost comically dejected. Understandably, he was disturbed by what I had done. He'd known Anna since she was a child; he regarded her almost as one of his own. I think he suspected that I'd deliberately set out to hurt her.

'She's going to be fine,' he said quietly.

'Bill, for Christ's sake!'

'She was worried about you. More than the dogs at first. What she saw in the box ... she thought some maniac – I'm sorry, but that's how it looked, like a maniac had gone on the rampage. She was afraid he'd killed you too.'

'How did she get out of the bedroom?'

'She climbed out onto the roof of the porch and lowered herself down by the wisteria. Must have been about an hour after you left. She'd gotten bored with waiting for something to happen – some sort of surprise, she said. The house was quiet. She wondered where the dogs had got to. She called them, and of course they didn't answer. Then as she was coming in through the front door, she saw blood on the hall carpet.

'Anna wouldn't talk about finding them, Martin, so don't ask me. The poor child was terrified the killer might still be in the house. When it became clear that she was there alone, she locked all the doors and was about to call the police. She was more anxious about what had happened to you than anything else. But then she found the birthday card.'

'But she saw me drive off. I waved to her.'

'She said she wasn't sure that was you.' There was anger in his voice. 'She wasn't sure of much by then.'

'I don't remember any birthday card.'

'It was enough to make her put the phone down. It was your handwriting, all right. She was in a pretty bad way by the time I got to her.'

'What else did she say?'

'I gave her a sedative. She didn't really talk much. She was asleep when I left, but not alone. The nurse arrived about five. I told you, there's nothing to worry about. She's in good hands now ... Mrs James will stay as long as Anna needs her. I considered asking her sister to fly in from Monterey, but I figured the fewer people who know about this the better.'

'Who took care of the the dogs?'

'I buried them in the garden.'

'I'm sorry it had to be you.' Turning away abruptly, I went over to the window and looked out. 'If I could explain any of it, believe me, Bill ... I'm sorry.'

'That's all right,' he said more gently. 'I'd do anything for Anna – for both of you. I don't have to tell you that. You're not just patients to me, you know.'

'You were there when she needed you.'

There was an awkward pause.

'Better get dressed.' It was the doctor speaking now. 'There's nothing wrong with you that a good rest won't cure. I want you to take it easy. Take a couple of weeks off. I'll square it with your office.'

'I already called my office,' I admitted hesitantly, as if it showed that I had my priorities confused. 'I said I had a bad case of flu.'

'Fine, I can easily elaborate on that – if necessary.' He smiled, but his eyes remained severe, watchful.

'Martin, I'm going to make an appointment for you to see a colleague of mine.'

'You mean a shrink?'

'A psychiatrist, yes.'

'You know what I think about all that.'

'And I know how anxious you are about your wife. We have to think of her too, don't we?'

He put it with customary bluntness: we were dealing here with something outside his province. It wasn't a question of my being off the wall. Probably I'd just been overdoing it at work. Stress. A minor psychogenic disorder. The sort of thing that could happen to anyone. But I owed it to Anna, as much as to myself, to 'seek professional guidance'.

It was more or less what I'd expected him to say.

'Are you going to tell her that I've seen you?'

'Should she ask – which, frankly, I doubt. She's still suffering from shock. There's no sense hurrying things. She'll come around in her own good time, don't worry. For the moment I think it's best that you don't try to get in touch – unless, of course, there's an emergency.'

If he had meant to reassure me, he didn't do a very good job of it; but I felt grateful nevertheless. At this point I couldn't bear the thought of seeing Anna. It was a relief – in a way – to know that she didn't want to see me either.

'You're the doctor,' I said.

It occurred to me then that it might be easier for Anna if she heard from some official source that I hadn't known what I was doing when I killed the dogs. I knew I was to blame, but it would help her, I thought, if she could see me as 'innocent'. For a while the idea of pleading insanity seemed the solution – dishonest, maybe, but not without honor.

That was before I met Marcelle Hartman.

The first moment I saw her, sitting up behind her desk in that antiseptic consulting room at the Lenox Hill psychiatric unit, I knew it wasn't going to work. Everything about her – the grim, accusing smile; the wire-wool hair scraped back into a gritty little bun with a pencil sticking out of it; the thick-lensed glasses that magnified and distorted her eyes, giving them a look of angry inquisition – combined to set my teeth on edge. I took an instant dislike to Dr Hartman. When she spoke, her small anxious mouth, compressed into a line as thin as trip wire, snapped open and shut with an obscene precision. She looked like a baleful nanny, eager to get her hands on a new charge.

Hartman must have had dogs of her own, or something. She made little attempt to disguise the fact that she found my crime absolutely repugnant – which was understandable, though of no great help. I made the mistake of telling her that I was frightened by the possibility of some kind of relapse. She seemed to take it literally, that's how bright she was – as if I might now become a threat to other people's pets. Before I knew it, she was suggesting in a very forceful way that I would find life a bit easier if I came and spent some time at the hospital.

Toward the end of my 'hour', when everything else seemed to have failed, Dr Hartman announced that she would like me to complete a standard psychological test, known as Rorschach. I agreed, with the same grudging compliance I had given throughout. Producing a sheaf of square white cards from a desk drawer, she explained in her dry, clipped voice the rules of the game.

'Rorschach is what we call a projection test, Mr Gregory. The purpose is to determine personality traits through attempting to measure the fertility of the subject's imagination.'

'A projection test,' I repeated dully.

'On these cards you will find a series of inkblots and paint splashes. In a moment, I will ask you to study them very carefully – in a moment, Mr Gregory – and tell me what objects you see in the figures. You are quite free to follow your own inclinations or fantasies, and, of course, you realize there is no right or wrong interpretation. Though I should warn you that the number of objects you report in a given time period may be significant. It's very simple really.'

'Child's play,' I murmured.

But when I looked at the first card she handed me, I saw in the irregular black stain that covered half its surface nothing more than an ink spill. I stared at the blot, but the shape refused to transform itself. I shook my head.

'Try another.' She turned a second card over onto the desk in front of me.

This time I studied it more carefully, moving the card around and examining it from different angles, concentrating on individual areas of the design, but in the end with no more success than the first. I could hear Hartman breathing heavily through her nose.

'Nothing doing, I'm afraid.' I looked up at her, laughing into that deeply repulsive face.

'I don't think you're trying very hard, Mr Gregory,' she said coldly. 'Everyone can see *something*.'

But I was trying. That was the trouble. She turned over more cards. A series of extravagant shapes passed under my barren gaze, each one different from the one before, some in color, most in black and white, all of them equally empty of suggestion. I could see splotches – that was it.

Across the desk, Dr Hartman's breathing was becoming more insistent. Finally her patience gave out.

'Since you don't seem prepared to cooperate, Mr Gregory, there's really not much point in our continuing.'

She began to gather up the scattered cards.

'Wait a second!' I held up a hand, still concentrating on the last inkblot. 'I think I've got something.'

She sighed. 'Very well, what is it you see?'

'It looks like an animal – a goat or maybe a donkey, lying on its back.'

'Yes?' She extracted the pencil from her hair. 'What else?'

'More of these animals lying around. There's water everywhere. Some of them are floating on the water. And all the animals are dead, drowned.

'I can see people, too – running through the streets – they're running away from something. They look back, falling over each other, fighting to get away, but whatever it is keeps coming. They seem terrified . . . God!'

'Go on,' Hartman said quietly.

'But I can *see*! This isn't what you think. I can actually see it happening. People are dying. Thousands, thousands of them.

'It keeps moving, changing all the time. The sky is dark, but it isn't night. There's a child, a young girl, half-naked, shivering with fear. Her body is horribly thin. Pitted with sores. These revolting boils everywhere. The bones are literally protruding from her chest. She's trying to get away like the others, but she can't. Too weak. They have to leave her behind.

'There's something over there in the corner, watching her . . . Christ Almighty!'

'What is it?'

'I don't know. I can't see her anymore. I can't see anything. No, wait! A face. But it keeps changing. God, it's horrible – ancient, moldering, like stone covered in lichen – I can't look at it.

'Now it's much darker all of a sudden. No face. Nothing there. Just a mask, an evil-looking mask – whatever was behind it has gone.'

'What else can you see?' Hartman leaned forward in her chair.

The slight movement must have broken my concentration. It

threw me off balance. I felt as if I'd been standing in a strong wind that had dropped without warning. I looked away from the desk and for a moment I had no idea where I was.

The room was full of mist. Behind the woman's head the pale green hospital wall was receding at vertiginous speed.

I closed my eyes, waiting for them to clear.

'Nothing else,' I managed to get out at last, conscious of having said too much.

'Why not try another card?'

There was a faint gleam now in the dealer's eye. She'd scented victory. But I realized from her question that I needn't have worried: she hadn't understood. She was pleased because she thought she'd gotten through to me. She'd no idea what had really happened.

No idea at all.

'I'm sorry, Dr Hartman,' I said without regret, 'but I don't believe you can help me.'

I must have walked fifteen blocks before I began to realize what was happening. They'd been there on the other side of the street when I came out of the hospital. I watched them cross over, and then I noticed them again a few minutes later when I happened to look around at a girl who'd reminded me a little of Anna. At first it didn't occur to me that there was anything odd about them: a blind man and his Seeing Eye dog.

The man was short and fat with a sallow skin – in his late twenties, maybe. He was wearing an ill-fitting denim suit, a baseball cap and dark glasses, and he was attached to a large black-and-tan German shepherd by an iridescent leash designed to reflect the lights of cars at night.

On the corner of Sixty-second Street I found myself stopping, waiting for them to catch up. A wind was gusting north on Park Avenue: I reckoned they had my scent ... It was absurd, of course, the whole idea of being tailed by a blind man. But after what had happened during the Rorschach, I wasn't taking any chances. Only the relief of getting out of that place – just to breathe air that didn't have Hartman in it – was holding me together right then. The experience had left me badly shaken, a prey to every anxiety.

As they drew near, I realized that the man had nothing to do with it. It was the dog I had to worry about. With a jerk of its big head it pulled its master up at the edge of the curb, a few feet from where I was standing. Through the sides of his shades I could see the flicker and play of the man's sightless eyes. Like rolling dice. The dog put back its ears and began sniffing my legs. I was wearing the same suit I'd had on the morning I killed the boys. Particles of their blood would still be on my trousers. I expected the animal at any moment to leap up and tear my throat out.

The light stayed red. Fighting off a sudden onslaught of panic, I forced myself to bend down and stroke the massive head. A test of both my own nerve and the dog's instinct. Neither of us gave way. The good shepherd licked my hand and wagged its tail. Apart from a little shock of revulsion at the touch of its wet tongue, I felt nothing.

SEVEN

As soon as I got back to the hotel, I called Heyworth to let him know what had happened at Lenox Hill. After hearing out my diatribe against Dr Hartman, he told me rather stiffly that he'd already spoken with her and that he'd gone ahead and arranged for me to see another psychiatrist.

And this without even asking whether I was prepared to go through with it all again. He just naturally assumed he had my continuing cooperation – for Anna's sake, if nothing else. R. M. Somerville, he reassured me, was a very different proposition from Marcelle Hartman. Heyworth's profile of the man – a 'free-thinking therapist, what you might call a latitudinarian' – filled me with misgivings. When I asked him why, if Somerville was so extraordinary, he hadn't sent me to see him in the first place, he hemmed and hawed, but could provide no satisfactory answer.

It seemed less trouble to go through with it.

That evening after checking out of the hotel – the idea of spending another night there had suddenly become unbearable – I moved into a kind of boardinghouse down on Mulberry Street. An ample Italian woman who spoke broken English showed me a room that bore scant resemblance to its description in the Classifieds. Although an improvement on the hotel, which wasn't difficult, it seemed barely adequate. I took it at once because it was available and because I considered it an advantage to be living so far downtown. There was very little chance there of running into anyone I knew.

The next morning, restored by twelve hours' oblivion induced by phenobarbital, I turned up for my appointment with Dr Somerville at his office in an elegant town house between Fifth and Madison in the low Nineties.

Before my thumb hits the bell, the door gives a hiss and swings back smoothly on its hinges. The profile of a girl appears in its shadow, her head turned away, bent in conversation with someone hidden from view. I have an impression of rapid movement behind her, but see nothing beyond the line of dark hair swirling up from the pale skin of her neck as she brings her eyes around to meet mine. An expression of distaste in the slight downturn of her mouth changes quickly to a cool smile of greeting.

'Mr Gregory?'

She didn't falter.

I nodded, aware of having witnessed something in that fleeting moment, however insubstantial, that I shouldn't have.

'I'm Penelope – Dr Somerville's assistant.' She offered her hand. It was startlingly white, as delicately boned as the wing of a bird.

I walked past her into the dim hallway, ignoring the outstretched arm. I was curious to see whom she had been talking to.

There was no one.

She closed the door behind her and came right up to where I stood waiting under the burnished skies of an overrestored Victorian landscape.

'Does anyone else live here,' I asked, 'aside from Dr Somerville?'

The girl didn't reply, but turned away and started up the broad, carpeted stairs. I followed, conscious of her surprisingly voluptuous figure, beginning to regret getting off to a frosty start with her. But something had put me on the defensive – the incident out front perhaps, or perhaps it was just that I found her attractive.

On the first landing she ushered me through a half-open door.

'This is Dr Somerville's study. If you'd care to go in and wait, I'll tell him you're here.'

I thought I detected a hint of sarcasm in her voice, but the look she gave me was merely professional. 'Used to dealing with all types,' it said.

A narrow, oak-paneled L-shape, the room looked more like an underused reception lounge than my idea of a study. There was a desk hidden away in the foot of the L beneath the windows and a couple of built-in bookcases – only the books appeared uniformly new and unread, and the desk lacked clutter. There was nothing in the room that didn't arouse my suspicion. The pictures, ranging from sporting prints to stark, geometrical abstracts, all carried the stamp of the 'collector's' dreary taste. The furniture, apart from two modern reclining chairs that faced each other suggestively in a corner, was imitation Louis XV, covered in a bilious saffron brocade that matched the carpet, the draperies, and a couple of sick-looking dragons who were chasing each other slowly around a big Japanese urn. Under a freshly gilded Venetian mirror, an imitation Colonial mantelpiece straddled one of the earlier models of 'live-coal' electric fires, completing the unhappy mixture of period flavors. The room was airless and claustrophobic. It had a depressingly impersonal atmosphere.

I went over and tried to open one of the windows, but they had all been safety-locked. I took off my tie and undid the top button of my shirt. It occurred to me that I could always leave. I was certainly under no obligation to be there. Only it would mean dealing with the receptionist again. I retrieved the image of her swaying haunches.

She mounts the stairs, white fingers trailing over the banister, incongruously fragile, arresting me with a single gesture ... No, I didn't have the energy; nor was I looking for complications of that kind. Staring gloomily out the window, I thought of Anna, feeling somewhat reassured by the accompanying access of guilt.

'Mr Gregory, I am sorry to have kept you waiting.'
The voice was deep and rich, modulated by a vestigial British accent. It seemed to fill the room.

I swung around.

'Ronald Somerville.' He advanced toward me holding out his clean, hairless hand.

For a moment I was convinced that I knew the man from somewhere; the jolt of recognition made me take an involuntary step forward. As he came closer, I realized that I'd made a mistake.

His handshake was pleasantly firm and left behind it a barely perceptible scent of almonds.

There was nothing even remotely familiar about him. He seemed courteous, smooth, altogether unobtrusive. Wearing a charcoal worsted suit, Brooks Brothers shirt and tasseled black loafers, he gave an impression of self-effacing suavity that hardly seemed to fit the 'latitudinarian' image. He blended in with his surroundings.

Of indeterminate age – I would have guessed mid-fifties, though he turned out to be older – he was like a stone that has been polished by other stones. All distinguishing marks had been removed, his features worn to a blur that stayed no longer in the memory than an unknown face in a group photograph.

'Why don't we go and sit over there by the window,' he said, holding out a shepherding arm.

I had a ludicrous sense of the inevitable as he steered me toward the two comfortable-looking chairs in the corner.

At least there was no couch.

I wrote it down on the back of a train schedule while Somerville and I were talking and handed it to him. I watched him as he read the note. His face remained impassive, but when he spoke I could tell from the tone of his voice that it had had an effect.

'If one can only discover *where* to look,' he said, leaning forward in earnest, 'there is an explanation for everything, Mr Gregory.'

'That's what you get paid for, isn't it?' I let out – I couldn't help myself – 'and the longer it takes you to find it, the more you get paid.'

He smiled, but said nothing.

'Okay, so no one is forcing me to be here. I just want you to know that –'

'Why exactly did you write this down?' he interrupted, waving the train schedule at me.

When I didn't answer, he made a steeple of his fingers and looked up to the ceiling. 'Was there a family dog when you lived in Boston?'

'*That's* why I wrote it,' I pounced.

'Ah! "No catalyst or precedent,"' he read aloud from the note. '"No explanation to be had from delving into the subject's history." It doesn't leave us much to work with, does it?'

'I'm just trying to save you the trouble of asking a bunch of useless questions.'

'The more you tell me now, of course, the less I'll need to ask later on. It could work out cheaper for you in the long run.' Somerville smiled.

'Who said anything about a long run?'

The skirmish had been lost and won.

I told my story, sticking to the facts as I knew them, but leaving out some of the details. I did not mention, for instance, that there was a bloody imprint left behind on the sheets in my hotel room. I suspected Heyworth might have told Somerville about the bruise, but he didn't bring up the subject. Nor did I say anything about the incident with the Rorschach. It made no sense to give him that kind of ammunition. If you once start talking to a shrink about 'seeing things', you're done for. That's meat and drink to them: it's what they really long to hear. I knew that Somerville would have discussed my case with Hartman – if only out of professional courtesy – so he probably had the results of the 'test'; but since she had totally failed to notice what was really happening to me, I assumed there was nothing in her report for him to get too excited about.

Somerville tried to draw me out, very tentatively, on my relationship with Anna. If it was too soon, I didn't have to talk about her ... I didn't. I let him make do with my curriculum vitae and the family history, which is enough to put anyone to sleep.

'What if I were to come back to the subject of dogs?' he asked.

I shrugged my shoulders.

'You don't have to talk about them ...'

'... if I don't want.' I was getting quite used to finishing that sentence.

'Okay, I've got something – a tragic little story about a dog. I've never told this to anyone before. Maybe I'm ashamed of it.

'It happened when we were out in the Philippines. My father was working in Manila at the time, and we lived in this big old army bungalow on the edge of town. The jungle started right at the bottom of our garden.'

'Go on,' Somerville said.

'I remember lying in bed at night listening to the calls of the birds and monkeys, trying to distinguish between the different species. Sometimes you could hear wild pigs crashing about through the undergrowth, or the cough of a leopard – they used to come prowling around our chickens. It was pretty exciting stuff for a nine-year-old, though in many ways life out there was restricted. I was never allowed to go anywhere unaccompanied; but being left alone in the house a lot, I sometimes managed to slip away.

'I used to go over to Johnson's farm, about a mile down the road, and do some fishing in their stream. There were a lot of dogs on the farm, every shape and size – strays, mostly, that had just shown up and that no one had had the heart to turn away. I made friends with them, particularly with a little terrier mix called Jeff. You see, we didn't have any dogs at our house. Father said there was a danger of rabies: no pets.

'One day when I was over at the farm, it started to rain. I'm not talking about a shower – this was a real tropical downpour. I ran for home, already soaked to the skin, hoping I wouldn't be found out. For some unknown reason, the dogs decided to follow me. I did everything I could to make them go back, but they stuck to my heels – a dozen of them at least. When *I* ran, *they* ran. If *I* stopped, *they* stopped. I yelled at them to go back, cursed them, pleaded with them. They just stood there. I even threw stones at them, but they just stood there in the pouring rain, a bedraggled bunch of dirty, mangy underfed ... The sight of them began to infuriate me.

'They followed me all the way back. They even came up onto our veranda and started barking to be let in. I shut all the doors and windows and did my best to ignore them. No one else was at home – except for the cook's little girl, who was in the shed out back. Her mother had forbidden her to go into the house when she wasn't there. She might have been a year or so older than me – I used to play with her sometimes.

'The rain was coming down in rods of glass, hammering on the roof, smashing up the flower beds, gouging holes out of the earth. The dogs were still milling about in front of the veranda, all twelve of them, as if they were having some kind of conference about what to do next. After a while they gave up, and just padded off through the mud and rain. All except for the little terrier mix, my friend Jeff.

'He kept it up for quite a while. I could hear him yapping away and scratching at the screen door – thin, maddening sounds that cut through the steady roar of the rain – but I was determined not to give in. I blocked my ears. It occurred to me that he might not know how to find his way home. I didn't care – I didn't care what happened to him as long as he let me alone. I guess I just didn't want the responsibility. He was a friendly enough little creature.

'Several days later I heard that Jeff had disappeared. Everyone just assumed he'd been taken by a leopard. I never said anything about seeing him that day. Nobody even knew that I'd been over to the farm.

'For a long time after that I felt utterly miserable.'

I looked at Somerville, expecting him to say something, but he just sat there.

The silence became oppressive.

'Well? Aren't you going to comment? See, I'm not suppressing anything. You're not going to find out that I caught my parents in flagrante with a German shepherd when I was two years old. I'm not neurotic or psychotic or *crazy*, you know!'

'Tell me, Mr Gregory, have you ever been to a psychiatrist before, apart from Dr Hartman?'

'Never.'

'Then why do you so resent the idea of being treated by one?'

'Because I'm not mentally ill, and I've always had a healthy resistance to ... self-indulgence. I was really beginning to get things together until this happened.'

'If you broke a leg, you wouldn't hesitate to call a doctor and, if necessary, be admitted to a hospital, would you?'

'That's different.'

'When you were living in California did you get involved in any therapy groups, est-type movements, religious cults, drugs, politics?'

'What's that got to do with anything? I was involved, yes, but not with any particular movement. I took drugs for a while because they were part of the scenery. I wasn't looking for "answers".'

'You'd given up trying to solve the world's problems?'

'Right.' I laughed. 'The problem out there was good living – and it was one I preferred not to solve.'

'And you never got depressed? You told me that in the hotel room, you suffered an acute attack of depression.'

'Yes, but that was like ... well, I can't describe what it was like. It really *was* something different. That's what they all say, I guess. How can I explain it? Everything I tell you, you're going to read something into.'

49

'Then how can I help you?'

'Look, I've killed two dogs that I loved more than almost anything in the world. I don't know why I did it. It was something I had no control over. What if there's a next time? What if I do something worse?'

'There was this mist. It filled my head. In the kitchen everything suddenly went cold and damp. The smell of mildew ... I knew afterwards, however much I tried to deny it, that I was responsible. It doesn't make much sense, does it? I had this feeling of being invaded, and yet I know that the force for the invasion came from somewhere within me.'

'You could be reacting to what happened on two different levels.'

'I'm not schizoid, if that's what you're getting at.' I could hear my voice beginning to rise. 'I'm not crazy, for Christ's sake! Don't you see?'

Somerville said nothing. He sat quietly, running a finger along the line of his jaw. I felt angry with myself, frustrated by his inertia, conscious of my failure to convince him. All my arguments seemed to whirl around and bite at their own tails.

Under no illusions that I'd won him round, I came away from the session with the feeling that I hadn't totally wasted my time. Somerville could see that I was serious about one thing: finding out why it had happened.

Against my every expectation, I ended up finding him sympathetic. He hadn't really tried to put anything over on me. The only advice he gave me was that I should begin to keep a diary. When he asked me if I would like to come back and see him the next day, I was surprised to hear myself say yes.

It may simply have been the relief of talking to someone. Although I was still wary of him and had kept a lot back, I was beginning to see Somerville as a potential ally. And there was something reassuring about that. It gave me a glimmer of hope.

EIGHT

I am lying by the edge of a green swimming pool on a hilltop in Southern California, looking out over the ocean. It's early afternoon, not a cloud in the sky, and I'm lying there daydreaming of Anna. I concentrate my thoughts, trying to summon her by telepathy. I'm not surprised when this instantly produces the desired result. Appearing from nowhere, she kneels down beside me on the blanket and slips off her beach robe.

The sun caresses her back. I feel the warmth of her skin under my hand. Traveling south, it finds a patch sticky with sweat at the base of her spine. She begins to squirm a little. I wonder if I am pressing the wrong button ... A touch of caudal nostalgia? She murmurs something about going inside. I shield my eyes, squinting up at her against the light, but I cannot read her face.

I roll over onto one elbow, which brings my head in close to her thighs – deliberately left ajar in case I should mistake her meaning. The skin there, matt, without blemish, is as soft and white as pipeclay; the hair, oiled and perfumed, hangs in glistening tendrils, dark like opium.

I am about to reach out for her when abruptly I remember that Anna's blonde ...

Warning lights begin to flash in my head. This is Hollywood, where a blonde still counts for something. A NATURAL BLONDE – I can see the pink neon lettering floating on the surface of the pool through the gap between her thighs. Up in the sky hangs a wispy scrawl of contrail: THINK GOLDEN.

She takes charge of my hand. Guides it toward her black, scented fleece. A shiver runs through me.

'No, wait ...' I draw back.

Without a word the girl rises off her haunches and walks slowly up towards the house. The invitation is still there in the languid trailing of her body as she passes under a white colonnade and melts back into the cool subfusc interior. But I am unable to move, pinned by indecision to the side of that ice-green pool.

The conflict arises not from a question of loyalty to my wife, but doubt as to the wisdom of screwing Dr Somerville's assistant.

The scene changes and I find myself in a room identical to the one I have rented at 245 Mulberry. It's uncomfortably old-fashioned, with heavy chintz curtains, yellowing wallpaper and a washbasin in the corner concealed by an olive-drab screen. Over the boarded-up fireplace hangs a lurid watercolor of the Bay of Naples. There's a table in front of the window with a folded piece of newspaper under one leg to keep it stable, a couple of upholstered chairs, a bureau, a rickety pharmacy lamp and two iron-frame beds – one behind the door, the other across the room in the corner opposite the washbasin.

It's pitch dark; the curtains are drawn, the lights out in the hallway. Although I am perfectly familiar with the contents and layout of the room, I have lost my bearings. I know that I am in bed – only I cannot be sure *which* bed. Of course, I could easily find out by reaching over and turning on the light, but something prevents me.

I lie hunched up under the blankets struggling to keep warm. It's cold for October; the night air feels damp against my face. I can't remember if I've left the window open – there's no draft, no noise from the street – but again I'm reluctant to get up and check. A faint musty odor about the place seems annoyingly familiar.

I lie there shivering, fighting the cold, trying to ignore a dismal feeling in the pit of my stomach.

In the pursuit of warmth I am constantly shifting position, twisting and turning, pulling the covers tighter around my neck. The old iron bedstead creaks in protest every time I move. When I lie still, not a sound: the house is steeped in silence. I hear only the rumor of my breathing and the heavy pulse of my heart.

So I concentrate on the breathing. It seems uneven. I try to regulate it. A sluggish response. It's as if I have lost control of my own lungs. Afraid of suffocating, I sit up in bed and take several deep breaths.

I am counting, totally absorbed now, like a doctor listening to some rare pulmonary disorder. In my ears a stethoscope to amplify the sound. I note the way the supply of air runs down to nothing before pumping up again till my breathing reaches a certain level of intensity. It stops short, then falls away to a low, tremulous growl, then starts over, gradually getting louder. The bed creaks in accompaniment ...

Abruptly, I realize that I'm not moving.

A soughing wheeze, stronger than before, harsher, more urgent.

It's no longer *my* breathing.

The girl! I listen intently.

It agitates the air, penetrates the darkness.

I can hear her – panting, gasping, sucking air; little moans escape her, little grunts and cries ...

All at once the bed on the other side begins to shake.

... piglike squealing.

It shudders, bucks and plunges. The walls, the floor, the ceiling, the whole room vibrates to her rhythm.

'Fuck me,' she howls against the din, 'under the *tail*, sweet Jesus!'

Faster, faster, rocking violently, to and fro, in, out – slipping it to herself, she reaches her solitary climax in a long defiant snarl of ecstasy.

I woke up ... I *must* have woken. Everything was quiet again. I remember listening, straining my ears for a familiar sound. Beyond the silence of the room I could make out a white, fuzzy noise, a low hum that came slowly into focus as the traffic on Houston. I looked at my watch. The red numerals glowed comfortingly. It was five to three.

But in the dark, lying wide awake, I realized that nothing had really changed.

I still didn't know which bed I was in. The room felt unnaturally cold, the air clammy; and there was that same dank smell, unmistakable now – the stench of mildew.

A quick blade of fear twisted up under my ribs. I reached out, groping for the light. Where the bedside table should have been my hand found empty space.

'Martin.' The voice came out of the darkness, scarcely audible, clotted with lust.

The sound of breathing again. The faint creak of iron. No dream, she was here with me in the room.

'Martin.' This time a low, urgent call.

The iron heaved, springs adjusting to the shift of her weight; then the rustle of bedclothes being pulled back and the soft plump of bare feet going down to the floor.

I sat bolt upright, skin prickling all over. The sweat ran off my forehead and stung my eyes. I peered into the darkness. At any moment I expected her.

She didn't stir.

I listened to her hot, ragged breath, imagining her body lying open on the edge of the bed.

White hands, delicately boned as the wings of birds.

'Over here,' she whispered.

I set out across the void guided only by the sound of her breathing. I could feel the carpet underfoot, threadbare, familiar. I stretched out an arm, brushed against something cold and hard. It was the back of a chair. I held on to it tightly, overwhelmed by the intensity of the darkness. I closed my eyes, trying to fix my position ... standing at the edge, looking down into the vortex of a monstrous ... I feel the room begin to turn with the current, slowly at first, then with gathering speed. I stumble, lurch forward, knocking into the table. It comes off its wedge and seesaws under my weight. I know at once where I am. The window! I reach up with both hands and fling back the drapes.

A howl of anguish rises from the corner.

The frantic sound of tearing cloth. I wheel around. A flurry of movement over by the far wall.

It is still too dark for me to see clearly. I have an impression of something white twisting up from the bed and sweeping toward the window. I back away, instinctively trying to cover my face. A blast of freezing air rushes by, knocking me to the floor with the force of a massive wave. For a moment I have the sensation of falling farther – as if the ground had given way beneath me. I feel a searing pain along the underside of one arm. Then nothing.

Protecting my eyes against the sudden glare, I looked back at the room, letting my gaze travel slowly around. Everything seemed normal, approximately where and how it should have been. The shabby furniture, the worn-out rugs, the dismal screen, the gay improbable blue of the Bay of Naples, the chintz drapes ... I stared at them in disbelief.

I come round, surprised at first to find myself spread-eagled on the carpet instead of lying on the bed. Unhurt but a little dazed, I pick myself up and with a few faltering steps make it over to the door. Fumble for the light switch ...

The curtains were drawn.

I distinctly remembered opening them.

The table I'd knocked into was back in place – I could see the wedge of newspaper still supporting its awkward leg.

I looked over at the beds. Only one of them had been disturbed, the same one I'd gone to sleep in a few hours before. Next to it stood the bedside table complete with books, glass of water, sleeping pills, photograph of Anna and reading light – all within arm's reach.

I crossed the room and examined the second bed more carefully. There was nothing to indicate it had been slept in. The counterpane was immaculate. Underneath were three gray blankets neatly folded and a pillow without a case. No sign of any sheets. I tested the springs. They were silent. I felt the wall behind the bed. Bone-dry. The temperature in the room seemed about normal. The smell of mildew had completely disappeared.

It had all been a dream.

There was no other possible explanation. I remembered waking earlier and looking at my watch. The time then was 2.55. Now it said only 2.30. It *must* have been a dream. Walking in my sleep I'd had an accident and fallen down.

Obviously the dream had to do with my being frustrated, and my feeling guilty and worried about Anna at the same time. Nothing startling in that. Hadn't I successfully resisted the temptation to be unfaithful to my wife? Doubtless Somerville would find it interesting that my subconscious had selected his receptionist to play the role of succubus. Of course, I had no intention of telling him. It wasn't that significant. The girl had seemed attractive enough, but I didn't even recall her name. In fact, I could only just remember what she looked like.

I felt relieved, almost pleased with myself. It had been a test, not unlike the Rorschach incident, an ordeal to be survived. And I had come through it with flying colors.

I went back to bed. For a moment, lying there, I considered taking another sleeping pill, but decided to try to get by without. I stared at the picture of Anna – a color snapshot of her, which earlier I'd taken out of my wallet for comfort. Now it inspired only a feeling of unease. I reached for it and felt a sharp pain at the back of my elbow. I twisted the arm around. There was a vivid red mark the size of a small cigar running up from the elbow towards the shoulder. It looked like a burn or a graze – presumably the result of my fall.

The arm felt sore when I bent it. I had some antihistamine cream which Heyworth had given me for the bruise on my chest. It hadn't done much good, but it would probably be better than nothing. The tube of ointment lay on a small glass shelf above the washbasin in the corner – 'the lavabo' the landlady had called it, drawing back a folding wing of the dilapidated screen with a little flourish.

From where I was sitting the screen looked a long way off and somehow forbidding, like a cliff rising out of a dark green stretch of ocean. Beyond it, a land of milk and honey and soothing aromatic balm . . . I had to summon the energy to get off the bed.

I rose wearily to my feet. The arm had begun to throb.

Halfway across the room I stopped. There was a peculiar scent in the air, heavy and sweet like the fragrance of lilac or some exotic creeping plant. It transported me for an instant to another place – an ancient courtyard, it might have been somewhere in Italy or Spain, surrounded by a high crenellated wall, part of a magnificent citadel. I look up at the wall, which seems to be covered in people, and realize that it's about to collapse.

No more than an impression, a forgotten image from some B movie perhaps. I cancelled it at once, determined now not to give way to suggestion of any kind.

I cannot afford to confuse what is real with what is not. The smell seems to be coming from the corner behind the screen. Yet now I detect a subtle change in its bouquet, as if the flowers, in blossom only a moment ago, have withered and died. I approach the screen in trepidation. The faint breath of decay rises in my nostrils.

My heart begins to race. The palms of my hands are damp with sweat. Surely it's only my imagination? Mold from the carpet? Drains? Suddenly the smell becomes overpowering.

I rounded the end of the screen.

It was lying huddled in the corner, partly swathed in a torn sheet. A thin bloody hand that gripped the rim of the washbasin, as if it had been trying to pull itself into an upright position, flew back out of sight, leaving a rust-colored smear on the porcelain. I took a step forward and it cowered away from me, pushing itself back into the angle of the wall.

The bones of the shoulders, showing white through skin flayed and darkened by corruption, were hunched up around its ragged ears. A small, emaciated creature, it was covered from head to foot in a rash of dark red tumors that stuck to its morbid flesh like glistening sea anemones. Protruding below the rib cage from a gaping vent in the abdomen loose grayish knots of intestine spilled over into its hardly pubescent groin. I realized to my disgust that I was looking at the body of a child.

A young girl, no more than ten or twelve.

I saw her for a moment as she must have been – fair-skinned, with long golden hair flowing down her back, a face like an up-turned flower.

Her face now, sucked empty of flesh, was shrunken back onto the bone. The skin, drawn tight over the skull's hollows, had been repeatedly punctured by burrowing maggots that tossed and heaved behind the perforated mask like rice in a sieve. From deep infested sockets a pair of tawny, crimson-veined eyes stared out at me full of hopeless entreaty.

A violent shudder passed through her body. Poisonous emanations filled the air with nauseating fumes. Her breathing quickened. She began to struggle, writhing and twisting in agony, as she tried to suck air into her lungs. Then, seized by a succession of paroxysms that seemed to carry her to the very brink of existence, she let out a muted shriek that subsided gradually in a long, halting whimper of pain.

I felt the vomit rise in my chest.

Was this what I'd heard from the other bed and mistaken in the dark for a woman's pleasure?

I recognized in the hideous spectacle before me something I'd witnessed during the Rorschach. It was the same girl – her frantic movements an attempt to get away from danger. Even now she was holding up her insufficient arms to fend off the oncoming horror.

Fear glittered in her eyes as they fixed themselves on mine. Almost involuntarily I turned and looked behind me.

I felt a momentary breathtaking pressure across my throat as if I'd been caught around the neck by a steel rope. But there was nothing . . .

When I looked around she was gone.

NINE

.

SESSION TWO
October 4
Length of interval since last session: 24 hours

A. INITIAL EXPECTATIONS

Less hostile atmosphere. Greater willingness to cooperate. Fewer attempts by patient to keep rigid control over the subjects discussed. Weakening resistance to the idea that he can be helped. Increased transference toward the therapist.

B. APPEARANCE AND MANNER OF PATIENT

Quite unexpected deterioration. Wild-eyed; pale, almost haggard complexion; somewhat disheveled. Evidently under mounting stress, he seemed very agitated and restless. His attempts at controlling himself were noticeably less successful than yesterday. I told him he should feel free to move about the room, if it made him feel better, or take off his coat, or whatever. He declined angrily, insisting that he felt perfectly all right. Later in the session, after he had unburdened himself of his cryptesthetic experiences, he became somewhat calmer, though never relaxed.

More than once during the interview I noticed him looking over his shoulder. At one point he got up and went to the door, opened it, then returned to his chair without offering any explanation.

C. SALIENT FEATURES OF INTERVIEW

Much of the first part was taken up with factual material which for one reason or another could not be touched on in the introductory session. Of his own accord the patient brought up the subject of his relationship with his wife, then dropped it again almost at once. He found it difficult to stay on any topic for long. Gave a disparaging account of his early hopes, ideals, political convictions – which amounted to a rather conventional flirtation with sixties radicalism – and his subsequent disillusionment, adding somewhat portentously that he belonged to a generation, born under the shadow of Hiroshima, that had never seriously believed it controlled its own destiny.

I hoped to steer the conversation back to the relationship with his wife, suggesting that their decision not to have children might have something to do with his currently pessimistic outlook. This produced an unexpected outburst from the patient, who recited a litany of statistics intended to illustrate that the world is a cesspool, civilization on the brink of collapse, nuclear war inevitable and so on. I intervened to remind him that yesterday he had given the impression of being quite content with life – that is, until the recent incident. For a moment he said nothing, then asked me quietly if I was accusing him of complacency, of having middle-class values, of only being concerned with his own material well-being at the expense of suffering humanity, etc. I denied making any accusations and changed the subject.

They argued about everything, they fought, they could get on each other's nerves, but he had never disagreed with his wife on any fundamental issue. At the outset both agreed that they didn't want to start a family. When the question was raised again after three years of marriage, they talked it over at length and decided they were happy as they were. It was about then that the patient bought his wife a dog. He admitted that he perhaps unconsciously hoped a pet would dispel any 'brooding thoughts' she might be having. Both he and his wife regarded the dogs with deep affection. The patient didn't deny that they became a substitute family, but insisted that I was wasting my time on that line of inquiry, he did not kill the dogs for any reason connected with his wife or their decision not to have children.

I withheld comment here. At a later stage it might be useful to have a talk with the wife.

D. THERAPEUTIC INTERVENTIONS GIVEN OR THOUGHT OF BUT NOT GIVEN

I read aloud the words found scrawled in blood on the surfaces of the white box and again in pencil on the back of the birthday card. At my request, the latter had been sent on to me by the G.P. I did not, of course, show the card, which was smeared with bloodstains. Nor did I preface the material in any way.

I studied the patient carefully. There was no immediate reaction. I asked him if the word 'Magmel' had any special meaning for him. Again negative. It was more or less as I'd expected.

In free association he produced the following : INSURANCE, ABDICATE, GUARDIAN, CRYSTAL, DESERT, FIRESTORM, RAIN, REDEEMER, DARKNESS, KEY, THRESHOLD, NAPLES, CLEANING FLUID, SCREEN, MIRROR . . . The progression seemed to cause the patient severe distress. He became very agitated, apprehensive, constantly looking over his shoulder, etc. I decided to discontinue.

At this point the patient announced that he had something important to tell me. The introduction of the coded material appeared to have precipitated a minor crisis, as I'd hoped it might. Although it was too soon to talk of transference, since the beginning of the session I had been aware of a conflict in which I was somehow involved. After a brief preamble explaining why he had not mentioned it before and imploring me not to dismiss what he had to say as the ravings of a lunatic, he informed me that since the incident with the dogs he had been having 'visions' of an alarming nature. These were of such intensity that while they lasted they blocked out all other perceptions and became the only reality. They were unlike anything he had experienced before: he referred here specifically to the type of hallucination or vivid fantasy associated with certain drugs. He listed a number of hallucinogens that he had occasionally indulged in – including opium, mescaline and lysergic acid – none of which, he claimed, had produced an effect remotely similar. He assured me that he was not now taking any of these or other drugs – apart from sleeping pills prescribed by his G.P. – nor had he been doing so in the recent past.

The patient believed to have had eidetic experiences on three separate occasions: 1) Saturday, September 30. After killing the dogs and returning to the city. Nightmarish vision of chaos and destruction. Physically overwhelmed. 2) Tuesday, October 3. During interview with Dr Hartman. Unable to complete Rorschach test, 'sees' in inkblot animated scenes of people trying to escape from unidentified danger. Sense of lurking evil, terror, but at a remove – not directly involved. 3) Last night. After waking from confused dream. Discovers a child, described as a living corpse, in a corner of his bedroom. This image recurring apparently from previous vision.

After all three incidents, patient experienced varying degrees of disorientation. More significantly, he was also overcome by feelings of guilt – particularly on the first occasion. When I pointed out that remorse over killing the dogs was not unnatural, he insisted on making a distinction. He spoke of a more generalized sense of guilt, though he had some difficulty in describing what he felt.

It occurred to me, though I didn't suggest it, that the patient's acceptance of responsibility for killing the dogs (irrational behavior) while denying that he was in any way ill might have extended the range of his guilt feelings and that the struggle with his conscience had given rise to delusions of persecution. Yet he was adamant that the only way he had 'survived' the experience (the attack in the hotel room) was by refusing to give in – by refusing to admit liability for what he had *not* done. He also maintained, apologizing if the idea seemed farfetched, that this 'massive burden of guilt' which he succeeded finally in rejecting had produced the bruises on his chest.

I did my best to reassure the patient on this point, without telling him that in states of anxiety, it is quite common for an individual to create a physical reaction in an attempt to defend himself against an impossible situation. I have never come across a case of bruising before – which rules out nothing. I deliberately did not try to explain this to the patient. An attempt at demystification would have been counterproductive, I felt. Particularly so since the moment seemed right to introduce the idea of hypnosis as therapy.

I brought up the subject in connection with the patient's hallucinations, suggesting that under hypnosis it might be possible to re-create his visions and investigate them more thoroughly. This idea seemed to please him, since it indicated that I was taking his more outlandish claims seriously. He was a little surprised that his G.P. had not told him about my practicing hypnotherapy, but I assured him that hypnosis has become routine clinical practice for a growing number of psychiatrists. He said he had no objection to being induced, though he expressed the usual doubts about whether he would make a good subject

E. OUTCOME OF THE INTERVIEW

In many respects real progress has been made. The patient has come a long way towards trusting the therapist. Signs of a developing conviction that he has found the right man to help him. A rather touching, almost childish confidence in the winning potential of our partnership − especially since the introduction of the hypnotic element. As sometimes happens, the simple mention of hypnosis has already begun to have therapeutic effect. The patient seems to think not only that it will prove him right − i.e., that he is not ill − but also, that it may provide the key to understanding what is happening to him. Motivation is good. He sees what is sometimes regarded as the unorthodox nature of treatment by hypnosis − the so-called 'magical' element − as being particularly suited to the uniqueness of his case. He went away much calmer and almost looking forward to tomorrow's session.

F. SUMMARY

There are some puzzling aspects to this case, but for the present I am treating it as a mild depressive psychosis. Depression clearly underlies anxiety neurosis − patient's fears reminiscent of what in the fifties we used to call 'nuclearosis'. In the circumstances, despite the presence of some paranoid features, hypnosis therapy seems justified. To probe further using conventional methods might precipitate acute manic depression and disassociation. Guilt feelings probably related to childhood trauma, which should emerge in age regression. Unless I'm much mistaken, the patient will prove highly susceptible.

TEN

10 p.m. – The landlady, Mrs Lombardi, a fat, greedy-looking person with little inquisitive black eyes, helped me move the other bed out. I told her I needed the space for a desk. She complained, of course, but I insisted – either the bed went or I did. I also tried to get her to take the screen away. That was asking too much: she had no place to store it, she said. The minute she left, I folded it up and leaned it against the wall where the bed had been. The place looks quite habitable now.

Feeling more relaxed tonight – largely thanks to Somerville. There is no question I feel better for having told him. He genuinely appears to believe me, which is a big relief. It's funny how only yesterday I thought he was a creep. Now it's almost as if my first impression, that I'd known him before from someplace, was the right one after all. I think this just means there's a strong affinity between the two of us, which is all to the good. The peculiar thing is that he even looks different to me now, though I still don't have a very clear picture of his face. When he told me about being a hypnotist, naturally I checked out the eyes. They're sort of a grayish yellow, with little flecks in them, not particularly dramatic. He has a rather disconcerting habit, though, of lowering his eyelids while he's talking, quite slowly, as if he were dropping off to sleep, then suddenly snapping them back open – like a lizard or something.

Before, I must have either avoided his eyes or simply not noticed them. Maybe it's just that – now he has eyes.

I asked Heyworth about hypnotism and he said there was really nothing to worry about. He even uses it himself for some clinical situations. That's how he got to know Somerville. They're both members of the American Society of Medical and Dental Hypnotists.

He gave me news of Anna. She's thinking of going over and staying with her mother in Vienna for a few weeks. Bill approves, of course. It was probably his idea in the first place, though he wouldn't admit it. I *think* I'm in favor. It might do her good to get away. It's just that I resent the way ... It feels as if there's been something going on behind my back. When I suggested that Anna and I might see each other briefly before she goes away, he said, 'Better not.'

Fuck him. I'm going to ask Somerville about this.

ELEVEN

The blinds in Somerville's study were drawn, the lighting subdued, the temperature a little warmer than usual; otherwise everything seemed much the same. One of the pictures had been taken down from the wall and a white chart scored with bold vertical lines hung in its place. It looked harmless enough. I was on the lookout for weird contraptions, flashing lights, pendulums, metronomes. There was nothing like that.

Somerville was sitting in the corner, his head back and his eyes shut, listening to Mozart. As I came up to him, he asked if the music bothered me, and then without waiting for an answer, reached over and turned down the volume on the stereo. He seemed friendly – over friendly, talking away about nothing in particular – which put me on my guard. I noticed he avoided any mention of hypnosis. This deliberate attempt to creat a relaxed atmosphere made me feel nervous. After a few minutes, he excused himself and left the room. Oddly, I had a disquieting sense of being abandoned.

I could hear him talking with someone in the hall: a low, conspiratorial murmur. Presently he reappeared, followed by the girl.

'Miss Tobin is going to audit the session, if that's all right with you,' Somerville announced. 'I always prefer to have a third party present – in fact, it's recommended procedure – but not if you have strong objections.'

'Well . . .' I hesitated, suddenly alarmed by the thought that under hypnosis I might reveal the intimate role his assistant had been playing in my dreams.

I glanced over at the girl. She was sitting demurely with her legs crossed and her delicate white hands folded in her lap, awaiting the instructions that would follow my reply. Our eyes met, and she smiled at me – provocatively, almost as if she were challenging me to object.

66

'I should explain that Miss Tobin is training to be a hypno-therapist,' Somerville added. 'Her discretion is naturally assured.'

'It's just that I hadn't expected anyone else,' I said, rather weakly.

'Remember what I told you yesterday – nothing can happen under hypnosis unless you want it to. If I were to try to make you do something against your will, it would result in the spontaneous termination of the hypnotic state. It can't work without your consent.'

'All right.' I resigned myself. 'I have no objections.'

What did it matter anyway? The girl might get off on it.

'I'm ready when you are,' I said with a touch of bravado.

It was simply a series of black stripes against a white background. In a frame it could have passed for one of the paintings on the wall opposite. I thought of asking Somerville how much he'd paid for it, but decided that the joke wouldn't be appreciated.

I was made to stand sideways to the chart so that the bridge of my nose was aligned with the center. It was explained that if I moved forward or backward, however, slightly, the chart would show the degree of 'postural sway'. I suspected this was just a gimmick, but Somerville seemed to take it seriously.

I was standing a few inches from the wall with my feet together, arms pulled close in to the sides, body straight and shoulders pushed back, head up and tilted slightly backward.

'Close your eyes.' He made it sound like a command. 'I want you to breathe deeply, in and out. That's good. Now listen carefully to what I'm going to say. This is simply a test of your ability to relax.'

He began to speak more slowly and in an even tone of voice, with long pauses between phrases. 'Imagine ... I want you to imagine you're standing on top of a tower ... high up in the air ... Are you there?'

'I think so.' I felt the touch of his hands on my shoulders.

'There's no danger ... no need to worry ... you won't fall. I'm standing right behind you. In a moment I'm going to take my hands away and you'll feel yourself swaying backwards. Now ... I want you to let go ... give yourself up completely to the idea of relaxing ... relaxing ... letting yourself go.'

After a minute or two – Somerville was silent during this time – I felt myself beginning to sway.

'There,' he said, sounding pleased, 'you're starting to relax. The chart shows three, four inches ... it's looking good. You're feeling very relaxed now ... swaying gently ... very relaxed ... gently backwards.'

Despite all attempts, mostly involuntary, to remain upright, I could feel myself leaning farther and farther over.

'Backwards you go.' His voice was firmer now. 'Backwards ... falling ... back, backwards ... falling, falling over backwards.'

I stumbled and put a foot behind to save myself, but I needn't have worried – Somerville had hold of my shoulders. I caught a light whiff of almond as I struggled quickly to regain my balance.

'Well done, Martin. You may sit down now.'

I went back to my chair feeling unreasonably pleased with myself, as if I'd achieved something rather more difficult than falling off my feet. I looked over to where the girl was sitting. Immersed in a book, she obviously hadn't been paying the slightest attention to what was going on. Her lack of interest was reassuring and at the same time a little irritating.

Somerville sat down opposite me. There was one more test to be completed before moving on to the real thing. He asked me to interlock the fingers of both hands and concentrate on them, to push them together and keep up a firm and constant pressure.

'I want you to feel,' he began again in his slow, rich voice, 'that all your fingers are joined together, as if they'd been glued one to another. Now, concentrate very hard. Don't stop looking or thinking about your hands even for an instant. As you concentrate, you will feel the boundaries between your fingers, becoming less and less distinct ... The fingers are bonded together ... stronger and stronger ... While this is happening, you will notice how the rest of your body is becoming more relaxed ... calm and relaxed. In a moment I am going to ask you to try to separate your hands – in a moment, not before. You will find it quite difficult to do so ... But then I will say, "Release them," and your fingers will part easily, leaving you feeling relaxed and very calm. Right now you feel them sticking together ... stronger and stronger ... glued to one another ... bonded together. Now separate your fingers.'

I pulled hard, trying to jerk them apart, but I couldn't shift them. I remember thinking, This is absurd. They were stuck fast.

'Release them!' Somerville gave the command and they parted like old enemies.

'That's really something.' I was laughing – out of surprise mostly, but also because I felt embarrassed, as if I'd been made the victim of a practical joke.

'You're a natural – see, there's nothing to worry about. You were awake the whole time, conscious of everything you were doing, and yet you were able to relax.

'It's only a question of relaxing, Martin. That's all there is to it.'

Yet I was still watching the proceedings with one mistrustful eye.

There was nothing mysterious about Somerville's technique; no penetrating stares, no esoteric passes. He worked with his voice, timing every phrase to coincide with the rise and fall of my breathing. It was firm and persuasive, but never overbearing. A well-tempered sound; I can hear it even now – the gentle, caressing resonance that promised with each gratifying syllable to lead the listener safely across to the other side, a place from which all care and pain had been banished. Yet part of my mind resisted the invitation. Evidently Somerville was aware of this. He gave me another pep talk about motivation, finally convincing me that if I wanted the induction to succeed I would have to let myself go, give in completely to his will.

My memory of the actual session is confined to the spoken word. Although I remained conscious throughout and remember everything that happened – up until the moment when Somerville intervened with amnesic suggestion – I gradually lost all awareness of my surroundings. It was a very odd sensation, something like that tranquil, twilight moment just before going to sleep, when the mind unloads its ballast and begins to soar gently upward. Yet at the same time it was a highly concentrated experience, like becoming absorbed in a good book or film to the exclusion of all else. I found it far from unpleasant, slipping easily and without fear into another world, where, apart from myself, only Somerville had the right to be. Although he soon faded as a presence on the physical plane, his voice accompanied me now wherever I went. It didn't matter which way I turned, it was always there, just ahead of me, leading the way.

'Let your head go back,' he began, 'close your eyes and listen carefully to what I say. I want you to listen to every word. Notice how I say things, how I pronounce words ... how I say things ... Concentrate on my voice ... my accent ... everything about the way I speak. Nothing else matters ... just concentrate on my voice.

'Now I want you to imagine that we are in a library – a quiet, peaceful room lined with books, leatherbound volumes, floor to ceiling. We are standing together by an open window ... looking out onto a garden. At the bottom of the garden you see an old stone wall overgrown with honeysuckle and jasmine. Beyond it, a green meadow that trails down to the sea ... The sun is shining on the water and the waves sparkle as they rise and fall ... We're feeling warm and relaxed, just standing there ... Far out to sea there's a lighthouse ... Can you see it? I want you to show me by raising your right hand ... Very good.

'Outside the window there's a balcony. A spiral staircase leads down into the garden. Now concentrate on my voice. We're going to go down the stairs ... down ... and around ... and into the garden. We can hear the murmur of the sea ... The sun feels so warm ... The air smells fragrant. Over there in the corner, between the trees, there's a hammock ... Raise your hand when you see it ... Good. Now I want you to walk over to the hammock and lie down in it. You feel it sway as you climb in ... swaying in the warm, the fragrant breeze. You're feeling very calm and relaxed ... You sink deeper and deeper into the hammock ... so calm and relaxed ... And now, you *sleep!*'

The voice grew loud abruptly, and then there was silence. For what seemed like a long time I could hear only the creaking of ropes as the hammock swung gently to and fro and the distant muffled roar of waves breaking on a beach. Later my guide came back and led me away from that infinitely restful place. We were setting off together on a voyage, he explained, a voyage of discovery. Of course, I wouldn't have to go anywhere I didn't want to. At any moment I could call a halt and we would abandon our journey or go somewhere else, or turn around and make our way back to the garden outside the library window. All I had to do was say the word – I could express myself now in ordinary speech – but he warned, the way would not always be easy. It would take us down through a seam in the mantle of darkness that covers the face of the unknown, down into the depths of my subconscious ... No, there was no need to be afraid. The light of truth would guide us, and together we would find what we were looking for, before returning safely to our garden sanctuary.

What followed this high-flown but, to the hypnotic subject, very compelling introduction comes as something of an anticlimax. After carefully evoking the imagery of my visions as I had described them to him, Somerville tried to re-create the circumstances in which they had occurred. In sequence he took me back to that Saturday morning when I killed the dogs. He walked me past the place where I had my first hallucination. He sat me down with Dr Hartman in front of the Rorschach inkblots. He woke me in the middle of Tuesday night and led me over to the screen in the corner of my room on Mulberry Street ... In each place he asked me what I saw, what I remembered, what I felt. But the answer was always the same. I knew nothing.

We returned to the library garden.

Once again I was lying in the hammock listening to the sea. I could smell the jasmine and honeysuckle and feel the warmth of the sun on my face.

'Feel the warmth, as you breathe in, spreading through your whole body. From your legs up to your stomach ... to your chest ... and up into your head ... relaxing you, unwinding you ... deeper and deeper. And as you breathe out, feel the warmth spread down your arms ... until it reaches the tips of your fingers ... deeper and deeper. You can feel all the muscles in your neck going loose, growing heavy ... relaxed and calm. From head to foot you are completely relaxed now. Your mind is calm. You only hear my voice ... only hear what I say.

'We're going to go back now, Martin ... back through ...'

A shutter comes down.

From here on I have no recollection of what happened. What follows is taken from a tape-recording.

At the end of the session, Somerville handed me a cassette – ostensibly a complete record of my induction – explaining that he wanted me to go over the material again in my own time. He failed to mention, however, that he had removed part of the tape from the cassette. It was not until several weeks later that I discovered he had censored the recording – for the same reason he chose to put a block on my memory while I was under hypnosis: he considered that I was not ready to handle the material in a waking state. He may well have been right. I reproduce the censored material here, rather than as chronologically revealed to me, because it affected the way Somerville treated the case in the weeks that followed.

'I want you to visualize,' the voice continues, 'a number that corresponds to your present age. You don't have to say anything, just raise your right hand when you can see the number ... Good. Now as I begin to count down from thirty-three you will visualize each number as I say it and you will become the age of that numeral. Thirty-two ... thirty-one ... thirty ... And as I count down, your memory will improve. Scenes from the past will unfold before your eyes. All the time your memory is becoming clearer ...' He continued counting down, pausing for about thirty seconds on each number.

'Twenty-two ... twenty-one ... You will enter fully into each year that I count. You will be able to see yourself when you were twenty ... Remember what it felt like to be ... nineteen ... and all the time you are becoming younger ... younger.

'You are returning toward childhood and your memory is steadily improving. As we go back in time, I want you to tell me – raise your right hand – when we reach the year that something happened. Fourteen ... thirteen ... twelve ... something that upset you very much ... eleven ... something that you have deliberately forgotten ... but now you *remember* ... nine ... you remember very clearly.

'How old are you, Martin? I want you to answer me this time.'
'I'm nine and a half.'
The voice, a little remote and uncertain, is my own – the voice of a man trying to imitate a child.

'Where are you?'

'At home, at our house.'

'Do you want to tell me what the house is like?'

'It's okay.'

'What have you been doing?'

'It's raining out. I'm soaking wet. If my mom catches me I'll be in trouble. You better not tell her.'

'No, I won't tell anybody. Where have you been?'

'Fishin', over at the Johnson place. It started to rain and I came home. Only they followed me.'

'Who followed you?'

'The dogs, of course. I *told* them to go back. I shouted at them, but they wouldn't listen to me.'

'Where are they now?'

'They've gone off back.'

'All of them, Martin?'

'I'm scared ...'

'What are you scared of?'

'It's dark ... the rain ... everything's rattling and banging ... oh ... the rain.'

'Is anyone with you in the house?'

'Nope. Only Missy, Tsu-lai's little girl. Tsu-lai's the lady who cooks and cleans up, but Missy's not allowed in the house, 'cept when her mother's there.'

'Where are your parents?'

'My mom's out visiting Mrs Greenlake and my dad's at work.'

'And your brothers?'

'At school. In Boston. We're going back there soon.'

'Are you looking forward to that?'

'I guess so.'

'Let's move on a little, Martin. What are you doing now?'

'Nothing ... I'm playing with this piece of wood. I found it in the shed.'

'Why are you crying, Martin? What's upsetting you?'

'He wouldn't stop barking.'

'You mean – ah – Jeff?'

'He wouldn't stop, he just wouldn't. All the others went back, but he kept on barking. He was scratching on the door. He wanted to come in. Out of the rain.'

'Has he gone now?'

'I let him in, but now he's ...'

'You let him into the house?'

'I took him through to the back. I put him in the shed and told Missy to look after him. But she wouldn't, she said she didn't want to. She said she would tell on me. He left muddy paw marks all over the house. He jumped up on the couch, but I've cleaned it off. No one's gonna know.'

'I won't tell. You can trust *me*, Martin. It's all right. But where is Jeff?'

'Out there someplace. Missy threw him out. I got mad at her ... real mad.'

'You did?'

'I called Jeff, but he didn't come. I made her take her clothes off ... (Pause) The hole kept filling up with water faster than I could dig. I gave up and carried the spade back to the shed.'

'Why were you digging a hole?'

'For her clothes, so no one would find them.'

'Where is Missy now, Martin?'

'I dunno. Not where I left her. She crawled away under some sacks, over in the corner. She was shivering all over and her eyes were moving around all white. I couldn't look at her. I hit her again with the spade. Again and again. She stopped shivering then. There was a bunch of blood on the floor; the ants were drinking it up. I covered them over with earth from the tubs. Then I dragged Missy out by her ankles – into the rain. She was heavy. It left a trail of blood across our lawn. The rain washed it all away. I pushed her under the fence into some bushes. Now the leopard'll get her.'

There is a pause.

'Why did you kill her, Martin?'

'I dunno.'

'Were you that mad at her?'

'I dunno.'

'Were you afraid your father would find out that you let a dog into the house? That you'd been over at the farm?'

'I didn't *want* to do it. Missy was my *friend*.'

'Was it Jeff's barking that made you angry?'

'I dunno ... I just had to *save* her. And Jeff too. We were the only ones left.'

'You mean you were frightened of being left on your own? Was it some kind of game?'

'I dunno. They were all dead – all the people, all the animals, everyone.'

'Who were they?'

'I dunno ... it was *dark*. I want my mom.'

'When did everyone die?'

'A long time ago. I dunno ... I didn't want to ... it wasn't my fault. Don't leave me here, *please!*'

'It's all right, Martin, you're perfectly safe. You don't have to say any more. You've done very well. There's nothing to be afraid of ... you're quite safe. We're going to go back now ... back to the garden outside the library window. You're lying in your hammock again ... calm, relaxed ... calm. You can rest there for a while.'

There follows a long pause, the only sound on the tape the steady rise and fall of my breathing.

BOOK TWO

THE
WHITE
BOX

ONE

9 p.m. – He said there would be no aftereffects, and there are none. I feel tired and have a dull, fuzzy kind of headache, but that could have been brought on by anything – like taking the subway from Ninety-sixth Street. When I finally got back here, I swallowed a couple of Excedrin and poured myself a large Scotch.

The whisky didn't seem to help, so rather than waste it I tried to siphon the stuff back into the bottle. Most of it ended up on Mrs Lombardi's carpet. I noticed then that my hands were shaking – Somerville did say I might experience 'a minimal reaction'.

Now I'm lying on the bed waiting for the pills to work.

The tremor has transferred itself to my left eyelid. I just checked the mirror – scarcely visible.

Should go out and get something to eat – I've had nothing since breakfast – but I don't have the energy. And the whole idea of sitting by myself in some friendly little neighborhood restaurant ... that Greek place on MacDougal Street where Anna always insists on going whenever we're anywhere near the Village. They're sure to ask where she is – they might even inquire politely after the boys. That's *just* what I need.

I haven't talked to Anna now in six days – the longest we've ever been out of touch.

While I can still keep my eyes open, I'd better make some notes on today's session.

On the subject of hypnosis ... Fuck it, I remember exactly what happened, plus it's all down on tape. Somerville gave me the cassette, pressed it into the palm of my hand. He suggested I play it over a few times – I might glean something, he said. He's even lent me his portable, a Sony TC-150.

* Extract from Martin Gregory's diary

Being hypnotized isn't so bad. To a certain extent I found it pleasurable, like getting a little stoned. But the fact is nothing useful has come out of it. Somerville's attempt to investigate my 'visions' was a complete failure.

I talked to Heyworth on the phone this morning. I asked him if he thought I should try to see Anna before she goes off to Europe Saturday. He says she doesn't feel up to seeing me yet; I'm supposed to find that 'yet' encouraging.

I know that Heyworth is doing his best to keep us apart. Not that I blame him – he thinks he's protecting her, of course. In Somerville's opinion, the longer Anna and I put off seeing each other, the harder it will be. I feel he's right. I told him I *wanted* to see her, just for a few minutes. He said he'd talk to Heyworth.

God knows I miss her.

It's hot in here. The J&B I spilled on the carpet is really stinking the place up. I need some air. Maybe I *will* go out and get something to eat.

Only now I'm not hungry. Too tired to move. There's still that tic in my eye, but it's quieting down. I feel good, relaxed.

Somerville was pretty insistent: play the cassette over and let me know what you think.

Play it over, he said. Play it over.

But the Sony is sitting over there on the table in front of the window.

Out of reach.

12.45 a.m. – An hour ago I woke up out of a sound sleep. My eyes just seemed to open. I was instantly alert.

I lay there for a long time, not moving, monitoring the room. The light was on. I was still in my clothes. My notebook and pen lay in the bed beside me. I must have let them fall. The pen had made a small stain on the sheet.

I felt a little apprehensive, remembering what happened here the other night. But this time I hadn't been dreaming. I've no idea why I woke up like that. I didn't need to take a leak. The light maybe.

I turned it off and tried to get back to sleep.

Lying there in the dark, I get this feeling there's something I've forgotten to do, a vague sense of liability.

Next week the planning group is to meet for discussions on a major productivity drive. I am scheduled to give a report on the feasibility of changing over from mainframe computers to the new small, low-cost data processors. The report is crucial to my career. A week ago that report was all that I could think about. Now it has nothing to do with me anymore.

I decided to sit up and read for a while, but found it almost impossible to concentrate. I lit a cigarette and tried to make a list of things I ought to have done – letters I've meant to write, bills I have to pay, Anna's parking tickets, getting Hawkins and Scott to finish work on the roof . . . None of it seemed to matter.

I can't locate the source of my anxiety.

Then I found myself going over to the table and pushing the Play button on the Sony.

The room filled with orchestral music. It reminded me of a TV commercial. I thought at first that Somerville must have given me the wrong tape. But then I recognized the first movement of the Mozart symphony he'd played at the beginning of our session.

The music soon began to fade, and as if the tape had been skillfully mixed, the diminuendo cued in Somerville's mellow baritone. The effect made me want to laugh.

Something prevented me from laughing.

'Close your eyes,' the machine said. 'I want you to breathe deeply, in and out . . . That's good. Now listen carefully to what I'm going to say. This is simply a test of your ability to relax . . .'

Just as I remembered.

My own voice, when it came on, sounded tinny and nervous, unsure of itself. As I went deeper into the trance it grew strong.

I listened to the rest of the recording, not paying too much attention. It crossed my mind that I might still be susceptible. When it was getting toward the end, where Somerville leads me back to the garden outside the library window, I realized that I'd forgotten how he brought me out of the trance.

Until now I'd been sitting on the edge of the bed. Funny, but I didn't want to get too close to the machine. But as he began to wind the session up, I moved to the chair in front of the table.

'You can feel all the muscles in your neck going loose, growing heavy . . . relaxed and calm. From head to foot you are completely relaxed now. Your mind is calm. You only hear my voice ... only hear what I say ...'

There was a long pause.

'We're going to go back now, Martin ... back through ...'

And then nothing. I waited for it to continue, but nothing happened. The tape gave a little hiccup and whirred on in silence. Nothing, not even the sound of breathing.

Slightly irritated, since it was the only part I really wanted to hear, I reached over to switch the machine off.

Just then the recording started up again.

'... want you to go deeper into hypnosis, focusing your mind on my voice ... with each breath ... deeper as we prepare to journey back in time.

'In a moment, Martin, I'm going to count down very slowly from eight to zero. Just as before, you will visualize each number as I say it and you will become that age. When I say one, you will see yourself as you were at the age of one. And then I will say, "Go back further, go further back," and you will begin to feel calm and relaxed ... even more relaxed, calmer even, even sleepier than before.

'You will gradually discover that there are parts of your memory that you didn't know about before – memories of another place, another time ... other times, other places ... There's nothing to be afraid of, Martin ...

'When I reach zero you will go into a deep, very deep sleep.'

TWO

'Where are you? Can you hear me? Where are you?'

'Ah ... ran [indistinct] ... cu ... aba.'

'Cuba? Tell me, in English. Where are you?'

'Cuyaba ... name of this town.'

'What is your name?'

'I ... I don't know ... can't remember.'

'Concentrate on your breathing. Now I'm going to count down from three to zero, and on the last count you will know your name. Three ... two ... one ... Whatever comes to mind, I want you to tell me. Zero.'

'I see P.H.F. ... my initials.'

'What do they stand for?'

'Percy ... Harrison ... Fawcett. Name's Fawcett.'

'Good. [Pause] Where is Cuyaba?'

'In Mato Grosso ... headwaters of the Rio del Paraguay. Last outpost of civilization – if you can call it that.'

'Can you describe it?'

'Miserable place. Some of the poorest, most wretched people I've seen in all Brazil. Been cooped up here for weeks now ... endless delays ... dealing with those damned bureaucrats. The sooner I can get away the better.'

'Where will you go?'

'Up country, north of here. North is where we're headed – that's all anyone needs to know.'

'What are you doing now?'

'We're waiting for the mules, sitting out on the veranda of the Hotel Gama. That damned liar Federico promised he'd have them for us two weeks ago.'

'Who else is with you?'

'Jack, my eldest boy ... and Raleigh. Raleigh Rimmel, a friend of his from England. Both of them are new to this game, but they have the makings of the right sort – in good physical condition, young enough to adapt. A few months on the trail will toughen them.'

'How old are you?'

'I am fifty-seven. Too old really to be setting off again, but I must.'

'Why must you?'

'My last journey. It's the end of a lifelong endeavor. If I do not achieve my objective this time, then all my work in South America amounts to nothing.'

'Can you tell me what that objective is?'

'I make no secret of *what* I'm looking for. Our destination is a city lost in the jungle. I call it "Z".'

'What do you expect to find there?'

'The remnants of an ancient civilization. A city still occupied, I have reason to believe, by descendants of its original inhabitants. For centuries now, millennia even, they have remained hidden ... surrounded by impenetrable jungle, protected from the outside world by a ring of savage tribes. The odds are not in our favor, but I know the risks better than any man. And now that the others are all dead, I alone have knowledge of where "Z" lies. If we don't come out, no one should look for us. But I have no fear of failure.'

'What about Jack and Raleigh? Are they aware of the danger?'

'[Pause] ... I would have preferred to undertake this journey alone, but unfortunately it was not within my power. I know I can rely on Jack. In an emergency his courage will stand – and Raleigh will follow him anywhere.'

'They accompany you willingly, then?'

'Of course. They regard it as the adventure of a lifetime. Jack is even more impatient to get started than I am. He spends his days practicing with the rifle and going for long training walks, though the heat is stifling. They've both been breaking in their boots; Raleigh's feet are covered in Johnson's plasters as a consequence.'

'How soon do you hope to set out?'

'Any day now ... as soon as we get the pack animals. Our provisions are all in order. The peons are engaged as far as Bacairy Post; after that they will be released and we go on alone.'

'The three of you?'

'And the dogs ...'

'The dogs?'

'I bought a pair of mutts in the market a week ago. Answer to the names of Pastor and Chulim. Neither of them a patch on Vagabundo, but they have bags of spirit. We'll be glad of their company soon enough, I expect.'

'Do you know what date it is?'

'April . . . nineteen twenty-five.'

'In a moment I'm going to ask you to move ahead in time. You're feeling calm and relaxed. Now I want you to concentrate on your breathing. I'm going to count you down again, and on zero it will be a month later.

'Three . . . two . . . one . . . zero. [Pause] Can you tell me where you are?'

'Dead Horse Camp.'

'What do you see?'

'White . . . whitened bones . . . I can see them lying in the clearing a few yards ahead of us. It was here that my horse died in nineteen twenty. A previous attempt to get through. Poor old Bravo. I had to turn back.'

'Are you making good progress?'

'If it weren't for these damned flies. We're pestered by them day and night. Flies that sting like wasps, small enough to get through our head nets. The pain is literally maddening. They follow us everywhere. A plague of vicious . . . I don't remember them ever being as bad as this. Must be the humidity. We're getting a lot of rain, and it's hot for this time of year. I seem to be perspiring more than usual. Thank God, in a few days we'll be out of this infernal region.'

'What lies ahead?'

'Dense jungle. We should be making contact with the Nefaquas within a couple of weeks. Soon after that I hope to reach the waterfall.'

'Another landmark? From an earlier trip?'

'No, tomorrow we venture into unexplored country. The waterfall is our first objective on the way to "Z".'

'How will you find it in the jungle? Do you travel by river?'

'By compass. I first heard about it from a Bacairy Indian several years ago. No one else knows the . . .'

'It's all right, you can trust me.'

'He told me that the roar of the waters can be heard from five miles distant. A figure carved out of white rock stands in the river below the falls. The Indian also spoke of a tower of stone in the forest nearby. He was frightened of it. He had seen a light there at night shining from a window. But the Bacairys would naturally fear the place – it's in the heart of Morcegos territory. They're enemies. Morcegos are primitive troglodytes who live in pits beneath the floor of the forest and venture out only at night to hunt and scavenge ... Other tribes call them the "Bat" people.'

'Do you count on befriending them?'

'There would be no point ... We shall try to avoid them altogether.'

'How will you do that if you intend to enter their territory?'

'I have a great deal of experience in dealing with forest Indians. Now that the peons have gone back, we travel lighter ... fewer animals ... less of a circus. If we are lucky, the Morcegos will let us alone.'

'How are Jack and Raleigh making out?'

'It's been hard on them, but on the whole they've taken to the *sertão* well. Jack is in fine shape, getting stronger every day.'

'And Raleigh?'

'Raleigh still has problems with his feet. Badly swollen now ... from scratching insect bites. I warned him. When he took his socks off today to bathe, strips of skin came away with the wool. He has a raw spot on his arm too. Don't like the look of it.'

'Will he be able to go on?'

'Nothing will induce him to go back. For the moment we have enough food and no need to walk, but I cannot say how long this will last. The real challenge lies ahead.'

'What about the dogs? Are they still with you?'

'Yes! ... They are well enough, though Pastor limps a little. I suspect he does it to gain sympathy.'

'I'm going to ask you again to move on in time. When I reach zero, another month will have passed. I want you to tell me what you are doing. Tell me what you see.'

'Everything is dark ... dark as Hades. It must be night still ... but it's time to be going, break camp; have to keep on.'

'Are you near to your objective? Have you found the waterfall?'

'That noise. Can't you hear? Today it seems . . .'

'No, I hear nothing. What is it?'

'I thought for a moment . . . It's always the same, the roaring never ceases, like an army on the move. I've been hearing it for a week now, only it never gets any closer.'

'Which direction are you headed?'

'Can't be certain any longer . . . nor'west, I think. Sound of the falls everywhere, all around me . . . Sometimes it plays tricks — marching tunes and nursery rhymes in my ears. I must find it soon. This time will be the last. I cannot fail them now.'

'Why don't you take a compass reading?'

'I had to let the compass go. They wouldn't have stood a chance without it.'

'What do you mean? Who wouldn't have stood a chance?'

'I had to send Jack and Raleigh back to Bacairy Post. Two weeks after we left Dead Horse Camp . . .'

'It's all right, take your time.'

'The mules could go no further for want of food. Had to abandon them. We shouldered our packs and set off towards the river on foot. Raleigh's leg hadn't healed . . . I tried to make them both turn back, but they wouldn't hear of it. We were constantly plagued by those damned insects — clouds of them. Raleigh's leg got worse, infected . . . he contracted blood poisoning. By then I didn't need to persuade Jack; it was clear that Raleigh would die if he didn't get help. They left me the two dogs and a little food. With luck, they should reach Bacairy Post . . . any day now.'

'Why didn't you accompany them?'

'Why? Because I had no choice. It's my duty to go on. I could have taken them back . . . Yes, it might have improved their chances. But I didn't. Those who know me will understand. All my life, I have sacrificed so much, demanded so much of others — for *this* moment. To give up now that I am near, so near to finding the way through . . .'

'What will you do?'

'It's getting lighter. I can make out a few trees up ahead . . . hanging, twisted shapes of lianas. Soon be dawn. Ghostly mist over the forest floor like a fallen veil. Such beauty defies . . .'

'Listen! . . . No, it was nothing. Some night bird. The slightest sound catches my attention. If there's any game about, it will be moving soon.'

'Are your supplies holding out?'

'Yesterday I ate the last of the *mandioca*, and a few unripe *paripou* nuts. Spent the whole day looking for food. The day before, I shot a toucan, but Pastor and Chulim got to it first. They're as hungry as I am, poor devils. I've decided that if I find nothing to eat by this evening I shall have to . . . They are becoming wild. It's either them or me.'

'You mean to kill the dogs?'

'Both together . . . easier that way. There's hardly any meat on the wretched animals. If I don't eat tomorrow, I shall be too weak to continue.'

'Now listen carefully: this is important. Concentrate on your breathing. That's good. I want you to move ahead in time to the moment when you have to kill Pastor and Chulim. Three . . . as before, on zero . . . two . . . one . . . zero.

'Describe what is happening.'

'They're watching me. The forest has eyes. I can tell . . . it's always like this. Only a matter of time now. Soon it will be dark. That's when they come.'

'The dogs are watching you?'

'Morcegos.'

'But where are the dogs? Have you . . .?'

'I didn't have the heart.'

'Are they still with you?'

'Who? Pastor and Chulim? Gone.'

'Did you try to kill them?'

'I couldn't . . . couldn't do it. They left me because there was no food.'

'You're quite sure? This is important.'

'I'm positive.'

'All right; I want you to come forward in time just a few hours. [Pause] What are you doing now?'

'Move very slowly. The path is difficult. Have to force myself to . . . Mustn't rest. I can't take another step. All I can think of is lying down . . . But I mustn't . . . *mustn't*. They're following me.'

'Who? Who is following you?'

'Can't see them, but they're all around me. If I could just find a way ... might have a chance. I can hear the falls, much closer now, like thunder. A light! There's a light ahead shining through the trees. Come on, by God ... it must be the tower. I am home, home at last.

'No! Please, no! Not yet. Let me through. They're ... God Almighty ... help me, help me. Let me *through* ... no, *no!*'

'What do you see? Tell me.'

'Everything is dark ... darkness ... darkness.'

THREE

PREAMBLE

I delayed dictating the write-up to include an informal note on the
patient's wife, who came to see me this morning (October 6) at her
own request – the arrangements were made somewhat reluctantly
by Dr Heyworth.

Her appearance and manner were generally subdued, though she
seemed more self-possessed than I'd been led to expect. A strikingly
beautiful girl, she was neatly if somberly dressed (drab, dark colors),
wore little or no makeup and kept her coat on and her head covered
throughout the visit. She avoided eye contact at all times. The look
of constrained despair in her face, however, left no doubt that she
has been, and still is, under severe stress. I got the impression that
she could be partly blaming herself for what happened – perhaps
without knowing it.

There is a strong resistance to the idea that the patient is unwell.
She is concerned about his welfare, asks how he's managing on his
own, whether he's looking after himself properly. But pretends to be
indifferent in all other respects, particularly with regard to patient's
state of mind, treatment, etc. Clearly finds it difficult to admit to
herself that she may still love him in spite of what he has done. She
spoke in a vague and confused way about her 'duties as a wife'. I
suggested it might be easier for her if she could learn to accept that
her husband is unwell.

She ignored the remark, but soon afterwards asked whether I
thought it would help if she agreed to see him. She seemed doubtful,
and I responded cautiously, making it clear that I felt there was

some risk involved. I also reminded her that Dr H. was against it. Without divulging the reasons for my concern – I said nothing to her about hypnosis or regression therapy – I warned her she might find her husband somewhat changed, that he might act strangely towards her. When she asked, in a desolate voice, what more could she expect, I told her – I told her again – that I believed Martin Gregory to be unwell.

On her way out she thanked me, but without much conviction. I asked her if she felt strong enough to see him before she went away; I suggested that it might be better if she waited until after her return. She said defiantly that she would always love her husband whatever he did and that yes, of course, she would see him.

The reaction I had been hoping for.

A. Initial Expectations

General improvement in patient and easing of tension. Develop-. ment of trust between patient and therapist. Proceedings dominated by introduction of hypnosis. No therapeutic interventions.

B. Atmosphere

Cooperative. Some nervousness – only to be expected.

C. Main Trends

The patient proved at once to be highly susceptible and had no difficulty in achieving both medium and somnambulistic trance. As I suspected, his somewhat militant view of himself as a self-sufficient, independent sort of person concealed an intense un-conscious need for passivity. The tranquilizing effect of the hypnoidal state soon overcame any resistance there may have been to the investigatory nature of the induction. An alliance with the therapist was gratefully accepted. The patient seemed to welcome the offer of refuge from his troubled world. Presence of neurosis a help here rather than a hindrance. Breathing pattern and other physiological correlates indicated that he was deriving therapeutic benefit from his temporary abdication from his life.

1. Visions: After a successful induction, the failure to re-create

his recent eidetic experiences under hypnosis was puzzling. Resistance appeared to be negligible, yet his subconscious managed to block all my questions. The possibility still exists that the patient's so-called visions were either drug-induced hallucinations or mere fantasy.

2. Regression to age nine: Story volunteered by patient about dogs in Philippines (Session One) retold with a different ending and highly dramatic abreaction – i.e., the killing of the little girl, Missy. Although it was Missy's refusal to look after the dog Jeff which apparently provoked the boy's murderous rage, causal motivation must lie elsewhere. But not within the family constellation.

3. Regression beyond birth to postulated former existence: The key to an unusually vivid and detailed account appeared to be the moment when 'Fawcett' declares his intention of killing the two dogs Pastor and Chulim. It seemed at first like a plausible and convenient explanation of the patient's actions last Saturday. Fawcett's decision to spare their lives, however, invalidates analogical procedure.

D. INTERPRETATIONS THOUGHT OF BUT NOT GIVEN

In other words, back to square one. It is difficult at this point to see any objective connection between a) the slaughter of the golden retrievers Caesar and Claus b) the 'visions' c) the Philippines story and d) the Fawcett material. If 'dogs' have emerged as an obsessional motif, then clearly it is only one of secondary importance. It may be worth noting there are no dogs in b). However, the girl 'seen' cowering in a corner of the patient's room, the living corpse (also mentioned in the Rorschach), may well be the same as in c), where Missy crawls into a corner of the shed to die after he attacks her with a spade.

The only consistent theme is water: In a) rain, moisture on the kitchen walls b) 1. flooded streets 2. drowned animals c) torrential rain and d) the waterfall. But at best the link is tenuous.

In order to protect the patient from his own potentially dangerous revelation that as a child he may have committed murder, I decided to suggest posthypnotic amnesia, and removed the relevant section of tape from the recording of the session. At a later stage in his treatment it should be possible to confront the patient with this material – but not now.

E. OUTCOME

In general terms the session can be rated a success. The patient has shown himself to be an excellent hypnotic subject, and the material revealed by regression, though in some respects confusing, leaves no doubt as to the direction treatment must take.

F. AFTERTHOUGHTS

Position in regard to the law: as far as I know, inviolate. I shall have to check with Siegel and Barse. But to protect all concerned it will be necessary from now on to keep a closer watch over the patient. The question of hospitalization may have to be reconsidered. For the moment I do not believe him to be a danger to himself or others.

N.B. The name Fawcett had a familiar ring. Out of curiosity I called O'Rorke at the Library and asked him to look it up for me in the British National Biography. It came as no surprise to learn that there was a Colonel Fawcett – a well-known explorer who has been the subject of several articles and books.

FOUR

*Friday, October 6

10.30 p.m. – I called him up about the tape this morning, demanding an explanation. He apologized for 'springing' Fawcett on me. He said he hadn't given a warning of his intention to regress me because he felt that I wouldn't have responded if I'd known about it beforehand – and that there was no sense in discussing Fawcett until after I'd listened to the tape.

I asked Somerville if he seriously expected me to take the Fawcett material for evidence of my having lived before.

'That's not important, Martin,' he said. 'The question of whether "previous existences" revealed under hypnosis are the product of fantasy or actual experience "revisited" does not affect its usefulness as an instrument of psychological healing. In a case like yours the symptoms might be the result of some event – the psychological term is an "exciting cause" – that took place in childhood, but the origin of the problem often lies buried in the uttermost recesses of the mind. Regression therapy provides a key to these vaults of the "deep unconscious".'

Then he asked me if I had ever heard the name P. H. Fawcett before I listened to the tape, read anything about him, possibly in books on South America, the First World War or the history of exploration: Did I realize that Colonel Fawcett was in fact a celebrated traveler who had set off in 1925 on an expedition into the jungles of Mato Grosso, an expedition from which he had never returned?

I answered no to all his questions. It came as a surprise to me to learn that Fawcett had actually existed. But it doesn't change how I feel about the tape: I never had much time for the salve of reincarna-

* *Extract from Martin Gregory's diary*

tion. Yet I resent Somerville's insinuating that I regurgitated the story straight from some history textbook. I countered with the suggestion that he might have dredged it all up himself, planted *his* fantasy in *my* head. He informed me in that mellifluous, understanding voice of his that technically it wasn't 'feasible'.

It particularly annoyed me when he asked me what I made of the passages about Fawcett's dogs. I answered without thinking: I said it didn't surprise me in the least that he hadn't killed them.

He didn't comment, just told me the good news about Anna . . .

FIVE

It was raining when I set off for the airport. Once more I'd awakened early with that nagging sense of obligation, the feeling that I had something important to do. Then I remembered that it was Saturday and I was going to see her again, and the feeling was replaced by an anxious kind of joy.

I arrived at Kennedy with an hour to spare and went straight to the departure lounge of the T W A terminal. We were to meet there by the main gate at a quarter of twelve. Somerville had arranged everything. Her flight to Vienna was at 12.30, which would give us a good half-hour together – if we needed that long. I hoped I might be able to persuade her to change her mind and stay.

I bought a newspaper and took up a strategic position under the departures board with my back to the observation windows. That way, I could see all I needed and at the same time remain partly hidden from view to anyone entering the lobby. I wanted to see her – have her in my sights awhile – before she saw me. I'm not sure why. I'd been over it so many times – how it would be, that first moment; what I would say to her; whether or not to embrace her; when to . . . I longed to see her.

The rain washed against the sheltering expanse of Plexiglas behind my head. I thought of Fawcett, alone and without compass, wandering through the jungle in search of his elusive falls. I thought of Fawcett, but I was skeptical of any suggestion that our lives were connected.

A sudden screeching of hydraulic brakes. Out across the water-logged taxiways the looming bulk of a silver 747 was nosing its way in toward the terminal. I watched until it came to a standstill. Somehow the whine of its jet engines brought home to me the simple fact of Anna's impending departure. I realized the meeting might not go the way I had planned. The idea that taking her in my arms and telling her I loved her would make everything all right seemed pitifully optimistic.

I thought about the boys: how they'd come trotting up to me that morning with their ears pricked and their tails wagging, their long golden coats dark from the rain. The idea that she could ever forgive me . . .

The feeling, the feeling of nagging obligation returned now with an urgency. There *was* something I'd failed to do, something so simple and obvious that I was surprised it hadn't struck me before – I'd forgotten to get Anna a going-away present.

In the airport gift shop the Muzak seemed louder. I found it difficult to concentrate as I drifted among the concession stands, carousels and counters piled high with useless glitter. The lights revolved to the strains of a Hawaiian Christmas. I couldn't make up my mind what to get her.

In the end I settled on an expensive trifle, a silver charm bracelet with enamel attachments, which I asked a tall black girl behind the counter to gift-wrap.

Carefully putting the bracelet back into its display box, she closed the lid and began very methodically to cut out a small square of plain gold wrapping paper. I glanced impatiently at my watch. It was almost 11.30. If Anna happened to turn up early, I wouldn't be back in position in time. I told the girl to forget about the gift wrapping.

She laid down her scissors with a sigh, then slipped the box into a brown paper bag. She handed it to me, and I thanked her, stuffing it into my coat pocket.

As I came out of the gift shop, I saw Anna standing at the top of the steps by the entrance to the departure lounge. She turned and looked at me. We were still some distance apart, separated by a party of Japanese tourists. The moment we saw each other, I realized – and I believe she did too – that our meeting was a mistake.

I waved to her, and she inclined her head. I couldn't see if she smiled.

I made my way toward her with a tight feeling in my chest. There was something about the way she looked . . . She seemed thinner. I put it down to the fact that she was standing at an angle to me, wearing travel clothes. She had on her riding boots, and the dark green Lodenmantel her mother had bought for her in

Salzburg two summers ago. I never liked the coat. Perhaps she had chosen to wear it for that reason.

When I reached the top of the steps, I suddenly saw what was different about Anna, what was wrong: she had had all her hair cut off.

I don't know why I didn't see it at once. Her hair was the first thing you noticed; so pale, almost white, the color of white sand. It really hurt me to see her looking like this. Then I realized it was meant to, that she had mutilated herself for my benefit.

'Hello, Martin,' she said quietly. I caught the eclipse of a dead smile.

For a moment I was unable to speak. I reached out a hand toward her, withdrawing it at once. The barriers were already up. If I was going to show her any sign of affection, she was making it very clear that this was out of the question.

'We might as well go and find somewhere to sit,' I said. 'Have we got time?'

She nodded.

We installed ourselves in the coffee shop overlooking the departure lounge. The table was close to the balcony – small and awkward. Looking down, I saw that the folded newspaper I had left to hold my seat under the observation windows was being read by a man in a tan raincoat with a matching rain hat pulled down over a long, fleshy face. Just then he happened to look up in our direction, and for a moment I thought it was Bill Heyworth sitting there – I wouldn't have put it past him, following her to the airport, to make sure she got on the plane all right.

But the man was a stranger to me. He must have felt me staring at him, because he looked away quickly and went right back to reading my newspaper.

Anna kept her eyes lowered. The light behind her shorn head revealed the outline of a small, fragile skull. She looked frighteningly vulnerable. I wanted to say something – anything – to reassure her. Tell her that I didn't *mind* about the hair, that it made her look more beautiful. But I could no more mention her hair now than I could tell her that I loved her.

'Are you going to be okay?' I asked.

'Yes, I think so.'

'Are you sure? How about money? Are you okay?'

'Yes.'

'Bill said your mother's going to meet you at the airport.'

'She said she'd try. She's hurt her back.'

'So you're all organized?' I smiled ruefully, using a pet expression of mine that she used to enjoy teasing me about.

She just looked at me.

I lit a cigarette and sat back in the small ironwork chair trying to keep our knees from touching under the table.

'Martin?' I could see she was treading cautiously. 'Are *you* going to be all right? I mean, it must be hard for you in that place – you know, you could always live at home while I'm gone.'

'I think I'd better stay where I am for a while. I'm seeing a head doctor.' I laughed, to make it easier.

'Yes ...' She hesitated. 'Bill said he was a good man. He could help you.'

'He's good,' I said.

The waitress brought the coffee then, and I paid the check.

An uncomfortable silence had grown up between us. We both reached for the sugar at the same moment. My hand brushed hers, and she pulled away. I could tell by the way she looked at me that I was suddenly repugnant to her. She offered me a pink sachet of Sweet 'n Low, then took one herself.

I kept my hands beneath the table, out of sight.

Sitting opposite her, I thought about the last time we'd slept together. Barely a week ago, it seemed an irretrievable memory.

We made stilted conversation, my wife of six years and I.

There were moments that generated a little of the old warmth, and a false kind of hope. We talked about the things that needed doing around the house, about starting work on the barn, about cutting down on the heating bills this winter. There was mention of Thanksgiving. But we both knew all along that it wasn't any good.

From the moment I'd laid eyes on her in the terminal I'd known that it wasn't going to work. What came as a surprise to me was that I didn't care the way I thought I would. After looking forward so intensely to seeing her again. I'd expected to feel more. I couldn't wholly admit it yet, but the truth was I felt very little. In a detached kind of way I found myself wishing it would be over, so that I could get back to the library.

The waitress offered us refills. We declined, and she cleared our cups away, giving the tabletop a quick wipe with a yellow cloth she took from the pocket of her apron. I glanced over at the clock on the departures board. It was five past twelve.

I put my hand into my coat pocket and with some difficulty removed the little box with the charm bracelet from its brown paper bag, holding it carefully in my lap. At a suitable break in the conversation I said, 'Look, I know it's not much, but it was all I could find. They're meant to be good luck. Here, it'll keep you safe on your journey.'

I placed the little box in front of her on the table.

She didn't look at it right away, just stared at me – as if she was frightened to look down.

'Don't you want to open it?' I smiled at her.

It was just a plain white cardboard box, but it looked enticing against the sea-green marble tabletop.

'Go ahead, open it!' I said, laughing. 'It won't bite you.'

Anna made a small, frantic move to get up from her chair, but she seemed to lack the resolve. She was staring at the little white box. I pushed it over to her. The blood drained from her face and she began to tremble.

'What's the matter?'

'Take it away,' she pleaded in a hoarse whisper. 'Take that away from me.'

'But aren't you going to open it?' I was irritated and a little hurt by the way she was behaving. 'It's just ... it's just something I ...'

But I could no longer be sure. My head was spinning. I could no longer be sure that I knew what was inside the box. And then abruptly I saw what it meant. I saw what I had done.

Slowly I reached out and picked up the tiny replica of the boys' coffin and without a word slid it back into my pocket.

SIX

The city looked cleansed after the heavy rain. The streets had been sluiced down, left slick and glistening. There was a fresh wind blowing, dispersing clouds that ran low and swiftly between the buildings, carrying a briny, petrolic smell of the sea in from the East River.

I picked up something to eat at a delicatessen on Sixth Avenue, then walked back to the Public Library along the north side of Bryant Park. The sidewalk under the trees was littered with debris. I kept my head down as I walked, making an idle inventory of everything that crossed my path: the fluttering wreckage of an umbrella, a gap-toothed metal comb, sodden inducements to visit a massage parlor, a crushed McDonald's container, sawdust around the base of a tree stump . . .

A hand touched mine.

I looked up, startled.

A young, thickset Hispanic girl stood there swinging a Lord and Taylor shopping bag between the legs of her jeans. She smiled, then blew a wad of bubble gum into a pink little proposition that snapped against her lips. Stupidly slow to understand what she wanted, I stared at her for a long moment. Then I started to apologize. She shrugged her shoulders and turned away.

Something was hovering in the back of my mind.

Gazing up at the Grace Building across the street, I followed the concave sweep of its black glass until it became lost in vaporish, driving cloud. I felt it move then, the whole gleaming structure begin to drift out over my head like the hull of a great liner slipping away from the dock. I closed my eyes and, stretching both arms to keep my balance, drew in deep lungfuls of air.

I looked down again at the sidewalk.

Something.

But still I couldn't . . .

It had been neatly cut close to the ground: the remains of a scrawny plane tree set in a plot of impacted earth at the curbside.

Somehow the stump seemed familiar. At the first sight of it I'd felt a jolt of recognition, as if an obscure memory, an apprehension of some thing, some place or some person were about to be revived.

I bent down to examine it more closely. But the moment had passed. Whatever it was had risen almost to the surface, then turned without showing itself and sunk back into the depths.

I walked on, trying to ignore a persistent feeling of unease.

I entered the Library by the Forty-second Street entrance and took the elevator to the third floor, setting off down the long marble passage to the Main Reading Room. The green walls of the passage were hung with an exhibition of antique maps, travel sketches and topographical prints.

I looked them over without particular interest.

Then I remembered seeing something in one of the prints. I'd noticed it last night on my way out: a peculiar outcrop of rock pushing up through a ring of paving stones in the middle of a plaza or garden of some kind. A rock shaped like the figure of a crouching man: at least, that was the impression the artist had managed to create. Coming across the stump there in the sidewalk must somehow have reminded me of the picture. Once I'd made this connection, it all seemed quite straightforward.

I found the picture without difficulty: a hand-colored engraving by a German painter named Johann Moritz Rugandas. It was a rather uninspired view of an eighteenth-century park titled *'Finsternpromenad: Grosstadt Nürnberg'*. The landscape had been conventionally furnished with elegant stands of trees, flower beds formally laid out, a fountain, some prosperous-looking citizens promenading along the shores of an artificial lake – and in the left foreground that curious, gnarled outcrop of rock, the man crouching ...

Only now he wasn't there.

At first I thought I'd made a mistake. I had to be looking at the wrong picture. But in all other respects it appeared exactly the way I remembered. I studied the landscape more carefully, poring over every detail, in case I'd missed something. But the only reason I'd noticed the engraving in the first place was that rock, featured so prominently. And now it had completely vanished. The corner where the crouching man ought to have been was covered over by the surface of the lake.

There was something else wrong.

I hadn't noticed it to begin with, but the figures in the landscape who had been walking along the lakeshore, and a little girl riding in a pony trap with a yellow parasol over her shoulder, were now strolling in another part of the park. They were now on higher ground. If they had remained where they were, they would have been up to their knees in water. Since yesterday evening, when I'd first looked at the picture, the level of the lake had risen about three feet.

It was not possible, of course. There had to be some explanation. This time I had to know that what I saw could be seen by others.

There was a grille door in the wall opposite, marked MANU-SCRIPTS AND ARCHIVES DIVISION. I went over to it and put my fingers through the wire mesh, rattling the grille. A fat boy in shirt sleeves emerged sideways from behind the stacks. He was eating a sandwich and stared out at me resentfully through glasses held together at the joints with Band-Aids.

'Do something for you?'

I said, 'There's a picture on the wall out here that I'd like to talk to someone about.'

'Mr O'Rorke,' he called out to the bookshelves behind him. Then, taking another bite of lunch, he heaved back out of sight.

'What, another one? You've got to be kidding. You know, you're the third person today.'

Shaking his head as he came up to the door, the librarian, a man in a light-colored tweed suit, unlocked the grille and stepped out into the corridor. He was in his early forties, slightly built, with thinning hair, a well-groomed mustache and warm brown insincere eyes.

'You want to know about the engraving?' He forced a little smile. 'They're so much alike is why people have noticed. You *do* want to know about the Rugandas?'

'Yes. I'm sorry to bother you with something so trivial.'

'There are two versions of *Finsternpromenad*,' he said, 'practically identical. We have'm both.'

Again the little smile.

'The other has some sort of rock formation in the foreground? People walking by the lake?'

He nodded. 'Something along those lines.'

'That explains it, then. But why?'

'We have a ridiculous amount of stock here and less hanging space than you'd believe. So we're always moving things around.' He coughed drily. 'Someone must have switched them.'

'When?'

'I'm sorry?'

'When were they changed?'

'I'm not exactly sure about that; I'd have to check. I believe they did some rehanging here last night. The person who could tell you isn't here right now, but if you'd care to come back ...'

'No, it's really not important. Thank you.' I gave an awkward laugh and started to back away. 'For a moment there I thought I was seeing things.'

'Anytime I can be of assistance,' the librarian said, looking at me hard, as if he were making an effort to remember my face, then withdrawing behind his grille. It clanged shut.

I found my seat in the cavernous South Hall of the Reading Room and settled down gratefully in front of the pile of books I'd reserved last night. It was a while, though, before I felt in the mood for reading. I couldn't get them out of my mind: the image of a sunken rock, the crouching figure, the strolling citizens of Nuremberg and the little girl trailing her yellow parasol from the back of the pony trap down by the blue-tinged water's edge.

I decided to say nothing to Somerville about any of this. After all, confusing the two engravings had been a genuine mistake, something that could happen to anyone. Hadn't the librarian complained that I was the third person today who wanted to know what was going on?

Having checked the details of the tape against any information I could dig up about Fawcett, I'd been able to verify from published sources almost everything that happened in the first part of the colonel's story. From the name of the man who had sold him the mules to the blisters on Raleigh Rimmel's feet, it was all there –

fully documented in the letters that Jack Fawcett and his father had sent back from Cuyaba and Bacairy Post to the family in England.

What I'd dreamed were facts ...

The second half of the interview with Fawcett – when he abandons Jack and Raleigh and goes on alone to look for the waterfall – posed a different kind of problem. It appeared to be all 'original' material: historically unverifiable.

No one has ever known what really happened to the Fawcett expedition. Like the story of the *Marie Celeste*, or more recently the Bermuda Triangle, it enjoyed a certain vogue in the thirties and forties as an 'unsolved mystery'. After the three men left Dead Horse Camp they were neither seen nor heard from again. The last communication ever received from them, a letter from Colonel Fawcett to his wife, dated May 29, 1925, was sent back with the peons to Bacairy Post. It contained a reference to the search for the waterfall and closed with the words 'You need have no fear of any failure ...'

As time went by, anxiety about the fate of the expedition increased. A half-hearted investigation by local government officials – the same 'damned bureaucrats' that Fawcett had grumbled about on the tape – yielded nothing. Then rumors began drifting in from the jungle of white men held captive by Indians, and the first rescue party set off on their elusive trail. In spite of Fawcett's explicit instructions – 'If we don't come out, no one should look for us' – several determined attempts were made, from Commander Dyott's heavily equipped expedition of 1928, sponsored by the North American Newspaper Alliance, to the discreet inquiries by the anthropologist Orlando Villas Boas among the Kalopolo Indians as late as 1950.

None of them were successful.

When I began my research I was drawn by curiosity, excitement even; the prospect of discovering something in Fawcett's story, or in his character, that might throw a little light on my own situation was a powerful incentive. Although skeptical, I was willing to consider the possibility that there existed between Fawcett and me a connection of some kind.

I kept a snapshot of P.H.F. taken in 1911 at Pelechucho, Bolivia, propped up on the desk in front of me while I worked. It showed a tall, bearded man in jodhpurs, an old army coat and a bizarre-looking native hat worn at an uncompromising angle. He was leaning against a wooden fence with his hands in his pockets, and chewing on the stem of a meerschaum pipe. The effect was all the more pronounced for the grimness of Fawcett's expression. His brow was furrowed with concentration, and his pale, resolute gaze seemed to be focused on some distant horizon.

There was a fierce intensity in the eyes that I found disconcerting, perhaps because they revealed a man who not only held passionate convictions but was ready to die for them.

If I were seeking an affinity with Fawcett, I didn't find it in that photograph. And the more research I did into his life, the clearer it became to me that I wasn't going to find it there either.

The celebrated explorer, who played cricket for Devon County; the exhibitor of drawings at the Royal Academy; a man who designed and built racing yachts and patented something called the 'Icthoid Curve'. The professional soldier decorated for bravery in the First World War; the amateur philosopher and archaeologist regarded by his contemporaries as an eccentric, a dreamer, something of a mystic . . .

To compare the life of a buttoned-down commuter from Bedford Hills, New York, who pushed the cart for his wife at the I.G.A. on Saturday mornings; the 'radical' sixties dropout, who used a college deferment to avoid the draft; the businessman who now worries nonstop about how inflation is eating up his income, and whether he can afford to join the Bedford Golf and Tennis Club this year; the talk-show addict, the amateur golfer, the amateur gardener . . .

Hardly fair, perhaps, but I couldn't pretend that my life amounted to much more. On the face of things, I found it difficult to identify with someone whose life experience had been so wildly different from my own; also, there had been nothing on the tape – not even the incident with the dogs, Pastor and Chulim – that had struck the meanest chord of recognition. And although I'd made an effort to find some sympathy with Fawcett's cause, I could no more share his enthusiasm for the remains of forgotten civilizations in South America than he could share mine for Phil Donahue.

*

It was a quarter of seven and already dark out when I decided to give up. Since I wasn't going to be able to prove anything about the tape one way or the other, I'd come to the conclusion that I was wasting my time on Fawcett. I'd developed a pain in the small of my back from sitting too long, and the undaunted look in his eyes was beginning to get on my nerves. I put the photograph away and began closing up books, removing the pink reserve slips as I arranged them in piles.

I'd discovered in the course of my research that the guy was really quite a crank, who dabbled in spiritualism and actually believed that his 'lost cities' of Brazil had once been part of Atlantis! He'd heard or read somewhere that there was a race of blond, fair-skinned people living among the Indians in the *sertão* north of Bacairy Post, and he felt certain these were descendants of the original Atlantans.

An acquaintance had once said of him, referring in particular to his obsessive meanderings in the jungles of Mato Grosso – 'As credulous an old dear as ever bought a gold brick!'

My feelings exactly.

The drama enacted in the regression, I decided, had been an accident. Hypnosis must have somehow triggered this third-rate historical fantasy, and by some weird coincidence it had turned out to correspond with fact. I'd almost begun to take it seriously. I blamed Somerville for that. The 'previous life' caper might be his idea of therapy, but it wasn't mine. I wanted nothing more to do with it – regression, reincarnation, hypnotism or any other tricks he might have up his sleeve. I made up my mind to tell him that I'd had enough – call him right up and tell him.

In the Reading Room foyer, beside a drinking fountain and a broken ball-point-pen dispenser, I remembered seeing a telephone. I wanted to get this over with as soon as possible, while I still had the energy.

I gathered the notes I'd made and folded them, tearing them neatly in half and dropping them into the wastepaper basket. So much for the intrepid explorer. In a defiant mood I stood up and started walking.

As I moved up the aisle toward the exit, leaving others still sitting at the long refectory tables in frozen slumps of concentration, each trapped in a brilliant little pool of reading light, I felt as if I were playing hooky, escaping.

Then I saw him.

At first I couldn't be sure. He'd been sitting at the left of the hall up near the front, maybe fifteen rows ahead of me. I didn't even notice him until he got up to leave his seat. He was gliding silently from the room. A sleek, older man in a blue blazer, his height. I caught no more than a glimpse, but the back was unmistakable, the slightly crouched back of my therapist.

It was him.

'Dr Somerville!' I called out, loud enough to be heard.

He didn't turn around.

'Somerville!' I shouted, and a worried-looking librarian detached herself from the wall and came hurrying toward me.

SEVEN

She stood there, a small woman with a sharp face, barring the way, one hand resting on a lectern that supported a huge, chained copy of *Webster's*. A notice beside the dictionary warned that THE USE OF LIBRARY BOOKS IN CONNECTION WITH CONTESTS AND PUZZLES IS PROHIBITED.

I stared over her shoulder, not listening to a word she was saying. There wasn't time to explain. I needed to find out if it was really Somerville. I pushed past her.

A security guard perched on a stool in the foyer looked up as I came through. I held out my hands to show I wasn't carrying any books, and he gave a sleepy nod. I walked quickly into the Public Catalog Room. There were a dozen people working from the card index and a few more standing by the information desk. None of them Somerville.

He was faster than I was. I ran out into the vestibule, a grandiose anteroom at the top of the central staircase (dark frescoes, carved stone benches, elaborate gilt sconces), and scanned the green, brightly lit corridor. Empty. I hesitated. He could have gone any one of several ways. I stood still for a moment, hoping to hear somewhere in the building the sound of footsteps hastening over marble floors. Everything was still. He must have on shoes with crepe soles.

I felt discouraged. There were too many places in that labyrinthine palace where a man could hide.

Hide from what? Why was he so anxious to avoid me? He couldn't *not* have heard me call his name. Had I dreamed that I'd seen him?

I took the stairs, three at a time, one hand skimming the oak rail. At the mezzanine I stopped to gaze down over a colonnaded balcony into the expanse of Astor Hall. Apart from the receptionist and a security guard, deep in conversation, there was no one. It looked like the deserted set of an old Hollywood epic. The massive bronze doors of the Fifth Avenue entrance had been closed for the night. Through a barred window I could see the head of one of the stone lions that guard the Library steps, silhouetted against the yellow glare of the street.

The chances of finding him now were diminishing. I climbed back up the stairs, crossed the vestibule and this time made a left into the green corridor. As I turned down it, there was a blur of movement at the far end, of someone disappearing around the corner toward the elevators. An afterimage. I couldn't quite tell if it was Somerville. I started to run, past MANUSCRIPTS AND ARCHIVES – there was no light now showing behind the grille door. I ran flat out.

He wheeled around, looked up in alarm as I came tearing into the elevator area. A bearded young rabbi in a homburg and black overcoat was waiting in front of the aluminum doors. When he saw that I wasn't about to mug him, he turned away in relief, still keeping a firm grip on his thin plastic briefcase. I checked the elevator indicators. One car was sitting down in the basement, the other just starting up to the third floor. I asked him, trying to catch my breath, if anyone else had been standing there when he arrived. The rabbi didn't answer or even look at me; he just shook his head slowly from side to side.

I walked back along the corridor to the Public Catalog Room, more or less resigned now to the fact that Somerville had given me the slip. I approached the information desk, intending to ask if any of the librarians there had seen a man in a blue blazer leave the Reading Room in a hurry a few minutes before. But before I could speak, I recognized, standing in the center of the group, hands in the pockets of his tweeds, the mannered O'Rorke talking to the sharp-faced woman who'd accused me earlier of creating a disturbance – and I thought better of it.

Feeling their eyes on my back, I walked stiffly by, turning right at the foyer into the North Hall of the Main Reading Room, which is separated from where I'd been sitting before by a heavy oak partition resembling the rood screen of a church. Behind it goes on all the weighty business of retrieving books from the stacks and issuing them to the readers. It struck me then that Somerville possibly had access to staff-only areas; it would help explain how he'd been able to vanish so suddenly. The man in the blue blazer certainly knew his way around the building.

I started walking slowly down the center aisle of the North Hall peering at faces under the uniform rows of the reading lamps. By now I was ready to accept that I'd made a mistake. It was understandable enough. God knows, Somerville had been very much on my mind.

If it hadn't been for the slight stoop of the shoulders and that peculiar ridge at the base of the skull, I doubt if I'd have even noticed the man in the blue blazer. I knew the back of Somerville's head better than I knew his face, which I could never picture clearly. During our sessions he would often go and stand by the windows and gaze out while I talked. And as I talked I'd watch the back of his head. A ridge of bone protruded a couple of inches above the nape, covered by what little hair he had left. It was like a brow.

I didn't really get a good enough look at the rest of the figure in the blue blazer.

Ahead, the doorway leading to LOCAL HISTORY AND GENE-ALOGY had been roped off. I'd reached the end of the hall.

As a last resort I checked the Microfilm Room, an open-plan section where a couple of dozen unwieldy projectors covered in plastic hoods stood crowded together behind a corral of wood and glass. Only two were being used: the nearer by an elderly woman who'd fallen asleep in front of her machine; the other by a girl in shirt sleeves, her head bent low over the viewfinder.

A hand with a narrow green ribbon tied around the wrist rested on the controls. I looked closer at the girl, trying to see her face. There was something about her. She turned her head a fraction, and the light from the projector caught her profile.

I recognized Somerville's assistant.

So I'd been right all along. Not imagining things.

I stepped between the hooded projectors and made my way to where she was working.

'Hello, Penelope,' I said, almost in a whisper. There was a librarian stationed nearby, observing my movements.

The girl looked up with an abstracted frown. Then she recognized me, registering what appeared to be genuine surprise.

'This is really strange,' she said. 'I was just thinking about you. Not a minute ago.'

'What are you doing here?'

'Research for Dr Somerville.'

'Aren't we all? I hope he pays you, at least.' I looked over at the microfilm in the projector. She was reading *The American Journal of Clinical Hypnosis*. The title of the article in the scanner was 'Anti-social compulsions induced under hypnotic trance'.

'Are you working on my case?' I laughed.

'Of course not.' She laughed too, shaking her head. A dark wing of hair fell across her face. She brushed it away with the back of her hand. 'Dr Somerville has to address a symposium next week at the University of Virginia. He's giving the introductory lecture. Only he got the dates mixed up, so now he wants it all done in a rush.'

'What's the lecture on?'

'He calls it "Fairy Tales, Hypnosis and Depth Psychology", if you really want to know.'

'Fairy tales? What's that got to do with hypnosis?'

'The different aspects of enchantment – something like that.'

'Doesn't he do his own research?'

'The lecture's already written. I'm just checking references, quotations, that type of thing. He's been so busy. He's seeing patients till nine o'clock tonight – and it's been like that for weeks.'

'So he's home now?'

'Yes, he's home.'

'I was going to call him.'

'You'll get the service. I told you, he's seeing patients.'

'I'll have to try him later, then.'

I wasn't sure whether to believe her or not. I felt like telling her that I'd just *seen* him, here in the Library, not five minutes ago. But what if I had made a mistake? – I didn't want them thinking I'd been hallucinating again. She could have been instructed to report back to him whatever I said. Perhaps the real reason for her being there was to keep an eye on me. More than once today I'd had the feeling that I was being followed. It was just too much of a coincidence, finding her there like that.

'Why don't you take a little breather and we can have a drink? You can tell me what it's like being a hypnotist's apprentice.'

I stood there smiling at her. It was bold, it was clumsy, but it had been a while since I'd asked a girl out.

She hesitated, turning and glancing down at the microfilm scanner.

'I still have work to do, but I guess it can wait. Yes. I mean, I'd love to.'

She switched off the projector and reached for her purse. I helped her on with her coat, a full-length domino of dark green leather trimmed with silver fox. It wasn't the kind of coat you pay for out of a receptionist's salary.

'Aren't you going to take your notes?'

'I'm coming back. I'll be here till the Library closes. He wants it all tonight.'

'I hope he's paying you overtime,' I said, taking her by the arm.

We sat in a corner of the Blue Bar at the Algonquin sipping Scotch-and-waters. It was a little awkward at first. I wasn't sure how much she knew. I felt like asking her point-blank if Somerville ever discussed his patients, or if she'd ever seen my file: but she already had the advantage, and I didn't want to give her that extra edge.

She asked too many questions: about living in the country, about my job, Anna. Boring questions that I suspected she already knew the answers to.

She kept on about my family, the past . . .

'You never go down to see them in Florida?'

'Have you ever been to Florida?'

'All right.' She smiled, and her mouth turned down quickly at the corners. 'But seriously, you don't keep in touch?'

'Sometimes you have to make a break. Before the nooses tighten. I can't say it bothers me. I just don't think about it.'

'Never?'

'No.'

'But you must think about it *sometimes*! Don't you see things that suddenly remind you of what you did, oh, ages ago, when you were a child . . . surely?'

'I've got a bad memory. Not that there's anything much to remember. How old are you – twenty-two, twenty-three?'

'Twenty-five. At least.' She looked down and began playing with the ice cubes at the bottom of her glass.

'Do you ever see *your* parents?'

'I was orphaned. My parents were killed in a car crash when I was twelve. I don't usually tell people this, but Dr Somerville is my guardian.'

I stared at her, at a loss for something to say.

'You live there with him in the house?' I didn't know what to ask. Her confidence had made me uneasy. I felt she'd forced it on me somehow, and for a reason.

'He doesn't like his patients to know. You won't say anything, will you?'

'Who would I tell?'

'Him.'

'I promise I won't. What was it that made you think of me in the Library?' I asked; it was time to change the subject.

'Oh, that,' she said. 'It was just something in his lecture notes. I wonder if I should have another drink?'

'You should. *Definitely.*' I signaled the waiter to bring two more Scotch-and-waters.

'I won't be able to focus the microfilm.'

'Do you really have to go back to the Library?'

'He says he needs those notes tonight. He's counting on me.'

'And what if you called him later, when the phone's hooked up again, and said that you'd been asked out to dinner?'

'You don't understand: this is a job. Just because he's my guardian doesn't mean I can . . .' She cut herself off. 'I'm sorry. Thanks for asking.'

'Another time?'

She nodded but said nothing.

'So tell me, what was in the notes?'

'Just a footnote he added yesterday on your regression – the story of Colonel Fawcett.'

'I'm not interested, then.'

'He says it's a unique example of historical recollection.'

'Look, I'm not interested. I've had enough, I'm sick of the whole business. That's what I want to call your guardian about. This is a good time to make a break. I'm going to tell him that I'm quitting therapy.'

There was a long silence.

Then she said, 'I'd give it another chance. Dr Somerville is a very brilliant man. He can help you, I know he can. You know what they say – that unless the doctor and patient become a problem to each other, you're not going to get a solution.'

'He's not the problem, it's his methods. Unless I've become a problem to him. Have I?'

She hesitated. 'He hasn't really spoken about you. But I wouldn't worry about it – about being regressed, I mean. It's part of the process. He knows what he's doing. Believe me. No one's asking you to commit yourself to anything.'

I wanted to ask if her being sent to the Library to keep an eye on me was 'part of the process' too. But she'd just assume that I was being paranoid. I didn't like the idea that she might think of me as sick in any way.

She drank the last of her whisky. It surprised me then how much I didn't want her to leave. I tried to think of ways to keep the conversation going, but by now it had lost all momentum. For what seemed a long time neither of us spoke. We sat and stared across the table at each other.

'You have a strange way of looking at people – did you know that?' she said in a voice that was bright, uncertain. 'Your eyes don't seem to take them in.'

'All I can see now is you.'

She smiled and her mouth opened a little, revealing a moist tip of tongue between her lips. In the dim light of the bar, it appeared livid, a bruised blue, the color of a chow's tongue.

My throat felt dry. At that moment I desired her so intensely, I thought I was going to pass out. I knew what it was I wanted her to do. But it couldn't be allowed to happen. I had an obligation to protect her from what we had already done, from what the two of us had perpetrated in my dreams. I gripped the edge of the table to steady myself.

'Aren't you feeling all right?' She reached over and touched my hand.

'I'm fine; I just – it's hot in here. I need some air, that's all.'

'I have to get back to the Library anyway.' She drew her hand back slowly, almost reluctantly. I caught it and held on to her thin wrist with the green ribbon tied around it. I held on so tightly that when I let go the skin showed angry red marks.

'What are you doing?' She gave a frightened laugh. 'That really hurt.'

'What am I doing? What are *you* doing?'

'I have to go.' She pushed back her chair and stood up. 'Will I be seeing you there on Monday?'

I couldn't answer; I didn't know.

EIGHT

11 p.m. – She took a cab back to the Library, wouldn't hear of my accompanying her. No good-night or anything, just jumped in the cab and was gone.

I needed to clear my head, so I decided to walk.

I thought of Anna – I made myself think of her, and not Penelope. But I could only imagine Anna clothed, sitting in a window seat of the 747, wearing her Lodenmantel, the strong sunlight at thirty thousand feet silhouetting her ragged head: sitting there motionless, face turned in against the white napkin of the headrest . . .

It's happened again. I had another attack, but this time literally.

I was walking from the Algonquin to Mulberry Street, moving diagonally across the city through Gramercy Park over to Second Avenue and down to the East Village. I stopped for something to eat at Kiev's, then headed downtown again on Third. As far as I could tell, I wasn't being followed.

It happened near the corner of the Bowery and Prince Street opposite a vacant lot where all the bums congregate. It's a couple of blocks from here, but since I've been living in Little Italy I try to avoid walking that way, especially at night. Now that the weather's turned, I find it increasingly difficult to ignore their plight – to go on telling myself that they're really so out of it they must be beyond feeling anything.

I remembered something Anna said when we first discussed moving to the country: 'And we won't have to deal anymore with all that misery on the streets.'

I'd gotten angry at her: 'What do you mean by "deal with"? Do you think it exists only in your mind, that it goes away when you're not looking?'

* Extract from Martin Gregory's diary

'Yes,' she said.

I didn't deliberately go by there, I just found myself taking that route.

The lot was deserted, not a zombie in sight, but it was dark, and to avoid the possibility of an unpleasant encounter I kept to the other side of the street. I crossed over almost without thinking – an automatic reflex.

Suddenly this bag lady, a tiny, wizened creature with toothless gums and bleary eyes, rolls out of a doorway and snatches at my sleeve. Dressed in grimy tatters of green plaid and lace that looked like the remains of a little girl's party frock, she was snarling at the night, dribbling with alcoholic rage. Her meager, bowed legs were covered in filthy bandages that had slipped down around her ankles. I could see dried blood and God-knows-what-else caking down inside them.

She began screeching at me, 'You cunt, you fucker, *you* pick up the fuckin' pieces! You pick 'em *up*, you bastard!'

I was so startled that I cursed right back at her. All the while she was clinging to my arm, plucking at the skin of my hand. The smell was quite intolerable. She *had* to be shaken off. I gave her a shove, harder than I'd intended, and she went down, smacking her head on the sidewalk. Seeing her sprawled out, still screaming her obscenities, crying for my help, I felt the weight again, the terrifying pressure beginning to build in my chest.

I wanted to put a match to her – God knows I'd have been doing her a favor. But I could feel my legs begin to buckle. I was being pressed down. I was about to go down on top of her, down into that fetid, kicking embrace.

For a moment I had the sensation of being able to see right through her. My eyes were like a CAT scanner's, revealing the condition of her internal organs, detecting hidden cancers, dormant contagion and other malignant secrets that she desired to share with me.

She was laughing ...

Then suddenly it passed. Like the time before at the hotel, the weight just lifted. I left her lying there, a trickle of blood seeping from her matted scalp, and went away trembling with guilty loathing.

Later, when I was taking a bath, I noticed that the old bruise, which had faded now to a dirty yellow-gray, seemed to have deepened again in places.

Why did I buy Anna that bracelet?

NINE

He rose from his desk and came forward to meet me, smiling easily, holding out his hands. I could hear the tiny slapping sound the tassels of his loafers made as he crossed the carpet. He didn't say anything, but his handshake was emphatic, glad. He put his arm around my shoulders and guided me back to the twin chairs under the windows. Buddies. I felt like telling him I could find my own way.

We stood for a moment looking out over the strip of garden behind the house. It seemed like an extension of the study, cloistral, dark, unpleasantly luxuriant.

I wanted to ask what had happened to Penelope – if it was her day off, if she was sick or something: a girl I'd never seen before had answered the front door. Only I thought it would be a mistake to show too much interest.

Along the far wall a trellis had subsided into what must once have been a bed of kitchen herbs. Borders and paved terraces had merged under a spreading shawl of weed. I could see a few sprigs of rosemary pushing up through the diamond-shaped lattices, feathery plumes of dill, shoots of sorrel and marjoram, all with long rank fingers reaching toward the light.

It gave me an uncomfortable feeling, Penelope not being there. It was only because of her that I'd kept the appointment. I felt cheated somehow. She must have said something to Somerville about our encounter at the Library. Had she told him that I'd made the decision to quit therapy and that she'd talked me out of it, talked me into coming back? I couldn't be sure.

I went over to my chair and sat down. Without any prompting I began to talk, giving a full, disparaging account of my research on Colonel Fawcett.

Somerville remained at the window with his back to me; a shaft of sunlight angled his shadow across the study floor. As I talked

I found myself seeking out the ridge of bone at the base of his skull, trying to picture him in a blue blazer instead of the fawn, hessian-weave sports jacket he was wearing. But what difference did it really make whether it had been Somerville at the Library that evening, or someone who happened to look like him?

It no longer seemed important.

In spite of myself I was beginning to feel the benefit of being with him again. It was always that way. Whenever I was with him, just sitting there talking, the misgivings I had about the man seemed to disappear. I had to make a conscious effort not to let myself fall under his spell.

Finally I came right out with it: was regression therapy really the answer in my case?

'Maybe we should try a different approach,' I suggested. 'Now that you know how I feel about Fawcett, couldn't we just forget this whole "previous life" business and start all over?'

Somerville made no reply. He stood with his head bowed, arms folded, one hand supporting his chin, apparently deep in thought. Then without turning around he asked me how the meeting with Anna had gone. It was as if he hadn't heard a word I'd been saying.

'You haven't answered my question.'

'We'll come to that in a moment,' he said.

'I think we should talk about it now.'

'Later,' he said. 'Tell me what happened with Anna.'

'I'd rather not.'

He raised his head a fraction. 'You don't have to tell me anything if you don't want to. Did you give your wife a *bon voyage* present?'

'How do you know about that?'

'You asked my advice.'

'Funny, I don't remember asking your advice.'

'Are you sure, Martin?'

'Yes, of course, I'm sure.' It was true – I *didn't* remember. I knew about it only because Anna had told me at the airport.

'You were thinking about giving her some flowers.' He began plucking at the slack skin along the line of his jaw. 'A bunch of roses. For obvious reasons I tried to convince you that this wasn't such a good idea, but you seemed –'

'For Christ's sake, why would I want to do a dumb thing like that?'

He turned around then and looked at me for the first time. 'What *did* you get her?'

'You're so sure I got her something – *you* tell *me*.'

'The roses?'

'Hell, no!'

'What did you get her, Martin?'

'Nothing . . . nothing much.'

It was still there, in my pocket. I hadn't even looked at it since the airport. In the taxi on the way uptown I'd made up my mind not to say anything to Somerville about giving Anna the bracelet, but it was beginning to bother me now that I couldn't remember things.

A bunch of roses?

Without looking down I reached into my pocket.

'I didn't mean to upset her,' I said weakly, handing him the little white box. 'Really, I had no idea.'

With the sun behind his back, his face in shadow appeared expressionless. He opened the box and glanced down at its contents, then tipped the lid shut with his thumb.

It lay there in the palm of his hand.

'What happened?' he asked.

There was no point holding back, so I went ahead and told him – everything. I even told him that I knew Anna had been to see him the day before she went away and that he'd warned her I might 'try something'. He didn't bat an eyelid. But I was already convinced that Somerville had nothing to do with my giving Anna the bracelet.

How could he have? How could he have instructed me to buy it for her unless he'd been out to the airport himself and chosen the bracelet in that white box *before* he hypnotized me Thursday evening? He *did* set up the meeting with Anna, and it *was* his idea that we use the TWA departure lounge as our rendezvous, but on Thursday he couldn't possibly have known that she would agree to see me, let alone which airline she was going to fly.

Somerville paid close attention to my description of Anna's departure. He stopped me several times with questions. Yet somehow I got the feeling that I wasn't telling him anything he didn't already know.

I finally asked him why he thought I'd done it.

He shook his head. 'I can't answer that yet, Martin. We're not dealing here with simple motive. I'm afraid the hostility you've shown toward your wife – whether or not *you* think you mean it – is very real.'

He reached out to give the box back to me.

'You keep it,' I said, waving his hand aside. 'I don't want the damned thing.'

He took the box over to his desk, wrote something on the lid and locked it away in a drawer. Then he came back and sat down opposite me.

'I love Anna,' I pleaded. 'Why would I want to hurt her?'

Somerville said nothing. His eyes half-hooded, he lay back in his chair, carefully arranging the creases of his trousers as he stretched his legs out in front of him.

'I love my wife,' I insisted, thinking only of Penelope, of a dark-stained tip of tongue emerging slyly between parted lips; "Will I be seeing you there on Monday?" She'd made it sound like an assignation.

'I said I love my wife. Doesn't that mean anything to you?'

Somerville's eyes flickered open. 'It's more serious than I think you realize, Martin,' he said quietly, sitting forward again. 'Anna's in Europe now.'

'I know where she is.'

'She's safe there.'

'You mean she's safe from me.'

'What happened at the airport changes things. If she were still here –'

'I couldn't hurt her. You *know* I couldn't. Christ! You were the one who said we should get back together. You said I wasn't crazy. You said it was . . . *something else*!'

And yet the last night I'd spent with Anna, the game we played in bed together – was that all it had been?

'It *is* something else, *isn't it?*'

Somerville said in a gentle voice, 'I know that you love your wife. Anyone can see that. But I'm afraid that's almost beside the point now. You loved her before. You also tried to harm her before. You say you want to find out why you do these things, why you killed the dogs, why you gave Anna the box, why you seem to want to destroy everything you care about. When you first came to me, you said you *had* to get to the bottom of this. Remember, Martin? Remember?'

Somerville leaned toward me. There was an intensity about his gaze now. I got a whiff of almond cologne and instinctively drew back, but he reached out and caught hold of my hand.

'Believe me, Martin. There's no other way.' The soft, enveloping grip on my hand tightened. 'Give it another chance. That's all I ask.'

'I don't know . . .'

'I never said it would be easy; but we can't give up now that we've come this far. Trust me.'

I could feel Penelope's dark little tongue licking at my memory, prompting me to let it happen, to say yes.

'Anna's just a child,' I blurted.

'Of course she is. That's why we have to take care of her. We *have* to go back again. Together. Don't you see? For *her* sake, Martin.'

BOOK THREE

SOMETHING HIDDEN

ONE

I waited till my third appointment that week before asking Somerville where Penelope was. I felt I had to make a joke of it, pretending that I'd only just noticed she wasn't sitting in on our sessions anymore: the new girl had not been admitted in her place.

'She went to Washington for a couple of days to see some friends.' Somerville smiled. He knew exactly what this was about. 'She said she needed a break. She couldn't have picked a worse time. Perhaps I've been working her too hard.' He shrugged and, thrusting both hands deep into his trouser pockets, turned again toward the windows. But he didn't say when he expected her back.

Maybe she did go away. I had no way of finding out. I had no reason to doubt that he was telling the truth. But I couldn't shake the feeling that she was still here, in New York. I suspected that Somerville's story about her taking off on the spur of the moment, his little show of irritation at being inconvenienced, was just a cover. More likely he'd released her from her regular duties so she could keep closer watch on me.

I made phone calls to Somerville's house at different times of day and night on the off chance that she'd pick up. During office hours it was always Somerville, or the girl; at night, usually the service. Whenever they answered I'd put the receiver down without saying anything.

I began to vary my route between Mulberry and Ninety-third Street, making elaborate detours, constantly backtracking to see if I was being followed – lying in wait for her on street corners, behind bus shelters, in storefronts, doorways . . .

There was never anyone.

And I kept going back to Somerville. I turned up for my appointment at the same time each day, always a few minutes early. I even began to look forward to our sessions. By degrees I had managed to convince myself that she was still there, living quietly with her guardian somewhere in the recesses of the house.

Sometimes on my way up to the study I'd hear footsteps hurrying overhead, as if someone who didn't want to be seen were climbing the stairs in front of me. Or on the way out I'd catch the sound of the front door closing a moment before I reached the bottom landing.

Once I thought I caught a glimpse of her.

Somerville had just finished with another patient and given the signal for me to go up. As I was coming out of the waiting room, I noticed that the crystal chandelier that hangs over the stairwell in the hall – a huge, multitiered affair that looks like an inverted wedding cake – was trembling for no apparent reason. There was no draft; the front door was firmly closed (the previous patient had left a few minutes before) and there was no one moving about on the landing above.

Halfway up the stairs I leaned over the banister and put out my hand to steady a pendant that was clinking softly against its neighbors, giving off tiny flashes of prismatic light. As I looked down, through a shimmering web of wire and glass, I thought I saw someone standing just inside the baize door at the end of the hallway; then the door shut. It happened so fast – a sudden gust of movement – I hardly knew what I'd seen. I couldn't be sure that it was Penelope. The image had been too diffuse, split up into a thousand shivering fragments by the lusters of the chandelier.

I ran down the stairs and across the marble floor to the back of the hallway. The door, covered in worn red felt, stood at the top of a flight of stone steps leading down into the basement. I'd no idea what was behind it – I'd never seen it open before. The room was directly beneath Somerville's study.

I tried the handle. Locked.

My hour ran over the usual forty-five minutes. When I came out of hypnosis, feeling a little dazed – I had no inkling yet of what had happened during the regression – the incident with the chandelier had gone completely out of my head.

I hardly knew who or where I was.

Somerville asked me if I wanted to lie down before going home.

But I was anxious just to get out of that house and breathe some fresh air into my lungs. I told him I felt fine.

On my way down I stopped on the landing to put on my coat in front of the hall mirror. As I struggled to get an arm into its sleeve, I looked up and saw in the mirror the glittering image of the chandelier above my head. It hung quite still, reflecting the pale glare of afternoon that poured in through the fanlight over the front door.

I remembered then.

I went over to the banister and looked down into the hall. At the far end of the passage the red baize door stood slightly ajar.

I could hear the girl typing away in Penelope's office upstairs. Somerville was locked in his study. It was lunchtime. There were no patients in the waiting room. I opened the front door, waited a few seconds, then slammed it shut so the girl upstairs could hear.

Then I crept back along the hallway.

I pushed and the red door swung open without a sound.

It was dark inside. I took a couple of steps forward – they echoed unexpectedly over the bare parquet. The windows were tightly shuttered. What dim light there was came from the passage behind my back.

I felt for the light switch. It didn't work.

As my eyes got accustomed to the gloom, I realized I was in a library. The walls from floor to ceiling were lined with books, some on open shelves, others in tall glass-fronted bookcases. The only furniture was an upholstered chair under a white dust cover pushed into a corner. There was a reading light behind it with no bulb in the socket.

I took out my lighter and held the flame up to the nearest glass case. The books that I could see, unlike the new uniform editions in Somerville's study, were a motley of old and new. Many of the older books were bound in leather; some, with obscure-sounding Latin titles, appeared to be rare.

I wondered if this could be the model for that other library, the quiet peaceful room with the spiral staircase outside the window leading down, down into a sun-drenched garden; the way station where Somerville transported me at the beginning and end of our hypnotic voyages into my unconscious past. I could all but see the garden wall overgrown with jasmine and honeysuckle; all but hear the creaking of hammock ropes, the murmur of the distant sea; I could feel the warm, scented breeze ...

There was a faint click.

I looked up – the front of the bookcase had come unlatched. As the glass panel swung outward, and I watched my reflection behind the flame of the lighter shift across its dusky surface, I thought of a gamekeeper holding up his lantern to the face of a stranger on a starless night.

A musty sweet odor came from the open cabinet.

In front of me, at eye level, I noticed that a book hadn't been put back properly in its place. It was a thin, elegant volume bound in green-and-black morocco and didn't seem to belong on a shelf that I saw was weighed down with psychology textbooks. Inscribed across the spine in faded gold leaf I could just make out the title: *Expositions Vaudoises*. I had no idea what it meant. The author's name was nowhere.

I reached up and took the book down from the shelf. Balancing it carefully in one hand, I wielded it open between thumb and forefinger. There was a bookplate attached to the flyleaf, a woodcut of a bearded ancient reading in the shade of an oak tree, the stylized leaves of the oak embowering the words 'Ex libris Ronald Somerville'.

I turned to the title page.

The book, written by one 'Le Chien' (a pseudonym?), had been privately printed in Paris in 1775. To judge from the chapter headings and some of the illustrations, it appeared to be a satire on the Church, conceived and executed as a work of pornography.

The frontispiece, so small and delicately etched as to be almost a miniature, offered a scene from the chapel of a convent.

A young novice in a white habit is kneeling at the altar rail to receive the Sacrament. The priest stands in front of her holding the gold paten under her chin, one hand resting in benediction on her shaven head. His eyes turn heavenward as the novice, hands clasped about his sturdy knees, devoutly blows him. She's also being screwed, mounted from behind – the skirts of her habit thrown up – by a girl wearing an ebony phallus strapped to her thighs, and a mask in the shape of a dog's head.

I stared at the tiny illustration, fascinated by the clarity and detail of the drawing. It was as sharp as a photograph, which made the image seem all the more obscene. It also had another deeply disturbing effect: I realized that the shorn scalp of the novice reminded me of Anna.

I fumbled the book shut and put it back onto its shelf. I felt uneasy about being in that room. As I reached up to close the front of the cabinet, the smell of dust and dry mold seemed stronger than before. The metal case of the lighter was starting to burn my fingers, but there was nowhere I could set it down.

I could see the door to the hallway mirrored in the glass panel. While I'd been standing there it had swung to without my noticing, making the room even darker. I inched the panel forward, checking out the area behind my back. To the left of the door stood another bookcase; then the dust-covered chair and broken reading lamp. Then an empty space. In the farthest corner of the library, I thought I saw something.

I jerked the panel back again and, holding the reflection steady, peered deep into the glass.

There was something there – hunkered down on all fours.

I watched it raise itself in my direction, as if to test the air. Then it seemed to stretch, and I saw the pale breasts, quite small, hanging forward in two tip-tilted points under the grizzled mane.

Slowly it rose up on two feet and came sidling toward me across the parquet. I could hear my heart pounding like a hammer against my ribs as I followed its soundless progress in the glass panel of the bookcase. When it got close – close enough so that I could catch its scent – it stopped, reached up with both hands and tore the top of its head off.

'Martin,' she whispered.

I wheeled around and for an instant I saw Penelope standing before me, naked, holding the dog's-head mask under her arm, a long bushy gray tail curling between her clenched thighs.

Then the flame went out.

'Martin?'

Somerville, silhouetted in the doorway, a hand resting on the light switch.

'Are you all right?' He clicked the switch up and down.

'The door was open, and I ... I was just looking at some of your books.'

He opened the door wide, letting more daylight into the room. 'You sure you're feeling all right?'

'I'm okay, really.'

'I had no idea you were still here.'

'I'm sorry, I didn't mean to ... You don't mind, do you – my looking at the books?'

'Of course not,' he said. 'You must think of this house as your own home.'

I couldn't think what to say. 'It's a very interesting library.'

He nodded. 'My grandfather did most of the collecting. *My* contribution was having it shipped over from Europe before the war. You say the door was open? We usually keep it locked. Some of these books are rather valuable, you see. It was probably the maid. I'm afraid when Penelope's not here to keep an eye on things ...'

'Do you expect her back soon?' I asked – then wished I hadn't.

Somerville smiled. 'I'll be seeing her this weekend. I'm giving a lecture in Richmond on Saturday. I'll leave my phone numbers with the girl. You'll always be able to get in touch if you need me.'

I shut the front of the bookcase and went over to where he was standing. 'I think I'll survive.'

'There's something I forgot to ask you, Martin. Have you ever been to Germany?'

'A few times. On business. I'm not crazy about the place.'

'Have you ever been to Nuremberg?'

'No,' I said, thinking of the Rugandas lithograph hanging in the green passage at the Public Library. 'Why do you ask?'

'You'll see when you play back the tape.'

I felt my pocket for the hard edges of the cassette case. 'Was there a lake? I mean, in the regression.'

He looked at me curiously. 'You remember that from this morning?'

'I'm not sure. I don't usually remember anything. But *was* there? A park somewhere outside the city walls with a lake in the middle surrounded by tall trees?'

'I think there may have been, yes,' he said gravely.

It couldn't be coincidence. Perhaps that was how the regressions worked. Like dreams. They just picked up odd scraps of information, took incidents from one's everyday life and wove them into some elaborate historical fantasy. It had been the same with the two dogs on the Fawcett tape.

'What century was it this time?' I asked. 'Early nineteenth, by any chance?'

Somerville shook his head. 'The end of the war, Spring 1945. You better go home and listen to the tape. I'll be here, if you want to call me later. You may find this one a little upsetting.'

TWO

'I used to spend all the time I wasn't in school runnin wild in the woods above the holler livin off berries, roots, hickory nuts, whatever I could catch in the way of game. I learned huntin from my uncle Joe, Ma's eldest brother. He always used to come by our house springtime of the year . . . He taught me how to set traps and lay nets for birds in the sycamore groves, showed me all the best fishin holes in the creek. At night I'd sleep out under the pines and watch the stars. 'Times I'd dream of flying right up among 'em – like old Rory rippin through a field of cocklebur.'

'Didn't anyone mind your taking off like that?'

'Pa would cuss me out some and call me a no-account fool. Like as not he'd give me a good whippin too. It didn't bother me none.'

'What's your name?'

'Begley . . . Print Begley. P-R-I-N-T . . .'

'Where are you from?'

'Indian Ridge. I ain't never goin back there, neither – not if I can help it.'

'Why? What kind of place is it?'

'Company town strung out along the bottom of a holler in the Cumberlands. In the old days, before they opened up the mines, used to be Cherokee. Now they call it a mining community. Ain't nothin but a lousy camp.'

'Where did you go to school?'

'In Pathfork. But, see, they didn't have much time for . . . Ma taught me how to read from stories in the Bible. She's a full-blood Cherokee, who got herself religion and some learnin. Most of the folks that live in the holler can't read nor write. They all end up becomin miners, so there ain't much call for it. My pa and his two brothers are miners, and their father before them – dirt-poor, dog-hole coal miners . . . At ten I decided I ain't never gonna be no dog-holer.'

'Did anyone pressure you to go down the mines?'

'Sure did ... specially Pa. He said I weren't no good on account of my bein a breed. Swore he never should have married Ma ... threatened to throw us both out, I weren't about to change my mind, though. See, that ain't the work I were chosen for.'

'What do you mean?'

'A few years back they had a revival meetin in the holler. Pa warned me not to get mixed up in it. He didn't hold with worship, specially them revivals. But I stole along and watched out of the pines. The flame of true religion were kindled up on Indian Ridge that night. Everyone hollerin and prayin. All of a sudden I got took by the spirit, got rollin in the dirt, dancin and barkin and babblin in tongues. Preacher said I burned with the sweet fire of Grace.

'After it left me, I knew – I knew for certain I was chose.'

'But what had you been chosen for?'

'When Pa found out what happened, he got real mad. He wanted to tear up the Bible that Ma gave me, but I hid it. There's an old cabin up on the hillside where we keep roosters. I made me a hole under the log floor aside the stove and I hid my Bible there. Once in a while I'd go to look. Sittin on the floor of the cabin among them birds, I'd talk aloud from the Scriptures. Then I'd go up in the mountains and wait. And wait for the Lord God to speak to me.

'One day some kids spied on me through the cabin window. They told everyone in the holler that Print Begley were talkin to chickens. Folks laughed, called me a crazy fool. Folk always said that – that I weren't right in the head.'

'Did you ever think of leaving?'

'I worked for the farmer five years when the war came. Scratchin that yellow dirt with Nate's bull-tongue plow ... I'd hear the airplanes fly over. At night I'd sit out on the ridge and watch those stars, lookin for a sign.'

'A sign?'

'A warnin ... See, I knowed about it since I was young, but I never figgered it were the Lord's will – what he had in mind for me all along. I heard it first from my uncle Joe. Out huntin one time, he told me what the old people said – how there were always one who kept watch ... The Cherokee believe that someday they'll see in the sky the signs that mean the end of the world. I read it in the

Bible too. Now it's Print the one that look for the warnin signs. See, that's what I was chose for – to keep watch.'

'How will you recognize these signs when they appear?'

'Near the time there'll be star showers, the stars'll change position and the moon show its back to the earth. Other signs come first that I ain't at liberty to reveal. But on the last day the sun'll turn every color in the rainbow. Then all a sudden everythin'll go dark ... darker than any eclipse. Pitch total darkness with no kind of light. The moon and sun and stars all disappear and the sky come down to earth ... Ain't *no one* gonna be saved.'

'What's the use, then?'

' "O generation of vipers, who hath warned ye to flee from the wrath to come?" '

'It'll give the righteous time to prepare, to work out their own salvation with fear and tremblin.'

'And the Cherokee?'

[Silence]

'When is all this to happen?'

'Soon.'

'What makes you think that?'

'The time is now.

'Why? Because of the war?'

[Silence]

'How can you be sure?'

'I already seen the first sign.'

People were beginning to emerge from cellars and basements, and pick their way through the rubble looking for food. Armed with sticks to ward off stray dogs and beat away rats that swarmed everywhere underfoot, they went about their work in exhausted silence, moving like shadows among the smoking ruins.

He watched them from where he stood sheltered from the rain on the steps of the old house. It was an official building of some kind, saved from the bombing by a wall of sandbags that reached to the first-floor balconies. Over the entrance a black-and-white banner hung in tatters from the splintered flagpole. Looking up, he could see gabled roofs leaning out against the sky like the wings of a great hunched bird.

Along with the others in his unit he'd been put in charge of a group of civilians detailed to bury the dead. It wasn't the kind of job men volunteered for. They were given masks to cover the lower halves of their faces, but the respirators were unpleasantly hot and didn't keep out the smell. The city reeked of death. The stench of decomposing bodies permeated the air. Some of the corpses they pulled out were victims of Allied air attacks, weeks old.

He remembers the sound of wooden handcarts creaking through the streets of Nuremberg, as they indiscriminately loaded the remains of the carnage. Dead Germans and Americans lying side by side in the charred soaking rubble; the loathsome task of picking up mangled corpses with bare hands.

He helped stack bodies in neat piles like the log rows the mountaineers made in the woods above the hollow. Later they'd be taken away by Red Cross trucks, sprinkled with lime and buried in trenches outside the city walls; or where there was immediate risk of contamination, burned with flame-throwers.

It was the smell that sickened him: the sickly-sweet smell of seared flesh mingled with smoke and gasoline.

Earlier he'd gone into the house with the rest of his detail to bring the dead out. The place was in a shambles. Offices and living quarters, moved to the basement during the battle, had been looted. Closets, trunks, filing cabinets, packing cases had all been smashed open, their contents scattered about. Crockery and glass had been swept off their shelves onto the stone floors. There were shoes, cigar boxes, women's underwear, silk stockings, wigs, cuckoo clocks, American cigarettes, leather gloves, bottles of brandy and perfume – all jumbled up and spattered with blood. Several corpses, mostly in SS uniform, lay sprawled among the debris. The floor felt sticky under his feet.

'I couldn't stand it down in that hole. The smell were that bad, the flies . . . I never seen so many goddamn flies. Had to come up and get some air.'

'What are you doing now?'

'Just gettin out here on the porch havin a smoke. I'll go back in a little while. If my sergeant catch me . . .'

'What outfit are you with?'

'Fifteenth Infantry. They kept us behind to clean up the mess. That's how come I got this stinkin job.'

'When did the fighting stop?'

'While back ... Wednesday, I guess. We had us a victory parade on the main square – what's left of it. Holes all over big enough to set a washtub in. Some general made a speech, told us how it were A-dolf Hitler's birthday. I bet that boy got sore as hell when he heard the news. All the men was cheerin and goin crazy. They sayin the war's as good as over.'

'Did you see much action?'

'Some.'

'Feel like telling me about it?'

[Silence]

'How old are you, Print?'

'Nineteen.'

'Have you ever been away from home before?'

'Last fall I went visitin with cousins that live in Rizton, about ten mile across the Tennessee line.'

'All right, let's go back a little. Just concentrate on your breathing ...'

One night during the first major assault on Nuremberg he'd killed a man in the window of a ruined tower. It was one of seven towers set at intervals along the medieval walls of the old town and used as sniper posts by the defenders. A light in the darkness – the flicker of a tiny flame behind cupped palms – had given him the other's position. There was a wind blowing, and the German had taken too long to light his cigarette. Begley hesitated before he fired – not out of conscience, but because the light in the tower window, infinitely fragile, had stirred in him some small, unfathomed resistance.

For a moment he'd felt afraid. Then he squeezed the trigger and the flame was extinguished.

'I can see him layin there under a mound of crushed cement. His helmet came off and what's left of his skull's burnin like a fuckin torch. The whole city look like it's on fire. Sky glowin red, full of swirlin dust and wrecked buildins standin out against the flames ... the wind fannin 'em higher and higher.'

'What did it remind you of?'

[Silence]

'The light in the tower window – it reminded you of something.'

'I dunno.'

'Was it one of the signs you were talking about?'

'I dunno, it just seemed like ... a door had closed somewhere.'

'A door?'

'This mornin, down by the lake.'

'What happened?'

'I seen a young girl ... walkin near the water. But I can't – she had no right to be there ... [Hesitates] I can't seem to ...'

'Go on. What happened?'

'I can't ... The door shut.'

'All right. Concentrate on your breathing. That's good. Now I want you to go back again to the moment when you first set eyes on this girl. Tell me what happened ... [Pause] What do you see?'

'Trees in the park all burned up blackened stumps ... branches layin scattered over foxholes and slit trenches. Even the *grass* is black. It's pourin down rain. Never stopped rainin since the day we shipped. Mist driftin off the water like smoke. You can't hardly tell where the grass end and the lake ...'

'What are you doing there?'

'Waitin for the order to advance. Settin in the mud ... I'm lookin out from behind this big crooked rock ... *Damn, missed!*'

'What were you aiming at?'

'Buncha mean-lookin dogs up on the hillside feastin off some dead G.I.s. One of the boys took a shot at them an they run off.'

'You mean, it wasn't you who fired the shot?'

'Waste of a slug. I can see her now ... down by the lakeshore.'

'All right, I want you to describe her to me.'

'She's just young. Kinda scrawny-lookin with big brown eyes, scarf tied around her head – carryin an umbrella too. Keeps walkin toward us slow, like she's daydreamin or somethin, comin on through the rain ... She don't watch out, she gonna get herself killed.'

'Isn't there anything you can do?'

'Try to pull her outa there before it's too late ... *Damn!* Okay, let's go!'

'What happened?'

'The signal. We're under fire. All hell's breakin loose ... Let's *go*, boys!'

'What about the girl?'

139

[Silence]

'Where is she?'

'I don't know ... can't see her no more. The mist come down thick, real sudden. She just disappeared.'

'Are you sure?'

'Let's go boys, time's a-wastin.'

'Do you see her now?'

'The door *shut* ... It shut and I can't open it.'

'What are you talking about?'

'I seen somethin floatin in the water, just below the surface.'

'Is it the girl? Did she drown?'

'I can't say. It's too ... too ... No! Don't go in there. Don't open it!'

'The door?'

[Silence]

'All right, I won't. There's nothing to worry about. Now listen carefully. We're going to go back to the house now. You're feeling calm and relaxed. Breathe deeply ... Once again you're standing on the steps of the old house with the sandbags all around it, and the broken flagpole. Only now it's later ...'

Begley takes a last drag on his cigarette, then flicks the butt out into the rain. Shouldering his rifle, he turns in under the pillared entrance, letting the door swing back on its hinges. It's dark in the hall. The ground-floor windows have been blacked out with tar paper and there's no electric current. At first he has to feel his way along the paneled walls. After a few steps he stops and listens. The sound of voices drifts up from the basement. They're still down there, arguing over what's left of the spoiled contraband. Somewhere he can hear a clock ticking. He moves slowly toward the staircase; his boots make a measured crunching that echoes through the empty hall. At his feet, lakes of shattered glass across the dusty marble floor. He reaches the bottom of the stairs and stands there gazing up at the remains of a crippled chandelier. Its lusters seem to flow down out of the dark stairwell in a single gleaming runnel of light.

'It's ... beautiful ... like a waterfall. I can see clear through to the other side.'

'What's there? What can you see?'

'The door.'

'Which door?'

'At the top of the stair ... ain't but one.'

'Is it open or shut?'

'Shut. It's kinda hard to tell in this light, but I *know* it's shut.'

'Are you going to go up?'

'I'm on the stair now ... just takin a look 'round.'

'Tell me what you see.'

'Nothin much ... piles of books, and junk everywhere. White patches on the walls, where pictures used to hang. This big brass clock with an eagle settin on top of it ... [Pause] There's a corner here open to the sky. Shell must have busted through.'

'All right, start climbing.'

'Okay, I'm climbin ... I'm climbin ... [Pause] Okay now, the door *is* shut. I come up them stairs and I can see ... uh ...'

'What's the matter?'

[Silence]

'Are you afraid?'

'I have to put on the mask. It smell pretty bad up here.'

'All right. You reach the top of the stairs ...'

'Okay, I reach the top and the door's shut and ... I [indistinct] ... I can't do it.'

'You can do it. Just concentrate on your breathing, the rhythm of your breathing. That's better ... Good, now open the door.'

'Not a sound anywhere but the rain beatin down on the roof. It ain't no use ... I can't do it.'

'Open the door.'

'I can't move my feet.'

'Yes, you can.'

'Lord, be my strength and my redeemer.'

'Open it!'

'I know what I'm gonna see in there.'

'I'm here beside you. You're quite safe. We'll go in together, but you have to open that door.'

'Okay, I open it. I kicked it open, only it got stuck – it *won't* open. Goddamn, the door hit on somethin. It jammed right on her ... on her hand. I can see her little fingernails peekin out under the bottom of the door ... scrabblin at the rug like she trying to *get out*! And then it – it – it shifted sudden like ... and the arm jump back and I can see it's been cut off ... at the ... her elbow ... and the blood *everywhere*. Jesus, help me, the blood!'

'How did it happen?'

[Silence]

'All right, let's go in. Together ... [Pause] We're in the room now. What can you see?'

'I see the arm layin there, the knuckles all scratched up from where I pushed the door over 'em. There's a piece of string tied around her wrist ... and someone's shoe. I'm starin at the arm, wonderin how it come to be there. Sick to my stomach. The smell ... blood everywhere ... and – and then I go over to the bed. She's lookin right at me – a cute little doll set up against the pillows, blond with blue eyes ... wide-open eyes ... lookin right at me. And that's ... that's ... I just barely can ... that's when I see over the other side of the bed ... in the corner. No, it *can't* be.'

'What do you mean? Is it the girl? The girl you saw down by the lake?'

'He just *butchered* her!'

'Who did?'

[Silence]

'Is it the same girl?'

'She were totally destroyed. He split her open like a hog, tore out her insides ... and then he musta done ... Jesus Lord ... *crazy!*'

'Look at the body and tell me if it's her.'

'I can't ... I can't look no more. Don't leave me here.'

'I won't. Just tell me if it's the same girl.'

'Don't leave me here, *please!*'

'It's all right. Everything's going to be all right. You're quite safe.'

'*Please, don't leave me here!*'

'Martin, you're quite safe. Concentrate on your breathing. The sound of my voice, Martin ... *Martin.* You're feeling calm and relaxed ... That's better. Now breathe deeply. We're going to go back home now, back to the garden outside the library window. You're lying in your hammock again ... calm and relaxed ... calm, relaxed.'

THREE

After a while, when Begley didn't come down to join the others in the basement, one of the civilians in his detail went upstairs to see what had happened to him, and then sent at once for the U.S. military police. They found him in an attic room of the Palmenhof, the local Gestapo and SS headquarters – by now he knows the name and function of the building – sitting cross-legged on the floor in the corner behind the bed, cradling in his arms the body of a young German girl.

Thin, dark-haired, about ten years old – whether it's the same girl he saw walking by the lake is never established – the child had been struck repeatedly on the back of the head with a trenching tool, which lay half-hidden under the bed, the bloody spade end curtained off by the lace valance. A faded print dress, torn and stained with blood, was hiked up over her meager thighs, exposing horrifying wounds to the abdomen and groin. One of her arms, severed above the elbow, lay like a discarded sock behind a closet door. It had been tied by the wrist with a length of yellow thread to the laces of a man's shoe.

Begley, still wearing his respirator, was humming softly to the girl as he rocked her to and fro, every now and then stopping to recite a passage from Revelations or the Book of Isaiah.

The M.P.s took the body out of his arms and ordered him to remove the respirator and identify himself. He was reluctant to let go of her. When they started to question him, he went over to the window and, pulling back the blind, looked down into the street. He saw a river of mud, clogged with refuse, heaps of pulverized brick, burned-out tanks, stalled cars, dead horses ... He couldn't remember what had happened. He couldn't remember anything, not even his own name.

Near the intersection a U.S. jeep had driven over the lip of a huge bomb crater and gotten stuck. He watched the driver climb out from behind the wheel. Red in the face, fanning himself with his helmet, he began shouting angrily at his buddy, who'd given up trying to push and was leaning against the side of the jeep, helpless with laughter. At the far end of the street he could see long lines of women waiting in the rain to get water from a broken standpipe.

One of the M.P.s flipped a cigarette from a pack of Chesterfields and offered it to him. While he was lighting it, shielding the flame of the Zippo with his cupped hand, it started to come back.

'I wanted to save her, see . . . only it were too late. I knew she were gonna die anyway. They all gonna be dead pretty soon. All the people, the animals, birds and fishes . . . trees, everythin. You and me too . . . dead. Even the dumb flies. It's comin. I already seen the sign . . . but I can't wait that long.'

'Do you mean she wasn't dead when you found her?'

[Silence]

The tears were running down his face. He wiped them away with the backs of his hands, which were bloody from holding the girl. When the M.P.s put the cuffs on him, he didn't try to resist.

'How could I leave her there to die all alone? I had to do it. The Lord didn't give me no choice. He wouldn't save her. I just wanted to put her out of her misery . . .'

After he was arrested, Corporal Print Begley was taken to the Seventh Army Headquarters in the Fortress of Nuremberg, where he was formally charged with the murder of a German civilian.

FOUR

2.30 p.m. – They delivered the TV early – a 19-inch late-model Zenith. Color. I plugged it right in and watched *Mike Douglas, The Munsters, I Dream of Jeannie* and half of *Hollywood Squares* before leaving for the office.

Today was the first time I've been anywhere near the place in two weeks. Before going up to the executive floor, I looked in on the 'Store' – just to reacclimatize. I'd forgotten how clean and peaceful it is down there. Console operators silently patrolling the skidproof gangways, gleaming banks of hardware, no noise, no smell, dust-free ...

The guys in the office all seemed glad to see me. A little too glad. Mrs P. *very* concerned over my health. There were a lot of jokes, mostly about the Pentagon's latest computer foul-up, which Al says nearly started W.W. III. An argument ensues over whether the error was technical, or merely human. I know nothing about it, since I haven't seen a newspaper in days. A note on my desk: *'We missed you – The Cleavage.'*

A half-hour or so with Diana clearing the backlog; then it's time to see Greenfield. As I come into the room he leaps to his feet – always a bad sign – and reaches out to me with both hands across that titanic desk. 'Great to have you back, Martin. Fully recovered, I hope ...'

When he's through, he sits there sucking on a mint – waiting for me to say something. I tell him that I've decided to take the two weeks' vacation – the two weeks I have coming to me from the summer – now.

'Something personal?' He's on to it right away, his little eyes glinting like silicon chips.

* Extract from Martin Gregory's diary

I know enough to say, 'No, no, it's nothing. I just need a holiday.'

Which somehow brings us around to the question of my promotion: 'The smooth running of any organization is dependent on everyone on the team pulling their weight, Gregory ... With so much hanging in the balance, this could be a bad time for you to be going away ... In our business, as you know, individual units are always replaceable ... Pity you had to miss the Planning Group conference ... I'm afraid I can't promise that when you get back ...' And so on.

I let him have his say, hardly listening now. When the moment comes to swear allegiance to the corporate flag, I do it – at least, I make the right noises, the sound of people eating shit being what turns Greenfield on – but I don't give an inch. I insist on my two weeks' vacation. Unhappy, but appeased, he tells me to have a good one.

7 p.m. – With every new 'life' Somerville and I draw another blank. Not that I've come to expect anything different. Therapy after all is just a game, a way of keeping the patient occupied, of killing his time. Since Anna left for Vienna I've been regressed five times in as many days. Counting Fawcett that makes six – six *lives*! And so far nothing, not a single lead, has come out of it. It might help if I knew what I was supposed to be looking for, but Somerville insists that 'It's the only way.'

I can't really explain it, but I'm beginning to get the feeling that he *wants* something from me. More than just his fee.

Over the past week I've noticed an odd thing. When we're sitting opposite each other, he's taken to assuming the identical position in his chair that I do in mine. If I slump down or cross my legs, or put my hands in my pockets, after a while he does the same. At first I found it slightly disconcerting, but then it just became ridiculous and I decided to say something to him. Only for some reason, I couldn't – I was too embarrassed to. Now he's started copying *all* my gestures, even my facial expressions.

It gives me an eerie sort of feeling, as if I'm looking at myself in a mirror, knowing that someone else is standing on the other side of the glass, watching me through my own reflection.

Since the Nuremberg regression last Tuesday we've hardly

talked. I told him I'd written to St Louis to find out if Print Begley really did serve in the U.S. Army, but he didn't seem in the least interested. Whenever I try to tell him about some piece of evidence I've managed to dig up at the Library, he listens quietly to what I have to say and then says nothing. On Friday I finally asked him if he thought we were making any progress.

He just said, 'Well, you're feeling better about yourself, aren't you?'

Maybe it's the cumulative effect of being hypnotized every day, but the truth is I *do* feel better. That is, I don't feel anything, except maybe a little numb, like I'm walking around with a head full of snow.

Transcribing the tapes is a slow business, so I don't get to bed till late; I haven't even had time to keep up my diary. But I sleep well. No more 'visions', no more dreams – at least, not since Tuesday – and no need for the little white friend, though Heyworth insisted on writing out another prescription. He asked me last night if I'd heard anything from Anna.

There's no one I want to see or hear from now, except Penelope. After my session this afternoon I tried the downstairs library again, but the red door was locked as usual. When I think about what happened in there, I realize I must have been hallucinating. But it amuses me to think I might have discovered Somerville's secret vice; I don't imagine he'd want the world to know about his taste for high pornography.

Looked up 'Vaudoises' at the Library – they were a heretical sect in medieval France accused of worshipping the Devil and holding orgies 'at which a dog appeared and sprinkled the worshipers with its tail'. They also had a reputation throughout Europe – right up until the end of the nineteenth century, apparently – for 'sorcery and cannibalism'.

Still no word from Somerville of when Penelope is expected back. When she does return – assuming she ever really went away – I'll ask her out to dinner, then bring her here afterward. Just to see what happens. If it's what I've been afraid of, what I've dreamed about so often, well then . . .

FIVE

All week I worked with the new tapes in the hope of discovering some sort of pattern to the regressions. After each session I'd take home the latest cassette, play it back a couple of times and then transcribe it. The next morning at 9.55 sharp I'd be sitting with 'Patience' and 'Fortitude', the two stone lions that overlook the steps of the Public Library, waiting for the doors to open. I started out full of enthusiasm, just as I'd done with the Fawcett tape, but the deeper I got into the research, the clearer it became to me that I was just wasting my time.

The lives of the six fell within a span of roughly a thousand years: the last millennium. None of them, apart from Fawcett, turned out to be a known historical figure, though three referred to, or took part in, recorded historical events which could be used to corroborate their testimony. There was no easy way of establishing whether they had actually existed – I was still working on Print Begley – but their stories did seem to be supported by the facts. In some instances the detail was remarkably accurate.

It was only when I tried to find a connection between the six different 'lives' and determine how they might be relevant to my own that I ran into trouble. There were enough superficial connections: themes, recurring images, certain phrases and catchwords, which appeared in some, though not all, the regressions. On the Begley tape, for instance, ceaseless rain, mist, flies, starving dogs, the light in the tower window, the word 'waterfall' all seemed to echo Fawcett's journey through the jungles of Mato Grosso. But that was as far as it went. The connections were meaningless in themselves, and although I tried to work it a hundred different ways, I couldn't seem to tie them in to any kind of overall structure or progression.

By the end of the week, I was seriously considering taking the problem to Al at the office and asking him to run it through one of our big computers. Mensa IV properly programmed was capable of shifting through a thousand years of history and coming up with the correct answer to *any* question in a few microseconds. I even got as far as trying to prepare input for the first run, but when it came down to it, my knowledge of the lives was so sketchy it proved impossible to compose a workable data base. There were simply too many variables.

At the time, I made the following brief summaries of the six regressions. Since, taken together, they provide all the information needed to understand what would happen in the weeks to come, I reproduce them here (rather than the transcripts of the tapes) in chronological order.

TAPE 4 – *Thorfinn*, born A.D. 947. Navigator, farmer. Leads group of Northmen from Vatnsfjord in Norway to settle small, remote island called Boreray (unable to locate on map). Hoped to live a simple, harmonious peaceful existence there – something no longer possible in his own country. Believed island to be sacred place – unclear why. Community does not prosper. Climate harsh; boats destroyed by storm; not enough to eat. No trees on the island to make another boat – no one can leave. Feuds and rivalries between settlers. Thorfinn and family, held responsible for community's failure, ostracized by the others. Take refuge in cave, slowly starve to death.

TAPE 3 – *Jean Cabet*, c. 1250–1288. Apothecary, alchemist. Lived and practiced medicine in Lyon and Aix. In secret, devotes himself to discovering the Stone, alchemical formula for ideal gold, said to confer true immortality by relieving adept of the burden of successive mortal incarnations. Wife and two children die of plague in epidemic; Cabet blames self for infecting them because of his work among the sick. Flooding in Provence spreads disease. Townspeople of Aix believe Cabet to be cause of plague, burn him to death in his laboratory for practicing witchcraft. At the point of death he sees 'a massive gate, behind which the Stone lies guarded', but it will not open for him.

TAPE 5 – *Tommaso Petacci*, 1558–1589. Poet, philosopher, friar. Born Naples, son of a fisherman. Joined Dominicans aged twelve. More interested in learning than religion. Shows too much independence of mind and soon clashes with religious authorities in Rome. Critical of the Church and political system. Believes the end of the century will bring violent social upheavals. Claims plans for a 'Universal Republic' have been revealed to him by God in a vivid dream. Writes them down in a tract titled *The City of the*

Stars – never published. Manuscript seized by the Pope's secret police and burned in public; Petacci arrested and convicted of heresy by the Roman Inquisition. Imprisoned in a tower near Fiesole. Tortured to death.

TAPE 2 – *Subhuto*, 1761–1821. Tibetan lama. Joins Order of Sangha, the gateway through which all men may enter on the Path. Achieves enlightenment, but realizes he does not wish to enter final Nirvana – becoming one with the eternal matrix, the 'boundless being of the Universe' – until the suffering of humanity has ended, until all other beings have been saved. Grows increasingly disillusioned with spiritual life, but knows he's unfit for any other. One day in despair he walks up into the snows of the Himalayas and doesn't return.

TAPE 1 – *P. H. Fawcett*, 1867–1925. Soldier, explorer, etc. Pursues obsessive quest for 'lost cities' in the jungles of Brazil. Believed these to have been part of a forgotten civilization, possibly Atlantis. On his last journey (delays, bad weather, sickness, etc.) sends his companions back, goes on alone. Searches for waterfall marked by stone tower in the forest – believes will lead him to 'Z', an ancient city surrounded by 'a ring of savage tribes'. Weak from lack of food. Talks of 'finding a way through'. Killed by Morcegos Indians on the verge of reaching his destination.

TAPE 6 – *Print Begley*, 1925–(?). Farmworker, G.I. Born Indian Ridge, poor mining community in eastern mountains of Kentucky. Considered simple-minded. Persecuted because he's a half-breed. Keeps to himself. Refuses to follow tradition and become a miner. Religious enthusiasm thwarted by father. Hides Bible in shack after attending revival meeting, where he discovers he's been 'chosen'. Takes on ancestral Cherokee role of watching the stars to foretell end of world. Drafted into Army and sent to Germany in February 1945. Short but intense war experience. Fought at Nuremberg – one of the fiercest and bloodiest engagements of the last days of the war. Stayed on afterward to garrison the town and bury the dead.

Among my detailed notes listing all possible connections between these six regressions, I noted several recurring images that could be traced directly to my own experience.

I had no doubt, for instance, that the chandelier in the Nuremberg Palmenhof, which makes Print Begley think of a waterfall, was inspired by the one that hangs in the hallway at Ninety-third Street. When Begley looks up and sees the door behind it – it can hardly be a coincidence. Any more than the image of the girl walking by the lake, or the rock shaped like a crouching man, or even Begley's use of the phrase 'out of her misery' can be a coincidence. Clearly they referred to incidents from my own very recent past, which meant that they invalidated whatever claim the 'lives' had to being genuine historical memories.

As far as I could see, regressions were made up of the same haphazard stuff as dreams: the unconscious mind embroidering on the trivial details of one's daily existence to produce a series of elaborate, marginally related fantasies. But then it occurred to me that there was another way of looking at this. If I counted my own life as one of the 'lives', making it the seventh in the series, as it were – for the computer I even tried adding my own curriculum vitae to the list of capsulated biographies – then all those images that showed up in the regressions, apparently lifted straight from my own experience, would appear no more or less valid than any of the other connections between the six 'lives'. In other words, we'd all be in it together: seven in one. Everything would fall into place.

But though the idea appealed to the programmer in me, it still didn't *explain* anything. Like why an obscure German engraving hanging in the corridor of the New York Public Library, or the chandelier in my therapist's office, should have taken such a sinuous hold of my imagination. The 'correlative data' still seemed just as arbitrary as ever; the overall pattern that I hoped to reveal remained just as elusive.

Print Begley was the only one of the six whose story had no ending. I had to find out what happened to him, so I asked Somerville if he could bring him back under hypnosis. He seemed doubtful at first. It could be done, he said, but the Begley regression had been so traumatic, it might be dangerous to pursue it further. The last time, just after Begley was arrested for murder, Somerville had had to pull me out of the trance because I was showing signs of having an 'acute panic reaction'. I argued that it didn't make any sense to leave unfinished what was probably the most interesting of the regressions. In the end Somerville reluctantly agreed to try to reach Begley again.

Unfortunately, the session was not a success. By one of those capricious 'synaptic lesions', as Somerville called them, instead of

Nuremberg or the hills of Kentucky, we found ourselves back on the grim little island of Boreray, holed up in a cave with Thorfinn and his family, sheltering from the icy blast of the north wind.

To be fair to Somerville, he never claimed to have total control over which incarnation would manifest itself. It was like turning a dial, he said, looking for a radio station that was always changing frequency and broadcast only when it felt like it. Sometimes in the middle of a regression, particularly when he moved a character back or forward in time within his own life-span, other voices, some of them familiar to us, others unidentified, would surface without warning. But never Print Begley's. His slow, hard-shelled Appalachian drawl had signed off the air for good.

A curious thing: no matter which identity I assumed, I always answered Somerville's questions in English. Sometimes I'd come up with words I hardly knew the meaning of, or that simply weren't in my vocabulary; on the other hand, I'd also use expressions that couldn't possibly have been known by any of my earlier selves. Petacci, for instance, in a glaring anachronism, suddenly announces that he's tired of being 'hassled' by the Vatican police! Somerville explained that being regressed was largely a visual experience, in which the subconscious naturally translated the incidents recalled into contemporary language.

In the case of Fawcett and Begley, where I seemed to have hit on the right accent and speech pattern (being a poor mimic, I was totally unable to imitate them afterward), he maintained that the intensity of the recollection had produced a more 'developed' response. I suggested it might have something to do with their being the closest to me in time and the fact that we had a common language, but Somerville insisted that it was because their stories – particularly Begley's – had a 'deeper significance at the subconscious level'.

I was far from convinced by his arguments. Admittedly, Begley's story had affected me more than the others. When I found out that he'd murdered the girl in the Palmenhof, I was depressed about it for a couple of days. But in spite of his crime I found him the most sympathetic of the six. And since Begley was my predecessor, and therefore the most accessible of all the regressions, it seemed only natural that I should concentrate my researches on him – on trying to establish whether he'd actually existed.

It was the librarian in the Genealogy and Local History section of the Public Library who suggested I apply to the Army for a copy of Print Begley's service record. I'd explained to her that I was trying to trace a distant relative from a small town in eastern Kentucky, and that all I really knew about him was that he'd fought as an enlisted man in World War II. She went out of her way to be helpful, showing me how to fill out the '180' application form, which I duly completed and sent off to Military Personnel Records in St Louis.

She also recommended that I write the clerk of the town or village where my relative was born. 'He must have had a birth certificate,' she said. 'And that's always a beginning.'

I'd already looked up Indian Ridge in an atlas and established, at least, that there was such a place. It lay in a secluded valley at the southern end of the Cumberland Mountains close to the Tennessee line, about eight miles east of a town named Pathfork in Bell County, which is where Print Begley said he had gone to school. According to an old Kentucky gazetteer, which the librarian produced from somewhere, Indian Ridge, formerly the site of a Cherokee village known as Tuskarora, was founded by the Cumberland Coal Company as a mining community in 1903. In 1937 it had a population of one hundred and five. It was described succinctly as 'a hamlet of little scenic interest'.

There were no civil institutions in Indian Ridge. I called the Town Clerk's office in Pathfork and was told by a secretary, who sounded half-asleep, that as far as she knew Indian Ridge came under her town's jurisdiction, but that all information concerning deaths, births and marriages had to be applied for in writing. I wrote to her the same day, though I had a feeling it would be a while before I got an answer back.

The next thing I did was look up the name Begley in the Bell County phone book. There were three listed – none of whom lived in Indian Ridge. The first two had never heard of any Begley named Print; the third, one Aaron Begley from Pineville, put down the phone as soon as I mentioned my 'cousin's' name.

The librarian finally suggested that I try to contact the minister of one of the churches in the district, explaining that 'in that part of the world, the clergy are still the chief repositories of local history'.

Under 'Churches' in the Bell County Yellow Pages, I could find no listings for Indian Ridge, though Pathfork seemed to have more than its fair share. I had to call most of them before I got my first lead.

The Reverend Charles F. Pennington, pastor of the Straight Creek Trinity Tabernacle Church, remembered hearing about a couple named Begley who used to live in Indian Ridge. He thought they'd either died or moved away about thirty years ago.

'They weren't churchgoing people, so I didn't have any contact with them. But I'm afraid the name *Print* Begley doesn't mean a thing to me. A lot of the boys from these parts went off to fight in the war and never came back.'

'I don't think he was killed,' I said. 'It's possible that he wound up in prison. Or even an institution. He may have been a bit simple-minded.'

'Have you considered getting in touch with the County Insane Asylum?'

'Yeah, I thought of that . . . as a last resort.'

'As I recall, the Begleys weren't too popular in the hollow, though I can't tell you just why. It was always a hard place – even in those days, when the mines were hiring.'

'Surely some of the people living there now, some of the older ones, must have known them?'

'You say you're researching a book?'

'About the war, yes. I'm doing a series of interviews with Seventh Army veterans.'

'I'm not so sure they're going to want to talk to you. Mountaineers are cagey when it comes to strangers asking questions. Can you hold the line a minute? I want to ask my wife – she was born and raised here, and knows the district better than I do.'

I heard his palm clamp over the mouthpiece, then the sound of muffled conversation.

'Mr Gregory? My wife tells me that the Begleys did have a boy, though she doesn't think he was named Print. That's a one-of-a-kind name, even for the Cumberlands. Of course, it may not have been the same family. There are no Begleys in the hollow now. But my wife says they do have kin here in Pathfork.'

'Do you think they'd agree to talk to me?'

'There's a young fellow by the name of Zach Scalf who runs a motel on the road to Pineville. He might be able to tell you something. But you'd have to come down here. I doubt you'll get much out of him on the telephone.'

'What's the name of the motel?'

'The Pineview Motor Lodge.'

SIX

October 17
Length of interval since last session: 24 hours

A. INITIAL EXPECTATIONS

Further progress and continued easing of tension without any change in our relationship.

B. ATMOSPHERE

Patient was restless to begin with and unusually talkative. He seemed keyed up over something and anxious to tell me about it, though he waited until late in the session. I realize now that he wanted to hear what I had to say about the regressions before letting me in on his discovery. The atmosphere remained somewhat tense.

His manner changed noticeably soon after he settled into his chair. On adopting the same posture as I had, which has now become an automatic reflex with him, he grew much calmer. We were soon making synchronous gestures and movements reflecting the rhythms of our conversation. Postural congruence, however, is less conspicuous than interactional synchrony, which suggests that some of the time he may be *consciously* copying my gestures.

My influence over the patient has grown recently, but the therapist can never escape completely from the impact of his patient's troubles. I had an unpleasant sense of foreboding about the proceedings.

C. MAIN TRENDS AND THERAPEUTIC INTERVENTIONS

I began by congratulating the patient on his performance as a hypnotic subject over the past week and told him that I had never regressed anyone so successfully or with such interesting results. He said impatiently that he would find the results interesting when he knew what they meant. Explained briefly the notion of metempsychosis: that after the soul leaves the body it is born again in a new body, and that its character, circumstances and station in each successive life are dependent on its performance in its previous lives. Sometimes a belief in Karma can be a useful therapeutic aid, but in this case I have been careful to avoid all references to rebirth except to mention that acceptance of past lives was not essential to regression therapy. I brought the subject up now chiefly to allay the patient's fears that I might be trying to indoctrinate him. Prejudice against the idea of reincarnation less marked than hitherto.

We both agreed that the following questions needed to be answered: a) Why *these* six lives? b) What do they have in common? c) How do they relate to his present difficulty?

a) In five out of the six cases – Begley's fate being still unknown – the lives end tragically and in violent circumstances. Put forward the argument that since we tend to remember best from our own lives what made greatest emotional impact at the time, the same principle may apply to memory of previous existences.

b) At first, not a great deal. A few inconsistent motifs of marginal interest only. All six might be described as 'seekers', each engaged in some kind of spiritual quest. Whether it's Thorfinn's attempt to regain lost innocence by getting back to nature, or Cabet's search for the true gold of metaphysical alchemy, or even Fawcett's mazed journeying to find the answer to an ancient riddle – all apear deeply committed to the pursuit of the unattainable. Perhaps what the six really have in common is that they set themselves Grail-like projects, which were inevitably doomed to failure.

Admitted I could see no sign of any Karmic progression between the lives.

c) Suggested to the patient that a possible connection with his own life might be the frustrated idealism of his student days (Session Two). He reacted scornfully.

As expected, the patient seemed disappointed by the above remarks. Despite my assurances that they were relevant, he dismissed them as 'superficial' and 'irrelevant'. I reminded him that this was an interim report, which I'd only made at his request, and that it was still too early to be talking about solutions.

Patient then produced from his pocket some papers which he handed to me without comment. They consisted of a buff-colored document and an attached letter on official notepaper. The document was headed 'Standard Form 180, Request Pertaining to Military Records' and had been filled out on behalf of Print Begley. I photocopied the letter, which appears to be authentic, before returning it to the patient:

Military Personnel Records (GSA)
9700 Page Boulevard
St Louis, Mo. 63132

October 13, 1981

Dear Mr Gregory,

Records of military personnel who served within the last 75 years are subject to restrictions imposed by the military under the Public Information Act of 1966. Records cannot be made available for public examination or copies provided, although information from them may be furnished.

Generally, other than requests from official sources, only those from members of veterans' immediate families are honored. However, in cases where there is a genuine need for identification, an exception is usually made.

According to his service record, Cpl Print Begley served with the 7th Army 15th Infantry, 'C' Company from February 2 through July 25, 1945. There is no record of criminal proceedings in Begley's 201 file. As you mention, he was arrested and charged with the murder of a German civilian, Effie Gastler, on April 23, 1945. However, he was released unconditionally after an investigation revealed that the victim had already been dead forty-eight hours when he found her. The girl's mother, who worked as a cook at the Palmenhof, told the U.S. authorities that two SS officers had tortured and then murdered her daughter the night before Nuremberg fell because they were under the mistaken impression that she was Jewish.

Begley was kept under medical supervision for several weeks with suspected battle fatigue and then sent back to his unit. After the war he applied to join the Air Force and enlist for pilot training, but was turned down on grounds of unsuitability.

Date and place of birth: Indian Ridge, Ky, May 5, 1925. Names of father and mother: Preston and Ida Begley. Status: Unmarried. For information as to whether he is still living I suggest you write to Washington National Records Center in Suitland, Md, and ask for his Social Security number.

I hope this has been of some help,

Sincerely,
(Sgt) Deborah B. Johnstone

After reading the above, I complimented the patient on a diligent piece of research. When he realized that I wasn't going to say anything more, he asked me if I considered the letter proof of his having lived before. I said no. Then he asked if I thought Begley might still be alive. I said that anything was possible, but I thought not. He laughed and said he was reassured to hear that, because if Begley were still alive, what would that make *him*?

D. INTERPRETATIONS THOUGHT OF BUT NOT GIVEN

The reappearance of the murdered girl in Begley's story (Session Four) is of great significance. The disclosure that he, or someone else, struck her with a trenching tool clearly parallels the homicidal attack on Missy with a spade in the Philippines. Although it turns out that Begley *did not* kill the girl, just as Fawcett in the end couldn't bring himself to kill his dogs, both stories must be regarded as subconscious attempts by the patient to deny responsibility for the crime he committed as a child.

He told me today that he felt better because he was no longer 'consumed by guilt'. When I asked him why not, he replied cryptically that it was because he realized now that he hadn't acted alone. I asked him if he meant that his 'other lives' were involved. He said, 'Something like that.'

He seemed to be quite satisfied with this explanation. When I made it clear to him that I was still at a loss to understand what he meant, he shrugged his shoulders and stared out of the window as if it was unimportant to him whether I understood or not.

If the patient's 'other lives' can be described as an imaginative response to the challenge of hypnosis, I'm afraid now that the evidence is beginning to suggest a mind on the verge of fragmentation.

E. Outcome

At the end of the session, patient announced that he wouldn't be coming again this week as he was planning to go to Kentucky to see if he could find out anything more about Begley. He told me that he was 'determined to prove this thing one way or another'. My first impulse was to warn him that he might be taking things too literally and try to talk him out of setting off on some wild-goose chase, but at this stage it would only have been counterproductive. I wished him luck instead. He reacted coolly; he said he felt we'd drifted apart during today's session, that we weren't as 'in tune' with each other as before. He certainly seemed remote and unapproachable now. He was no longer making any attempt, conscious or unconscious, to imitate my movements. When he left, I got the distinct impression that he wanted the break to be a permanent one.

F. Afterthoughts

I am not altogether certain how to interpret this sudden deterioration in the patient's behaviour. One possibility is to consider his paranoia as an irresistibly advancing process, which may have grown so strong as to be beyond my influence.

Patient's tendency to retreat from relationships in order to adopt a position of self-sufficiency – a defensive mechanism that has an ominous quality about it – is marked. The patient's flight suggests that his fantasy of total independence – from wife, family, friends, work and now from me – can only be achieved at the cost of a total break with reality.

SEVEN

9.30 p.m. – As I sit here waiting for Scalf to get back from town, I have to ask myself what the hell I'm doing in this sleazy backwoods motel room in the middle of nowhere ...

From La Guardia this afternoon I flew Republic (never heard of them before) to Knoxville in Tennessee, where I rented a car and then drove on up through the mountains to Pineville. It was already dark by the time I crossed the state line, so I haven't exactly seen Kentucky yet. I stopped for a hamburger at a greasy spoon diner in downtown Middlesboro and got to the motel at about 8.30.

As far as I know I wasn't followed.

I seem to be the only guest, which is not really surprising – the Pineview Motor Lodge has definitely seen better days. The cabins look as if they could all use a little basic renovating. Scalf blames the low occupancy on the weather – says it's been bad all week. You can be sure that even on a good day anyone in his right mind passing this place would keep on driving.

The first thing I did when I got in was open up all the windows and run a check for any trace of former occupants. Under the bed I found a rusted Bumble Bee tuna can overflowing with cigarette butts and dead roaches, one cheap earring, a little heap of yellow nail parings and an empty bottle of Nehi soda. In the bathroom there was a white plastic spermicide applicator lying on the soap holder in the shower stall. I've sprayed deodorant everywhere, but the room still stinks of feet and stale sex.

The sooner I get this over with and get the hell out of here the better.

Scalf seems friendly enough, though I'll have to wait till he sobers

* Extract from Martin Gregory's diary

161

up before I start explaining things. When I arrived he was standing behind the reception desk in the office talking on the phone. There was an open pint of Wild Turkey next to the cash register. I walked through the door and he raised a slow hand half in greeting, half telling me to wait, and then a little unsteadily sauntered off into the back room taking the phone and the bottle with him. He was in there about ten minutes. I couldn't hear what he was saying, but he sounded angry about something.

While I was waiting I read the blurbs of some old postcards on exhibit under the dusty glass of the counter top. One said: 'Each June lovely mountain rosebay covers hill and cliff with bell-shaped, rose-purple flowers.' At the bottom of every card was printed, 'THE PINEVIEW MOTOR LODGE. GOOD FOOD AND A WARM WELCOME! ONLY 15 MILES EAST OF PINEVILLE ON U.S. 25E.

When he came back into the office, he insisted on shaking hands and 'welcoming' me, introducing himself rather formally as Zachariah Scalf. I asked him if he had a room, but he seemed more interested in just standing there and shooting the breeze. He spoke excruciatingly slowly, carefully enunciating each word to avoid slurring it, always explaining more than he needed to. It wasn't the moment to be asking questions about Print Begley.

If he's a relative, then it has to be on the father's side because there's no trace of Indian blood in this man. Everything about Scalf is white and seedy – just like his motel. Somehow not at all what I expected. He's a real slob. In his late forties maybe, grossly over-weight, pale and unhealthy-looking – wearing cowboy boots, an old pair of jeans held up by an enormous leather belt to support his beer gut and a filthy Allman Brothers T-shirt. Long reddish-gray hair swept back and hanging down his shoulders in rattails – looks like a holdover from a sixties bike gang. He appears to be just a good ol' boy, but his eyes have a shrewd, mean little slant to them that I don't like. At one point he told me he was a helicopter pilot in Vietnam, which I find hard to believe.

After we'd been talking awhile, he suddenly announced that he had to go into town right that minute. He took a key off the board and slapped it down on the desk in front of me, breathing in deeply, as if the familiar action had stabilized him. Then he picked up a green down vest that was lying draped over an ancient water cooler, slung it across his shoulders and went lumbering out back. A moment later I heard a car drive off.

P.S. Just discovered there's no lock on the door to my cabin, so I've stuck a chair under the handle and dragged the bureau up behind it as a support. It won't keep anyone out for long, but it should give me some warning at least.

Now I wish I'd brought something to read. The TV doesn't work, and the Gideon Bible on the bedside table won't do the trick. Which leaves sleep.

EIGHT

When I woke, I was surprised to find that it was still dark out. I looked at my watch: 12.13. I'd slept for less than two hours. I got up off the bed and a little disoriented wandered over to the window and pulled back the drapes. There were no lights on in the rest of the motel, no other cars in the parking lot. The place looked utterly deserted, like a miniature ghost town.

I tugged on a pair of sneakers, dismantled the makeshift barricade in front of the door and went outside.

The night was warm and clear. I stood for a while gazing up at a bright field of stars above the cabin roofs. The air smelled of pine trees; somewhere close by I could hear the low murmur of running water. As I made my way over to the office, I stopped more than once to glance back at the row of empty white cabins and the dark mass of the hill rising up behind them. It reminded me of walking in my garden in Bedford, doing the rounds last thing at night.

The screen door hung half-open, a hinge squeaking with mournful regularity as it plied with the breeze. There was no one home. Scalf must still be out propping up a bar in Pathfork or some other watering hole – probably dead drunk by now. I pulled the door back and went inside. The walls of the office reflected the red glow from the neon VACANCY sign in the window, but it wasn't enough to see by. I wanted to use the phone. I wanted to call Somerville's, just to see if Penelope would answer. I reached for the light switch, then for some reason thought better of it. A moment later I heard a car approaching along the highway.

An old white Chrysler turned into the driveway, sweeping around the parking lot to the rear of the office. I ducked down out of sight until it had gone by, then slipped back out the front and started walking quickly toward the cabins.

Strains of bluegrass came drifting through the darkness. The music cut out suddenly and I heard a door slam.

As I reached my cabin, I turned and looked behind. The lights were on in the office, and I could see the burly silhouette of Zach Scalf framed behind the screen door. He was standing quite still, watching me.

'It's a beautiful night,' I called out, making as if I'd just stepped outside for a breath of air.

After a long pause, Scalf said, 'You and me has some business to tend to, boy.' He sounded no drunker than when he'd left, but there was an aggressive tone to his voice now. 'You didn't register yet. And if it's all the same to you, I like the money in advance.'

'I'll be right over,' I said, feeling inside my jacket for my wallet. Then I started across the lot.

The smell of liquor and sour sweat assaulted me as I came near. 'How you doing?' I said pleasantly.

Scalf turned away without a word and I followed him into the office.

There was television going in the back room, throwing up shadows that flickered against the doorframe like firelight. He went behind the desk and started rummaging around, finally producing an old shoe box, from which he drew a sheaf of faded blue registration cards and several ball point pens.

'Place is a fuckin mess!' he muttered. 'Never can find a damn thing.'

Then, unexpectedly, he said, 'My old lady walked out on me last week. Bitch! Well, she didn't exactly walk out. Went visitin her folks in Lexington, only she forgot to tell me, see.' He belched as if to emphasize his grievance. 'And the goddamn maid's off sick.'

'It's twenty dollars even, right?' I held out the bill, which he took from me and dropped into the shoe box.

'A fuckin mess. *Look* at this shit!' He waved at a clutch of empty beer cans and a plate of congealed food sitting on a redwood coffee table in the living half of the room. 'Damn!'

While I was standing at the desk filling out the registration form, he disappeared into the back, only to reappear a moment later with a fresh six-pack. He tore off a can and handed it to me, then carried the rest over to the table.

After he'd had a drink, he let out a deep sigh and, hooking his thumbs into the armholes of his green vest, declared, 'I'd like to ask you somethin, boy.'

'Sure, go ahead,' I said lightly, glancing over at him as he lay back on the couch, his feet up on the table.

'What were you doin over here in the house while I was out?'

'How do you mean?' I gave a nervous laugh. 'I was just taking a walk.'

'Lookin for somethin in particular?' He screwed up his eyes at me, pushing a hand through his long, greasy red hair.

'Okay, I wanted to make a phone call. But it wasn't that important. When I saw there was no one in the office, I –'

'Kinda late ain't it to be botherin folks on the phone?' he interrupted softly.

'– I went back to my cabin.'

Scalf grinned. 'Is that a fact?'

Collecting my beer, I walked over to the table and sat down uninvited in the chair opposite him.

'I'm looking for someone,' I said. 'A man named Print Begley. I thought you might know where I could find him.'

'You're lookin for *what*?' He took a quick swig of beer and burst out laughing. '*Print Begley?* Now, what in hell's name would you be wantin with *him*?'

'Does that mean he's still alive?'

Scalf didn't answer. He just sat there shaking with wheezy laughter.

'The reason I'm trying to trace him' – I waited to get his attention – 'is that I'm doing research for a book on World War Two. I've been interviewing Seventh Army vets who fought at the Battle of Nuremberg.'

'What makes you think I might know something about that?'

'I was talking earlier to the Reverend Pennington, the minister of the Tabernacle church in Pathfork. He said you were related to the Begleys.'

'Is that a fact? And you came all the way down here from New York City to ask me about Print?' He leaned forward and suddenly slapped the table. 'Well, I'll be *damned*!'

'Do you know where he is?'

'Are you kiddin? I ain't seen hide nor hair of that ol' boy in thirty-five years. Left Indian Ridge a few days after he came home from the war, took off across the hill one mornin and no one's heard a peep out of him since. He were kind of crazy, see, so people just said the good Lord took him away ... Well, anyhow, that's what they 'said.'

'But where did he go? What happened to him?'

'Don't know, I said. I was only young at the time, maybe fourteen, fifteen year old. Print and me was cousins, but my folks never did hold with my keepin company with him. I were told to stay away from the holler because people up there was poor and ignorant and no good could ever come out of that place. And by no good they meant Print Begley.'

'I heard from some of the other guys in his outfit that he kept to himself pretty much.'

'You could say. A loner. But we were buddies just the same. He used to call me "Little Zee"! How *about* that?' Scalf guffawed and slapped the table again, and this time I laughed with him.

'He used to take me out huntin in the mountains. It were like religion with him. Had to leave our shoes behind at his mammy's house so we could move up through the wood real stealthy like. Weren't nothin he couldn't teach you about trackin game. I see him walk right up on squirrels and cottontails and catch 'em with his bare hands. He'd skin 'em with his bare hands too. Then he'd eat the flesh – didn't bother throwin it on the fire, just chewed it up raw. Claimed it were better for you that way. He were a strange one, Print. Didn't say an awful lot. You never really knew what was goin on inside his head.

'My pa didn't like him. "That boy were nothin but trouble from the day he were born," he'd say. "Ya'll stay away from him, hear?" And when he found out I'd been huntin with him, he'd get madder than hell and start callin Print ever' kind of bad name he could lay his tongue to. 'Round here they looked on him like he were the hind wheels of bad luck. I figgered maybe it had somethin to do with him being a breed: his ma was a squaw, see – Cherokee Indian. But that were only a part of it. It weren't the real reason.'

Scalf paused and, giving me a significant stare, took a long, steady pull at his beer. 'Folks was *scared* of Cousin Begley,' he said at last.

'Why?'

'I'm gonna show you somethin, buddy. Sit tight.'

With surprising agility he swung himself up from the couch and went off into the other room. When he came back he was carrying an old brown scrapbook, its tattered covers held together by strips of adhesive tape. He cleared a space among the beer cans and carefully wiped the table dry with the underside of his arm before laying down the book.

'This belonged to my ma,' he said with a kind of wary pride. 'She were always cuttin stuff out of the local paper, stories, poems, pictures – whatever toook her fancy. Specially any item that concerned her kin. Kept it like a family album.'

He wiped his hands on his jeans and, licking his thumb, started slowly turning over the pages.

'Here now,' he said. 'May 30, 1925. That were the day Print Begley were born. See, she wrote it in right next to the article. Now you read what it says.'

He slewed the book around and indicated with a dirty fingernail the clipping he wanted me to read. Taken from the Pineville *Courier*, it was dated May 31:

Last evening in the Cumberland Mountains one of the worst flash floods in living memory claimed the lives of more than 100 people from the coal-mining district of Bell County. Thousands of head of livestock were destroyed in the flood and untold damage done to property, crops and the mines, many of which, according to the owners, will have to be closed down. The full extent of the devastation and the effect on the livelihood of the mountaineers may not be known for several days. The death toll also is expected to go higher when the waters abate.

Yesterday in Bell County the warm spring weather gave little warning of impending disaster. At dusk a few clouds began to collect on the horizon. Occasional lightning flashes and the sullen rumbling of thunder as cumulus clouds began to pile up over the mountains indicated that a storm was to be expected, but not one of any great magnitude.

At 8.30 p.m. the storm broke over Pathfork and Indian Ridge, and at once the downpour of water was extraordinary. But as it moved eastward and north along the valley of the Cumberland River, where most of the casualties occurred, its volume steadily increased.

Here beside the column of yellowed newsprint, a handwritten note in a neat copperplate script gave the details of Print Begley's birth. The hour of his delivery, 8.30 p.m., had been heavily under-

scored in red ink and arrowed to the time in the text when the
storm began.

The water ran down the hillsides in broad sheets. Hollows and ravines
became roaring torrents carrying away log cabins and washing frame
houses off their foundations. People took refuge on rooftops as landslides
brought tons of rock and slate and mud crashing down into the valley
with hollow roars that could be heard above the fury of the storm. By
11.00 p.m. the rain had already exceeded anything in the memory of living
men ...

I tried to go on reading, but the words had blurred over. The
page was receding in front of my eyes, the walls of the room closing
in on every side, until it seemed as though I were looking down
at the tiny square of the coffee table through a long, narrowing
tunnel. Scalf was saying something to me, but it didn't make sense.
A whirring, glutting sound filled my ears. Then suddenly everything went black. For a moment I thought I was going to pass
out. Closing my eyes, I held on tightly to the armrests of the
chair.

'They blamed him for it. Blamed him for what you might call
an act of God. Do you see what I'm sayin? Here you go.'

Something pale and bloated was drifting toward me through
the darkness. It swam lazily into focus and I realized I was staring
at Scalf, leaning forward across the table to me, holding out another
beer.

I shook my head No thanks. The words wouldn't come.

'He didn't do nothin, just happened he got born that night.' He
shrugged, opening the can of beer for himself. 'It were nothin but
damn-fool superstition. And when the boy grew up kind of different,
that just went to prove it: they *knew* they was right. My ma told
me after Print went away that some of the folks in the holler
believed he was visited upon them, like an angel of destruction.
Maybe for the Devil, maybe for the Lord.'

'Do you think he could still be alive?' I heard myself say.

'He's *dead*. I don't know that for a fact, mind you. I just feel it.
After he came back from Germany he never were the same.
Somethin musta happened over there. I can remember him actin
real peculiar, even toward me. And we were *buddies*. Talkin to

himself and all that type of carry-on. He didn't do a lick of work, just sat up on the hill and watched the clouds roll by.

'There weren't no jobs anyway, 'cept for the mines. And that were one thing he swore he'd never do. I remember the day he left, he said to me, "Zee, I ain't got no education much and just barely can read and write, but I won't never creep like no mole to earn my feed."'

'Do you remember when he went away? The date?'

'It were in the summertime, I know that. Musta been '45.'

'August? The *sixth* of August? Does that mean anything to you?'

Scalf shook his head. 'You'd need to ask ol' Ida 'bout that. *She'd* know the answer. Only she wouldn't tell you nothin.'

'You mean his mother? His mother's still alive?'

'Yep. She's pretty old by now. Preston died a while back with nothin to show for his life but a chestful of coal dust, but she's still livin up there in the holler. The company reclaimed the house and twenty acres of wore-out hillside that was rightfully hers. They took the coal and totally destroyed the land – didn't leave her nothin but a beat-up old shack stuck out on the ridge where they kept roosters in better days. That's where she's livin now.'

So it was still there. I felt a tightening in my throat. 'Does she live alone?'

He looked at me curiously and nodded. 'But if you're fixin to pay her a call, you be wastin your time. She don't speak much to anyone now.'

'Maybe if you came with me she might want to talk about Print.'

'Maybe. He was her pride.'

Scalf lay back on the couch with his hands clasped behind his head. He stared up at the ceiling for a long while, as if he were having difficulty making up his mind. Finally he yawned and said, 'Ida don't like company.'

'Is it all right if I go myself?'

'There's no harm in tryin,' he smiled. 'If you like, you can tell her I sent you.' Then he made another small concession. 'Anyone ask you what you're doin up there, you just tell 'em you're a friend of Zach Scalf's.'

'Thanks, I will.' I stood up to go, and the room swayed alarmingly. 'It's been interesting talking to you. And thanks for the beer.'

As I reached the door, anxious now just to get back to my cabin, he called after me, 'When he went away that last time, some folks said we'd get another flood. But it never come.'

NINE

At the mouth of the hollow the asphalt came to an end. A winding dirt road continued along the bottom of the ravine, following the course of a stream littered with rubbish and the rusting skeletons of junked machinery. A few decrepit old frame houses were set back among the trees on either side of the creek; most of them looked as if they'd been abandoned long ago, yet I could see they still had curtains in the windows, coal in the sheds, even washing hanging on the line. From the safety of the car I scrutinized each one in the hope that I would recognize something. But I experienced nothing stronger than a mild feeling of oppression. The hollow seemed a dismal place – rank, sunless, a valley of stones and neglect. It was sealed off from the world outside by dark-forested slopes that rose steeply toward the high ridges, reaching for a narrow vault of sky.

I pulled over to the side of the road and parked behind a battered Dodge pickup that had an empty gun rack in the rear window and a bumper sticker that said, TAKE THIS JOB AND SHOVE IT! Suddenly the idea that I'd ever lived in this godforsaken hole as a half-bred, half-crazy Cherokee Indian seemed to me hilarious, and I burst out laughing; then looked around quickly to see if anyone had heard. There wasn't a soul in sight.

I lit a cigarette and sat in the car smoking awhile, trying to figure out the best way of approaching Ida Begley; though I was less interested in talking to her than I was in getting inside her cabin. Maybe I could pretend to be from the Department of Public Safety, an exterminator looking for vermin – something like that. How else could I persuade an old woman living alone to let a perfect stranger come in out of the woods and start digging up the floor of her home?

After changing into a pair of rubber boots that I'd bought earlier in Pineville, I locked the car and set off down the dirt road toward the village. In front of the nearest house, two small and dusty children I hadn't noticed before were playing in a vegetable patch overgrown with ragweed and surrounded by a broken rail fence. They stopped to watch me approach, then bolted and went scampering inside. Feeling like a tourist, I looked up at the house with an amiable half-smile in case I was being observed from behind the narrow, small-paned windows. But there was no sign of life.

A dog started barking some place farther along the hollow. I began to walk a little faster. As I came within view of the main group of houses, from Scalf's instructions, I recognized the turnoff for Ida's cabin. Much to my relief, I made it down to the creek without running into anybody. The less explaining I had to do the better.

I crossed the stream by hopping some flattish rocks put there for that purpose and found myself on a rough, twisting trail that led up through the woods toward the ridge. The path was steep and awkward, made slippery by layers of fallen pine needles. Before I'd gone a hundred yards I had to stop to catch my breath. I realized that I was badly out of shape, and wondered how the old woman – she had to be over seventy – managed to get up and down the hill to her cabin. Maybe she never left the place; maybe someone brought her whatever she needed. The thought that I might not find her alone began to bother me. It would only complicate things.

It was still early. The air in the hollow where the sun hadn't reached felt cool. A heartening scent of woodsmoke drifted down from the ridge. I imagined it coming from Ida's cabin and took this as a sign that she was home. It had another, much greater significance for me, and I felt an uneasy sense of expectation. On tape, Print Begley had talked about an iron stove at the rear of the cabin, which his mother had used for storing chicken feed. It was underneath the floorplate of that stove that the boy claimed to have hidden his Bible.

The nearer I drew to my objective, the more apprehensive I became. Maybe I was afraid of what I'd find up there – or not find. Afraid of what I might discover about myself. But it wasn't only that. I stopped for another rest and, leaning heavily against a tree, looked back down into the hollow, thinking of Print's story about hiding out among the pines to watch the revival meetings. Perhaps there were some things better left undisturbed, some immutable laws of time that should never be broken. I almost considered turning back – only I knew that it wasn't my decision anymore.

As I began to climb again, the path grew steeper at every turn. I kept on up the hill now at a strong steady pace. Far above I glimpsed the crest of the ridge hovering beyond the tree line against a wash of pale sky. I wanted to get up there to where it was light. Climb right out of this loathsome valley before it closed in over my head.

Then suddenly in front of me I saw the cabin, looming through the trees like a dilapidated old pier, gaunt and moss-grown. It was built out over the slope on tall wooden piles worn thin with age. At the gable end, above a broken window boarded up on the inside with Sheetrock, a chimney stuck up from under the roof like a crooked black finger.

There wasn't a trace of smoke coming from it.

I was convinced now that something was wrong. Making as little noise as possible, I continued up the path and followed it around to the front of the cabin.

Outside the door, I stood for a moment and listened, trying to steady my breathing as I wiped the sweat from my face and hands. A long way off at the other end of the valley I heard the cough and stutter of a chain saw coming to life. There was no sound from inside the cabin. Everything would be so much simpler if the old lady wasn't home.

I rapped a couple of times. She didn't answer. I tried the handle. It was made of an old horseshoe, rusted through so badly I was afraid it would break off in my hand.

The handle turned, and the door grated open a few inches.

'Mrs Begley?' I gave the door a little shove. 'Anyone home?'

It felt peculiarly stiff, as if someone without much strength were resisting on the other side.

'Mrs Begley,' I repeated.

A smell of damp, leafy rot wafted out from the dark interior. With a sinking feeling I realized that the place was empty. I'd got the wrong cabin: or else Scalf was mistaken about Ida still being alive. No one had lived here for a very long time.

I put my shoulder to the door and forced it open.

Then I saw the stove.

It stood like a throne at the far end of the room, a potbellied relic of the last century, gray with dust and covered with cobwebs. Looking around to make sure there wasn't anyone watching, I stepped inside the hut. There was an ominous creaking, as if the whole structure were about to collapse and go sliding down the mountain. Advancing a few steps at a time, I went over to the stove and knelt down at its claw-shaped feet.

With a piece of charred wood I found in the burner, I began brushing away the layers of leaves and impacted cinders that covered the iron plate on which the stove rested. As the dirt came loose, I saw that the edges of the plate were bolted to the floor with heavy coach screws set about three inches apart. At the front of the stove, where the floorboards ran under the plate at right angles, I noticed that two of the screws were missing.

It was exactly the way Begley had described it on the tape.

I scraped the area around the missing screws as clean as I could get it, then set to work on the floorboards, using the piece of wood to pry them loose. One of them, cut much shorter than the others, came up almost at once.

I threw down the stick and began to slide the plank out with my hands. The room seemed to grow darker, as if a shadow had fallen over the floor of the cabin. Suddenly aware of feeling exposed, I glanced behind me. Stationed outside the door with a shotgun under one arm, his bulky frame blocking out most of the daylight, stood Zach Scalf.

'Well, look what we got here!' he crowed. 'Now, just what do you think you're doin in there, boy? This here's private property. Or ain't you never heard 'bout the laws of trespass?'

'Hey, wait a minute,' I protested, laughing, 'you didn't tell me I was ...' Then I realized that he wasn't joking. I started to get to my feet, but he quickly brought the gun up to his shoulder.

'Easy, now! Take it *easy* ... Stay right where you are, where I can see you. On your knees, both hands touchin the floor. That's better.'

'What is this? Isn't this the place you meant?'

'You see Ida anywhere?'

'Look, why don't you put the gun down so we can talk? It's making me nervous.'

He chortled, lowering the gun but keeping it level with my chest. 'Now you better tell me why you come down here from New York askin all them questions about Cousin Begley. And don't give me any more of that horseshit about writin a book, 'cause it ain't worth a good goddamn.'

'It's the *truth*. I can prove it. When we get back to the motel –'

'Who said anythin about going back to the motel?' Scalf smirked. 'I seen you foolin around under that ol' stove. What you lookin for?'

'A Bible.'

'Don't fuck with me, boy,' he said softly. Then, jerking the shotgun, 'What's in there, anyway?'

'A Bible. Honest to God! When Print was a kid – if this is the right cabin – he used to come up here sometimes to read his Bible in peace. He kept it buried under the stove.'

'So how come *you* know about it?'

'One of his Army buddies told me.'

'About a *Bible*?' he sneered.

'Look, I don't even know if it's still here. Or what else he kept . . .' I hesitated. 'He may have taken everything with him when he went – the last time.'

'Is that a fact?' Scalf's eyes narrowed with interest.

'You saw him that day. Do you remember if he was carrying anything?'

He shook his head; then, thinking there might be some advantage in answering the question, volunteered. 'He were carryin a rope and a miner's helmet and a lamp that belonged to his pa. I asked him where he were headed with all that equipment, if he'd maybe changed his mind about workin in the mines. That's when he said about crawlin like a mole, only he wouldn't tell me where he were goin. He had his dog with him, too.'

'What kind of dog?'

'Brown dog. Used to take him with us when we went huntin, only he were gettin old and blind by then.'

'Was he named Rory?' Print had mentioned the name a couple of times on the tape.

Scalf nodded. 'It was on account of that dog we finally learned what happened to Print.'

'What do you mean?' I stared at him. 'I thought you said he just disappeared.'

'He *did* disappear. Only I guess he didn't reckon on his dog followin him.' Scalf leaned up against the door, still keeping me covered with the gun. 'They found ol' Rory twenty mile north of here sittin out in the rain by the entrance to Lost Hope – that's a big cave up around Springfield. They call it a cavern now, with lights and tour guides, motel and everythin. Back then the entrance were just a hole in the ground. They found ol' Rory 'bout three weeks after Print went away. The dog were half-starved. Wouldn't let anyone near him. Preston Begley and some of the other miners went down into that cave to look for his son. They never did find anythin.'

Scalf paused and scratched doubtfully at his stubble, as if he weren't quite sure why he was telling me this.

'Hell of a way to die for someone who were scared of the dark ... Son of a *bitch*! I don't like to think what happened to him down there. Lost Hope's deeper than the pit of Hell and it goes on forever. They ain't found no end to it yet. Maybe that's why his body never showed up in all these years.'

'What happened to Rory?'

'He wouldn't leave that cave mouth, so Preston done shot him.'

'Why didn't you tell me all this last night?'

'Why didn't I *tell* you?' Scalf repeated incredulously, then threw his head back and stood there braying with laughter.

'What's so funny? I asked.

'You must take me for a damn fool, boy,' he said at last, wiping tears from his eyes. 'The minute you walked in my door I knew you had somethin goin on. You think I were gonna let you keep it all to yourself? Now, why don't you quit stallin and show me what Print got buried under there.'

'What if there's nothing here?'

Scalf didn't answer right away. Raising the shotgun to his shoulder, he squinted down the barrels at me. A loutish grin slowly spread across his face. He looked up suddenly and said, 'You're dead, asshole.'

I wheeled around on my knees and faced the stove. Keeping my back to him so he couldn't see what I was doing, I began working nervously at the loose floorboards. As soon as I'd levered one end up, I pulled the plank out from under the iron plate and laid it against the side of the stove. Underneath, between the floor and the cabin shell, there was a cavity about a foot deep.

Peering down into the hole, I saw something stowed there. It was a book, wrapped in a caul of spiderweb, its dog-eared cover mottled green and black like the skin of a lizard. 'Do you remember that date now?' I asked, anxious to keep the conversation going. 'The day Print went away?'

'Second of August, 1945,' Scalf answered, still wheezing from his bout of laughter. 'I looked up the story last night in the *Courier*. They wrote about him, see, on account of the search party goin down Lost Hope.'

'Then he must have died four days later.'

'How can you know that?' he scoffed.

The incontestable proof of my having lived before lay on a bed of little white bones – the skeletons of countless small animals. Some of the bones had been carved into different shapes and objects; others had simply been whittled thin, then polished till they shone like straw. He must have spent a lot of time, I thought, sitting up there on that ridge, just waiting.

'I was born on August sixth at eight fifteen in the morning,' I said, almost to myself, the significance of the discovery I'd made still sinking in. 'On the other side of the world, at the *exact* same time – it's a coincidence I've always found hard to accept – a B-29 cruising at an altitude of twenty-five thousand feet – out of a clear blue sky – dropped a nuclear device on Hiroshima. It was called 'Little Boy' – the bomb, I mean.'

'What the fuck you talkin about?'

'That's when Print Begley died. He must have known it was going to happen. You see, he was watching for signs that would foretell the end of the world. It's all beginning to come clear now. I was sent to take his place.'

'Shit, you're crazier than Print ever were. Ain't you found nothing yet?' I heard Scalf impatiently take a step forward into the cabin, but the timbers groaning under his weight seemed to discourage him from coming in.

I put a hand down into the cavity and felt around.

'There's something in here,' I said, glancing back at him over my shoulder. 'Feels like a lot of stuff. You better have a look.'

'Wrong, friend! *You* bring it to *me*.'

As I lifted the book out of the hole, carefully dusting off the mold and cobwebs, I managed to scoop up one of the larger bones from the heap, concealed it in my left hand so that it lay snug along the book's missing spine. It was about six inches in length and half an inch thick, knotted at one end and whittled down to a hollowed curving point – it looked like some kind of primitive surgical instrument.

Opening the book flat across my hands, I rose and slowly turned to face him. 'It's Print's Bible. It was here, just as he said it would be. Christ, if you only knew what this means . . .'

Scalf was watching me closely now.

'There's even an inscription in the front. "To Print Begley, from his mother, Ida Rose Begley. May 18, 1932." Then a list of family names and dates.'

'Well, I'll be . . . Let me see that!' He motioned me forward with the gun. 'Now move on over here nice and easy.'

I walked toward him across the creaking floor, keeping my eyes lowered, trying to look as if I were still poring over the book. Under its cover I maneuvered the slender bone into my right fist, keeping the sharp end pointed toward my stomach.

'Okay, that's far enough.' He made another abrupt gesture with the gun. 'Give it to me.'

I waited a few seconds, then looked up at him absently, as if I hadn't quite taken in what he'd said. We were standing less than two yards apart. An oily sheen of sweat covered his face and neck. Under his narrow gaze I looked for the place in his throat, the soft-looking hollow between the Adam's apple and the tufts of reddish hair that grew out of the top of his shirt. I concentrated on that one spot, praying that the bone would be sharp enough, that it wouldn't break.

'What the hell you waitin for, boy? Give it to me,' he said with a puzzled frown.

As I reached out to hand him the Bible, I took a step forward, and for one careless moment Scalf lowered the barrels of the gun.

I let the Bible fall and I lunged, turning the wrist of my right hand and striking upward at his throat with a backhanded blow that had the whole weight of my body behind it. The shard of bone pierced his larynx and sank in all the way. A warm jet of blood leaped through my fingers, splashing down the front of his green vest. Scalf gave a grunt of surprise and dropped the shotgun. Clutching both hands to his throat, he lurched backwards out of the cabin.

He stumbled around out there under the trees, making a kind of harsh croaking noise. Then slowly he fell to his knees, scrabbling at the hilt of the bone with his thick, clumsy fingers. But it was wedged so tightly in his windpipe he couldn't tug it free. His face turned a deep dusty red, and his eyes, bulging from their sockets, rolled up into his skull. He kept shaking his head, as if he couldn't understand what was happening, tossing it violently to and fro in a desperate attempt to get air into his lungs. The stubborn knob of bone protruded from his neck like a tiny bloodied fist that had punched its way out through the prison of flesh.

In a last despairing gesture he held up his hands, clasping them together under his chin, as if he were imploring me to help him. for a moment I thought he was going to get to his feet. I snatched up the shotgun and aimed it at his head. But there was no need. With a dreadful chuckling sound, a shiny red flag of blood unfurled from his gaping mouth and he just pitched forward onto his face and lay still.

TEN

I wiped my hands clean on the inside of my sweat shirt, lit a cigarette and sat down on the bare floorboards near the door of the cabin. It wasn't cold, but I had to hug myself to keep from shivering. From the pit of my stomach I could feel a numbness spreading slowly outward.

At the moment of stabbing him I'd experienced a surge of exhilaration, like the sudden working of a drug, an adrenaline high, from which I was still coming down. It had left me feeling drained, strung out.

To calm myself I picked up Print Begley's Bible and started to turn over its mildewed pages.

It was either him or me. I really didn't feel I'd done anything wrong. It was just that I'd never killed anyone before. Through the door I could see the worn soles of Scalf's boots turned in toward the ground at an odd angle. He was dead, and the irreversibility of that fact, the absolute effectiveness of what I'd just done, seemed shocking.

But if I accepted the implications of what I now held in my hands – the evidence I'd killed to get – then I had to consider the possibility that Scalf had died here only to begin life again somewhere else. As the tenant of another body with a different personality, living in completely different circumstances. Perhaps this time around he would land himself a better deal. Who knows, I might even have done him a favor.

I found it a difficult idea to get used to nonetheless.

After reading in the Bible for a while and smoking another cigarette, I began to feel more relaxed. The chill had worn off. I knew I should have left by now, but I had no sense of urgency about my situation. No one had seen me; no one knew I was here. I felt confident that if I were just to walk down to the car now, everything would be all right. Once I got gack to the Pineview, it would be easy enough to remove whatever traces there were of my visit. Then all

I had to do was drive to Knoxville, catch the next plane to New York and forget that any of this had ever happened.

I went out and dragged Scalf into the cabin. I dragged him in by the ankles, just as he lay, face down in the dirt. He was heavy. He left a trail of blood that I had to cover up afterwards with leaves. I thought of going through his pockets to make it look like robbery, but I didn't feel much like touching him again. I took the shotgun and pushed it down into the cavity under the floorboards; then I replaced the loose plank and smoothed the dirt back over the footplate of the stove.

I checked for blood on my hands and clothes, picked up the Bible and, making quite sure I'd left nothing behind, stepped out into the woods, pulling the door tightly shut.

As I came away from the cabin, I found myself not turning back along the path that led down into the hollow, but keeping on up the hill toward the crest of the ridge. Long shafts of hazy sunlight were beginning to filter down between the trees. I wanted to see the place where Print Begley had kept vigil all those years, watching the stars and whittling away at bones, while he waited for the end.

The day he left for good, he must have believed the time had come. Why else would he have gone down into the cave? In his Bible there was a passage from the book of Isaiah that he'd underlined: *'And they shall go into the holes of the rocks, and into the caves of the earth, for fear of the Lord.'*

Only Print had made a slight miscalculation. The great cataclysmic event that he awaited had never happened. The stars didn't alter their courses, nor the sun grow dim, nor the sky come down to earth, the way he had predicted. Hiroshima, extreme as it was, could hardly be described as the end of the world. It was more like a beginning . . .

Near the top of the ridge the trees grew farther apart, till soon I was walking in the open, with the sun at my back now, across a high grassy plateau. Gradually the path became stonier and more rugged, rising steeply to a rocky pinnacle that stood out in majestic isolation above the countryside. A desolate view of narrow boat-shaped valleys still shrouded in mist, of barren yellow hillsides, blackened here and there by the scars of strip mining, stretched away to the indefinite horizon.

It was a haunted landscape, vaporish and melancholy, ravaged, yet still grand under its broad sweep of sky. In the thrall of so much space I felt my spirit begin to soar. This was the place, the sentinel's eyrie where Print used to sit by night and gaze up at the constellations, looking for the signs that would herald Armageddon.

I lifted up my arms and closed my eyes, breathing in deep lungfuls of the sharp mountain air. It was as if I'd come home, and nothing had changed. Then I sat down on a rock and placed Print Begley's Bible under my feet, and waited.

BOOK FOUR

MAGMEL

ONE

PREAMBLE

The patient called up late last night in a very excited mood and asked if he could drop by and see me in the morning. He explained that he had just returned from Kentucky and had something of great importance to show me. I agreed to see him, but only briefly, as I had a very full schedule and he hadn't made an appointment.

A. INITIAL EXPECTATIONS

Uncertain in view of extended absence. For two weeks he had been coming here on a daily basis. At the end of the last session he seemed forbiddingly remote, and I had serious doubts about the usefulness of his continuing therapy. Rapid acceleration of the pathological process indicated.

B. ATMOSPHERE

Friendly, but far from relaxed. Patient seemed pleased to see me and grateful that I was able to fit him in at such short notice. Exuded self-confidence, a positiveness about everything which seemed almost too good to be true. This new manner, however, was undermined by his squalid appearance. He showed up in sneakers, an old pair of combat fatigues and a red sweat shirt with a torn hood; on top of that, he was unshaven and looked as if he could use a bath. All too clearly he hadn't been sleeping well: eyes sunken, unnaturally bright, pupils dilated. I asked him if he'd been taking any drugs. He gave me an enigmatic smile, but didn't answer. Later

187

in the session, when I repeated the question, he denied it scornfully. Sat quietly throughout, this time making no attempt to synchronize his movements or gestures with mine.

C. Main Trends and Therapeutic Interventions

Patient reached into a plastic shopping bag he had with him and produced what he claimed was 'proof' of his having lived before: a Bible. It appeared authentic enough: without a spine, its pages ripped and stuck together, mildewed – even the inscription looked old. I congratulated him on his find.

He was eager to discuss its implications. On making this discovery, he told me, he had experienced an almost mystical sense of wonder. With the enthusiasm of a recent convert he described to me how everything had suddenly 'fallen into place', how he had seen all his 'previous existences' as different stages in his 'soul's journey toward the light'. Now he understood that his own search for the truth was no more and no less than a continuation of the quest he had sequentially undertaken as Thorfinn, Cabet, Petacci *et al.*, throughout history. He believed that in his present incarnation, as Martin Gregory, he was destined to find 'the way through' that had eluded his past selves for so many centuries.

I interrupted to remind the patient that as yet we had seen no sign of Karmic development in his cycle. I asked him if he had discovered a progressive link between his former lives. Did he know what had motivated them all in their reaching out after the unattainable; did he know what had precipitated his own recent crisis? The patient appeared crestfallen and offered no reply. A long silence ensued, which I did not attempt to relieve. He sat slumped in his chair. I pretended not to notice his distress.

When he finally looked up, he asked me in a low voice if there was something I could do to help him.

This was the moment I'd been waiting for. At last, I felt the patient was ready to listen to an 'orthodox' interpretation of his ontogenetic history. I explained that according to the law of Karma, man must sometimes face a repetition of the situation which led to his downfall in a previous life so that he can overcome it in this life, graduating to a happier, more enlightened state. In the patient's

188

case the evidence seemed to indicate he had failed to do so in every one of his previous lives. A possible explanation for this might be that in one of his earliest existences – one we had yet to touch on – something had happened which at no cost could he allow to happen again. Denied the opportunity of redemption and enlightenment, he had been condemned to the static destiny of an unending quest. I suggested that his only hope of release lay in our working together to locate the original trauma that had been tormenting him through all his successive incarnations.

I warned him that it would be difficult – that it might even be dangerous – but he said he was willing to take almost any risk.

D. Interpretations Thought of but Not Given

A phone call to Military Personnel Records in St Louis confirmed that the Begley letter (submitted by the patient last session) is genuine, but I'm not at all convinced that he followed up on it by actually going to Kentucky. My bet is that Begley is some distant relation of the patient's, whose story he was already at least partly familiar with. I'm certain the Bible is a forgery, though an extremely skillful one. That he should have gone to so much trouble to delude himself, as well as the therapist, is thoroughly in keeping with the function-complex of his persona.

E. Outcome and Afterthoughts

On the whole, I feel that we've made progress and that my prognosis at the end of the last report may turn out to have been too hasty. Now that the patient has accepted the idea of an original crime, long suppressed, which must be brought to light, the moment is approaching when I will be able to confront him with the incident in the Philippines.

TWO

.   After what I'd been through, I'd fully intended to stay away from Somerville for a while – at least until I got everything straight in my own mind – but I realized my absence might look suspicious. So the morning after I got back from Kentucky I went to see him, and gave a carefully censored account of what had happened up on Indian Ridge.

I showed him Print's Bible and told him roughly how and where I'd found it, but without mentioning the Pineview Motor Lodge or Zach Scalf. I figured that his body would be discovered in the next few days and the murder routinely reported in the local papers, but I knew I was safe. The chance of Somerville hearing about it seemed remote. The only other person who might conceivably connect me with Scalf was the Reverend Pennington in Pathfork, and he had no way of tracing me. His only contact with me had been one long-distance phone conversation, when I'd taken care to give the name Gregory Martin and to say I was a war historian.

Somerville was obviously impressed by the evidence I put before him. After examining Print Begley's Bible, he said it was the most convincing proof of someone's having lived before that he had ever come across. I tried to explain to him that even if I had lived before – and proof or no proof, there would always be some question in my mind – it didn't make me feel any different. All I'd really done was satisfy my need to prove what millions of people on this earth accepted as a matter of faith. I certainly wasn't any the wiser for it. Somerville smiled and said that everything would change once we discovered the 'true source of your unhappiness'.

We made an appointment for the following day. Against my better judgment – I was afraid I might say something about Scalf during the induction – I agreed to being regressed one last time. Somerville suggested an evening session so we wouldn't be disturbed. He asked me not to eat anything or drink any alcohol for four hours beforehand. I didn't much like the sound of that: it sounded as if I were being prepared for surgery.

Then he casually informed me that Penelope was back and would be assisting him during the session.

He was standing in his usual place at the window with his back turned, yet I could feel him watching me, waiting for my reaction. It was almost as if he were putting her out for bait. Just the thought of Somerville's knowing that I was interested in her disturbed me.

As I was coming out of the study, uncertain whether I'd made the right decision, I ran into Penelope on the stairs. She was standing under the chandelier on the bottom landing, fixing her hair in the mirror. Her coat was thrown over the banister and there were expensive-looking packages scattered everywhere, as if she'd just come in from shopping.

From the top of the stairs I watched her get out her makeup and start putting on lipstick. When her eyes caught mine in the mirror, she stared back at first with a completely blank expression, seeming not to recognize me. Then she began to smile. And making a mischievous face, she wrote with her lipstick on the glass, 'How was Kentucky?'

I laughed and said, 'All right, I guess, if you like coal mines.'

I walked down to her and we stood on the landing making polite conversation. There was still that certain awkwardness between us. I kept looking over her shoulder at the mirror, wondering when she was going to remove the red scrawl of lipstick.

'If you're not working late,' I said – the moment seemed right – 'how about having some dinner tonight?'

'I'd like that,' said Penelope, smiling; then, slipping her arms around my neck, she kissed me on the lips.

I was so surprised I just stood there, watching it happen in the mirror. Her splendid back arched up between my outstretched arms, a river of dark hair cascading over her shoulders – I might have been watching a movie.

She clung to me, pressing her body against me; slowly her hands rose above my head.

In the mirror I could see her blue sleeve slip back off her forearm; something silver shimmered at the wrist. It was the lucky charm bracelet I'd bought for Anna at Kennedy Airport.

191

I grabbed her hands and pulled them down from around my neck.

'Where did you get this?' I demanded. 'The bracelet.'

She looked up at me with a startled expression. 'You gave it to me.'

'*When* did I give it to you?'

'You don't remember?'

'*When?*'

'The night we met in the Library ... You're hurting my hands, Martin. We had a drink at the Algonquin. You remember ...' Her eyes opened wide. 'I love it. I wear it all the time.'

'I remember perfectly well.'

'You don't remember, do you?' She shook her head slowly.

'I wasn't feeling so great. I ...' I hesitated. 'Maybe I had too much to drink.'

I remembered that I'd *thought* of giving her the bracelet. She was wearing a green ribbon around her wrist and I'd thought of giving her the bracelet to wear instead – the box was in my pocket – but then I decided against it. I'd put Anna on the plane just a few hours before, and it seemed a disloyal, a tasteless thing to do.

I'd left the bracelet with Somerville. I remembered showing it to him that following Monday; we talked about what happened at the airport, and I left it in his study. Penelope must have found it there and taken it for herself, or else *he'd* given it to her.

Either way she was lying.

'I never really thanked you for it, did I?' she said.

'It looks good on you,' I said. 'You might as well keep it.'

'Martin, you *gave* it to me.'

'If you say so.' I smiled. 'I really have to go.'

I started down the stairs.

'What about dinner?' she called after me.

I didn't turn around. 'Let's take a rain check, Penelope. I've got a lot of work to do, I just remembered. I'll call you.'

I stood for a moment outside on the steps, wiping her lipstick from my mouth, wondering if I hadn't overreacted. Perhaps my memory had been playing tricks on me. Hadn't I forgotten things before? Like telling Somerville I was thinking of giving Anna a going-away present.

But this was different. It was one thing to simply forget. This time

I had a very clear impression of what had happened. It wasn't just that I didn't remember giving Penelope the bracelet: I *knew* I'd left it with Somerville. I remembered watching him open the little white box and look inside – I remembered he tried to give it back to me, that I said no – then I saw him put it away in the drawer of his desk.

Unless the box had been empty.

The minute I got to the Library I called Somerville and asked him if he still had the bracelet. He sounded surprised. Did I mean the present I'd bought for Anna at the airport? We'd discussed it, yes, of course, though he'd never actually seen it. The box, yes, but . . . Was I quite sure I'd left it there? When he had a moment he'd take a look around, talk to the cleaning lady about it in the morning.

'Don't bother,' I snapped; 'I must have made a mistake.'

Silence from the other end.

I was about to hang up when Somerville said, 'It's just conceivable that this might have something to do with therapy, Martin. I'm afraid memory lapse is one of the more common side effects associated with hypnosis. Flashes of amnesia, forgetting some things, remembering others that never happened . . . But it's really nothing to worry about. The condition is only temporary, I assure you.'

He sounded almost apologetic.

It was still basically the same view. Although perspectives had been altered, everything was in the right place – the bones of the landscape still showed through. Only it was no longer a view of a park, but of a wide body of water dotted with half-submerged trees and patches of green ground. What used to be small rounded hills had become islands. The flower beds, the fountain, the paths, the shrubbery, the people – including the little girl in the pony trap – had all disappeared.

I calculated that the level of the lake had risen this time by nearly twenty-five feet.

My first reaction was that Rugandas must have done yet another version of *Finsternpromenad* and that the prints had been switched again. Maybe Nuremberg had been flooded in 1826 and the artist decided to sketch the same view of the park to show different stages of the deluge. It seemed a curiously experimental project for an early-nineteenth-century landscape artist who appeared perfectly conventional in every other respect; but O'Rorke, I thought, might know something more about that.

Before going across to Manuscripts and Archives, I studied the hand-colored engraving more carefully. It was then I realized that the flood had claimed victims. One of the smaller trees in the middle distance, which must have stood near the edge of the lake originally, was not quite submerged. Its top-most branches, like a floating clump of weed, were just visible above the surface. I noticed a daub of yellow caught in the greenery.

It was the little girl's parasol.

Peering up closer, I began to see other things. Under the surface of the water there were shapes concealed in the lines of the drawing. They looked like bodies drifting in the current. I thought I saw faces with fish eyes and gaping mouths and contorted limbs that came twisting up from the depths. Offshore from the nearest island, a thin crooked arm seemed to reach up out of the water. It might just have been a branch, but there was something about the angle at which the hand emerged from the lake. There was a strand of green around the wrist that looked like a garland – and whoever the hand belonged to wasn't drowning, but waving, beckoning.

Of course, I couldn't be sure. One minute the bodies were there and the next they were lost. Sometimes it seemed as if the surface of the lake were one roiling mass of drowned or drowning people. But when I looked again, everything was clear and calm.

O'Rorke came to the door himself this time, looking suitably pre-occupied. 'Yes, can I help?'

'So they've gone and switched them again,' I said with a breezy familiarity.

'Switched what?' O'Rorke sighed, folding his arms across his chest. 'I'm sorry, I'm not quite with you.'

'The Rugandas. The view of Nuremberg on the wall out here. Remember, I asked you about it last week – or was it the week before? You didn't tell me there was a third.'

'Do I know you?' He was peering out at me suspiciously from behind the grille.

'Well, yes,' I said, slightly disconcerted. 'You may have forgotten. I think you said there were two or three people who'd asked you the same question, just that morning.'

O'Rorke shook his head. 'You're going to have to explain.'

'I wanted to know why the engraving, the one of the park outside Nuremberg, looked different. There was a tree stump – I'm sorry, I mean a *rock* – in the foreground that was missing. And you told me that the Library owned two different prints by the same artist of an almost identical view, and that they'd been changed around.'

'You must be thinking of someone else.' O'Rorke managed a little smile. 'You never talked to *me*. And I never talked to *you*, or anybody, about an engraving. The Rugandas out there is the only one we have. It's been up for the past month from a collection on loan to the Library. We don't own any of the pictures. I think if you look at it closely, you'll see that it's not a view of a park, but a lake. Now, if you'll excuse me . . .'

He began to turn away.

'No, wait!' I almost shouted at him. 'O'Rorke . . . There, you see, I know your name. And there was a fat boy with glasses held together by Band-Aids. He works here with you. I talked to him too. He'll remember me.'

'I'm sorry, *sir*,' O'Rorke said, 'I've never seen you before. There are no fat persons working here and no boys. I think you must have made some kind of mistake.'

'He was standing *right* where you are now, a fat slob eating a sandwich. I didn't make this up. I was talking to him. And it's *not* the same picture, goddammit! It's been changed – you know it has.'

'Wait here,' O'Rorke said, disappearing behind the stacks. He came back a moment later with a printed sheet in his hand.

'This is the catalogue for the exhibition. What I suggest you do is contact the owner of the print. Let's see . . .'

He ran a finger down the list.

'Here we are. Johann Moritz Rugandas, *Finsternpromenad: Grossstadt Nürnberg.* Lent by Dr R. M. Somerville. I'm afraid we're not at liberty to give out the address; but you can always try the phone book.'

'I know Dr Somerville's address,' I said.

THREE

A dry cool hand on my forehead, giving off a faint scent of almonds. Lying back in the chair, I stare up at my usual spot on the ceiling. Blinds drawn; candles burning on the mantelpiece; soft music coming from the stereo. Out of the corner of an eye I can see Penelope in her usual place beside the desk, sitting very correctly, like a stenographer poised for dictation. She's wearing a short black evening dress cinched at the waist with a thin gold belt. Her legs are crossed and tucked primly under her chair – she doesn't seem to have any stockings on. The back of a shoe has slipped off her heel; a marbling of tiny blue veins visible beneath the white, almost translucent skin of her ankle.

'In ancient civilizations,' Somerville is saying, 'the priest-physician understood the important role that music plays in the healing arts . . .'

'Do you want me to dim the lights?' Penelope asks.

She's smiling at me now, as if there were something between us. I look at her wrists. She's not wearing the bracelet. My eye travels back to her legs. On the inside of her upper knee close to the crease, there's a little dribble of moisture. I watch the muscles of her thighs tighten – she must have sensed the direction of my gaze – and the wetness on her skin catch the light.

'Lights?'

Somerville clears his throat. 'Anytime you're ready.'

She gets up from her chair and disappears from view. It gets darker suddenly and the stain on the ceiling is swallowed up. A smell of candle grease hangs on the warm air.

'Listen to me, Martin . . .' Somerville's voice close to my ear. 'We've got a long and difficult journey ahead of us. There's no guarantee of success, you know. It could be very rough on you this time. If you don't want to go through with this, tell me now.'

I hear myself say, 'I'm ready.'
Then the music begins to fade.

Earlier in the evening I'd called Somerville to cancel my appointment. I told him that I didn't think I could handle another session,
that I was very much concerned about what hypnosis was doing
to my memory.

'I won't try to pressure you, Martin,' Somerville said, 'but it's
important that we find out what happened. And one more session
isn't going to hurt your memory – in fact, it'll probably help it.'

As always, he seemed perfectly reasonable and understanding,
assuring me once again that the amnesia was only a temporary
condition and really nothing to worry about.

It had been five days since my last regression. I felt my resistance
beginning to weaken.

Before hanging up, I asked him – I couldn't hold back any longer
– if he had ever lent an engraving of Nuremberg to the New York
Public Library. He said he didn't have the slightest idea what I
was talking about, that he'd never heard of an artist named
Rugandas, and that he looked forward to seeing me at 8.30.

'Outside the library window there's a balcony ... A spiral staircase leads down into the garden ... Concentrate on my voice;
nothing else matters. We're going to go down the stairs ... down
... into the garden. You know it well; we've been here before many
times. We can hear the murmur of the sea ... the sun feels warm
... the air is fragrant. Over there between the trees, your hammock
... Can you see it? I want you to walk over to the hammock and
lie down in it. You feel it sway a little as you climb in ... swaying
... swaying in the warm, fragrant breeze. You're feeling very calm
now, very relaxed ... You sink deeper into the hammock ...'

I sank back gratefully, oblivious to everything but the sound of
Somerville's voice and the faint creaking of the guy ropes.

'Feel the warmth as you breathe in; feel it spread through your
whole body ... relaxing you ... deeper and deeper.

'We're going to leave here now, Martin ... and travel back down
through the years ... further back than we've ever been before
... back through history ... and beyond history ... down ... down
to the very dawn of time.'

Those are the last words Somerville spoke which I actually remember. From here on I have to rely on the tape recording and on what Penelope told me about the session afterward.

On the tape there follows a silence of maybe three or four minutes. All that can be heard is the sound of my breathing, slowed way down and regular. No different from the other times, really, except that the silence lasts longer. At one point Somerville says something I can't make out to Penelope. Suddenly he begins again in a voice so low it's almost a whisper:

'Can you hear me, Martin? It's dark outside. Raining. The rain's coming down in sheets; water everywhere. It never lets up ... Remember? You wanted to run away and leave them, but you couldn't. No, there's something you have to do first. There, over there in the corner ... see her? Cowering behind the bed. She's frightened of *you*, Martin – only Martin is not your name. You can see it in her eyes. See how she's holding up those thin, wretched arms of hers to keep you from ... Do you remember now? Where are the dogs? You had to do it, didn't you? That's all right – I understand. You can tell me all about it now ... You can trust me.

'[Pause] ... Where are you now? *Who* are you? What's your name?'

On the tape a low moan breaks the rhythm of my breathing; then I try to say something, but words don't come. Penelope said that I began to pour with sweat, and that she had to fetch a towel to wipe my face and hands.

'Where are you now? What is your name?'

There's no answer – just several rapid intakes of breath, then a scuffling sound, followed by a scream. Then the familiar click on the tape indicating a cut.

Penelope explained later that Somerville had turned the machine off at that moment because he thought I was trying to break out of the trance.

The tape continues.

'Who are you?'

'I'm cold ... It's dark. I can't ... the river ...' The voice is very faint.

'Who are you? What's your name?'

'I . . . am Magnus.'

'Magnus? Tell me where you are.'

'On the ... bank. Can't reach the water ... don't have the strength. Must ... have to get up ... [Pause] Up to the cave ... get it back.'

'Isn't there anyone there who can help you?'

'[Pause] I'm all alone now; the others are all dead ... dead. I'm so thirsty ... can't reach ... If she comes for me, I'm ... No, no, I *gave* it to her ... my fault.'

'Where are you? What's the name of this place?'

'Magmel.'

'Where is that? In what country?'

[Silence]

'Can you hear me?'

'Too far ...'

'Listen to me, Magnus. Concentrate on your breathing. Now listen carefully. In a moment I'm going to ask you to go further back – back to when it all began. I want you to tell me exactly what happened. [Pause] It will make you feel better. I'm going to count down from three. On zero you will go back to the moment you first set out on the path.'

FOUR

The city stood at the end of the valley, perched on a high red sandstone bluff and surrounded on three sides by a protective loop of the river. Across the river a road ran out between orchards and vineyards to the farmlands beyond. There, open country began and stretched away to the north, where the valley grew narrow.

The river flowed from north to south, leaving Magmel by an underground channel below the cliffs of Tlanuwa. There was no natural break in the walls of the valley; they were almost uniformly steep and rugged. Behind the cliffs mountainous peaks rose up on every side. Had anyone wanted to leave Magmel, or enter it from outside, he would have had to scale those heights. As far as Magnus knew, only one person had found his way into the valley, and nobody had ever wanted to leave.

'Once, a long time ago, a stranger arrived here from the Outside – my father told me this. The stranger had lost his way in the mountains. After a few days here recovering from his ordeal, he asked if he could stay. "Paradise" he called our valley ... Nobody knew what he meant when he tried to explain. He was told that he was welcome to stay on one condition: that he never speak again of the Outside.

'I asked my father what would have happened if the stranger wanted to go back where he'd come from. He said it would not have been possible: "The stranger understood that there would never be any reason to leave." '

In Magmel, where there was neither rank nor privilege, one family – at first Magnus was reluctant to admit it was his own – held a hereditary title in the male line. The Kendal, or Guardian of the Valley, enjoyed a great and time-honored prestige. He was venerated for a wisdom which the Kendalship automatically conferred. But he had no power. What duties he had were known only to himself, to his wife and to their eldest son when he came of age.

For centuries the Kendals had lived in the great house on the edge of the city. Alone of all the dwellings in Magmel it was surrounded by a high wall. A marble tower rose above the green roofs of the city, affording a view of the whole valley. At all times a light, a sign of peace and security, was kept burning in the tower window.

'In a few days I'll be seventeen – the most important day of my life ... My father says I must accept my fate without a question.'

As his seventeenth birthday approached, Magnus spent most of his time alone, fishing on the river up at the northernmost end of the valley.

He would sit for hours on the bank, staring upstream into the rocky, barren Tlenamaw – the one place in all Magmel where nobody was allowed. There was nothing much to see there, yet the Tlenamaw beckoned. As he watched the wild goats picking their way among the boulders down by the water's edge, or gazed out at the dusty hills pitted with shadows that marked the entrances to caves, in his mind's eye he trespassed, measuring out the route of his escape. It was an act of defiance just to let his gaze wander over that landscape, following the course of the valley as it tapered to a narrow, winding gorge that ran back under the cliffs till it was lost from sight, its head buried among the dark red folds of the mountain.

One evening when Magnus was fishing on the river, he saw something silver flash through the water. Thinking it might have been the belly of a large fish catching the light as it turned over under the surface, he climbed up onto the highest part of the bank to get a better view. The water below him ran deep, without a ripple. He had to hold a hand up in front of his eyes to see beneath the cloudless reflections of the sky.

At the bend in the river which marked the beginning of the forbidden territory, a long flat rock projected into the stream like a jetty, creating a still, narrow backwater. Magnus was looking over the water, searching for the signs that might give away the lie of the fish, when he noticed a small white hand reach out of the pool and cling to the edge of the rock. It slipped back with a faint splash. Turning, he saw the gleam of pale shoulders and a round, glistening head, black and sleek like an otter's, as the creature swam out from under the shadow of the bank.

Magnus stood staring down at a girl in the river. He waved. Very timidly she raised an arm half out of the water, then dived beneath the surface, her nakedness revealed to him for a moment before being covered by a swirl of ripples. She came up again a little farther out, and looked back at him.

'What's your name?' he called out to her.

'Nuala,' she answered. Then she turned in the water and set off upstream, swimming very fast. He watched her until her silvery wake had disappeared from sight.

Magnus knew that no one could live in the Tlenamaw, not even this strange-looking creature. Her skin had been white as a dead person's, and the hair on her head blue-black, the color of grapes. Her eyes, when she'd looked at him, had been full of golden light, but in the shade of the riverbank he'd noticed that they too were almost black.

'Nuala' – he said the name over to himself.

The next morning Magnus returned to the same place on the river, and he waited there all day in the hope that she would show herself again. It was only at dusk, when he'd all but given up hope and was on the point of turning for home, that he recognized the faint rhythmic splashing of a swimmer coming toward him through the water.

FIVE

'I walked home through the fields as dawn was breaking. When I looked back, I could see a dark trail among the waving corn where I'd brushed away the dew in passing. The air was filled with the sweet heaviness of blossom ... All I could think of was when would I see her again.

'When I reached home everyone was still asleep. Only my sister Fala's hounds were about. They came rushing up to me, joyfully wagging their tails and licking my hands as they always did. Then for some reason they cringed and backed away from me making little whimpering sounds. I laughed aloud and whispered to them that they were a pair of cowardly fools.

'When I woke, the sun stood high above the city. Fala came into my room and sat down on the edge of the bed. She looked so pretty sitting there – like a little gold-and-blue flower sparkling with dew. She demanded to know where I'd been all night. I wanted to tell her what had happened, but I knew she wouldn't understand.

'After I'd had something to eat, I quickly left the house. I told my mother I was going fishing again and wouldn't be back till late.

'My father never spoke a word to me all morning, but I felt his eyes on me whenever I wasn't looking in his direction – as if he suspected that I would soon betray him.

'I'm leaving the valley ...

'Nuala told me how long ago her family was unjustly banished from Magmel and forced to hide out in the Tlenamaw. Her parents died when she was young, and she's lived there ever since with her grandfather in a cave at the head of the river. The old man's almost blind, and she takes care of him. She's always wanted to leave Magmel, but never had the courage to try the climb alone. Now we can go together. It's the only way we can be together.

'Her grandfather won't leave. Nuala says he'll manage without her – he can see in ways other people can't. She says he may be able to help us.'

Nuala was waiting near the border, sitting under a tree on the far side of the river. Her night-dark hair was threaded with yellow flowers. He swam over to join her, holding his clothes in a bundle over his head. He followed Nuala across the boundary into the forbidden territory. Only once, when, looking behind him, he realized he could no longer see any part of the valley he knew, did he have a moment's doubt. Nuala took his hand, and together they skirted the river up through the narrow canyon under the red cliffs that shut out more and more of the sky.

The ground rose steeply before them. At every step the way became more difficult. The river, a wild torrent now, twisted and turned between fantastic compilations of fallen rock. The air was stale and thick, filled with the squeaking of bats which flew out from hidden caves in dark spiraling clouds as they passed underneath.

The torrent's roar grew steadily louder until Magnus, rounding a rocky promontory shaped like the prow of a boat, saw that they'd reached the end of the valley. A sheer barrier of red sandstone confronted them. High above the ground a shelf of rock projected from the perpendicular face of the mountain. Behind it the cliffs closed in – a bare wall, broken only by the entrance of a cavern from which the river flowed in a broad dark stream.

The water thundered down onto the rocks, sending up clouds of spray that filled the gorge with misty prismatic light.

A flight of steps hewn out of the cliff led up to the lip of the cave mouth. The steps were worn smooth, and the spray from the falls made them slippery. When they reached the platform, Nuala pointed to a narrow path that led back under the huge fissured rock out of which the river flowed.

Nuala went on ahead. For a time they walked in single file by the river. Behind them the thunder of the waterfall grew less till all they could hear was the sound of their own footsteps. When it became too dark to see, Nuala turned to him and, touching her hand to his face, said, 'Wait here. My grandfather will come for you in a little while. He wishes to speak to you alone.'

Magnus started to protest, reaching out for her in the dark, but she was gone. He couldn't even tell in which direction. He listened for footsteps, and heard nothing but a steady dripping of water onto rock.

'Don't be frightened.' The voice of an old man echoed around the walls of the cave. 'I would bring light for you, but I have lived in this place too long and it hurts my eyes.'

Magnus peered into the blackness. The voice seemed to come from somewhere above his head.

'You want to take my granddaughter away. I give you my blessing. It's always been my wish that one day she would leave the valley . . .'

'Come with us.'

'I'm old; the journey is too perilous. I have all I need here.'

The old man became silent.

'But there is one thing you could do for me.'

Magnus waited, thinking only of the moment when Nuala would return and they could leave.

'Your father has in his possession – perhaps without even being aware of it – a thing that belongs to me. It's an object of no value, a specimen of quartz crystal that lies forgotten somewhere in the attic of his house.'

'You want me to ask my father for it?'

'No, he must never know that you have been to see me. I want you to bring me the crystal without telling him – or anyone.'

'You're asking me to steal it.'

'How can it be stealing when the crystal is rightfully mine?'

'I have only your word for that.'

'It belongs to me, Magnus. I know its every facet, I know its every glistening plane. It is of no more value than a scrap of glass, but to one who has devoted his life to the study of minerals and the appreciation of beauty in crystalline form, it is rarer than any jewel.'

'I don't know.' Magnus hesitated. 'I need time to think about it.'

'There is no time. I hardly need remind you that tomorrow is your seventeenth birthday.'

'What do you mean?'

'Only that if you wish to leave the valley with my granddaughter, then you must leave tomorrow before dawn. Once you have been initiated into the Kendalship, it will be too late. If you want to take Nuala away with you, you must bring me the crystal tonight.'

'What if I can't find it?'

'You shall find it. It's only a question of knowing where to look.' The old man laughed, going on to describe where exactly the crystal lay forgotten in the Kendal's house. Once more he urged Magnus not to tell anyone of his plan.

'When will I see Nuala again?'

'She will be waiting for you at the bend in the river when you return with the crystal. It's getting late; I'll show you the way.'

Magnus felt a hand close around his arm just above the elbow. The old man's grip was firm, his fingers cold and smooth against the boy's flesh. As the old man led him through the darkness at a swift pace, Magnus had no sense of another being at his side.

Alone now, with the roar of the waterfall growing loud in his ears again, he hurried on down the path. Ahead of him, a faint circle of light; he could make out the cold glint of the river as it flowed on toward the mouth of the cave.

'I waited until the middle of the night when everything was quiet. Then, carrying my shoes in one hand, I crept into my father's room. After making sure that he was asleep, I removed the key to the tower from the ring on his belt.

'I found the crystal in the attic exactly where the old man had said it would be – at the bottom of the cistern that collects rainwater from the roof. My fingers grew numb feeling around for it in the cold water. When I saw how ordinary it looked – a six-sided obelisk, about as long as a scroll and no thicker than a child's arm – I didn't feel so guilty about taking it. Following the old man's instructions, I wrapped it carefully in a leather cloth, then hid it in the bundle of clothing and provisions I'd prepared for my journey.

'I put the key back on my father's belt. Then I went into Fala's room; I had to see her one last time. She was sound asleep, her face buried in the crook of an arm. She looked so peaceful lying there. The dogs were curled beside her on the bed. I made a tacit pact with them to look after their mistress for me. Then, careful not to wake her, I leaned over and kissed her forehead.

'The streets were deserted. Everything was white and still, graven in the moonlight. I ran down the flight of marble steps leading from our garden to the bathing places in the river. Looking up at our house, I noticed that there was no light now showing in the tower window – I must have put it out. There wasn't time to go back.

'The night was oppressively warm, but I didn't stop once to rest until I reached the border of the Tlenamaw.

'Nuala, as the old man had promised, was waiting for me at the river bend, sitting on the bank near the pool with the flat stone where I'd first set eyes on her. She was staring down into the water holding her head in her hands – I was afraid for a moment that she might have changed her mind about leaving with me. But when she saw me, she jumped up, flinging her arms around my neck.

' "I'd begun to think you weren't coming," she whispered. "Did you bring it? Did you bring the crystal?"

' "I had to wait till everyone was asleep," I said. "Yes, I have it."

' "Show it to me." She laughed with delight and clapped her hands as she watched me unravel the bundle.

'I removed the crystal from its leather cloth and held it up to her. It felt cold and heavy in my hand, but for the first time I saw how truly beautiful it was. As it caught the light of the stars, living sparks of fire seemed to leap from it, until I was holding up a flaming torch against the night. I understood then what had possessed the old man to barter his granddaughter for its return.

'Nuala kept asking me if she could hold the crystal. Reluctantly I handed it to her. She took it from me with a little smile, and I saw its mysterious light mirrored for a moment in her eyes. She looked at me, and her mouth opened – I thought she was going to say something. She leaned forward instead and touched my lips with hers. I saw then that there were tears in her eyes.

'After that everything happened so quickly. A rapid movement just behind her – something in the river. A splash ... An eddy of dark hair swirling up from the line of her neck – Nuala turning away from me. Gone.

'Moments later I saw her surface again midstream holding the crystal high in one hand. She was swimming toward the Tlenamaw.'

'I called out to her, but if she heard me she didn't answer. I plunged in after her and tried to follow, still calling her name. But she was stronger than I was in the water and drew steadily ahead ... the light of the crystal and the pale gleam of her shoulders becoming fainter and fainter until they were swallowed up by the night.

'I kept swimming – even when I could no longer see her, I kept on swimming. But the current was too fierce. I was swept downstream.

'Finally I crawled up onto the bank, utterly exhausted, almost at the point where I'd started from. I could see the flat rock with my wretched bundle lying open on top of it – a cruel reminder of how I'd been tricked. I thought of trying to cut her off by land before she could reach the cave, but I knew I didn't have the time, or the strength.

'I buried my head in my arms and wept.

'When I looked up again, I noticed something strange about the river. It seemed fuller than before; it seemed to run faster and deeper. Then I noticed that my bundle had disappeared. The flat rock where it had been lying only moments before was now completely covered over by water. Since I crawled out onto the bank, the level of the river has risen – it's still rising, creeping up over the stones toward me.'

SIX

Lower down the valley, the river had already begun to flood its banks. Imagining people still asleep in their houses, unaware of the danger, Magnus tried to warn them, shouting from the fields as he hurried home. But his cries were lost on the wind.

Although the night was almost over, the sky stayed dark. Storm clouds gathered overhead, piling up behind the mountains with deep rumblings of thunder. A warm rain spattered down in gusts. Lightning flashes arced through the dimness, thickening the air with sulfurous fumes, luridly illuminating groups of cattle that stood huddled together under the trees.

Dogs howled in the farmyards. As he came past, they ran out and barked at him. Then one or two gave chase, and soon there was a ragged pack at his heels. He stopped several times, shouting at them to go back, but they didn't, and when he ran on they followed.

As he drew near to the city, he heard the faint clang of the alarum across the river. The thin, jarring sound, barely audible above the rising storm, gave him a moment's hope: it meant that his father, at least, was alert to the danger.

It was his father's duty as Kendal to summon the people into the city in times of trouble, but in all of Magmel's history there had never before been occasion to sound the alarum. Rusted green and dulled by time, it had developed a crack that deadened its tone, rendering it next to useless. Even within the city itself its muffled voice didn't carry far. In the shape of a reclining crescent made of copper and iron, the alarum rested on a conical pivot at the center of the tower roof. From the street below it looked like a moon that some deranged person was trying to hammer down out of the sky.

After making sure that his mother and Fala were safe, Magnus ran up to the top of the tower and mounted the ladder that led from the attic out onto the battlements. Climbing up through the roof, he saw the Kendal raise an iron clapper above his head ready to strike the alarum.

'It's no good, Father,' he cried. 'They can't hear anything out there. I've just come from the fields.'

The Kendal brought the iron bar down with all his might against the inner rim of the crescent. It made a small, muted sound that was instantly swallowed up by the rushing wind.

He raised the iron club to strike the crescent again, and the boy caught the look of anguish in his father's face. 'What have you done, Magnus?'

'I don't know,' he said wretchedly. 'What *have* I done?'

The Kendal gave a bitter laugh, and the iron club came crashing down. 'You shouldn't have taken it.'

'The old man said it belonged to him. No one told me it was wrong to take it.'

'If you had only asked me. If you had only waited one more day.'

'Forgive me,' the boy sobbed, and threw himself down at the Kendal's feet. 'What's going to happen to us?'

The Kendal didn't answer, but gently pushing him away, returned to his futile tolling.

As Magnus rose to his feet, tears streaming down his face, a tremendous flash of lightning forked over their heads. Like an inverted tree hanging against the sky, it lit up the whole city and surrounding countryside with a shadowless glow. It was followed a moment later by a roll of deafening thunderclaps, as the storm finally broke over the valley.

During the first hour of the storm, the rain fell with devastating result. Because it was the dry season and the ground was hard, the water ran right off the slopes and quickly filled every streambed, gully and ravine that fed into the river. As the volume of water coming down from the mountains increased, the spate swelled to a mile-wide torrent that swept through the valley carrying everything in its path. Low-lying farms and hamlets were washed away; fields of crops, orchards, vineyards, pasture and livestock were all destroyed. Within a short span of time the floodwaters were backing up against the cliffs of Tlanuwa, and the valley began to fill like a sink.

Caught unawares, hundreds of people living outside the city drowned, either in their beds as they slept, or trying to escape from their flooded homes. Some, awakened earlier by the noises of the storm, had climbed up onto the roofs of their houses in the vain hope that the waters wouldn't reach them. Others, seeking the protection of higher ground, tried to make their way into the city.

By daybreak the southern half of the valley had become completely submerged, leaving the red sandstone bluff on which the city stood a solitary island in the middle of an immense black lake.

Magnus ran out into the turmoil of the streets. The rain beat down on the backs of the crowds and the wind shrieked about their ears as they surged through the main thoroughfares. Outside the walls of the Kendal's house the bedraggled pack of dogs that had followed the boy into the city was still milling around, waiting for his instructions.

Barely able to make himself heard above the fury of the storm, he shouted himself hoarse trying to direct the refugees from the countryside toward the main square. In their panic to find shelter, they ignored him – it was almost as if he were invisible to them. Only the dogs seemed ready to listen. They stuck to his heels now wherever he went.

As the storm centered on the city, drawn by some irresistible force to this last eminence, pandemonium broke loose. Lightning crackled down through the boiling clouds in chains of zigzag flashes, while the crash and roll of thunder, so loud it was painful to the ears, set up a continuous booming sound like the roar of the waterfall. Magnus saw a woman he knew who was holding a child in her arms struck by a lightning bolt that enveloped them both in a mantle of blue-and-white flame, before it pitched them over dead. People were screaming, charging headlong through the streets, falling down and treading one another underfoot, crowding into buildings, courtyards, doorways, seeking any kind of refuge.

Then, above the din of storm and panic, Magnus heard a low, soft rumbling sound. Looking out over the lake in the direction of the Tlenamaw, he saw what appeared to be a dark green hillside advancing slowly down the length of the valley.

He turned and started to run for home. The dogs followed him as far as the gates of the Kendal's house. They were still barking at the monstrous wave when it engulfed the city.

SEVEN

'I don't know how long it's been. We've lost track of the days. What does it matter now? I buried her next to my father in the garden. I had to open up his grave because I didn't have the strength to dig another.

'She died in agony. I watched them both die ... [Pause] My mother forgave me. There's no one left now except us two, and Fala can't last much longer. I hope she doesn't, for her sake. All of Maginel is covered in a thick, clinging mist. I saw it from the tower roof. Sometimes it lifts and you can see the ruins of the city. There are dead people and animals lying everywhere.

'I've been out of the house only once since the waters receded. Fala thought she heard someone tapping at the door. I went down to investigate. I knew that if others had survived the flood, it meant there was hope.

'There was someone out there. They didn't answer when I called, but the tapping grew more insistent. And I could hear an odd scraping noise. It took me a while to dismantle the barricade in front of the door. Everything down below was soaking wet, cold and dank. Mud oozing everywhere. One of the walls in the kitchen had collapsed, and all the ceilings were covered with green mold hanging down in strands like riverweed. The place stinks.

'As soon as I got the door open the tapping stopped. At first I couldn't see anything for the mist. I took a few steps outside. Then it cleared a little, and out of the swirling haze grew shapes of men. One came very close ... He was tall, and – I thought it was a trick of the mist at first – he had a white cloth wrapped around his head. They didn't make a sound, the others – they were like statues slowly moving up behind him. I saw his face as he turned toward me.

'It was raw and bloody – a crimson mask with slits for eyes. He reached out a hand, and I saw that it was covered in sores.

The whole of his wrist had been eaten away, and the sinews and bones showed through white. I took a step back ... He tried to speak, but he no longer had lips, and his tongue stuck out blackened and rigid between his teeth. That scraping sound was coming up from his throat. I went back into the house and barricaded the door.

'There was nothing we could do to help them. Presently the tapping started up again. It kept on like that, never very loud, for a long time. Then one evening it just stopped. They're all dead now ... [Pause] There's no food out there, anyway. How could there be? Everything's been contaminated.

'This morning, when I was opening the grave to bury my mother, I noticed that my sweat had turned red, speckled with blood – just like the others. It's the first sign. I haven't much time.

'The only hope is to get the crystal back. If I'm to reach the cave, I'll need all my strength. Fala can't last beyond tonight. She mustn't.'

Magnus had decided to wait until Fala was dead before setting out for the Tlenamaw. Until he was the only one left. He couldn't bear the thought of leaving her there to die alone.

But she clung to life with unknowing tenacity.

During the day he watched over her, trying to comfort her, always having to remind himself that the emaciated creature he held in his arms, her body now a mass of foulest corruption, was his beloved Fala. At night he listened to her struggling to stay alive, fighting for air, her every breath accompanied by a long-drawn-out whimper of pain.

He longed for her release even more than for his own.

When he noticed the first purplish swellings pushing up under the skin behind his knees and on the inside of his upper arms, he realized that he could wait no longer.

The dogs wouldn't leave Fala's side. They were thin and weakened by lack of food, but unaffected by the plague. She lay with them on a mattress, all three huddled together in the darkest corner of the attic. He had to pull them away from her by the scruff of their necks. He told her that he was taking them down to the stable to let them feed on the bodies of the horses. The horses had kicked down their stalls and escaped during the storm, but she would never know.

He was starved.

He cut the dogs' throats with a knife in the kitchen. He let their blood collect in a bowl. Then he drank the blood and ate as much of their flesh as he could stomach.

Later, he wandered from room to room trying to find the resolve to go upstairs with the knife. He couldn't just leave her there to die alone. After all, he'd only be putting her out of her misery ... But she was still Fala, still his sister. How could he think of harming her? He threw the knife away in disgust and went outside.

He walked the streets of the city, picking his way through the mist-shrouded ruins, stepping over corpses of flood and plague victims, many of whom he recognized as his friends. In his despair Magnus wondered if fate had not made him the last survivor just so that he might contemplate fully the deadly harvest he had sown.

When he got back to the house, he went into the kitchen and forced himself to eat more from the remains of the dogs. He had to preserve what little strength he had left. After he'd eaten his fill, he sat down and waited.

Although he rarely allowed himself to think about Nuala, she was never far from his mind. He couldn't accept that she hadn't really existed, that she was just an illusion, who'd only seemed real to him because he believed in her. He still loved her – in spite of what she'd done, or been forced to do. Against all reason he had hopes of finding her again and persuading her to help him get the crystal back from her grandfather.

If he could only survive long enough to reach the river.

When it was nearly dark he went up to the tower, praying he'd find Fala already dead. He pushed open the door of the attic. She had crawled out into the middle of the room, leaving snail-like tracks of blood and slime across the floor.

She asked him where the dogs were. Asleep after their feast, he said. She tried to smile, but the skin around her mouth, shrunken back to the bone, scarcely moved.

He carried her back to the mattress in the corner and covered her with a blanket.

*

'Near the end, I couldn't bear to be in the same room with her. I climbed the ladder and went up onto the tower roof to get some air. A sea of mist stretched away toward the Tlenamaw. It seemed hopelessly far. I knew then that I couldn't put off the decision any longer. I had to leave at once.

'I began looking for the iron bar that my father had used to toll the alarum. It wasn't there, so I decided to try the crescent itself. I managed somehow to lift it off its pivot. Balancing it carefully on my shoulders, I carried it down the ladder into the attic ... [Pause] It was so heavy. When I reached the bottom, I had to rest for a while. Fala wanted to know what I was doing. I told her she must try to sleep; but I could hear her sobbing quietly in her corner. She asked again about the dogs. This time, I didn't answer. I couldn't ... I knew that if I hesitated now, I would never be able to go through with it.

'I dragged the crescent over to where she lay. It made a dull scraping noise on the floor. With both hands gripping the shaft, I succeeded in raising the cumbersome weapon above my head. For a moment I saw the uncomprehending look in her eyes as she cowered away from me. She screamed, holding out her thin raw arms in terror to fend off the blow.

'Remembering her as she was that morning when she came in from the river and sat on the edge of my bed – a little blue-and-gold flower sparkling with dew, so full of life and happiness and laughter – I brought the heavy verdigris moon down through its executioner's arc.

'At the last moment I shut my eyes, and cried out with all the strength of my lungs so that I wouldn't hear the impact.

'The first blow took off her arm above the elbow. I had to hit her twice more before she finally stopped moving.

'When it was over, drenched in my sister's blood – in the blood of all my family, my friends and everyone who had ever lived in this valley – I set out for the cave to try to redeem the crystal, to mend the wrong that I'd done ...'

EIGHT

A white cloth floats up over my eyes. The hand reaches out and wipes the moisture away.

'Don't try to speak, Martin. Not yet. You're going to be fine.' She leans over, and I feel her cool, soft lips on my forehead.

Penelope.

I want to ask her where I am, what happened, what day it is. Behind the curtains it's light, or neon. I can hear whispering. A door closes. Footsteps move away down the passage.

I remember nothing, as usual.

When I open my eyes again, Somerville is standing there at the foot of the bed. Wearing a white doctor's coat with a stethoscope around his neck, he's looking down at me with a sympathetic expression – phony as hell.

'Hello, Martin. How are we feeling?'

I see his lips move before I hear the words.

'Am I in the hospital?' My voice sounds as if it were coming from a million miles away. 'What happened?'

'No, you're not in any hospital. You're a guest in my house. Everything went splendidly. As we expected, it wasn't an easy session, but a very useful one. I thought it best that you stay here for a while, just so we could keep an eye on you. Just till you feel yourself again. You've been asleep for about eighteen hours. You're all right; there's nothing to worry about. It went very, very well.'

'But what happened?'

'We'll talk about that later, when you're stronger. Right now I want you to get all the rest you can. I'll pop in and see you again in the morning.'

He glides from the room before I can say anything.

Penelope comes back with a glass of fresh orange juice and some capsules. Naked under the sheet, figuring it must have been she who undressed me and put me to bed, I feel slightly embarrassed.

I drink the orange juice and, when she's not looking, manage to get rid of the capsules.

That night when everything in Somerville's house was quiet, I slipped out of bed and made my way downstairs to the study. After rummaging through his desk and the file cabinets in Penelope's office, I found the tapes of my last session still lying on top of the tape deck. Sitting in the dark, I played them back with the sound turned as low as possible so as not to wake anyone. But the range of the voices was unpredictable and I had to keep adjusting the volume control.

About halfway through the third cassette, the lights in the study came on. Looking up, I saw Somerville standing by the door with his hand on the switch. He was dressed in a green silk robe and monogrammed slippers. A wattled throat sagged out from the vee of his pajamas. He looked tired and disgruntled, like an old lizard that had been poked from its lair by a kid with a stick.

'What are you doing down here, Martin?' he asked. 'Do you have any idea what time it is?'

I stopped the tape. 'What does it look like I'm doing?'

'You can listen to that in the morning.' Somerville gave a grunt of impatience. 'You need your rest.'

'I'm sorry, but I have to hear it now.'

Somerville shrugged and said nothing. He didn't try to persuade me any further. I switched the machine back on, and within a few moments I'd become so engrossed in the tapes again, I forgot all about his being there. Later, when I was changing over to the last cassette, I noticed that he was sitting motionless in his chair under the windows. He remained, not saying a word, until I reached the end.

With Magnus' anguished cry still ringing in my ears, I watched the dawn creep up behind the blinds in Somerville's study. Recognizing myself in Magnus, as I hadn't done with the others, seeing in his story the origin of mine, I felt a tremendous and exhilarating sense of release. It all made sense now; everything had finally come clear; the pieces of the puzzle had fallen into place. Still, I knew that nothing had really changed.

I played the last five minutes of the tape over again. It was a long time before I felt able to talk.

'It doesn't really change anything,' I began hesitantly. 'I mean, I'm still the same ... No, I guess I'm not. Not if I understand *why*.'

I looked across at Somerville, who showed no sign of having heard me. He was lying back in the chair with his head to one side, his eyes closed. Gray light from the windows caught the smoothness of his forehead and made it gleam like polished stone.

'The fact that I know what happened' – I spoke louder to get his attention – 'doesn't make it suddenly all right. I did something – something so appalling that I can never –'

'We mustn't let things get out of perspective,' Somerville yawned. He stretched himself, then sat up and looked at his watch. 'Magnus' story is certainly a dramatic and very painful one, but I don't think what he did was so dreadful. He was young, curious about the world out there – he fell in love.'

'You have to judge what I did by the consequences.'

'What *you* did, Martin?' Somerville smiled. 'Aren't we identifying a little too closely with the past? Taking things a bit too literally? All this happened a long time ago, by your own account. Right now it's seven o'clock on a Monday morning in Manhattan, 1981. If you like, we could take a walk in the park, or go and get a cup of coffee somewhere. Martin, do you hear what I'm saying?'

'Remember at the beginning of the tape, when Magnus is lying by the riverbank close to death? He never made it, did he? He never reached the cave, he never got the crystal back. That's why they were all driven – Fawcett, Begley, Petacci and the others: because the old man still has the crystal. Nothing's changed. It's still going on – *now*. Don't you see? When I handed it over to him, I unleashed something on the world, an enduring evil. And now it's my responsibility ... my responsibility to –'

'Come down off the cross, Martin. You didn't unleash *anything* on the world. Now listen to me. I don't think we want to go for a literal interpretation of Magnus' story. Clearly the symbolic content is what counts here. We're not asking each other to believe in crystal talismans, in magic powers, or anything of the kind. The crucial thing here is the story. In "Magmel" you've created your own legend, something between a myth and a fairy tale – with many obvious parallels in Western folklore and mythology – to help explain the world, or rather your disillusionment with the world, to yourself. You've constructed a model of Paradise, a regular Garden of Eden, Utopia, call it what you will – so you can deliberately destroy it.'

'What would I want to do that for?'

' "How art thou fallen from heaven, O Lucifer, son of the morning!" Magnus. A rebel in Paradise. The only *true* paradises are the ones we have lost. At some point in your childhood – perhaps when you were living in the Philippines – you may have found a happiness you've never been able to recover.'

'Are you trying to tell me that I simply *invented* Magmel?'

'I think the time has come for us to consider the real significance of your "previous lives"; to look at them in the context of what it was that brought you to me in the first place. In regression therapy, Martin, we're dealing with a highly specialized ability of the psyche to extract itself from a conflict situation: a psychological mechanism, if you like, by which the subconscious creates a fictitious personality in order to shed some light on the darker side of the hypnotic subject's character. In your case, it found a way to ease the burden of your guilt.'

'But I already told you I don't *feel* guilty about killing the boys. Not anymore. And now this explains everything.'

'Precisely.' Somerville smiled.

I looked at him in disbelief. 'What do you mean?'

'You found a way to explain things.'

'You mean you don't believe it really happened? You don't believe that I've lived before? All this time you've led me to think ... And you don't believe *any* of it? For Christ's sake, it was you who got me into all this. You conned me!'

'No, Martin,' Somerville said quietly. 'You went to very great lengths to persuade yourself. I didn't stop you from doing so. And for a very good reason. Your "previous lives" have at last revealed to me the structure of your illness. I also think you have derived considerable therapeutic benefit –'

'Crap! What about Print Begley's Bible? Do you think I made that up?'

'I don't believe in reincarnation; I never claimed that I did. I usually make this clear to my patients at an early stage, but in your case it would have been counterproductive. I consider regression beyond birth to be nothing more than dramatized fantasies created by the subconscious. The technical term for it is cryptomnesia.'

'But I have proof, don't I? What about Print's Bible?' I shouted at him. 'What *about* that, fuckhead?'

Somerville held up his hands in a gesture of mock surrender. 'You showed me a Bible, which you claimed to have found under the floorboards of a hut in Kentucky. I have to take your word for it.'

'You forget I have a witness,' I blurted out.

'*Do* you?'

I thought of Zach Scalf with the knot of bone sticking up out of his throat, of Zach Scalf lying dead under the pines.

'That's right, a witness.' It was all I could do to control the rage I felt building up inside me.

'I don't believe you,' he said calmly.

'I suppose if I told you that what *you* think doesn't make the slightest difference to me anymore, you'd say it was just another symptom of my "illness". That's *your* problem, Somerville. Now that I know what happened, I really don't need your help anymore.'

'Very well, if that's how you feel.' He unfolded himself from his chair and with a quick movement of his wrist, reached out and pulled the cord of one of the blinds. It rattled up toward the ceiling, flooding the room with daylight. 'You know where to find me, should you happen to change your mind.'

He held out a hand to me, smiling down at me, his eyes unblinking in the sudden brightness. I got up slowly, taken aback by the speed and ease with which our relationship had been terminated. He was letting me go so lightly.

'If you don't have any objection, I think I'll take them with me,' I said, holding up the four Magmel tapes.

'Ah!' Somerville closed his outstretched hand and brought it up

221

to his chin. The wide sleeve of his robe fell back, revealing a hairless arm raddled with liver-colored age spots. 'I'd like to hang on to those for a little while longer. Perhaps when I've had a chance to study them ... It's really a very remarkable regression.'

'I need them *now*,' I said defiantly.

He stood for a moment stroking the line of his jaw, then slowly began advancing toward me, holding out his hand again, but palm up this time. 'I think you'd better leave the tapes here. They'll be quite safe.'

His smile now was very intense.

'But I *need* them. If I'm to find my way back ... They're the only lead I have. Please. I can have copies made.'

'Find your way *back*, Martin?'

'Fuck you!' I shouted.

Somerville hesitated. 'I think you'll feel happier if you do as I say. Martin. You've been through a lot lately. When you're feeling better – calmer, more relaxed – drop by and we'll talk about it. But Martin, take things slowly for a while.'

Whatever resistance I meant to offer him suddenly evaporated. I looked at Somerville and realized to my shame that I couldn't oppose his will. Without another word I placed the cassettes in his outstretched palm and turned away.

'Martin.'

I stopped by the door and looked back at him. He was still holding the tapes, standing with his back to the light so that his face was in shadow.

'You told me that when you were a child in the Philippines, you used to play with – I think you said she was the cook's daughter. What was her name?'

'Missy. We called her Missy. What the hell has that got to do with anything?'

'What kind of games did you play?'

'How should I know? It was a long time ago.'

'Try to remember.'

'I suppose you think this is important.'

'It just might be, yes.'

'We played – the usual kinds of games kids play. I don't know. Games.'

'Where did you play with her? In the house?'

'The garden. There was a shed in the garden right on the edge of the jungle. That was our place. Missy wasn't really allowed in the house – except in the kitchen, when Tsu-lai, her mother, was there. In those days ... well, you know how it was.'

'Did your parents object to your playing with her?'

'On the contrary. They were glad that I'd found a friend. There weren't any American kids living anywhere around.'

'What did Missy look like?'

'I don't have a clear picture of her in my mind. She was part Chinese, part Filipino. Kind of cute-looking, a couple of years older than I was, quite tall. She was always laughing, I remember, and she had this wild streak. I was quite taken with her, and also slightly ...'

'Yes,' he said, 'go on.'

'She didn't speak much English, so we made up sort of a language of our own. We'd imitate the cries of different animals, monkeys, birds. She was much better at it than I was. She used to get on my nerves sometimes. I think I might have been in love with her – except you can't really call it love at that age.'

'Did you find a way of ...' Somerville paused. 'Was your love reciprocated?'

'Oh, I had my first sexual experience with Missy, if that's what you're getting at. We were both kind of young, so it was relatively innocent. I can't even remember what we did exactly. But I guess girls do mature earlier in the tropics. Isn't that what they say?'

'Did your parents realize what was going on? Did Missy's mother?'

'No way! I don't think it would even have occurred to them to suspect. And we were always pretty careful. It was part of the game.'

'Do you remember the first time it happened? Did she seduce you?'

'It wasn't such a big deal. Look, I really don't see the point of discussing this.'

'Just one more thing,' Somerville said. 'Do you have any idea what happened to Missy after you left Manila and came back to the United States?'

'I didn't want to leave, but I was ten years old. I forgot all about her. I have a vague recollection of my mother saying something to me about her getting married. But I really can't remember. Anyway, I don't see that this need concern you anymore.'

'It was just a thought.' Somerville smiled.

NINE

7.45 p.m. – This morning after getting back from Somerville's I took a phenob. and slept for seven hours straight. I dreamed for the first time since I started hypnosis – can't remember what about. Slight headache when I woke, but feel much better now. Stayed in bed all afternoon watching TV with the sound turned down and rereading some of the transcripts of the original six regressions.

While sorting through the Begley material, I had a revelation: Print didn't go down Lost Hope because he was afraid the world was coming to an end, but to try to *prevent* it from coming to an end. He may not have known himself exactly why he went into the cave – almost certainly he didn't – but I'm convinced now that subconsciously he was driven, just as Fawcett, Cabet, Petacci and the others were driven, by the need to find Magmel and redeem the crystal.

I decided not to ask Somerville again for the Magmel tapes back. I don't really need them anymore. Besides, he'll be expecting me to try something.

An hour ago I called Heyworth to find out if he'd heard from Anna. Also to tell him that Somerville and I had parted company. He said he had no news from Vienna. I wonder if I'll ever see her again.

Heyworth tried to give me a hard time as usual. He'd already talked with Somerville. I don't know how much he knows – he'd be the *last* person to understand – but obviously he thinks this time I've flipped out completely. I told him that I've had it up to here with sixty-dollar-an-hour mindfucks.

Anyway, God helps those who help themselves.

*Extract from Martin Gregory's diary

Earlier I'd thought of taking the train out to Bedford to pick up some clothes and other stuff I'll be needing for the journey. But I just couldn't face it: an empty house full of memories. Instead I called the office and asked Al where to find the equipment. He recommended Ben Seminoff's Camp and Trail Outfitters down on Chambers Street.

My flight doesn't leave until tomorrow afternoon so I've got all morning to get organized.

TEN

Mrs Lombardi waylaid me in the hall. She came padding out of her ground-floor apartment in an old chenille Mother Hubbard and a skullfull of rollers, her little black eyes beady with intrigue.

'You gotta visitor, Mr Gregory,' she announced in a loud whisper, pointing at the ceiling. 'She come here eight-thirty, maybe nine o'clock. I tell her you just gone out, but she wanna wait for you.'

'You let her in my room?'

'Sure.' Mrs Lombardi smiled complacently. 'Is your wife.'

'My *wife?*' I repeated, and shook my head. 'Impossible. She's in Europe.'

Anna must have decided to come home on the spur of the moment. I felt a surge of affection for her that too readily became confused with longing, then turned to resentment as I realized how inconvenient a reunion this was going to be: the awkwardness, the pain, the absolving tears, the spending of an emotion I could not afford to indulge right now. She couldn't have picked a worse time.

The door to my room was ajar. I stood outside for a moment, my head spinning from climbing the stairs, noticing how the light slashed my shoes on the diagonal. Earlier I'd treated myself to dinner at Luchow's, where I'd had one too many.

I pushed the door back.

Penelope was sitting on the bed in a Lotus position, both pillows stuffed between her and the wall, leafing through a magazine. She looked up at me with a faintly amused expression and said, 'Ciao.'

'I might have guessed.' I leaned heavily against the doorframe. 'What the hell do you think you're doing?'

'Waiting for you.' She went back to her magazine. 'You weren't in when I got here, so I told the woman downstairs I was your wife ... You don't mind, do you? I certainly wasn't going to wait for you on the street.'

'Why did you come?' I asked coldly.

'Oh.' She looked up again, the slight smile tugging at the corners of her mouth. 'I came to give you these.'

Penelope opened her handbag and took out a block of cassettes held together by a thick rubber band. She tossed them down beside her on the bed. 'They're the tapes of your last session.'

'Somerville sent you, didn't he? To persuade me not to quit therapy. Right?' I gave a snide little laugh.

'He doesn't even know I've taken them.'

'Do you really expect me to believe that?'

'I thought you wanted the tapes.' She hesitated, lowering her eyes. 'I couldn't help overhearing what you said this morning, about trying to find Magmel ...'

'Magmel doesn't *exist*. Didn't he explain that to you?'

'I just feel that you should have them.'

'Okay, now that you've done your good deed for the day, why don't you run along home?'

'I thought you'd be ...' She didn't finish the sentence, just sat there looking down at her hands.

'You thought I'd be what?'

She shook her head. 'Nothing.'

After a while I said, 'Penelope, it's late. I'm tired.'

She jumped off the bed, snatched her handbag and coat, and made for the door. I stepped aside to let her by, but at the last moment her face crumpled, and with a little cry she buried her head in my shoulder, bursting into a flood of tears.

'You don't understand,' she managed to get out; 'when he finds out that I've taken them, he'll ... I can't go back there. Let me stay here tonight, *please*. Just for tonight.'

I held her, trying not to surrender to her tears, trying not to surrender to the soft warmth of her body.

When I knocked at Mrs Lombardi's door to ask her if I could have the second bed back – the same bed I'd insisted on moving out a couple of weeks before – she looked at me at first as if I were crazy. Then, squeezing her pudgy little hands together, she suddenly beamed: 'For your wife!'

She helped me carry the bed in by sections from the storeroom and set it up in the corner of my room, exactly where it had been before. You could see the marks on the wall where the iron frame had rubbed away several layers of paper. Mrs Lombardi brought sheets, pillows and blankets. She kept fussing over Penelope, who sat by the boarded-up fireplace, a bit subdued after her crying fit, ignoring her completely. As soon as Mrs Lombardi had finished making up the bed, I told her thank you and good-night. At the door she turned and gave me a broad wink.

It didn't dawn on me till later that there was anything unusual about the arrangements I'd just made. I didn't believe for a moment that Penelope was really afraid to go home to Somerville. But I wanted her to think she'd persuaded me to let her spend the night on that account. I felt sure that Somerville had made an issue of keeping the tapes only so that she could bring them to me later, as a way of gaining my confidence. But I was curious to find out what it was they wanted from me – at least, that's what I told myself.

I insisted on putting the screen back up so that Penelope would have some privacy. She looked at it and started to laugh.

'Isn't this a bit Victorian?' she asked. And then, when I said nothing: 'I didn't know you could still find places like this in New York.'

She went on talking to me from the other side of the screen as she took off her clothes. She said it made her feel like a saloon girl in an old Western. Already in bed, I lit a cigarette and stared up at the ceiling, paying close attention to every little sound she made.

She came out from behind the screen with her hair up and wearing only the robe I'd lent her. Which was much too big for her.

While she was in the bathroom at the end of the hall, I went over to her bed and examined her clothes, expecting to find I don't know what.

I lay in the dark, listening to the uneven sound of her breathing and the faint squeaking of iron whenever she moved.

I remembered the dream I'd had the first night I spent in this place. The girl in the other bed: I'd only just met her then, Somerville's assistant, but it was she I'd dreamed of that night.

Penelope.

The whole room shuddering to the rhythms of her solitary frenzy.

Was it just coincidence that she was here now? Or the fulfillment of a wish? Could I be responsible somehow, without knowing it perhaps, for re-creating the conditions of the dream? An erotic fantasy that had turned with little warning into a grisly, sweat-soaked nightmare . . .

It seemed too absurd. I hadn't exactly invited her here tonight: it was Somerville who'd sent her; it was Somerville who'd sent me Penelope.

I lay there waiting for it to begin, listening for the low, urgent voice that I knew at any moment would call me over to her side of the room.

Nothing.

Her breathing gradually deepened and grew regular. No sound of movement now from the other bed.

I whispered her name.

Nothing.

I must have dozed off soon afterward. Drunker than I thought. When I woke, it was still dark. I could hear singing, a thin reedy sound that set my teeth on edge. I knew I should ignore it and try to get back to sleep, but I couldn't.

I sat up in bed shivering all over.

Penelope was standing at the window. She had nothing on. The window was open wide and she was leaning out into the night, her elbows resting on the sill, the curtains billowing around her like an unruly cloak. She stood quite still, as if she didn't even notice the cold. The whiteness of her body, bathed in neon from the streetlights, gave off a radiance that seemed almost ethereal. When the wind dropped, the curtains settled, and the room grew darker, and the upper half of her torso became obscured.

I threw off the covers, got out of bed and went over to the window.

At once the singing stopped. I parted the curtains and touched her gently on the shoulder. Her skin felt as smooth and cold as marble.

'What are you looking at?' I said softly, following her gaze out over the warehouse roofs, only to lose it somewhere at the dirty yellow edge of the sky.

She didn't answer. I leaned forward and kissed her between the shoulder blades. She shuddered, moving away from me. Something jangled at her feet. I glanced down.

She was wearing Anna's bracelet around one of her ankles.

'Don't speak,' she whispered. I saw that she was smiling. Her dark, pointed tongue came sliding out of the corner of her mouth, seeking mine.

I closed both hands around her icy little breasts and let my lips travel slowly the length of her spine, slicking down the mane of fine hairs that ran from the nape of her neck to the top of her buttocks – noticing how the hair grew thickest at the point where the tail should have been. All the way down I traveled, breathing in the faint scent of lavender, tasting the inky bitterness of her, as I knelt between her legs and came up under the taut swell of her partly shaved belly. Then suddenly I found myself swimming through a warm, fetid swamp, thick with sodden weed and full of quick, tangled creatures darting tentacles laden with juice down my parched throat.

Moisture ran down the inside of her thighs, gushing out of her like the dark stream that flowed from the mouth of Nuala's cave. I entered and was drawn up into the surprising heat, pulled deep inside her. She gave a tense cry and arched her body into mine, letting her head fall back on my shoulder; her hands gripped the edges of the window frame.

Bucking, she pushed hard against me with a flurry of rapid thrusts that made a fat hollow sound like waves slapping against a jetty. Rocking, legs and arms intertwined; tongues dueling, jazzing, jabbing sideways in a crazed froth of saliva. I got my hands up to her throat and began to squeeze. The curtains were blowing all around us; the night wind was sailing in our faces. She fought free and sank her teeth into the base of my thumb. I struck her with my open fist across the side of her head. She laughed, a wild laugh that rang out over the deserted streets. Then I hit her a second time and she fell to the floor, dragging me with her.

We rolled apart and lay panting on our stomachs, facing each other across the threadbare carpet. She was shivering un-controllably. Little moans escaped her, little grunts and cries. She got up and began to circle around me on all fours, nosing and nipping and licking me all over. Grabbing a handful of her hair and pulling her head down, biting into the damp skin of her neck, I mounted her from behind.

She gave a howl of anguish, starting somewhere in the back of her throat and rising, as she was transported by the first spasms, to a shrill wail. The sound went right through me. My head blew open, and suddenly I was with her. I let out a deep, bellowing cry that joined hers, wavering between unison and an eerie harmony, then soared like a bird through the open window out into the blue metallic night.

'Can't I come with you?' she whispered.

'You'd just be in the way.'

'I suppose you think I'm in your way *now*.' Penelope sighed and sat down heavily on the bed. A wing of dark hair fell over her face.

'I didn't mean it that way.'

'Can I at least come with you to the airport?'

'What for?' I said sharply. 'Is that another of *his* ideas?'

She shook her head. 'I came here to give you the tapes. I already told you, I . . .' She hesitated, biting her lower lip. 'I thought you needed someone. Martin, please let me help you.'

'You know you can't.'

'I could wait for you outside the cave.'

I laughed at that. 'You mean like Rory? The faithful brown dog! If you didn't starve to death, they'd shoot you.'

'Let me,' she pleaded.

'What makes you so sure I'm coming back? Print never made it back. None of the others did either.'

She reached up, encircling my neck with her arms. Her eyes, tilted half-shut, glistened through a sooty smear of lashes.

'You'll come back,' she said.

ELEVEN

The drive up into the mountains took longer than I remembered. After touching down in Knoxville a little after 5, I picked up the foam-green Honda Accord that Avis had waiting for me at the airport and followed the same route to Pineville that I'd taken last week. As before, I'd flown Republic from La Guardia – same flight, same everything, I even thought of going back to the same diner in Middlesboro, just to prove to myself I couldn't be recognized. In the end I decided not to push my luck.

At Pathfork I made an elaborate detour to avoid the Pineview Motor Lodge: I had an irrational fear that the Honda would break down in front of the motel and I'd be forced to ask Scalf's widow if I could use her phone. As a result, I missed the turnoff for Pine Mountain and got really lost.

It was almost 9.30 by the time I reached Springfield. I had to stop at the town's only bar to ask the way to the cave – I've always disliked asking directions. It turned out to be only a couple of miles down the road and, as the bartender and his cronies enjoyed pointing out, was signposted as clear as day. At the edge of town, peeling billboards loomed up in the Honda's headlights, wearily proclaiming the Lost Hope Cavern as the eighth wonder of the world.

I didn't have any trouble finding a room at the Caver's Rest Motel, a low white frame setup with a central office and a dining room built into the side of a mountain. There were no more than ten cars parked outside, but it looked a cut above the Pineview.

While I was checking in, I got into conversation with a young gray-haired woman behind the desk, who turned out to be the owner. She wore gold-rimmed glasses and had a pinched, weather-beaten face. I asked her how many people visited the cave on an average day.

'It's getting near the end of the season now,' she said a little defensively. 'Maybe fifty, a hundred. We get a lot of rain and snow up here in winter. Belowground that means flooding, so we have to close the cave down from the first week in November till the end of April.'

'Then I only just made it,' I said, smiling.

The office walls were hung with framed color photographs of the cave's principal attractions and a large-scale underground map of the Springfield system, which I went over to examine more closely.

'What's the busiest time of day belowground?' I asked.

'Well, that depends. We got a couple of busloads from Des Moines coming in tomorrow morning early. If you want to avoid a crush, better take the eleven-o'clock. The complete tour lasts about two hours. Less than that when it's only a small group.'

'I have to be in Lexington by early afternoon for a meeting,' I explained with an easy lie. 'I think maybe just to be on the safe side I should book the nine-o'clock.'

'If that's what you want,' she said with a friendly grin; 'but I warn you it'll be a crowd.'

'Too bad,' I laughed.

A crowd was exactly what I wanted.

The main entrance to the cave was less than fifty yards from the motel dining room. A man-made opening had been carved out of the rocky hillside and fortified with concrete overlay. It looked like the doorway of a modern cathedral. An orange ticket booth and small souvenir shop stood on either side of the entrance, where the bus party from Des Moines was slowly gathering now. I noted with satisfaction that many of the new arrivals carried shoulder bags and bulky camera cases. My army-green canvas tote bag from Ben Seminoff's wouldn't attract attention.

I watched through the dining-room window, waiting until the tour group had started to move into the cave mouth; then I got up from the table and walked quickly down to my room at the other end of the building to collect my things. On the way back, I turned in my room key at the office, explaining to the girl that I wanted to get away as soon as the tour was over. Before breakfast I'd taken the precaution of parking the Honda on a back road about half a mile from the Caver's Rest. It seemed unlikely that anyone would notice that my car was no longer in the motel lot

– at least until after the tour had returned to the surface, when it would look as if I'd just left, in a hurry.

With a feeling of mild euphoria I joined the others under the cave entrance and moved unobtrusively to the center of the group. After their overnight haul from Indianapolis, the tourists looked gray and pouchy in the bright October sunlight. An elderly couple standing in front of me were complaining about the schedule being too arduous for senior citizens and making unfavorable comparisons with a 'leafin' tour' they'd taken of Vermont the previous fall. As we prepared to negotiate the long flight of steps that led gently down an artificial rockfall into the floodlit cave, I took a last look behind us at the closing circle of blue sky and decided that if I was leaving this world for good, then I was doing so without much regret. When my turn came, the boy at the gate okayed my ticket and wished me a nice day, without giving the canvas tote bag a second glance.

The tickets weren't even numbered. There could be no body count.

'Hi, everybody! I'm Karen Dare, your guide for today,' a dumpy blonde coed in a red blazer screeched through a microphone from the back of the chamber, 'and I'd like to welcome y'all to Lost Hope Cavern! Our tour this morning will last approximately two hours and ten minutes, and as we proceed through this ... Please, sir, I must request you do not smoke ... this underworld fairyland, which acquired its remarkable beauty by the dripping of limestone water over innumerable centuries, I'll be telling you about the geological history of the cave, pointing out features of special interest and answering any questions you may have.'

Near the front of the group, a woman wearing a weather-proof Inverness cape raised her hand and asked in a muffled voice if there were comfort stations belowground.

''Fraid not,' the guide sang back into the mike, her adenoidal Southern twang echoing relentlessly around the walls of the chamber.

'Okay, let's move her on out!' She raised a short, red-sleeved arm and waved us forward with the kind of gesture John Wayne would have used to signal a cavalry charge.

235

The troop from Des Moines began to shuffle off along the pathway that sloped easily down toward the opening of a tunnel at the far end of the chamber. I hung back so that I could position myself somewhere near the rear of the column. The woman in the plastic cape had had the same idea, but at the last moment she changed her mind and, breaking ranks, suddenly darted back toward the entrance. No one seemed to notice that she'd deserted us.

As we moved along the tunnel, our shadows, enlarged to enormous size by the floodlighting, made grotesque patterns on the arched roof. People talked in hushed tones, as though they were in church, pausing with reverence before the dramatic rock formations: stalactites, stalagmites, translucent dripstone and flowing stone draperies – all illuminated by concealed fixtures that suffused the rock with unnatural brilliance. Pin spots and colored beacons played gaily over clusters of soda straws, calcite crystals and sprays of glittering gypsum. Every eye-catching specimen had been Disneyfied to a greater or lesser extent, drawing proportional gasps of wonder and delight.

In front of us, the rock formations came to an end, leaving only the curving sculpture of water on the limestone walls. A clear, shallow stream, fenced off by an iron guardrail, flowed along one side of the tunnel, here and there forming mirror-calm pools that covered the floor. We crossed over by wooden Japanese-style bridges, stopping to admire what Karen, our guide, called the Lilies of the Cave – stalagmites rising up from the bottom of a pool and expanding at the surface of the water like lily pads. On top of one of these stone saucers someone had carefully arranged a family of green Styrofoam frogs. They earned a spontaneous burst of applause.

Anxious to get started, I'd already begun looking out for a suitable place to hide; but I wanted to wait until we were closer to the center of the cave. By studying the map hanging in the motel office, I'd discovered that the route we were now taking would eventually lead to a crossways known as Shatter Fork. Beyond it lay the Little Hall of Thirteen, the most spectacular chamber in the Springfield cave system, where the tour group was scheduled to stop for a ten-minute rest. That was when I planned to make my move.

Because it describes vertical as well as horizontal dimensions, a cave map can be difficult to read. As far as I could make out, Shatter Fork was the only intersection between the show cavern and the wild parts of the cave – much of it apparently still unexplored, unmapped and restricted to all but experienced spelunkers – that didn't involve a long and difficult descent by ladder or rope. I was carrying minimum equipment and had no caving or climbing experience, other than a visit to a small cave near Boston on a school outing; and once, when I was at Brown, a backpacking expedition with my brother in the Adirondacks.

Somehow I knew that my lack of experience didn't matter. When Print Begley had walked into Lost Hope with nothing but a miner's helmet and a thirty-foot rope slung over his shoulder, he'd never been belowground before. He was scared of the dark, Scalf had said. Following in his footsteps – or rather, as I saw it, retracing my own – I had no idea where they would lead me, nor indeed what I was meant to be looking for; yet I was convinced that this time around – my seventh, and perhaps my last – I would find the way through.

Karen Dare was standing on hallowed ground. Under a white dripstone cascade that poured off the wall behind her like melting ice cream, a flat-topped boulder, also white, about the size of a concert grand, jutted out over the water. The minister usually stood to the side of the altar, Karen explained, facing the bridal pair and the congregation, gathered, as we were now, on the farther shores of Lake Bliss.

'The Chapel was consecrated by an ecumenical synod in 1975. Since then it has been used chiefly for weddings, christenings and memorial services. We had a couple from Tampa Bay get married here only last month,' she added brightly.

'It was a truly beautiful ceremony. The bride and groom both wore white, and a chamber-music ensemble played right over there by the water's edge.' She pointed to a sandy beach on the far side of the lake. 'That's where we're headed now, folks. We're going to take a short break before continuing on our tour. Just follow the path around and I'll meet y'all on the other side.'

The main party moved off obediently, but the group was not

as tightly bunched as before and there were quite a few stragglers. It meant that I was able to linger on in the 'Chapel' without drawing attention to myself. As soon as the last person had reached the opening to the passage that led into the Little Hall of Thirteen, I ducked down behind the altar.

It was even easier than I'd expected.

I waited a few minutes until everything was quiet, then stood up and walked back around the edge of the lake to Shatter Fork. Stepping over the low railing that closed off the restricted part of the cave, I climbed down a short rockfall to the bottom of a narrow cutting, which led past an outcrop of overhanging rock and then made a right-angled turn into total darkness. Just before the turn, where there was still enough light to see by, but I could no longer be observed from the passageway above, I put down my bag and changed quickly into caving gear.

I had prepared everything beforehand. All I had to do now was slip a pair of coveralls over my jeans and put on a helmet. The coveralls had protective leather pads at the knees and elbows and large pockets that held food rations, canteen, a two-pound water-tight can of carbide and a flashlight attached by a lanyard to my belt. I was already wearing boots with rubber-cleated soles; I'd been wearing them since Monday to get them broken in. Around my waist I had a short length of nylon rope spliced with a snap link to form an endless loop. I had another, longer rope tied across one shoulder like a bandolier. The equipment seemed heavier than I remembered when I'd tried it out at Ben Seminoff's, but it felt reasonably comfortable.

Since there was a good chance I'd be spending longer than twelve hours in the cave, I'd decided to use an acetylene lamp for light rather than one of the more modern electric headlamps. Acetylene was supposed to be less efficient; it was awkward to load and had a naked flame that could easily be put out by water; but for a long haul underground I was told it would provide the most reliable source of illumination. It was also the type of lamp Print Begley would have used in 1945.

I spooned the gray lumps of carbide into the lower chamber of the lamp and filled the top half with water. Then I closed it up and slotted the metal tongue into the grooved rigging at the front of my helmet. Holding the palm of one hand over the lamp's reflector to create a combustion chamber for the gas, I spun the wheel to get a spark. After a couple of tries there was a low popping sound and the gas ignited. A thin flame sprang up yellow and sure in the center of the reflector. I adjusted the nozzle, and the flame turned a brilliant blue-white.

With the helmet on, I found that whichever way I turned my head the darkness receded magically. It was as if the light were coming from my own eyes. It gave me a strange feeling of power. Nothing can exist down here, I told myself, unless I choose to look in its direction.

So far, everything had gone according to plan; I'd gotten off to a good start. It was almost 10.30. In three quarters of an hour the group from Des Moines would be reaching the surface. I reckoned that even if the worst happened and someone realized that I'd been left behind in the cave, it would be another half-hour before anyone was sent down to look for me, and probably much longer than that before it could be discovered which route I'd taken.

I covered my traces, smoothing out footprints in the sandy floor and hiding the green canvas tote bag behind a rock. Then I set off along the cutting. Beyond the turn, the path began to slope gently downhill.

TWELVE

The walls of the cutting soared up at either hand like the sides of a ravine, as if they would never meet in the darkness overhead. The air felt fresh and cool against my face, and I had to remind myself that I was down a cave, not out walking by night somewhere in the mountains.

Soon enough, the going got more difficult. The path, strewn with random stone and loose piles of scree, became narrow and steep; the rocks underfoot, grown fewer but larger, began stacking up one on top of another; and before I knew it, I was clambering down a chaotic staircase of massive wedge-shaped boulders. Then the walls closed in, becoming almost perpendicular; the floor dropped away, and I found myself without any foothold squeezing through a chasm so narrow there was barely room to turn my head. After twenty minutes or so of hard chimneying, which left me pouring sweat and aching all over, my feet touched ground again and I emerged unexpectedly from the cutting into the anteroom of a vast, silent hall.

The floor of the chamber continued on a downward slope by a series of rough terraces, littered with gigantic boulders and splintered fragments of stalactite that must have fallen from the roof. Even with the help of the flashlight I couldn't make out the ceiling or the far walls. It was that big. The darkness seemed to press in from all sides, held back only for a moment by the thin, wavering beam of light. The confidence I'd placed earlier in the power of my lamp quickly evaporated. For the first time I felt awed by my surroundings.

It took me a long time to work my way around the walls of the great hall. Where I'd hoped to find a way out at the bottom of the incline, I came up against a sheer rock face. According to the map there should have been a tunnel leading out of the chamber and on to a whole series of decorated caves, but I couldn't find any trace of it. Following the wall around, I began to climb wearily back up toward the cutting. If there wasn't another exit, I would have to go back to Shatter Fork, or what I'd assumed was Shatter Fork, and start over.

Suddenly I felt discouraged. The equipment seemed to weigh heavier at every step, my clothes under the coveralls were drenched in sweat and a large blister was forming on the heel of my left foot. I found myself thinking about Penelope; wondering if she'd spent last night at Mulberry Street or gone home to Somerville's. What the hell was I doing anyway fooling around down a lousy cave, when I could have been with her?

All I wanted now was to get back to the point from which I'd set out. I'd given up any hope of finding another exit from the hall. But after making so many turns and detours trying to follow its perimeter, I'd completely lost my bearings. I had no idea where I was in relation to the cutting. The thought that I might have missed it and would have to go all the way around again filled me with despair.

Then ahead, through the gloom, my headlamp picked up the dim outline of a rock formation that looked vaguely familiar. Hoping to find that I'd come full circle, I climbed the sloping face of an enormous slab of limestone and scrambled up onto the next ledge to get a better view.

On a small plateau, under an overhang of white calcite that curved up gracefully from the ground like a snowdrift hollowed by the wind, stood a group of dome-shaped stalagmites. Beyond them I could make out a patch of concentrated shadows in the wall which marked the entrance of a passage. I realized at once that it wasn't the cutting – I'd found another way out.

I gave a triumphant shout that echoed briefly and was swallowed by the vast silence of the hall. When I got closer, I saw that the shadows had concealed a second tunnel set next to the first and about the same size, but leading off in a different direction. Faced with the decision as to which tunnel to follow, I examined both entrances, carefully looking for some distinguishing feature, hoping I might have an instinctive feeling about one or the other. But there was nothing to choose between them. Unable to make up my mind, I had to settle for flipping a coin. I began to unzip the front of my coveralls to get at some loose change I had in my jeans, when I noticed that the stalagmites on the plateau behind me seemed to have changed position.

It was only an illusion, a simple parallax effect. I was seeing them now from a different angle, and instead of being a random group, they appeared to form an untidy line that straggled out from the tunnel entrance toward the center of the chamber. I went over and studied them more carefully: six gray, dome-shaped figures, about my height, standing silently by under their white canopy like cowled voyagers waiting without hope on the deck of an ice-bound ship.

Perhaps that was why they'd seemed familiar. There were six of them: Begley, Fawcett, Subhuto, Petacci, Cabet and Thorfinn . . .

I would make it seven.

As I formed up behind them and looked down the line toward the tunnels, I saw clearly that if they could have advanced, it would have been in the direction of the left-hand passageway.

It was no more than a vibration, a low humming that I could feel as much as hear, coming from somewhere far behind the tunnel walls. Imagining it to be caused by one of the many underground streams that run through the Springfield system, I didn't pay much attention to it at first.

For the better part of an hour, I'd been walking down a dry sandy path that descended at an easy angle between smooth faces of rock, leading deeper and deeper into the bowels of the earth. There were few turns or developments in the tunnel's steady course, and almost no obstructions. Sometimes I'd pass through small unadorned chambers that might have lain in perpetual darkness until the beam of my light disturbed them, and I'd stop to look for signs of earlier visitors; but neither the rooms nor the passage itself revealed any secrets, and I'd continue on my monotonous way. It was like strolling down a shelving beach at night, hearing the surf beating on the shore, expecting at any moment to find the ocean at one's feet – but never reaching it.

I was beginning to think I'd made the wrong choice after all, and that I should turn back, when the humming began to get louder.

It seemed to be coming up the tunnel towards me now, filling the air with a dull throbbing. The ground began to tremble, and I noticed that the walls and roof, glistening in the beam of my headlamp like the inside of a gun barrel, were dripping with moisture. The sandy floor was turning to mud beneath my feet.

The noise, somewhere between a growl and the rumble of nearing thunder, grew steadily more intense. As the passage bottomed out, making a sharp rightward turn and leading up to a fork, it suddenly developed into a full-throated roar.

Stupefied by the din, I advanced slowly toward the junction. One passageway continued on for twenty yards or so before the ceiling dipped, then terminated abruptly in a choke of stones and rubble. The other opened out into a low circular chamber in the middle of which a gaping black pit, as wide as the floor itself and overshadowed by dripping rocks, barred the way to the passage beyond. The dreadful roar was coming from the depths of this hole, intensified by a hollow booming sound that echoed and crashed back against the vaulted roof of the cavern.

I crept up to the edge of the pit on hands and knees and peered down over its slippery rim. Using the flashlight as a backup for my headlamp, I followed the sides down into the thick wet darkness until the two beams became dissipated. There was no telling how much farther below lay the bottom; I remembered Scalf's saying, 'Lost Hope's deeper than the pit of Hell, and it goes on forever.' I imagined a vortex of gigantic capacity, somewhere far beneath the shelving recesses and impending ledges of rock, turning implacably, thundering around the smooth caldron walls . . .

I knew it was there. Suddenly I knew.

I'd come this way before.

My head started to throb so violently I had to move away from the edge. As I crawled backward, the leg of my coveralls caught on something. I glanced down. Next to where I'd been kneeling, a rusty iron peg had been hammered into the projecting rock. Attached to it was a length of rope with a frayed end. Immediately beneath the rock, not more than twenty-five feet down, I could just make out the opening of a lateral tunnel in the wall of the pit.

I didn't hesitate. If I'd stopped for a moment to consider what

I was about to do, I'd never have gone through with it. I removed the old knot from the peg, tied on one end of my nylon rope in a primitive clove hitch and pulled it tight, testing it against my weight, then threw the coils over the edge. It hung down just right, and with line to spare. I attached the rope to the snap link on my waist line, gripped it firmly with both hands and, backing out over the edge of the pit, lowered myself into the abyss.

Crouched precariously on a narrow ledge above the opening in the pit wall, I rested for a moment before attempting to maneuver myself into the breach. After figuring out the best angle of approach, I began to wonder if Print Begley had done the same. At some point the rope he was using must have given way, sending him to his death.

This time I'd come better equipped.

Against my will, I glanced down. Far below, I could see the dull gleam of the whirlpool – like a monstrous spinning eye staring up at me through the blackness. Then the eye became still and the walls of the pit began to turn, and suddenly everything reeled sickeningly out of kilter. I lost my footing and lurched off into space. The whole weight of my body was thrown onto my arms; the nylon rope, slick with moisture, sped up through my hands as I tried frantically to grip it.

If it hadn't been for the breaking action of the waist line, I would certainly have fallen. But somehow I managed to hold on and to pull myself back up hand over hand till I was level with the mouth of the tunnel. Once safely inside, I lay down flat on my stomach hugging the cold wet rock until my head stopped spinning and the terror gradually subsided.

After freeing myself from the rope, I ate some of the rations I'd brought with me, then refilled my headlamp with carbide and water before setting off along the tunnel. It was smaller than it had seemed from above – I had barely room to turn around – and it was too low for walking; the only comfortable means of progress was on hands and knees. Before I'd gone fifty yards, even that became impossible.

The passage narrowed to a few feet, and the roof came down to a height where I could touch it with my fingertips when my elbows were resting on the ground. When I moved, snaking forward now on my belly, my shoulders scraped the sides of the crawlway, and I could feel the rock against my back pressing down from above.

I had to stop and rest every few yards, taking in lungfuls of mephitic air, trying to control the feeling of panic that surged in my gut. The fear of getting wedged in or being crushed or buried alive never loosened its grip. At times the urge to go back became almost overwhelming. While I still could. While there was still time. But with no room to turn around in now, it seemed easier to keep going.

Then, as I was coming out of an awkward turn, a few yards up ahead the lamp revealed a smooth bulkhead sealing off the crawlway. I moved in close, feeling around the edge of the walls where they met the obstructing rock. The join was practically seamless. I tried pushing against it, but there wasn't the slightest give.

Even though I knew it was hopeless, I kept on pushing, cursing and hammering on the rock with my bare fists until the strength went out of my arms and finally I had to admit defeat. There was nothing I could do now except go back the way I'd come. But the thought of having to back up all the way to the pit and then climb that rope over the abyss was more than I could stand. I just lay there face down in the mud.

The thin hiss of the carbide bug seemed unbearably loud in the narrow confines of the tunnel. Loosening the chin strap, I eased off my helmet and pushed it away from me. As I did so, I saw the blue-white flame in the center of the lamp's reflector waver. I held my breath, watching it closely. The flame continued to tremble, ever now and then turning yellow at the edge.

It could mean only one thing: there was a draft coming down the crawlway.

As tightly wedged in as I was, I managed to roll over onto my side and look back toward the turn. Less than ten feet away I could see the dark shadow of an opening in the roof. Somehow I must have missed it as I came through. I reached behind me in a frenzy for the helmet and wormed my way, feet first, back up the tunnel, sliding into position underneath the opening. My heart pounding, I looked up inside the chimney.

Any hope I'd had of finding another way out evaporated

instantly. A mass of gray flowstone drapery hung down above my head, partly blocking the flue. Behind it, a large boulder sealed off the top of the shaft completely.

I stared up in desolation.

Then I began to see shapes in the folds of the flowstone: the bend of a ragged-trousered knee, a head sunken between hunched shoulders, an inky recess that from a certain angle suggested a mouth shrieking with laughter.

It was just like the Rorschach.

And then lower down, a blunt formation that reminded me absurdly of an old boot . . .

I was laughing myself now, uncontrollably.

There was writing on the sole of the boot. It was upside down, etched in phosphorescence – a U.S. Army serial number.

He was hanging from his wrists; the boulder that blocked the top of the shaft had trapped both his hands. It must have fallen back and crushed them as he tried to push it away. Afterward, he would have pulled himself up into the chimney, perhaps to go on pushing with his head and shoulders in a vain attempt at freeing his shattered hands, or simply to take the weight off his wrists. How long had he stayed alive, I wondered, hanging there like that?

Poor Begley – all bunched together, the knees drawn up to his chest, his head fallen forward, a bundle of bone and rags suspended from his upstretched arms like a sleeping bat. Except for the hands, the skeleton appeared to be intact. What I could see of it was covered with wizened, pumice-gray skin, preserved by the constant temperature of the cave. The glaze of phosphorus, the semblance of petrification no longer concealed from me the horror and agony of his death. Now I understood why I'd reacted so strongly under hypnosis whenever Somerville had tried to find out what had happened to him. Print would have been better off dying in the whirlpool. Yet it was strange: confronted with the gruesome evidence of an ordeal that I believed had been mine, I felt neither pity, nor revulsion, nor fear – only a determination to succeed this time where I had failed before.

Closing my eyes, I prayed to God, as I hadn't done since I was a child, and asked for strength.

Then I pulled myself into a sitting position and slowly squeezed up into the chimney beside Print's skeleton. There wasn't room for both of us at the top of the shaft; I had to get him out of there before I could take his place. His body came easily away, snapping off at the wrists with a dry, brittle squawk. It unfolded against me, surprisingly light and small, then clattered to the floor, where it lay in a moldering heap. I shoved it along with my feet to create more space, then reached up to tackle the boulder.

I was still feeling stiff and sore after the long crawl, and it took me a while to get used to standing again. But I discovered at once that I had a considerable advantage over Begley: I must have been nearly a foot taller than he was. Not being able to stand up straight inside the shaft, I could get a better leverage on the rock.

At first I tried to raise it with just my hands; it barely moved. Then, getting my head and the top of my shoulders underneath it, I slowly took the strain and straightened up inch by inch till I reached a standing position. The rock lifted, and a cool draft of air faintly scented with limestone was drawn into the chimney. I pushed now with every ounce of strength I possessed. Then suddenly I heard a loud rumbling, and for a moment I was afraid the roof would cave in. But the weight had gone, the boulder had rolled back – and I was looking up at the dim outline of a low vaulted ceiling.

I pulled myself up on the rim of the chimney until my head and shoulders were through the opening, then clambered out onto the floor of a narrow chamber. It was little more than a temporary widening of a stream passage. Along the length of the far wall a broad, dark river, which had reached this point independently of the route that I had taken, sped on silently down a smooth tunnel of sculptured rock.

I followed the stream a little way by the path that ran beside it. Stopping, I stood near the edge and looked down into the water, trying to gauge its depth beneath the reflections that the beam of my lamp sent shivering across the surface. I felt a breath of wind against my cheek. The air tasted sweet and carried a fragrance of blossom ... At that moment I became conscious of someone standing behind me on the path.

I swung around. There was no one.

Then, unaccountably, my headlamp spluttered and went out.

I reached for the flashlight in the hip pocket of my coveralls, but as my eyes became accustomed to the darkness I realized that I didn't need a lamp anymore. Ahead now, as though looking down the wrong end of a telescope, I could make out a faint circle of light and the cold glint of the river flowing toward the mouth of the cave.

BOOK FIVE

LEST
DARKNESS
COME

ONE

FILE   Martin Gregory
DATE   November 20
TAPE   G/M h3
SUBJECT Conversation with Anna Gregory

On Friday evening the patient's wife called and asked if she could come see me early in the week. She sounded anxious, almost distraught, on the phone and requested more than once that I say nothing to her husband about her getting in touch with me again. Explained to her that since I've had no contact with the patient for more than a month – apart from a note he'd sent letting me know that he did not wish to continue treatment I was pretty much out of the picture, but that if she felt I could help in any way, I'd be glad to talk with her.

According to the G.P., Mrs Gregory returned from Europe three weeks ago – as soon as she heard what had happened – and went straight home to be with her husband, who by then had moved back to Westchester. Dr Heyworth examined the patient shortly after his return from Kentucky, found nothing physically wrong with him apart from a few minor cuts and bruises, but felt that his behavior, although normal on the surface, was very disturbed. He called Mrs Gregory in Vienna and told her that in his opinion her husband's accident was a suicide attempt, and that he didn't think it advisable that he continue to live alone. Finding some pretext, Heyworth was able to examine the patient a second time during a social visit to the Gregorys. On this occasion he tried to persuade him to resume therapy, but without much success. At my suggestion, he also raised the possibility of Voluntary Admission. Apparently this provoked a violent outburst.

Heyworth's main concern seems to be the welfare of the patient's wife; he told me recently that he was becoming increasingly worried about her. Referred to her as 'a sensitive creature, very highly strung, not up to the strain of coping with her husband's illness'. He feels there's a real danger of *her* having a breakdown. In spite of this, I found Mrs Gregory much improved – Heyworth certainly has a tendency to be overprotective where she is concerned – but there was no question that the situation at home has deteriorated.

N.B. An informal discussion; the proceedings have been written up accordingly. Excerpts from the tape reproduced verbatim.

Notes/Transcript
Section A (123–287)

R.M.S.: ... We'll get on to that in a moment. Does he seem particularly depressed?

ANNA: Not depressed so much. I'm not sure how to describe it.

R.M.S.: Withdrawn?

ANNA: He seems, yes, well, more contained in himself. But things aren't easy between us. I didn't expect them to be easy. I thought after that morning at the airport – I thought I'd never be able to face him again. I really believed it was the end for us. Did he tell you what he did?

R.M.S.: What made you change your mind?

ANNA: I realized that he needed me, that I still love him. It's so wonderful to have him home. He's home all the time now. He's on a long vacation. Only sometimes – it feels like I'm living there with a person I don't know. Even the house feels different.

R.M.S.: What do you mean?

ANNA: He doesn't confide in me the way he used to. But it's more than that. He won't go out, he won't have people in – not even our old friends. He doesn't bother about the way he dresses anymore. Sometimes he goes into New York wearing his gardening clothes. He's grown a beard. People in the village stare at him, but he doesn't care.

R.M.S.: How often does he come to New York?

ANNA: Once or twice a week.

R.M.S.: Do you know why?

ANNA: I'm not sure. He says it's business. Otherwise he never leaves the house, except last thing at night he takes a walk around the garden. When I first got back, he used to come shopping with me in the village. Not anymore. Last weekend I tried to get him to take me out to dinner at a little restaurant we both like. I booked a table and got all dressed up and everything, but he wouldn't budge.

R.M.S.: What does he do with himself all day?

ANNA: He goes around the house checking doors and windows, checking the alarm system – he had a new one put in while I was away. I hate to think what it must have cost to install. He showed me how it all works, but I still haven't got the hang of it. The house is like a fortress. He's become obsessed by security. I mean, what have we got to protect? I asked him that and he said he just wanted me to feel safe.

R.M.S.: Does he keep the alarm on during the day?

ANNA: It's on the whole time. Yes. Now he wants to get new dogs.

R.M.S.: Does he?

ANNA: Guard dogs. Dobermans! I hate them. We had a big argument about it . . . He seemed surprised that I should mind so much.

R.M.S.: Does he ever mention Claus or Caesar?

ANNA: Never.

R.M.S.: Tell me more about how he spends his days.

ANNA: He says he's working on a writing project. But I don't know. He works up in the attic, and he keeps the door to the attic locked, *bolted* – even when he's in there. He's moved some of his things up there. That's where he'd been sleeping while I was away. He still sleeps there sometimes.

R.M.S.: In the attic?

ANNA: Yes, when he doesn't want to be disturbed. If I want to talk to him, I have to knock on the door at the bottom of the attic stairs and he comes down. He won't let me up.

R.M.S.: I see.

ANNA: I asked him for the key one day, so the cleaning woman could get in and dust. He got upset; he said he didn't want *anybody* to go up there *ever*! He was really furious. Then later he came down and said he was sorry. I'm worried about him, Dr Somerville. I get the feeling that . . . Dr Somerville, why did my husband go down the cave?

*

253

Rather than attempt to review the whole case, or outline the 'mythical' background to the incident in the cave, I explained it to her in broad, symbolic terms – i.e., as a voyage of exploration the patient had felt compelled to undertake through the subterranes of his own psyche. She seemed more or less to accept this, but wanted to know if besides acting out 'some dark and morbid fantasy', he'd had a more tangible reason for nearly getting himself killed: she feels quite unable to share Dr H.'s view that it was a suicide attempt. Without going into irrelevant detail, I could only answer that it was a search for self-knowledge and as such an end in itself. While agreeing that her husband had not tried to kill himself on this occasion, I made it clear that I was far from sanguine about his future intentions. By her own account – and I pointed this out to her – the impetus of the patient's paranoia seems to be gathering a dangerous momentum.

Suggested as tactfully as possible the coming need for institutional care and treatment. Mrs Gregory became very upset; refused point-blank to discuss.

Section B (369–522)

R.M.S.: ... Fine, but if you won't accept the fact that Martin needs professional help, why did you bother to come see me?

ANNA: You're the one he talks to.

R.M.S.: Not for some time now.

ANNA: I thought you could advise me what to do.

R.M.S.: Did you ask him why he quit therapy?

ANNA: He said he felt it was a waste of his time. I know that Bill – Dr Heyworth – tried to get him to go back to you, but ...

R.M.S.: Do you support that?

ANNA: Yes. Look, *I* can't help him. He won't let me.

R.M.S.: I'm afraid that makes two of us.

ANNA: Oh, God, he just needs to talk to someone. You *have* to help him, Dr Somerville.

R.M.S.: I'd like to, Anna ... you don't mind if I call you Anna, do, you?

ANNA: Please. Just tell me that you'll help him.

R.M.S.: I'm afraid it may be too late for me to help him.

ANNA: What do you mean too late? How can it be too late?

R.M.S.: I have to ask you a few more questions before I can explain. I need to ask about your personal life. If you find this at all awkward ...

ANNA: I'll tell you.

R.M.S.: How old are you?

ANNA: Twenty-eight. Last ... month was my birthday.

R.M.S.: You look much younger. Have you always worn your hair so short?

ANNA: What? Oh, no, I had it cut just before I went away. It used to be long – down to here.

R.M.S.: It's very becoming, Anna. Was it Martin's idea that you get it cut short?

ANNA: No, it was mine.

R.M.S.: I see ... Did Martin make any comment?

ANNA: No.

R.M.S.: You don't wear makeup, do you?

ANNA: Look, I don't see what ... Martin doesn't like me to put anything on my face. He wants me to look 'natural'. I really don't see what this has to do with anything.

R.M.S.: How has he treated you since you got back from Europe?

ANNA: I told you, we're not as close.

R.M.S.: What about sex?

ANNA: That too.

R.M.S.: You mean –

ANNA: Is this really necessary?

R.M.S.: Yes, I'm afraid it is.

ANNA: He hasn't slept with me since I came home. Oh, we sleep in the same bed – usually – but he never touches me. At first I thought it was because he was worried about how I felt – after what happened. But it isn't that.

R.M.S.: Perhaps *you* should take the initiative. Have you thought of that?

ANNA: I'd really rather not discuss it, Dr Somerville, if you don't mind.

R.M.S.: I understand.

ANNA: What did you mean when you said it was too late to help Martin?

R.M.S.: Tell me about your house in the country.

ANNA: The *house?*

R.M.S.: You told me it feels 'different' ... Please, it might be important.

ANNA: Well, it's an old farmhouse. It sits on top of a hill – it's very pretty, really – with trees all around. It's just a typical New England farmhouse – Victorian, made of wood. It has five bedrooms – no, *six.* Much too big for us, of course, but ...

R.M.S.: Yes, go on.

ANNA: We had it painted a rusty sort of red with a white trim. The proportions are rather odd, but there's an entrance porch with lovely twisting pillars, and there's a long veranda in back, and a bay window that looks out across the valley.

R.M.S.: How many floors?

ANNA: Two. And the attic.

R.M.S.: It sounds charming. Does it have turrets or a belvedere? A lot of those Victorian houses do.

ANNA: Not really a turret. There's a widow's walk, and a cupola in the middle of it with windows all around. Is that what you mean? It's a hexagonal – I think that's what Martin said.

R.M.S.: Is it difficult to get up there?

ANNA: You just go up through the attic. There's a ladder – if you want to climb up inside the cupola, or go out on the roof. The view is wonderful.

R.M.S.: The cupola's directly over the attic, then?

ANNA: Yes, it gives a good light. That's why Martin likes to work up there. There's a butcher-block table right underneath it; that's probably where he's sitting right now. It's so peaceful. You look up and all you see is sky – on all sides, sky. Why are you asking me this?

R.M.S.: Just bear with me a little longer, Anna. Tell me about the roof. Is there any kind of ornamentation? Ironwork, crestings, figures, motifs – anything like that?

ANNA: The widow's walk has an iron railing around it. And I think the top of the cupola does too. That's where we put the TV antenna. Oh, and there's a weathervane ...

R.M.S.: Is that above the cupola also?

ANNA: The other end of the walk.

R.M.S.: By any chance is it rather an unusual design?

ANNA: How did you know?

R.M.S.: Sickle-shaped, like a crescent moon lying on its back?

ANNA: Did Martin tell you about it?

R.M.S.: In a way ... yes, he told me.

ANNA: Then why are you asking *me?* I don't understand.

R.M.S.: And the weathervane, is it made of copper, covered with verdigris? Is it a greenish color?

ANNA: *No!* How should *I* know what it's made of? It's painted black, the same as the iron railing. It spins around, points north, points south – wherever the wind blows. Just like any *other* weathervane.

R.M.S.: I want you to think carefully now, Anna. In the past few months has Martin mentioned the weathervane to you at all?

ANNA: Mentioned the weathervane? No, of course not.

R.M.S.: You're quite sure?

ANNA: Positive.

R.M.S.: If he does ever mention it, in any context whatsoever, I want you to get in touch with me right away. Is that understood?

ANNA: Look, you're going to have to tell me what this is all about.

R.M.S.: In just a moment.

ANNA: *Now.*

R.M.S.: Will you promise to do that?

ANNA: Not until you tell me what this is all about.

R.M.S.: I'm afraid that Martin is seriously ill, Anna. He needs help. He needs the kind of help that I couldn't give him now, even if he'd let me. That's what I meant when I said it was too late. You came here to ask my advice, Anna. *Sign* a petitioner form so that he can be admitted to a hospital where he will receive the complete psychiatric care and treatment that he so desperately needs.

ANNA: I don't even want to hear about it.

R.M.S.: In that case I think you should move out of the house as soon as possible. For your own safety.

ANNA: I won't leave him.

R.M.S.: Very well, then. But please try to remember what I said – get in touch with me immediately if –

ANNA: All right, all right.

R.M.S.: If he says *anything* about it at all. Do you promise?

ANNA: All right, I promise.

R.M.S.: One more question. Does he keep a light burning in the attic? A candle, a lamp, any kind of naked flame?

ANNA: I've seen a light up in the cupola, yes. I remember I thought it was a star the first time I saw it, only it was a cloudy night. Why? What does it mean?

R.M.S.: It means that he has taken something of value which belongs to me.

TWO

*Monday, November 20

11.30 p.m. – Anna seemed subdued tonight. Barely said a word at dinner that I didn't have to drag out of her. It's the first time she's been into the city since she came back, and I was sure she'd want to tell me about her little excursion. I'd encouraged her to make the trip; I thought it would do her good to get out of the house. Apparently not. The only information she volunteered was that she'd had lunch with Sheila at McMullen's . . . I asked her how she'd spent the rest of the day – she didn't get back here till 7. She mentioned some stores and a couple of galleries. But I could feel her resentment, as if she sensed that I was making her account for her time. Can I really blame her?

Of course, I know perfectly well what happened. She went to see Bill Heyworth and doesn't want to tell me because they talked about 'my Problem', and it made her depressed. She didn't eat much, either, which is unusual for her. I asked if anything was the matter. She said she had a headache and felt exhausted, so I sent her up to bed.

They delivered the safe this afternoon – a 400-pound field-gray 'Key and Combo Knight' from Acme, to replace that piece of crap I bought at the hardware store in the village. The men didn't arrive until 4.30, and it took the two of them nearly half an hour to get it up the stairs with a hand truck. They weren't exactly overjoyed when I told them where I wanted it.

The 'Knight' is a tough-looking mother. Stalwart hinges, self-snap handle, top and bottom locking bolts, all heavy-gauge steel. I had them put it behind the cistern and bolt it to the floor. Before they left, the older of the two men ceremoniously handed me a

*Extract from Martin Gregory's diary

sealed envelope containing the combination, which I immediately memorized. The key has joined the others at the ring on my belt.

I can relax now. I made the transfer and all is well. The logo over the dial has a man in armor holding up a naked sword. Seems just right. Total cost works out at around $850. Worth every cent.

All I have to do now is link up the safe to the alarm system. Ademco has what it calls an 'under-the-carpet switch mat', which might do the trick. Better, though more expensive, is its '450 Ultrasonic Motion Detector', which would protect the whole attic. I could even install a separate control up here. Since I'm going to be around Canal Street tomorrow, I might as well drop by and get an estimate.

When that's all done, the house should be damn near impregnable. Who knows? I may even end up being able to lead a normal life again. Go out, find a new job – maybe something around here. Sooner or later I'm going to have to, if only for practical reasons.

But sometimes I wonder. When I think of the last time I went shopping with Anna: those women at the I.G.A., trading whispers in the pet-food aisle, staring at us, pointing with their barnacled old fingers. How did they find out? Who told them? Not Anna, for sure. That nurse woman who took care of Anna after I killed the dogs? The mailman? Heyworth maybe? Whenever I do go into the village now – and it's only to get to the railroad station – there's always somebody giving me queer looks. I pretend not to notice, try not to feel threatened.

I know Somerville would say that I'm just being paranoid, that I'm suffering from some kind of persecution complex. But what does he know? I can't afford to take any chances. I'm not ready yet. I don't feel strong enough.

I brought back *certain knowledge* from Kentucky. Yet I still find it difficult to accept what has happened. Was I really chosen? Print Begley would certainly have seen it that way. No accident that he died and I was born at the precise moment when the fire storm burst over Hiroshima. But chosen for what? To *warn* people? In the thirty-six years we have lived in Hiroshima's shadow, lived with the constant threat of annihilation only minutes away, the power of the world's nuclear arsenal has grown a millionfold.

People know this, and they know that the next time will be the last time – and that like the first, there will be no warning. But no one can be expected to take seriously what he cannot imagine. If I were to look into the crystal now and foresee the end of the world, what good would it do? Who would *believe* me? No, I was chosen to bear another – a far greater responsibility.

I must admit the idea takes a lot of getting used to. Doubt is the one weak spot in my defenses.

There are days – and today was one of them – when I just can't deal with it. When I woke up this morning and saw Anna beside me in the bed, still asleep, she looked so like a child, so *trusting*, I had to think, Well maybe I did go crazy down there in the hole.

Poor Anna! I do still love her, but as a person in my life she seems reduced somehow. It's as if I can only see her now from a great distance.

THREE

*Tuesday, November 21

Midnight – It's been nearly a week. I wonder if Penelope will notice the difference – that I'm growing stronger. Can I really do it this time? Break with her once and for all? It'll be like cutting my last tie with the outside world. Maybe I'd find it easier if I didn't think of it that way. Now more than ever I must be firm. This *has* to end.

I don't have any real feeling for her. It's just sex. Nothing more. And I'm pretty sure that's mutual. Despite her act. Think of it this way: saying goodbye to Penelope will mean that I've *finally* severed all connection with Somerville.

It was Penelope's idea to move the beds into the window. Soon after I got back from Kentucky – I didn't make a note of this at the time for fear of Anna's getting hold of my diary – we started using Mulberry Street as a meeting place. That awful little room!

We pushed the beds up alongside each other against the wall where the table used to stand, and I lashed the frames together with rope I brought out of the cave, transforming those creaky iron twins into a high, swaybacked double. It's comfortable enough – though we've never spent the night there – and fits neatly into the window alcove. Penelope even asked Mrs Lombardi to provide the right-size bedclothes. It was Mrs L. who suggested spreading a blanket under the bottom sheet so that we wouldn't feel the join between the mattresses.

We moved the screen out from the corner and pulled it around the front of the bed – the way they do in a hospital ward when doctors come to examine a patient – creating a sort of makeshift cubicle, a room within a room. We took down the drapes from the narrow dormer window to let in more light, and set the TV on a chair at the foot of the bed. .

*Extract from Martin Gregory's diary

She likes to lie up there in the window on top of the covers, usually stark naked, one hand curled between her thighs, staring out over those squalid warehouse roofs, I watch her from behind the screen sometimes. I see the view and Penelope in it, her alabaster tail exposed like a roadside shrine under a wide margin of sky.

She makes a great deal of noise *in extremis*, so we have to leave the TV on while we're screwing ... How can I pretend that I'm indifferent to her when I'm sitting here right now with a colossal hard-on? I can hear her howl in my ears. She's getting hot; she begins to shiver all over like someone with fever. I don't see how she can fake *that*: it makes her look ugly, for one thing, with her livid tongue lolling out of the corner of her mouth, lips all frothy with white stuff and her skin just burning up. And afterward, when those tiny droplets start to form around her nostrils and in the hollows of her eyes, and every crease and fold of her body begins to run with sweat ...

It's no good; I have to stop this. Time to do the rounds.

12.20 a.m. – All clear.

FOUR

Even before I learned where it had come from, the rose made me suspicious – a single red rose in a glass balanced on the window ledge over the bed. It filled the alcove with a sweet, cloying smell. I felt like throwing it out, only I didn't want to upset Penelope. I don't know why, but suddenly I got the feeling that Somerville was up to something. Penelope claimed that he didn't know about us, but she insisted too much. He knew everything, that old fraud – watched every move I made through her eyes.

There was a note on the pillow saying he had asked her to work late, and that she'd come to me as soon as she could get away.

The arrangement we had, if either one of us couldn't make it or got held up for any reason, was to leave a message with Mrs Lombardi. Why bother to trek halfway across town when a simple phone call would have done the job? Mrs Lombardi was always home.

While I waited for her, I checked the room to see if anything had been disturbed: not that I kept much there now, but a couple of weeks ago I noticed that someone had gone through the bureau drawers. At the time, I just assumed it was Mrs Lombardi snooping around. But now I wondered.

Penelope appeared at 7, an hour and a half late. I'd fallen asleep waiting for her, and she woke me with her mouth.

After we'd made love, I asked her about the note. She said she'd been lunching with a friend nearby, at Angelo's, and that it had seemed 'just as easy' to stop by the house. Besides, she felt embarrassed always using the landlady as a go-between. And didn't I think the rose particularly beautiful? She'd picked it herself that morning from Somerville's garden. Odd: I couldn't remember ever seeing any flowers growing there; but I said nothing.

The interesting thing is that I almost believed her.

We made love again, more intensely than before, the noise she made drowning out everything. I saw then the extent to which I had allowed myself to become enthralled by her. The affair was not going to be so easy to terminate.

We usually didn't talk much after we'd had sex. We'd lie together in front of that blazing TV until it was almost too late for me to catch the train, so that there was always a last-minute dash to Grand Central. But tonight was different. Penelope was in a strange mood – talking about Kentucky, and what a lucky escape I'd had, and how if she hadn't called the motel and told them I must still be down the cave, I'd never have come out alive. It was as if she wanted to remind me that she'd saved my life.

I was only half-listening. My head was between her legs, and her open flesh was spreading like a soothing compress against the back of my neck. I tried to think of the right words to tell her that I couldn't see her ever again.

'What happened after you found Print Begley's remains?' she asked. 'You've never really told me, you know.' She squeezed her legs together to get my attention. 'Martin?' I felt a little gush of warmth against my neck.

'I don't *remember* what happened. Why do you keep asking? If I knew I'd tell you.' More than ever now I was conscious that anything I might say to Penelope would be duly reported to Somerville.

'You must remember *something*.'

'I already told you what I know.'

'Then tell me again.'

I drew a deep breath and wearily recited: 'I pushed back the stone. I climbed up into the vaulted chamber with the river running through it and started to walk along the path. I was following the river downstream. I thought I saw a circle of light at the end of the passage, where the river seemed to flow out of the cave. I was walking toward the light when my lamp went out. That's when I realized I didn't need it anymore – I could *see* ... All of which I've told you. And that's the last thing I remember. Only now I can't be sure that the circle of light at the end of the passage wasn't just the beam of a flashlight from the rescue party. The next thing I knew, I was lying on a stretcher being carried up to the surface.'

'But they didn't find you near any river.'

'What difference does it make where they found me?'

Penelope reached forward and clasped her hands around my forehead. 'You could remember if you wanted to. He could help you to remember.'

'No.'

'He's worried about you, Martin.'

'I said *no*, for Christ's sake!'

'He really wants to see you. Just to talk. You don't have to be hypnotized again if you don't want.'

'Why is he so worried about me *now* all of a sudden? It's been more than a month and I haven't heard a word from him.' I didn't count Heyworth's misguided attempt to persuade me to commit myself, though I was sure Somerville had a lot to do with that.

'I think he was hoping that *you* would get in touch with *him* ...'

'I quit therapy. Remember? Didn't he show you the letter I wrote him? I quit therapy the same day I quit my job. Everyone thinks I'm on vacation, but I quit. Even if I wanted to see him now, I couldn't afford it.'

'You wouldn't have to pay him anything. He sincerely wants to help.'

'Bullshit!'

'Why don't you at least *talk* to him?'

'There wouldn't be any point; he wouldn't hear what I was saying.'

She pulled my head back against her. '*I* can hear you.'

'Look, I'm fine. I don't need help. So I can't remember. Maybe I'm not supposed to ...'

'What do you mean by that?'

'I found what I was looking for. I had to hide it from them – the cavers, the people at the motel, all those old fossils in the bus party. I had to hide it from everyone until I knew it was quite safe.'

'Hide what?'

'I guess there's no reason I can't tell you now. You're the only person I *can* tell. I brought it back, Penelope – I've *got* the crystal! ... And you can pass that on to *Dr* Somerville.'

She said nothing.

'Do you *realize* what this means?'

Penelope didn't answer. The back of my head suddenly felt unprotected. I looked around at her. She was sitting very still, her head erect like an alert bird's, staring at me.

'Tell me,' she said.

'All I remember is that moment in the cave when I first understood that my journey had been successful. It was while they were bringing me back up on the stretcher. I must have lost consciousness. I came to in the middle of a steep pitch; the stretcher was at a crazy angle – my feet were up here somewhere – and I remember thinking, *'Do I have it safe?'* I wasn't even aware of having *seen* it yet. And I couldn't use my hands to check that it was there – I was strapped in so tight. But I could feel something, this weight lying on my chest. It was in one of the long inside pockets of my overalls. You can't even imagine what it was like – the sudden triumph of that realization: of knowing that I'd found it, that I'd finally got it back.'

Penelope gave a little sigh and leaned back against the pillows. 'What does it look like?'

'Exactly how I described it on the tape. It's the most beautiful thing I've ever seen.'

'What shape is it?'

'An obelisk, six-sided – all its motifs are repeated regularly in three dimensions. It's like a perfectly cut diamond, flawless, full of fire and –'

'Do you have it with you?'

'Are you mad?'

For a moment neither of us spoke. Then she said, 'Martin, there's something I have to tell you. I don't quite know how to put this.' She looked down, crossing her arms over her small, pointed breasts. '*I* believe you; I believe that you brought it out of the cave. I've always believed you – you know that. But I'm afraid there may be another explanation.'

'What are you talking about?'

'You know the chandelier that hangs over the stairs at Ninety-third Street? Don't be angry with me, please. The center pendant is missing. Dr Somerville thinks you took it.'

'*What?*' I burst out laughing. 'You can't be serious.'

'*He's* serious. He's not blaming you. He said you probably didn't know what you were doing at the time.'

'He must really think I'm crazy.'

'He just wants to help you.'

'But the pendant isn't even the right shape ... and I told you, the crystal's flawless. Don't you see? The lusters of a chandelier are always *pierced*. There are little holes at the end, so the wires can go through. That's what holds them together. The crystal is flawless.'

'I know it is.' She reached out her hand for mine. 'Maybe if you *showed* it to him, he'd believe you. Tell him what happened.'

'Forget it,' I snapped.

'Martin, *please*.'

'Why don't *you* tell him? *You* convince him.'

'I still think you should talk to him.'

'No.'

'You see, it's not just any chandelier. It's a very valuable antique, a family heirloom. Apparently it's made of the finest old Waterford crystal.'

'Oh, yeah? It looks like a piece of shit to me.'

'He wants it back, Martin.'

'He wants *what* back? I don't know what you're talking about.' I pulled my hand away.

Penelope lowered her eyes. 'He's – I'm afraid of what'll happen.'

'Why? What's he going to do? Call the cops on me? Tell them one of his patients stole a piece of his lousy chandelier? Come off it!'

'You don't understand; he has the power –'

'You think he can afford *that* kind of publicity? He may be a total quack, but he's no fool.'

'Martin, let's go away together. Tonight. I have money. Let's just take off – we could go to California, Mexico ...'

I laughed.

She leaned forward and whispered fiercely in my ear. 'Then go yourself. It's not safe for you to stay.'

'Don't be absurd. I can't just leave. I have a wife at home.'

'Anna's hardly going to miss you.'

'It's got nothing to do with ... You know perfectly well why I can't go.' Unaccountably, I felt myself beginning to get hard again. I pulled a blanket over my lap so she wouldn't notice.

'I *don't* know.' She shook her head.

'We better get dressed,' I said 'Anna's expecting me to be home for dinner.'

But I didn't tell Penelope that I couldn't see her again; I just couldn't do it.

FIVE

*Wednesday, November 22

11.45 p.m. – At last I found what I was looking for, lying in a corner of the attic under a pile of old *Life* magazines – an encyclopedia of science I used as a kid when we were living in the Philippines. Page 251 of *The Wonderful World Around Us:*

> A crystal is a solid, or occasionally liquid substance in which atoms are arranged in a highly ordered structure, something like the framework of a skyscraper. Glass, on the other hand, is a chaos in which atoms or molecules have no ordered structure ... *Most chandeliers called 'crystal' are in fact cut glass with a high lead content.*

I'm going to clip this and send it to Somerville on a postcard. He's lying about the missing pendant. It's a ploy to get me back into therapy. He doesn't believe that I've got the crystal, and he knows I didn't take anything from his house. He just wants to goad me into some kind of reaction. Why can't he accept the idea that he's not needed anymore? ... Because it's true: I *don't* need him. I'm free of you, Somerville; finally and forever free of you!

Maybe Penelope's right; maybe we should go away together – before he tries something.

I've decided to sleep up here tonight. Anna had already gone to bed by the time I got back, and there's no point disturbing her.

2.10 a.m. – About half an hour ago I went down to the kitchen to fix myself a sandwich and a glass of milk. I wasn't able to sleep; I just lay there thinking about Penelope, and the rose ...

After I'd eaten, as I was closing the refrigerator door, I got a sudden urge to run upstairs and check the crystal – just to see it again and feel that cold, reassuring weight in my hand.

*Extract from Martin Gregory's diary

I turned off the alarm system at the control panel under the stairs and came back up here. I went right to the safe and unlocked it; took the crystal, still wrapped in its leather cloth, and climbed out through the cupola onto the roof. It was beautiful out, a classic fall night, cold and clear. The sky, a deep fluorescent blue, was sown through with stars. Looking out across the valley, I stood and breathed it all in; then I removed the crystal from its cloth and held it up to the night, just as Magnus had done that other time. I saw again how it caught the light of the stars, reflecting their faint glittering rays through all its facets and prisms until they seemed to converge along the length of its central plane in a silvery filament of incredible luminosity. For a long time I just stood there contemplating its beauty.

As I watched, the crystal seemed to grow colder in my hand. The silver filament of starlight became brighter, almost incandescent, then so brilliant suddenly that I could no longer bear to look at it and I had to shield my eyes with my free arm. I realized then that all the light of the universe was concentrated in my hand and that I was holding the crystal up as a torch to the darkness which would otherwise engulf the whole of creation.

At that moment I knew that I'd been chosen for this purpose. I'd been called again to be the light-bearer, as the ancient Kendals – guardians of the Valley and keepers of the Crystal – had been called before me until that fateful night long ago when I betrayed their sacred trust. I'd been called in time of urgent danger to keep alight the flame of consciousness among men and, by the power of the crystal, to prevent the nuclear holocaust which threatened to bring about the extinction of all life on earth.

I felt totally isolated by the awesome responsibility that was mine; yet I was also filled with joy and an exhilarating sense of my own destiny. I, Martin Gregory, had been chosen to be the saviour of mankind.

For the first time in my life I saw clearly what it was I had to do ... And I understood then that love, the chronic need to link the futilities of life to the Infinite, is nothing more than the desire to be alone.

Standing there on the roof, the flame burning in the tower behind me, the dark crescent of the horned moon outlined against the sky, I realized that it can have been no accident that Anna and I came to live in this house; and no accident either that I was allowed to bring the crystal back from Lost Hope. The conditions for my ascendancy to the Kendalship have been re-created here in Bedford, but my dominion, and the sphere of the crystal's influence, extend now to all the world.

SIX

*Thursday, November 23

10.30 p.m. – About 7.30 tonight I went downstairs to take a bath. Anna usually has her bath around 7 and I just assumed that she'd be in the kitchen preparing dinner. The door to the bathroom was closed. Lately we've been respecting each other's privacy, so to speak. Anyway, not realizing she was still in there, I entered without knocking.

Anna was standing in front of the washbasin, putting on make-up. As our eyes met in the mirror, she gave me a guilty smile. 'Only a little mascara,' she said quickly. 'Do you want me to run your bath?'

Over her shoulder, I noticed the cord of my electric shaver hanging down from the inside of the medicine cabinet. I noticed it because since I've stopped shaving I don't keep it there anymore.

'I'll do it,' I said, coming up behind her. She stepped aside so that I could reach over to turn on the faucets. She was wearing her long white terry-cloth robe, but hadn't tied it properly, so that when she moved out of my way it slid open for a second below the waist. I caught a glimpse of her smooth, pinkish thighs, still flushed from the bath, and the fluffy blond triangle I used to call her golden fleece. Maybe because I no longer feel any desire for her, or because I really was trying not to look, the impression of her nakedness hardly registered. But there was something poignant, almost pathetic about the way Anna hurried to cover herself up. I felt so sorry for her.

God knows, I love her. Only not in that way. Not anymore.

Anna had obviously made a big effort over dinner. She'd even gotten all dressed up for it, as if we were celebrating some special

* Extract from Martin Gregory's diary

occasion. But she seemed nervous and drank more than usual, which put her in an embarrassingly flirtatious mood. It made me very uncomfortable. When I told her I was coming up here to do some work, she looked disappointed and asked me with a wistful smile not to be too long.

11.15 p.m – Strong wind blowing. Cold out. I've made the rounds, checked the safe. All clear. But I still can't shake the feeling that something's missing.

SEVEN

'Your hands are frozen. Are you sure you're warm enough?'

'Just hold me, Martin.'

'I could turn the heat up.'

'Hold me. Don't get out of bed.'

'It feels like winter in here.' I made a little show of snuggling up to her, nuzzling the nape of her neck. 'Listen to that wind.'

'I always think, when it blows like this, one of the trees is going to fall on the house.'

I hugged her, and she turned around in bed so that we were facing each other. Holding her face between my hands, I kissed her gently on the lips. They tasted of the wine she'd been drinking. There was no way out now, and I wanted her not to have to make the first move. But she didn't respond. I kissed her again, this time slipping my tongue into her mouth. It came up against the bar of her clenched teeth.

'Is something the matter?' I whispered.

'It's not that. It's just that it's been so long.'

'Come on, baby.'

She leaned up onto one elbow and looked at me, her eyes wide open, earnestly searching my face.

'Do you still love me, Martin?'

'What kind of a question is that? For Christ's sake, you *know* I do.'

'Something's happened between us.'

'I haven't felt like it lately, that's all. Would it help if I turned out the light?'

'Maybe you'd better,' she said shyly. Sitting up in bed, she began to tug at the hem of her nightgown, which had rucked up beneath her. As she worked the gown over the top of her head, I watched how her breasts, caught in the gathered folds of the red flannel, were drawn upward for a moment before they dropped loosely into view. Feeling no stir of desire, I turned over and reached for the light. Perhaps in the dark it would be easier.

A branch of wisteria blew against the window, tapping out a brief, halting rhythm on the glass.

'What's that noise?' Anna shivered and drew closer.

'Nothing. It's the wind.'

She felt for my hand, pulled it to her breasts. I trailed my fingers lightly back and forth across the tips of her nipples. Dutifully I put one and then the other into my mouth, sucking them into little crusted erections. She began to moan softly and, taking charge of my hand again, guided it down across the slope of her belly.

I pretended to be impatient now, wanting to hide from her my lack of interest. I slid my tongue into her ear and grabbed down hard between her legs.

'Oh, my God!' I heard the sharp intake of breath. Her knees fell open and she strained upward with her pelvis.

I felt a jolt go through me and pulled my hand back.

'What the ... *Anna!*' I gasped. '*Anna, what have you done?*'

'I ... I don't understand.'

'It's gone.'

'What do you mean? What's gone?'

'You shaved your hair.'

'Martin, *please*,' she whispered.

'But ... it's impossible.' I'd seen it only moments before, when she was taking off her nightgown; and in the bathroom before dinner – her golden fleece. Then I remembered the razor cord dangling from the medicine cabinet.

'I have to turn the light on.'

'No, don't,' she said. 'It's nothing. You're imagining things. Here.' She took my hand and pulled it back down between her legs, trapping it there with her thighs.

I touched her again. She squirmed under my fingers.

I was getting an erection.

She laughed, a laugh that I hardly recognized.

'Anna, wait.' I tried to get up.

'Just lie still. Let me ...'

She throws a leg over mine, crawls over on top of me, straddles both my legs. Then, standing on her knees, kneeling over me, she begins to ease herself down, whimpering, dribbling saliva onto my chest. It's difficult at first, she's so incredibly tight.

I slip a finger into the sticky cleft of her buttocks, and pull her down fiercely on top of me. She lets out a sweet piglike squeal.

Suddenly afraid, I reach up to feel the shape of her face, her ears, the corners of her mouth, the soft spikes of her hair – just to make sure it's still Anna.

She begins to post, rising up and down in the darkness above me, slowly at first, almost gently.

She finds her pace, settles into a steady rhythm; our hands rest lightly on each other's shoulders.

But something keeps turning inside my head, whirling around, each revolution coinciding with the measured slap of our bodies' coming together.

I begin to feel dizzy – the darkness is spinning, wheeling inexorably on the axis of my prick. We're moving now as one, gathering speed.

Then I begin to hear – cutting through everything – the faint whir and squeak of unaligned metal parts.

It was coming from above. Immediately I thought of the safe, the crystal: somebody was trying to break into the attic through the roof!

'Listen,' I whispered. 'Anna, listen!' I pulled her down by her shoulders and held her still.

'What is it?'

'That noise! Can't you hear it?'

'No, I can't hear anything.'

'But it's so loud. You *must* be able to hear it. It sounds like it's coming from the roof. Don't you hear that squeaking? *There!*'

'It's nothing.' She began to move again. 'Don't pay any attention to it.'

But I couldn't not. It was driving everything else out. She tried to cover my mouth with hers. Her tongue flailed wetly about my ears. I rolled over on top of her.

'What are you doing?' she moaned.

Already I'd lost interest. I felt myself growing soft inside her. 'It's no good, Anna. I'm sorry. I have to go.'

'Go *where?*'

I reached over and turned on the light. We looked at each other, blinking in the sudden glare. I started to get out of bed.

'I can hear it now,' she whispered, clinging to me. 'It's just a rusty hinge or something. It's probably that screen door on the porch. You know how it's always blowing open.'

'*That's* what it is – of course!' I tried to sound convinced; I didn't want to frighten her. 'But I'm not going to lie here and listen to that thing all night. It's driving me crazy. I won't be long.'

'Don't go, Martin,' she pleaded.

'I'll be right back, I promise.'

I pulled on my jeans and sweat shirt and went into the bathroom. I couldn't hear anything now. The house was quiet. Perhaps Anna was right and it *had* been the screen door after all. Only I was sure that noise had come from the roof. The TV antenna? At first there hadn't been any sound, just that spinning feeling inside my head. I'd felt the shadow of its horns, the horns of the moon, turning in the night.

Suddenly I realized what it was I'd heard, and I had to laugh.

Without turning on any lights, I went downstairs to the entrance hall and checked the alarm control panel. Everything in order. The tiny A.C. ON light glowed red, which meant the system was fully armed. If any intruder did try to break in through the roof – or any other part of the house, for that matter – the outdoor arc lights would come on, and the howler alarm, with any luck, would waken half the village.

But, of course, no system is foolproof.

Outside the door to the attic I stopped and listened. The wind had dropped. The noise from the roof seemed less now, but it was still that same relentless grinding sound, punctuated each time it went around by a sharp squeal like chalk scratching across a blackboard. It set my teeth on edge.

I had a little trouble locating the right key in the dark. When I did, I unlocked the door and, trying to tread quietly on the wooden stairs, went up into the attic.

Everything there seemed to be in order too. I checked the safe first, then climbed up inside the cupola.

At the top of the ladder that gives access to the roof, I stood peering out through the lancet windows into the blackness. There was no moon out, no stars. At the far end of the widow's walk I could just make out the gleaming horns of the weathervane silhouetted against the sky, revolving like a radar scanner through its prescribed arc. But almost silently now. The squeaking had stopped. The pivot probably just needed greasing, though I figured something was a bit off, either with the balance of the crescent or with the alignment of the compass sights beneath it: something was keeping the whole thing spinning around and preventing the pointer from holding steady, as it should, in the direction of the prevailing wind. I'd have to get someone to come and fix it in the morning. In the meantime all I could do was take it down off its pivot.

As I reached up to unfasten the window, the magnetic contacts under the latch caught my eye, and I remembered - just in time - that the alarm system was still activated. I was going to have to go downstairs first and turn it off at the control panel.

I started to climb back down the ladder.

Since there no longer seemed to be any danger, I turned on the reading lamp and, pulling back the hood of my sweat shirt, sat down in front of the butcher-block table to smoke a cigarette. I looked at my watch: ten to twelve. I decided to wait and see what happened when the wind came up again - if the gremlin in the weathervane would maybe go away by itself. I didn't feel much like going out on the roof.

I picked up the key ring from the table and began looking for the key to shut off the alarm. It was a hefty bunch - I had as many keys on that ring now as a janitor. None were labeled, but I knew them all by sight, and most of them by feel; it came as quite a surprise to discover a new addition.

I can't understand how I hadn't noticed it before. It wasn't even a key, but a thin silver amulet in the shape of a heart. I recognized it at once: it was one of the charms from the bracelet I'd bought for Anna at Kennedy Airport.

Penelope must have done it yesterday at Mrs Lombardi's, while I was asleep. But why? Why would she remove a charm from a bracelet I'd given her - if I really *did* give it to her - and thread it onto my key ring? Was it supposed to be some kind of joke? Or something to remind me of her? She was hardly the sentimental type.

I stubbed out my cigarette and started to work the charm off the ring.

Once I'd detached it, I worked at the hair-thin crack around the edge of the charm with a fingernail until it snapped open. A tiny cavity appeared between the two silver halves of the heart, and a little dark pill of desiccated vegetable matter rolled out on the table. It had an unpleasantly rancid odor. I crumbled it with the ball of my thumb and from a mess of seeds and petals – and God knows what else – extracted three minute coils of black hair.

EIGHT

FILE   Martin Gregory
DATE   November 23
TAPE   G/M b4
SUBJECT Telephone conversation with Anna Gregory – recorded
        at 11.47 p.m.

ANNA: Is Dr Somerville there, please?

P.T.: I'm afraid he's not available right now. Would you like to leave a message?

ANNA: I have to speak to him. It's urgent.

P.T.: I'm Dr Somerville's assistant. Perhaps I can help.

ANNA: I know it's late, but he said it would be all right to call anytime.

P.T.: May I have your name?

ANNA: Mrs Gregory. Anna Gregory.

P.T.: Are you a patient of Dr Somerville's?

ANNA: No, my husband is ... was. *Please!* This is an emergency.

P.T.: If you'll hold on, I'll see what I can do.

ANNA: *Please* hurry!

P.T.: Mrs Gregory? He'll be with you in just a second.

R.M.S.: Hello, Anna?

ANNA: Dr Somerville, thank God!

R.M.S.: Is something wrong?

ANNA: I don't know. It's Martin – I'm worried about him. You said get in touch with you right away if he –

R.M.S.: You're going to have to speak up, Anna. I can't hear you very well. Where are you?

ANNA: I'm at home. I don't have much time. He'll be coming back any minute.

R.M.S.: Which room are you in?

ANNA: I'm in the bedroom.

R.M.S.: Where is Martin?

ANNA: He went up to the attic. He was hearing noises coming from the roof – they were getting on his nerves. I pretended I could hear them too because I didn't want to upset him. He's been acting strangely all evening. I couldn't hear a *thing*, Dr Somerville.

R.M.S.: What kind of noises? Did he say?

ANNA: Like a whirring, squealing sound. I mean, it was all in his head, wasn't it, but then he seemed to ... oh, God.

R.M.S.: Listen carefully, Anna. I want you to leave the house *tonight* and come to New York.

ANNA: But you don't understand. Even if I wanted to leave I couldn't. The alarm system is on. Martin has the keys. If I open any of the doors or windows, it'll go off.

R.M.S.: Couldn't you make some excuse – tell him you feel like going for a drive or something?

ANNA: He wouldn't believe me.

R.M.S.: Then go to your neighbors'. Don't worry about setting off the alarm. Just get out of the house.

ANNA: But he's got the keys to the garage, and the car keys. The nearest people live a mile away ... I have to go now.

R.M.S.: Wait a moment.

ANNA: I can hear him on the stairs. He's coming back. I *have* to go. Goodbye.

R.M.S.: Wait, Anna. Let me have a word with him.

ANNA: With Martin? He won't speak to you.

R.M.S.: Tell him that *I* called *him* – that it's important.

ANNA: It won't work. Please ...

R.M.S.: Do as I say.

ANNA: Hold on, Dr Somerville, he's just coming ... Martin, it's for you.

MARTIN: Yeah, what is it?

R.M.S.: I know this is a little irregular, Martin, and I apologize for calling so late.

MARTIN: I have nothing to say to you, Somerville.

R.M.S.: Don't hang up just yet.

MARTIN: What do you want from me?

R.M.S.: I'm about to tell you. I have some good news for you, Martin. I think I may have had a breakthrough on our case. I was listening to the tapes again this evening, and I heard something at the end of the Magmel regression —

MARTIN: *Our* case? What are you talking about? I thought I'd made it clear to you that I'm not your patient anymore.

R.M.S.: I think it would be very much to your advantage if you listened to what I have to say, Martin.

MARTIN: I've heard it all before. There's nothing you can tell me that I want to hear.

R.M.S.: Why don't you just listen, Martin ... Try to relax.

MARTIN: I don't want to hear it. Now, let me *alone.*

NINE

The voices I'd heard as I was coming down the stairs: I didn't imagine them – they were real. But then I realized there was only one voice and it belonged to my wife. Very gently I opened the door to the bedroom. Anna was sitting on the edge of the bed hunched over the telephone. She looked up at me with an anxious little frown, hugging the receiver to her chest.

'It's for you.' She held the receiver out to me, the palm of her hand covering the mouthpiece.

'Who is it?'

'Dr Somerville.'

'For Christ's sake! What does *he* want? I don't want to talk to him.'

'Martin, please. He says it's important.' I noticed her hand was shaking.

'Is that what he says?' In spite of myself I was curious to know why he was calling. 'Oh, all right.'

I took the phone from her and sat down on the bed, hanging an arm across her shoulders, pulling her close.

'Yeah,' I said, 'what is it?'

We talked for a moment; then I heard a muffled sound of the receiver changing hands at the other end. I rose quickly from the bed and, picking up the phone, carried it as far away from Anna as the extension cord would allow.

'I know what you've been thinking,' Penelope whispered in my ear. 'Even when she was going around the ring and you were up there behind her in the saddle, you were thinking about us. Weren't you?'

'I don't know what you're talking about,' I said loudly.

'Oh, yes, you do. Don't deny it, Martin.' Penelope laughed. 'I just want you to know how happy I am that you and Anna are getting back together. You won't believe me when I tell you this,

Martin, but I'm the one responsible for everything that's happening between the two of you tonight.'

'I don't have to listen to this.'

'You found the charm, didn't you? When you opened it, I felt as if you were opening me, touching *me*. Martin, screw her good this time. Screw her for me. For *us* ...'

'I thought I made it clear that I didn't want to continue therapy.' I heard the tremor in my voice. 'I'm not your patient anymore. You have no right to keep pestering me.'

There was a crackle of static as if the connection were about to be broken. Then the line cleared and I heard Somerville's voice again.

'Why don't you just listen, Martin ... Try to relax. Listen to the sound of my voice ... For Anna's sake, Martin ... She's only a child; she needs our protection ... Concentrate on my voice ... My voice is all that matters ... You're beginning to feel deeply relaxed now ...'

The phone suddenly went out of my hand and crashed to the floor. Cursing, I bent down and picked it up, replacing the receiver in its cradle. Then I took it over to the bedside table. I stood there a moment, waiting for my head to stop spinning.

'Darling.' Anna came up behind me and, slipping her arms around my waist, pressed herself to my back. 'Darling, I'm sorry. I should have told him you were asleep or out or something.'

'I didn't hear the phone,' I said, turning to look at her.

Anna kept her eyes lowered. 'I picked up right away. I was so surprised to hear it ring – it startled me.'

'Anna.' I put my hand under her chin and tilted her face up to mine. 'Is this the first time you've talked to him since you got back? You haven't been to see him again, have you?'

She shook her head. 'That man gives me the creeps.'

'Me too.' I smiled and kissed her lightly on the lips. 'I love you. You know that, don't you?'

'And I you ...'

'That's all that matters.'

Her eyes filled with tears.

'What's wrong, honey? You're crying. Don't cry.'

'I'm happy.' She clung to me and I felt her give a little shudder.
'I'm happy. That's all.'

Outside, the wind had died down. The night had grown still.
There wasn't a sound coming from the roof now. All was calm,
all was peaceful. The golden fleece lay soft under my hand. It was
as if none of it had happened: I hadn't heard Penelope's voice just
now on the telephone; I hadn't found any good-luck charm attached to my key ring ... The images I was afraid would rise up
and torment me as soon as I closed my eyes never took shape.

In the dark, as we lay together, I thought of us as children gently
drifting off to sleep in each other's arms. In the end we hadn't
made love. It didn't seem necessary. The time for making love had
passed.

'What are you thinking about?'

'Us,' I said. 'When we were kids. Just the two of us. We were
the only ones left.'

'But we didn't know each other when we were children.'

'Maybe we didn't, maybe we did. Who knows? People who love
each other often find a way to be together again, not always in
this life.'

'Since when have you started ... Were we very much in love?'
She snuggled up closer.

'Maybe. Or we might have been together in another way. You
know, like family.'

'That would have been nice too. I wish I could believe in it.
It's such a comforting idea to think you're never really going to
lose anybody.'

'You were my sister once.'

'I was?'

'You were younger than me – about four years. But we were
very close.'

'When you said we were the only ones left ...'

'Apart from your dogs.'

'My dogs?'

'Everyone else was dead.'

'Oh, Martin,' She began to cry again. She buried her face in
my shoulder. I felt the tears flow.

I did my best to comfort Anna, holding her in my arms, rocking her gently, shushing her like a baby until at last she cried herself to sleep.

For a long time I just lay there staring up at the ceiling, my mind a perfect blank. I remember looking at my watch, seeing the red glow of the digital numerals: 2.39. Soon after that I must have dozed off.

I woke up out of a dream: I'd had the sensation of drifting through space, a blue-black darkness that had no limit. I was aware only of a tiny pinprick of light ahead of me. I was trying to reach it, swimming toward the light through this sea of nothingness. And the light was growing and becoming more brilliant as I approached. It was indescribably bright, with a bluish aura – the center was pure white – yet it didn't dazzle or hurt my eyes. Irresistibly drawn toward it, I felt it giving out warmth and a kind of all-understanding love that surrounded and enveloped me so that I became a part of it, conscious only of the sheer ecstasy of being alone in that place, a region of perfect clarity, where the only existence was in the pure geometrical image of the crystal.

When I woke, it felt as if I had died and been brought back to life against my will.

I woke with a gritty taste in my mouth and removed something from my tongue. It was a little coil of hair.

I looked at my watch again: 3.10.

It was really cold and damp now in the room, and stuffy too – the air felt all used up. I was finding it difficult to breathe.

Extricating myself from the sprawl of Anna's limbs, careful not to wake her, I sat up in bed and tried to get some air into my lungs. On the third or fourth breath I began to feel dizzy. I felt a kind of clicking sensation in the lower part of my throat, a strong, erratic pulse. Then the first twinge of nausea.

Thinking it would pass, I continued to breathe deeply, holding each breath and then releasing it, till I realized it wasn't doing the slightest good. I felt sure I was going to throw up. I got out of bed and started to make my way in the dark toward the bathroom, when the pulse in my throat suddenly grew frenzied, clicking wildly like a Geiger counter. I felt a pain in my chest, an acute tearing pain, as if someone had forced a hand down my gullet and was trying to rip my lungs out. I sank down on the floor and rolled over, hugging my knees to my chin. I couldn't breathe. I'm going to choke to death, I thought, like Zach Scalf.

I must have cried out then, because I woke Anna. I heard her call my name. She couldn't see where I was.

The light came on.

'Martin! My God, what's the matter?' She ran over and knelt down beside me, her eyes wide with alarm.

By now the worst of the pain had passed and I was able to breathe normally again, though I still felt sick.

'I'll be okay,' I groaned, irritated by her reaction. 'It must have been something I ate.'

I saw the worried, pitying look in her eyes as she helped me. She gathered my sweat shirt from the chair and draped it over my shoulders. She even tried to come with me into the bathroom, but I wouldn't let her.

'Go back to bed. I'll be okay.'

I shut the bathroom door and leaned up against it for a moment, closing my eyes as waves of nausea swept over me. I knelt in front of the toilet and pushed a finger to the back of my throat trying to make myself throw up. I began to gag, coughing and dry-retching, each spasm more violent and painful than the last, but I couldn't vomit. It felt as if there were some obstruction in my throat.

Then I must have blacked out.

The next thing I remember is staring down into a swirling vortex of bright blue water. I wasn't sure if I'd been sick. I felt a kind of relief, more a numbness; I felt clammy all over, and my head ached. I went over to the washbasin, turned on the faucet and scooped up some water to rinse my face.

I saw my reflection in the mirror – ghostly pale under a beaded gloss of sweat. There was a little crimson thread hanging down under my left ear. It was a piece of lint from Anna's nightgown, but when I tried to pull it away it smeared under my fingers.

I must have cut myself.

Afterward, I wiped my face and hands on a towel. They left a pinkish stain. More blood. I searched in the mirror, but I couldn't find where the blood had come from.

I heard the sound of a door handle being turned softly. Thinking it was Anna coming in from the bedroom to see how I was, I looked for her in the mirror over my shoulder. I saw her white beach robe hanging on the back of the door, but the door didn't open.

Then I heard something else, a small scuffling noise I couldn't identify. It seemed to come from below, from the kitchen – Anna must have gone down to get a drink or something. But only a moment before, I'd heard her moving about in the bedroom. She wouldn't have had time to get downstairs.

A feeling of intense cold rose up from the pit of my stomach. There *was* somebody else in the house besides us. I thought of calling out to Anna, but I didn't want to frighten her. I zipped the front of my sweat shirt up and pulled the hood over my head. Then I went out through the other door onto the landing.

At the top of the stairs I stood in the dark and listened. I thought I could hear footsteps, and a dull, scraping sound, as if something heavy were being dragged across the tiled kitchen floor.

I turned on the lights and the noises stopped.

Halfway down the hall passage, gripping the shaft of an iron niblick I'd taken from the umbrella stand, I paused and listened again. Ahead of me, rocking gently on its hinges, stood the swing door that leads into the kitchen. I felt a cool draft against my ankles, but there was no sound coming from behind it. All I could hear now was the steady patter of rain on the porch roof.

Putting my shoulder to the door, I pushed it open and quickly reached inside for the light switch.

The overhead strip flickered on, fixing the kitchen surfaces with a cold fluorescent sheen. The room was empty. Everything seemed to be in order, neat and tidy as always – except for a pool of moisture darkening the terra-cotta tiles where the rain had come in.

The back door was standing wide open

Puzzled, I went over and closed it, hurriedly turning the key in the lock. The door was unmarked: it didn't appear to have been forced. Had the wind blown it open? If Anna forgot to lock it, surely I would have noticed when I made my rounds before bed?

And why hadn't the alarm gone off?

I felt a cold wetness underfoot and looked down. My bare feet were leaving damp footprints on the tiles. There were no other marks on the floor. Anyone coming in from the outside must have done so before the rain started.

Then suddenly I understood what had happened. The back door was standing open not thanks to any intruder, but because somebody had *gone out* that way and not bothered to close it. It was Anna after all that I'd heard.

She must have taken the keys from my belt while I was still in the bathroom, turned off the alarm and slipped out of the house. But *why?* Why would she want to go out on a night like this – and without telling me? For a walk in the rain, a breath of fresh air? It didn't make sense.

Realizing she couldn't have gotten very far, I came back into the hall, put the golf club away in the umbrella stand and went to check the control panel under the stairs, just to make sure the system had been deactivated.

It had. The little red warning light was dead; the key to the alarm had been turned to the shut-off position and then removed. As I reached up to open the panel, my hand touched metal, there was a blinding flash and the house was plunged into darkness.

TEN

FILE   Martin Gregory
DATE   November 24
TAPE   G/M b5
SUBJECT   Telephone conversation with Anna Gregory – recorded
         at 3.28 a.m.

ANNA: Dr Somerville, is that you? Can you hear me?

R.M.S.: Yes, I can hear you. Are you all right?

ANNA: Thank God! You've got to help me, *please*, Dr Somerville. Something terrible's going to happen, I know it. He's gone again and ... I don't know what to do.

R.M.S.: Try to keep calm, Anna. Tell me what's happened.

ANNA: I shouldn't be talking to you. He'll *kill* me if he finds out.

R.M.S.: You did the right thing to call me. I tried to call you several times, but the phone must have been off the hook.

ANNA: It was? I didn't know.

R.M.S.: When I talked to Martin earlier, he seemed less disturbed than I'd expected. Has he gotten worse?

ANNA: He's had some kind of fit. It just happened about ten minutes ago. I found him doubled up on the floor, writhing in agony. He said it was something he ate, but that's impossible. He could hardly make it to the bathroom.

R.M.S.: Why didn't you leave the house then when you could?

ANNA: Because I *couldn't*! He was sick. After a while everything went quiet. When he didn't come back – I began to worry.

R.M.S.: Is he in the bathroom now?

ANNA: No, he's downstairs. I knocked on the door, but there wasn't any answer. So I went in. It wasn't locked or anything. He'd just gone out the other side ... Dr Somerville, he left a message for me.

R.S.M.: What do you mean 'the other side'?

ANNA: The medicine cabinet was open, so I shut it. Then I saw myself in the mirror. It was there, written across my forehead ...

R.S.M.: What was? What did he write?

ANNA: Scrawled up in red. He found my lipstick – the one he never lets me wear. Oh, *God*, I'm scared.

R.M.S.: Anna, tell me what he wrote.

ANNA: *'Out of her misery'!* Just like on the white box, only this time it's for me! Don't you see?

R.M.S.: Listen carefully and do exactly as I tell you. Go now immediately and lock both doors.

ANNA: I already have.

R.M.S.: Good. Now, under no circumstances let Martin back into the bedroom. However reasonable he seems. Even if he begs you. Is that clear?

ANNA: Yes, all right.

R.M.S.: Are you dressed?

ANNA: No.

R.M.S.: Then quickly put on some clothes. You may not have much time. Open the bedroom window and climb out. You did it once before, didn't you?

ANNA: In broad daylight.

R.M.S.: It'll set off the alarm but so much the better. Somebody will hear it and come over to investigate.

ANNA: It'll take me too long to climb down.

R.M.S.: You don't have any choice, Anna.

ANNA: All right, but ... *Oh, God! The lights just went out!*

R.M.S.: Are you sure? Try the switch.

ANNA: I'm trying the switch ... It's just the way he said it would happen. He must have fused the lights deliberately. I can hear him moving about below. Oh, God, *no* ... It's stopped. The noises have stopped. He *said* this would happen. It was only meant to be a game. Please don't let him do it. Help me. No ... *Martin!*

R.M.S.: Anna, can you hear me? Hello Anna. *Hello* ... Are you still there? Hello, hello ...

ELEVEN

She must have screwed up the wiring. Christ knows how! It's the simplest thing in the world to turn off a burglar alarm. But then, Anna was never mechanically minded. I cursed her under my breath for messing with things she didn't understand – if she wanted to go out, all she had to do was *ask*. Then I opened the door to the broom closet and felt along the top shelf for a flashlight I kept there in case of emergency. It wasn't where it should have been, but I found it easily enough. In the light of the beam, I picked out a box of fuses and circuit breakers.

As I was backing out of the closet into the hall, I heard a muffled cry.

It was Anna. But the sound didn't come from outside. She was upstairs in the bedroom.

'Help me ... No ... *Martin!*'

Somebody was up there with her. In a panic, I looked around for the niblick. But then, just as I remembered that I'd put it back in the umbrella stand, I heard Anna's voice again. Suddenly I realized there wasn't anyone else up there: she was talking on the phone.

I shone the flashlight at the hall table. The telephone extension was half-buried under a pile of sweaters and coats. I swept them aside and picked up.

'Hello, hello ... Dr Somerville? ...' I could hear Anna's voice, frantic, at the other end. She began clicking the button up and down. 'Oh, God, it's gone dead. Please, no ... Dr Somerville, the phone's been cut. He cut the phone ...'

'It's *me*, Anna,' I interrupted her. 'Are you okay? Now, take it easy, honey. I'll be right up. The fuses just blew.'

I heard her give a despairing cry and then she hung up.

I took the stairs three at a time.

'Anna? Are you in there? Are you all right?' The bedroom door was locked. 'Talk to me, Anna.' I twisted and rattled the handle, hammering on the door with my fists, but she didn't answer. I ran across the landing and tried the door to the bathroom. That was locked too. I came back again and shone the flashlight under the bedroom door, waving the beam back and forth.

'Anna, what's going on here?' I could hear her sobbing quietly now. 'Why have you locked yourself in? It's all right, honey, there's nothing to worry about. There's been a power failure – that's all. Hey, let me in!'

I shook the handle. Then I heard her moving up close to the inside of the door.

In a low, cracked voice that I hardly recognized, she whispered, 'Keep *away*.'

'C'mon honey, open the door. It's cold out here.'

'Keep away from me, Martin, or I'll call the ... I know what you're trying to do. You want me to open the door so that you can cut me up just like you did the boys. You want to cut me up and *put me in a box*!'

'Honey, take it easy. You don't know what you're saying. You've been talking to that creep Somerville, and he's got you all mixed up with that psychological shit he's always spouting.'

'It's no good, Martin. I *saw* it.'

'You saw it? What did you see? What are you talking about?'

'I saw what you wrote *on the mirror*!' Her voice rose to a hoarse shriek.

'I didn't write anything on the mirror. You're becoming hysterical. Now calm down and open this door. Be a good girl. I'm not going to hurt you. Anna, I *love* you.'

'Go away ... and leave me alone.' She moved back from the door. A moment later I heard her slump down on the bed, sobbing without restraint.

'I'm going to stay right here until you decide to be reasonable and let me in.'

I switched off the flashlight and stuffed it into the pocket of my sweat shirt. There was a clink of metal The keys... I still had the keys! Their weight, the feel of them in my pocket, was so familiar I hadn't noticed them till now. Then I remembered I hadn't put them back on my belt after I came down from the attic; I must have had them with me all along.

So it couldn't have been Anna who turned off the alarm.

I rose slowly to my feet, seized now with a horrible feeling of uncertainty. My throat was dry. I felt the pulse starting up again. There was no sound from the bedroom. Anna had stopped crying. I could still hear the rain outside, but it wasn't coming down as hard. I began to shiver ... It was the same smell, a cold mephitic odor that clogged the air and made it hard to breathe. Thick and muddy. I felt hemmed in, trapped – as if I were back down the cave, with rock pressing in from all sides. Panic reared up inside me. I looked around for a way out. In the swirling darkness, shadows seemed to gather in every corner seeking form and substance, about to take shape at any moment.

I pulled the flashlight from my pocket, but out of anxiety let it slip, and it fell to the floor. As I reached down to pick it up, groping around on the carpet, my hand brushed over a cold, damp patch: something had spilled there. I turned on the flashlight, shining it at my feet, and saw that there were several patches darkening the carpet around the two doors that led into the bedroom. I traced them back with the beam and discovered that they ran from the top of the stairs across the landing and disappeared down the passage in the direction of the attic.

A sudden loud crash came from the bedroom.

'What was that? Are you all right?' There was a brief pause, and then I heard the sound of a heavy object being moved across the floor. 'For God's sake, Anna, what's going on in there?'

It sounded as if she'd toppled the bureau and was trying to push it up against the door.

'You're behaving like an idiot, Anna,' I yelled. 'Anytime I want to, I can break in through the bathroom – now come on, open up!'

She didn't answer. The dragging noise had stopped, and I could hear her panting.

'Honey, please. Let me in.'

The silence lengthened. Then I heard her voice, faint – from the very back of the bedroom – yet clear and defiant:

'"For he shall deliver thee from the snare of the hunter" ...'

'Stop it.'

'"He shall defend thee under his wings and thou shalt be safe" ...'

'Cut it *out*, Anna!'

'"Thou shalt not be afraid for the terror by night; nor for the arrow that flieth by day; nor for the pestilence that walketh in darkness; nor for the destruction that wasteth at noonday" . . .'

I shouted at her through the door: '*Anna!* Stop this *fucking* nonsense! Stop it at once!'

For an answer came another massive crash, much louder than the first. It shook the floor under my feet and reverberated through the house, rattling the doors and windows. Only this time it didn't come from the bedroom.

My heart pounding, I ran to the head of the stairs and waved the flashlight all around. But I could see nothing.

I stood there gripping the rail of the banister.

There was a sharp splintering sound, followed by a shatter of glass; I couldn't tell where it came from. Then a deep, rhythmic booming from the attic.

All around me now I could hear nothing but noise. My head sang with echoes: from the beams and rafters of the roof, under the floorboards and in the posts and joints of the walls there rose a hideous clamor of creaking, tearing, rapping, groaning – as if the whole house were slowly being wrenched from its foundations.

'"There shall no evil happen unto thee: neither shall any plague come nigh thy dwelling. For he shall give his angels power over thee: to help thee in all thy ways" . . .'

Anna's voice, small and calm, sounded closer now.

A series of shuddering crashes rang out through the house. Over the stairs in rapid succession pictures slithered from the wall and smacked down onto the treads below. A heavy china bowl came spinning off the table outside the bedroom and flew across the land-ind, disintegrating as it hit the floor.

I could hear furniture being flung about downstairs, crockery, glasses, jars breaking, bottles exploding, light bulbs popping off like gunfire, cutlery jangling in the kitchen drawers. Doors banging open and shut. I cowered behind the banister, putting my hands over my ears to shut out the din as it rose to a furious crescendo.

Then quite suddenly, as if a conductor had raised his baton, everything went quiet.

My ears still ringing, I waited for it to start up again – but there was nothing. A bated hush had returned to the house. All I could hear was the sound of my own breathing and the erratic pulse of my heart.

Anna had stopped her infernal praying.

My hand shook as I aimed the flashlight along the passage and started slowly toward the attic stairs. I had to force myself every step of the way – yet at the same time, I was drawn irresistibly; I know now that I never had any choice. Ahead, the walls and ceiling were dripping with moisture that glistened in the wavering yellow beam. The door to the attic stood ajar, not locked the way I'd left it. Everything smelled of mildew. At the bottom of the stairs I paused to wipe away the sweat that was stinging my eyes.

Thank God, I'm not too late. The lamp is still lit, though guttering feebly. I can feel the rain blowing in through the cupola, spotting down onto the butcher-block table underneath. One of the lancet windows must be open ... Swinging the beam around the floor of the attic, I search among the flickering shadows, constantly looking over my shoulder, expecting at any moment to see – I don't even know.

As far as I can make out, nothing up here has been disturbed. The live flame should mean that the crystal is unharmed. But I don't trust the signs yet: I have to make absolutely sure.

I kneel down in front of the safe, holding the flash between my teeth so that I can read the numbers on the dial: I need both hands to pull open the heavy door. Yes, thank God, it's still there, lying in back of the top shelf. I take it out and, removing it from its leather sheath, hold it up to the light. It appears to be intact. I put it back and quickly close the door of the safe, then spin the combination dial and lock it.

Now I can breathe again. Sitting back on my haunches, I let the flashlight fall to the floor and wipe my face on the sleeve of my sweat shirt. Then, clasping both hands behind by neck, I try to stretch out a bit, taking deep, regular breaths. While doing so, I notice out of the corner of my eye something sticking up behind the top of the cistern. Something that shouldn't be there ... I don't know how I could have missed it before, but I see it now shining in the beam of the flashlight: a great curving horn of black iron, still wet from the rain.

I must have taken it down after all.

When I'd checked the weathervane earlier, instead of leaving it and going to bed, I must have gone downstairs, turned off the alarm, then come back up here. Just as I'd intended to do in the first place, only I couldn't be bothered – at least, I *thought* I couldn't be bothered . . .

I remember sitting down at the table and smoking a cigarette. It was then that I discovered the silver amulet on my key ring. I remember opening it . . . But if that's the case, where is the amulet now? And where are its foul contents? Not on my key ring, not in the wastebasket, not lying up there on the table – I *must* have imagined the whole thing. And talking to Penelope on the phone. That too. An illusion. Like my thinking Anna had shaved off her golden fleece . . .

Somerville's to blame for all this. He's the one who fucked my mind.

When I go downstairs now, I expect I'll find the door to the bedroom open and Anna curled up in bed sleeping peacefully – as if nothing had happened.

I get up off the floor and walk slowly over to the cistern.

The cusp of the weathervane reaches almost to my chin. It's much bigger than it seems from the ground. Bending a little, I fit my shoulder into the curve of the crescent and lift it up, holding it by the shaft under the compass sights. Although it's made of cast iron, it doesn't feel that heavy. It's so well balanced that the weight sits comfortably. I could easily have carried it down the ladder . . .

The smell of mildew rises in my nostrils.

God knows, I *do* love her.

I'm about to put the weathervane down, when I hear a scream. A scream so piercing, this time I know it's the real thing.

In the few seconds it took me to get downstairs, the scream didn't stop. When I banged on the bedroom door shouting her name, it still didn't stop. She kept on screaming. The sound went right through me. I couldn't stand it. *What were they doing to her?* The door *was* locked: that part I hadn't imagined. The passage walls, too, were still oozing moisture; the carpet was still damp and littered with shards of broken glass and china.

I found myself praying that I would be in time.

I forced the sharp pivot end of the weathervane between the door and the doorframe and levered back. It burst open with a loud splintering sound as I heard the scream die in her throat.

I pushed the door back. It seemed to stick on something, but I got my weight behind it and shouldered my way through into the bedroom.

Everything happened so fast after that, I'm not sure how much I took in at that first glance, or whether I put it all together afterward. I remember the overturned wardrobe, drawerfuls of clothes tipped upside down in the middle of the floor, the open drapes billowing around the smashed windows, the mattress half dragged off the bed, a chair pushed up against the bathroom door – all of Anna's pathetic attempts to keep me out, or to escape. She'd lit a cluster of votive candles and left them burning on the bedside table, filling the room with a strong churchy odor of tallow.

At first I didn't see her. I thought she must have climbed out onto the porch. I ran straight to the windows; but before I was even halfway across the room, I heard a little whimpering cry behind me. I wheeled around clumsily, brandishing the weathervane.

In the deeper shadows behind the door, as it swung slowly back, I saw Anna squatting down on the floor. She was only partly dressed, squeezed into the corner, her thin shoulders hunched around her ears. Standing over her was a tall hooded figure all in red, dripping water, raising a huge curved instrument like a giant scimitar above his head. As I turned, I saw, as if in slow motion, the muscles working on the man's back as he put all his strength into bringing the weapon down on top of her. I could see the glitter of fear, the desperate pleading look in Anna's eyes, as they found mine.

I swung the weathervane at the head of her attacker. She screamed. I remember glancing down at her then, but even as I struck, the figure vanished. I saw to my horror that there was no longer anyone standing between us. It was already too late to deflect the blow. In that split second I realized with a terrible feeling of helplessness that I was going to kill her. I shut my eyes. At the last moment I cried out so that I wouldn't hear the impact.

I felt the shock of the blow run up my arms. I couldn't tell if I'd hit her or not. For a long time I didn't dare look.

When I finally opened my eyes, she was gone. At first I thought I'd destroyed her altogether. Then I heard her stumbling down the stairs. She must have jerked sideways and rolled out underneath the blow. The iron crescent had smashed into the wall above the spot where her head had been, embedding itself in the plaster.

I heard the front door slam.

I sat down on the edge of the bed. I began to shiver uncontrollably. I pulled off my red sweat shirt and pajama bottoms. They were soaking wet. Then I wrapped myself in a blanket and waited for the night to end.

TWELVE

PREAMBLE

An hour ago – I'm dictating these notes immediately after seeing the patient – I got a call from Dr Heyworth confirming that the patient's wife had arrived safely at his office. He examined her, administered a mild sedative and left his wife to put her to bed in their apartment on Gramercy Park.

Anna had already called me herself at about 4 this morning – shortly after the patient's homicidal attack on her – from a neighbor's house to let me know she was all right. She naturally sounded very distressed on the phone, but was coherent enough to give some account of what had happened. During our conversation, in a moment of exhausted resignation, she finally agreed to see reason about the kind of help and care her husband really needs.

A. INITIAL EXPECTATIONS

Very uncertain. The patient turned up on my doorstep without notice at 7.30 this morning. After last night's events I'd anticipated seeing him again, but didn't expect him to come here of his own accord. Prepared for great tension, psychotic behavior, even the possibility of violence.

B. ATMOSPHERE

Oddly reminiscent of our very first meeting – formal, somber, restrained – at least at the start. Patient seemed tired and clearly under great stress, though controlling it reasonably well. His appearance was unusual. Neatly dressed in a dark business suit, white shirt and tie, but appeared to be wearing another set of quite bulky clothes underneath. No explanation offered, nor could I think of one myself.

His manner, deceptively calm and rational to begin with, became increasingly peremptory and hostile as the session progressed. He avoided eye contact throughout and on more than one occasion put his hands over his ears to indicate that he didn't wish to hear what I had to say. He even accused me of trying to hypnotize him against his will. Tolerance of contra-argument low. When opposed or contradicted in any way, he began shouting, refused to let me speak and threatened to leave. Several paranoid features were present, including a constant febrile motion, looking over his shoulder, insistence on locking the door to the study (then getting up to check it every few minutes), obsessive ruminations and fear of being pursued. By the end of the hour he was distraught, quite unapproachable, indeed almost mad.

C. MAIN TRENDS AND THERAPEUTIC INTERVENTIONS

Pretending complete ignorance of what happened last night, I asked the patient why he'd come to see me. He began by saying that he'd been feeling anxious and depressed lately, then announced in an angry tone that he would prefer it if I didn't 'get together with' his wife behind his back because she was very 'impressionable'. Later he admitted that he'd come to me because he was afraid that Anna's life was in danger. 'They' had mounted a 'psychic attack' on the house during the night in an attempt to get at 'the crystal' through her. When I asked him to explain what he meant, he left his chair and went to the window, turning his back on me.

After a long silence he gave a desultory, garbled account of his 'spiritual transformation', which amounts to a delusional alienation founded on the Magmel myth. Patient believes he has been entrusted with the crystal for a special purpose. He has been appointed 'a guardian of the universe', whose sacred duty it is, as keeper of 'the Light', to prevent mankind from destroying itself in the last decades of this century and the world from being plunged into another, perhaps interminable Dark Age.

After this portentous disclosure, during which he referred to himself several times as 'the Kendal', his attention began to wander. He went over to check the door, then turned suddenly and shouted: 'You think I made this whole thing up, don't you – that I took the crystal from that cheap *glass* chandelier of yours out there? You think I'm crazy. You've always thought I was crazy. You just lied to me about it before – lied and *lied*!'

Despite the high degree of tension, I decided to introduce the Philippines material at this point and confront the patient with his taped confession (Session Three) of what I am now convinced was an authentic murder. There was a risk that the patient would abreact severely, but I felt the chances of his experiencing some catharsis were at least fair. Before playing the tape, I explained to him how I had censored the recording of his first induction and suggested posthypnotic amnesia, because at the time I didn't consider he was ready to handle the material. He made no comment.

He listened to the tape in silence, sitting with his back turned so that I couldn't see how he was reacting. When it was over, he shook his head and said quietly:

'I didn't kill Missy. Why would I want to kill her? She was my friend, my only friend out there: I loved her. The idea that I could ever have harmed her is absurd. I mean I can see why you might have thought otherwise. But no, there's nothing in it. It's just a fantasy. For one thing, Missy is alive – I told you: she got married and went to live in London. What's more, I can prove it.'

It was a bold, skillful defense, calmly and rationally presented by the patient, who even seemed quite tolerant of my 'wrong interpretation'. But when finally I showed no sign of changing my opinion, or coming around to his point of view, his manner became aggressive and minatory. He accused me of *wanting* to believe that he was 'a murderer'.

That's when I introduced the question of motive. I didn't mention that I'd already regressed him to that period of his childhood on several occasions (during earlier sessions, but without his knowledge) in the hope of discovering more about his relationship with Missy – and that each time his unconscious had successfully blocked my questions; but I did stress the importance, if he was to derive any real or lasting benefit from the releasing of this traumatic memory, of trying to establish why he killed her.

Patient loosened his tie and undid the top button of his shirt, revealing under it the neck of what looked like a gray coverall. He began to rock backwards and forwards in his chair. Then suddenly he stood up, trembling with rage, waving his arms and shouting that it was all irrelevant and that I was never going to find a motive because he 'didn't kill her in the first place'. Careful not to contradict him now, I suggested that the only means of settling the matter – now that he was cognizant of the story – would be to return to the incident under hypnosis and try to find out what really happened.

For a moment I was convinced the patient was going to attack me. Instead, he simply went on strike. He put his hands over his ears and refused to talk or listen on the ground that I was an 'evil manipulator' trying to take possession of his mind.

D. INTERPRETATION

In spite of the deadlock, I decided to go ahead and share with the patient some of my perceptions on his case. First, I had to get him to accept the idea that the 'long-suppressed crime', which I always knew to be at the center of his guilt and hostility feelings towards his wife, was not another dramatized reincarnation fantasy out of the mythical past, but an actual, traumatic event from his own childhood.

I began explaining to the patient that strongly sexualized behavior in preadolescence tends to be pathological, usually because of abnormal constitutional drives; but that in his case it seemed more likely that his precocity was the result of unusual circumstances – i.e., his being left alone for long periods of time with a sexually mature native girl in a 'tropical paradise'. The latency period, from the age of eight to ten years, dismissed by Freud as nonsexual, is highly significant psychologically since it is the time in our lives when we first make friends, when someone other than ourselves and outside the family constellation becomes important to us, when we are first exposed in our vernal innocence to the uncertainties of love. I suggested that it was in this area that a motive – possibly arising from some disappointment or sense of loss or betrayal – might be found for his wanting to kill Missy.

Patient's hands still pressed over his ears. Gave no sign of listening to what I was saying. I continued nevertheless: The first time I regressed him, patient revealed that as a nine-year-old child he'd committed murder, but wouldn't let me find out *why*. In subsequent hypnotic sessions he resisted all my attempts at probing his unconscious mind. Responding to the challenge of hypnosis, however, he produced several elaborate fantasies, indeed a whole system of belief (interlacing myth, history and the real world), in his quest *not* for some long-lost Grail-like talisman – the 'crystal' is clearly a symbol of transcendence – but for an acceptable story which would explain and perhaps exonerate his killing of the girl. He succeeded with the story of Magmel, where he cast Missy in the role of an adored younger sister, whom he is forced to destroy. As a result of *his* mistake, an innocent mistake, she has become mortally ill, so infested with plague that he feels justified in administering the *coup de grâce*, amounting in this case to an act of love.

By now the patient was beginning to pay attention. I went on to explain that about the time he began therapy, he found a way to transfer and externalize the burden of his unfathomed guilt by shifting its focus onto the killing of the dogs. Although at the time he didn't know why he killed them, when the motivating force later emerged as a compulsion to re-enact the end of the Magmel regression, his explanation not only satisfied him, he believed it to be literally true. Attention had been successfully deflected from the real motive – which was to destroy his wife.

The story of Magmel, formerly an internal metaphor for his own life, which he must have carried in his subconscious for some time (*vide* dreams, visions, hallucinations), once revealed to him became the new and only 'truth'. But the real conflict, still unresolved, lay festering beneath the surface.

His unconscious aim had always been to murder Anna – he felt compelled to do so for the same reason, no doubt, that he killed Missy. When he finally made the attempt, in a part of his mind he was acting out the last scene of the Magmel story, which he'd furnished with appropriate detail 'borrowed' from his own surroundings: e.g., the Kendal's house overlooking the valley (Croton Mill), the watchtower (cupola), the tower room (attic), the crescent alarum (weathervane), etc. It was as if Magmel had ultimately been created for this purpose. Myth and reality had finally become one. 'They' were attacking the house. He had to save Anna – to put her 'out of her misery'.

But why?

At this point the patient rose from his chair.

E. OUTCOME

Very agitated now, patient denied repeatedly that he had ever tried to kill his wife. Wanted to know where she was because he had to 'explain things to her'. I warned him that he could face criminal charges over what happened last night and urged him to seek voluntary admission to a hospital. He began shouting again. He said he would *prove* that Missy was still alive and that then I would have to acknowledge that he was both 'innocent and perfectly sane'. The so-called proof was in Bedford, and he proposed going there immediately and coming back with it. Since there was no way of keeping him here against his will, I agreed, suggesting that he also return the pendant which he took from the chandelier in the hall here.

We made an appointment for 1 p.m.

F. AFTERTHOUGHTS

The patient's wife is coming by at 11 with the completed petitioner form. As the patient's G.P., Heyworth has agreed to be the second signatory on the 2PC.

THIRTEEN

11.25 a.m. – Just to keep the record straight, I'm jotting down these notes on the train to New York. There's no telling when I'll get another chance. My only defense against the case Somerville has been building against me – from the very beginning, it seems now – is right here in these pages ... and the letter, of course. The letter is *external evidence.*

It would be much easier to have a Xerox made and simply send it to him, but I can't resist the satisfaction of seeing his face when he reads it. The moment he reads that letter, his analytical house of cards will come tumbling down and he'll know I've won. Then from my briefcase – the same battered Samsonite I've been carrying on this train for eight soul-sucking years – I shall draw out the crystal like a fiery sword, a terrible swift sword, with which to smite mine enemies ...

The letter is from my mother, dated May 21, 1964 – one of her infrequent, but comprehensive newscasts from the Gulfstream Key. Took me long enough to retrieve from that apology for a filing system, but I found it. Here, in case anything should happen to me before I can get it to a Xerox machine, is the relevant passage:

'The other day we had a letter out of the blue from Tsu-lai. You'll remember Tsu-lai? She used to be our cook in Manila, when we lived at "Wit's End". She wants to know if we can help her immigrate to the United States with *all* her family! You know, there were quite a few of them besides Missy. Your father and I would like to do anything we can to help, of course, but it may be rather complicated. Tsu-lai also wrote that Missy went to London last year to become an *au pair* to a 'good Catholic family', only it seems after a few months there she fell in love with this terribly dashing young Irishman – an accountant, I think. Anyway, now they're getting married! It doesn't surprise me one bit. Missy was always a very pleasing little girl, bright as a button and pretty too, in her way. She's done awfully well for herself, don't you think?'

It was still dark this morning when I left the house to drive into the city. I got home again at about 10 and went for a walk, hoping to find when I came back that last night had been a bad dream. It was so quiet in the garden, not even a bird singing. Then I pushed open the front door and just stood there gaping at the scene of destruction, as if I were seeing it for the first time.

In the daylight it looked much worse. The house had been ransacked, literally torn apart. There was water everywhere, bits of wood, plaster, food, clothing, broken glass. Every step I took, the mess crunched sickeningly underfoot. It reminded me of Print Begley walking though the deserted rooms of the Palmenhof. Then I began to imagine Anna lying upstairs somewhere with her head bashed in ... what *might* have been.

Through the splintered door to the bedroom I could see the pivot of the weathervane half buried in the pile of the carpet. I tried to remember exactly what happened last night, but the details wouldn't come clear.

The phone was on again; not the power. I called Heyworth and asked to speak to Anna. 'She's sleeping now, my friend,' he said in that comforting bedside voice of his. 'Why don't you call back later? I know she'll want to talk to you.'

Maybe I'll try again from Grand Central.

I haven't decided yet what to do after I see Somerville. I obviously can't go back home, not until I've explained everthing to Anna. I left the station wagon for her in the garage, the keys under the dash – she'll know where to look. If I could only get her to come with me to Somerville's. I want her to be my witness – I need her to witness his humiliation, to see him exposed for the charlatan he really is. Whatever he's said to her, poisoning her mind against me, when he reads that letter he'll have to take it all back. Then maybe she'll realize that I'm not the crazy one.

One day I'll tell her the whole story. I'll put all the evidence before her: the crystal, the tapes, Print Begley's Bible, even this diary – I won't hide anything from her. Someone once said it takes two to tell the truth: one to speak it and the other to hear it. I need someone who can hear me, whom I can trust.

Anna.

... Someone's just sat down in the seat opposite. I'm pretty sure it's him. This is *all* I need. If I keep my head low, maybe he won't recognize me and I can get away before ... No, it's too late. He's seen me. He's actually starting to speak to me ... Jesus Christ!

FOURTEEN

R. M. Somerville, M.D., Psy.
15 East 93rd Street
New York, N.Y. 10028

MEMO

Friday, 12.15 p.m.

Penelope – In case I have to go out before you get back and we don't get a chance to discuss: the certification is complete and ready to be filed with Oceanside Sanitarium. You'll find the documents on your desk, including Mrs Gregory's signed petition. She has now gone back to Gramercy Park with Dr Heyworth; they are both standing by in case we should need them.

I've arranged for the ambulance to come at 12.30. I want you to make sure they *don't* park in front of the house. I've already impressed on Mercaid the necessity of keeping a low profile; the dispatcher assured me that they would send two of their best men. Put them in the waiting room until after Gregory gets here. He's coming now at 1. If the patient turns up early, show him directly into my study. Once we're in there together you can have the ambulance men come up to your office. I'll buzz twice when I want them.

N.B.: The patient most likely will have to be subdued.

FIFTEEN

'Don't I know you from somewhere?' The man in the gray pinstripe suit leaned forward in his seat and tapped me on the knee with his rolled newspaper. 'Hey!'

Reluctantly I looked up and stared at him.

'Hey! I *thought* it was you.' His chubby pink face broke into a friendly grin. 'Even recognized you behind the disguise – the beard, I mean. Ha-ha! How you doin'?'

'We know each other?' I said blankly.

'Are you kidding? We've only been doing this run together for the last Christ-knows-how-long. Where you been hiding?'

'Of course! I'm sorry, I remember now.' I forced a smile.

'You know, this is a real coincidence. I was just talking to my wife about you this morning.'

'I've been away – on vacation.'

'She says, Harry, you may as well take it with you. He may be riding on a later train too these days. And she was *right*! She always claimed she had ESP.'

'I don't get it.'

The man opened his briefcase across his knees and began rummaging about inside. 'Remember that day we were both running for the four forty-eight? We only just made it? It must have been a Friday, a couple of months ago. You were carrying all those packages.'

'It was my wife's birthday,' I said quickly.

'You sure know how to celebrate in your family. Anyway *this* is the one that got away! You left it on your seat.' Beaming, he brought out a flat package loosely wrapped in blue tissue paper and handed it to me.

'Thanks, but . . .' I didn't recognize the package; it felt like a book.

'I was coming back from the bar when you got out at Bedford and I noticed it lying there. It was too late to catch you, but I figured what the hell, we'd run into each other Monday and I'd give it to you then.'

'Thanks a lot,' I said.

''Fraid I opened it. After a week or so and I didn't see you, I thought maybe I'd better check – in case there was a name or an address inside. That's a pretty interesting book you got there. Can't say I understand much French, but . . .' He grinned and gave me a knowing look. 'Don't worry, I didn't show it around. A present for your wife?'

'Yes.' I nodded, desperately trying to think how to end the conversation and get away from him.

'The picture in the front – that's you, right?' He laughed uproariously. 'Looked the name up in the phone book, but I couldn't find any Somerville.'

'*Somerville?*'

'The name that was inside the cover.'

I tore open the package. It was the same book – a cheaper, cloth-bound edition, but the same *Expositions Vaudoises* with the porno-graphic illustrations that I'd looked at that day in Somerville's library. On the flyleaf was the woodcut of the old bearded man reading in the shade of an oak tree – and the Ex Libris of Ronald M. Somerville.

'Where did you get this?'

'What do you mean?' The smile faded instantly from his pink, good-natured face. 'Hey, take it easy, pal. I just told you. You left it on the train. Are you feeling okay?'

'I didn't leave this on the fucking train!'

'It was right on the seat,' he protested. 'The guy sitting next to you told me you forgot it. The guy who helped you get all that stuff off the train.'

A shiver ran through me. No one had helped me getting off the train. 'All what stuff? What did he look like?'

'Jeez, I can't remember now. It was awhile back. An older guy. Good dresser. Had on a blue blazer . . . There was a girl with him – that's right. I think she was dark, not bad-looking, young – could have been his daughter. They helped you get that big package down from the rack . . .'

'Wait a minute. Was this *after* the train had stopped?'

'No, we were just coming into the station. I was standing at the back of the car. I don't mind telling you I'd had a few, but I remember when the train stopped you were already over by the door with all your packages. I was coming down the aisle and I saw you get off. Your wife was there to meet you on the platform with the yellow Labs – I recognized her from seeing her before, you know.'

'They're golden retrievers. What did the guy say to you? Why did he give *you* the book?'

'How should I know? He just handed it to me as I came by – said you forgot it. So I said Okay, sure, I'd give it to you first thing Monday morning.'

'Did he say anything else? Anything at all.'

'That was it.'

'Thanks, I really appreciate it,' I said, and put the book away in my briefcase.

'No problem.' The man smiled. Then, screwing up his eyes, he leaned forward. 'Look, if you're interested in more books like that one, I have a friend –'

'You don't understand. It's all a mistake. Excuse me, I'll be right back.' I stood up and edged out into the aisle, starting to move away. But he wasn't ready to let me go just yet.

'Hey, I thought you knew those people. The way the three of you were acting together.'

'Never saw them before in my life.'

He looked puzzled. 'Didn't they give you that big package? You sure didn't have it with you when you got on at Grand Central.'

'*What?*' I stopped and stared down at him. 'Are you *positive* about that?'

'Sure I am! Boy, you must have been dreaming or something. You could never have managed it with all that other stuff you had.'

'You're right,' I said quietly, 'it must have slipped my mind. Thanks again for the book. I'll see you later.'

'Take it easy.' He laughed. He was still laughing when I left the car.

*

I made my way to the front of the train and found an empty seat. Hunched down so I couldn't be seen from behind – in case my friend decided to come looking for me – I began to think about what he'd just told me. The implications were overwhelming. All I could immediately grasp was the idea that Somerville and Penelope – it had to be them – had been a part of all this, involved somehow in my story even before I knew it had begun.

He must have hypnotized me the very first time we met and then erased the memory from my mind. That would explain the feeling I'd always had of knowing him from before, yet never being able to recognize him, almost of forgetting what he looked like when I wasn't with him.

But then how did Somerville find his professional way into my life? And why? One thing was clear: it had nothing to do with Heyworth's referring me to a 'brilliant' psychotherapist he had happened to meet at a hypnotists' convention in Chicago. They must have arranged all of that.

They must have arranged *everything*.

If it was Somerville who provided me with the white box I put the boys in – I still couldn't remember where I got it – then almost certainly it was Somerville who had instructed me to kill them. It seemed incredible, but once I accepted the idea that I wasn't responsible for their deaths, everything else began to fall into place. The lucky charm bracelet I bought for Anna at the airport, the figure in the blue blazer, the prints of Nuremberg hanging in the Public Library ... They *wanted* me to think I was paranoid. That's why they had me followed. I didn't *imagine* any of it. They had to convince me I was crazy, that I needed help – from *them*, so that whichever way I turned would deliver me deeper and deeper into their clutches.

When I returned from Kentucky the last time, Somerville was smart enough not to put any pressure on me to see him or try to persuade me to reenter therapy. He left that to the others: Penelope, Heyworth, even Anna. He had Penelope suggest very tactfully that I bring back what I'd 'taken from his house', the missing pendant from his damn 'Waterford' chandelier. I almost believed her, I almost believed her.

Last night they made another attempt to recover the crystal.

They tried to make me kill Anna. I don't understand how exactly; it doesn't really matter, since, thank God, I didn't succeed. But they did get me to go back to see Somerville.

He just sat there spinning his web of lies, calling me a murderer, threatening to have me committed to a mental institution. He knew I'd have to prove him wrong once and for all, this time by bringing him what he wanted – the final proof.

History was repeating itself. I saw now the full significance of what was about to happen. At last I face a repetition of the situation that led to the destruction of Magmel. Just as Magnus unknowingly surrendered the talisman to the old man in the cave, so was I about to hand it over to Somerville *of my own free will*.

The train lurched coming up out of the tunnel and swung south through the city. The grimy tenements and shoddy high-rises of Harlem sped by on either side as we headed toward 125th Street, last stop before Grand Central. What if they were waiting for me at the terminal? I had to make a decision *now* whether or not to go through with it: to walk into the trap with my eyes open.

There was still so much that I didn't understand. Who was Somerville? Or Penelope? How did they *find* me? Had our paths crossed before in an earlier life? Was he an incarnation of the old man? And she of Nuala? Or were they his twentieth-century disciples, a magus and his accomplice bent on summoning their master's power from a mist-covered valley lost in time and unleashing it upon our own fragile, self-deceiving world? All I knew for certain was that Somerville had used me to retrieve the crystal – a task he was unable for some reason to perform himself – and that at all costs I had to prevent it from falling into his hands.

The fate of the earth hung in the balance.

On an impulse, I picked up my briefcase and walked back along the aisle toward the doors.

A guard came through the car announcing our arrival at the 125th Street station, and the train shivered to a halt. The doors hissed open. I stepped out onto the platform into bright sunlight and stood for a moment taking in deep breaths of the sharp, invigorating air. The doors slid shut behind me. As the train began to pull out, I looked around and caught a glimpse of my friend in the gray suit sitting motionless in a window. He saw me and turned his head, pale blue eyes staring, mouth open, his jaw working frantically as if he were trying to say something.

It was 12.30. My appointment with Somerville was for one. I walked down the iron stairs to street level and found a telephone under the elevated tracks. I dialed Heyworth's number. On the other side of the street a man leaning against a red-and-white-striped Coney Island hot dog stand was watching me. I moved deeper into the phone booth, keeping my briefcase close to my body so he wouldn't see the half-inch chain securing it to my belt. I let the phone ring a few times, then hung up.

I waited five minutes. The man across the street moved away. I dialed again. This time it rang only once. Anna answered.

'Don't say anything. Is there anyone else with you? In the room?'

'No, but –' I heard her catch her breath at the sound of my voice.

'Don't say my name.'

'All right.'

'There's a reason for what happened last night. I can't tell you over the phone.'

'Where are you?'

'Uptown.'

'On your way to see Dr Somerville?'

'No. I want you to meet me. Will you?'

'I . . .'

'Anna, *please*. I'm not going to hurt you. We can meet anywhere you say – out in the open, where there are people – anywhere you like. I just want the chance to explain. That's all I ask. Please.'

'Don't you think you should keep the appointment?' Her voice softened. 'You're not well, darling. We can talk later.'

'When you've heard what I have to tell, you may want to change your mind about *Dr* Somerville. *He* killed the boys, Anna – not me. I was just his instrument.'

Silence from the other end.

'Anna?'

'I'm still here. I just . . . I don't know what to say.'

316

'Just say you'll see me. Please say you'll see me.'

Another long pause; then, in a rush, 'All right, I'll see you. I'll meet you at Riverside Church.'

'How soon can you be there?'

'Half an hour.'

'I'll be waiting. Don't tell anyone where you're going. *Anyone.* Do you understand?'

'Yes, all right.'

'I love you.'

'Goodbye, Martin.'

SIXTEEN

It was cold in Riverside Park. A wind out of the north freshened off the Hudson, stirring up piles of dead leaves along the deserted avenue. I looked back at the thin steel-blue line of water glinting through the trees. There was no one around – just a couple of kids playing handball against the graffiti-scarred wall of Grant's Tomb.

I was sitting on a park bench across the street from the church, waiting for Anna's taxi. Every Sunday morning when we lived in the city I used to walk up Riverside Drive with the boys and meet Anna after church. Was that why she'd suggested it?

It seemed a long time ago now.

The cold had begun to penetrate the double layer of clothes I was wearing. I looked at my watch. It was two minutes to one. Still no sign of Anna. Soon enough Somerville would realize that something had gone wrong with his plan. I smiled at the thought of him pacing his study, looking at *his* watch.

I stood up, shivering, and walked slowly toward the church. As I crossed the street the carillon began to peal the hour. I stopped to listen for a moment, gazing up at the bell tower until it seemed to sway against the driving clouds and I began to feel dizzy.

Looking back down, I noticed a figure at the top of the steps. Impassive as one of the Church Fathers carved in the stone over the doorway, he stood quite still, watching me approach. Behind his back the revolving oak door was still spinning.

He was a man of about forty, tall, clean-cut, with an unlined boyish face. He wore blue jeans, sneakers and a tweed jacket with the collar turned up. I recognized him as the priest whom Anna used to call her 'spiritual counselor', and whom I'd dubbed the 'Skypilot'. He was Minister of Outreach at Riverside, though I could never remember his name. The few times we'd met, I'd found him heavy going. For once I was pleased to see him.

'How are you?' He grinned, holding out his hand to me as I mounted the steps. 'It's Martin, isn't it? This is a pleasant surprise. Haven't seen you around in goodness knows how long. How's Anna?'

'Fine,' I said; it was typical that *he* remembered. 'She's just fine.' I wondered if Anna had been in touch with him again.

The hour bell struck a deep, reverberative one. I looked up again at the tower, but it was the sky behind it that seemed to tremble.

'Are you coming in? It's a bit nippy out here. Come in and tell me all your news.'

'I'm here to meet Anna,' I said.

His mild, steady gaze crinkled with affection. He smiled: 'We can wait for her in my office. She'll know where to find us.'

I followed him through the revolving door into the dark, stone-scented interior of the church. It felt as cold inside as out. Signaling me to wait, he strode over to the information desk and said something I didn't catch to the receptionist. I saw her look in my direction and nod. Then he came back across the narthex, his sneakers making a light squeaking noise on the marble floor.

'Someone's booked it for a conference. Let's use the chapel. We'll wait for her there.'

An old woman dressed in black who'd been kneeling by the altar rail rose to her feet and came shuffling down the aisle toward us. We were sitting on hard wooden chairs at the very back of the chapel, conversing in whispers. At her approach the priest sprang up and pushed open one of the heavy bronze doors for her.

The woman murmured, 'Thank you, Father. God bless you.'

The chapel was empty now. Dust motes floated up in the gold-and-blue shafts of light that fell from the stained-glass windows. It reminded me of being in a show cave. I felt like shouting to test the echo.

'I wonder what's happened to Anna,' I said, raising my voice slightly. 'Maybe she's waiting outside.'

'She'll find us, don't worry. I told the girl at the desk to keep an eye out for her.' The priest cleared his throat. 'You said you had something you wanted to ask me.'

'I know I did. Now I'm not so sure . . .' I hesitated. 'I don't mean to be rude or anything – I just don't think you'd understand what I was talking about.'

He shrugged. 'Try me.'

'Even if you did understand, you wouldn't believe me.'

'Aren't you going to give me the chance to find out?'

'Do you believe in prophecy?'

'Oh, dear.' He smiled. 'You mean like the Book of Revelations, or the sayings of Edgar Cayce – that kind of thing?'

'I'll try again. Do you believe in myth?'

'As the revelation of a divine purpose in man, yes. A sort of archetypal truth. Truth out of time, if you like. But not literally.'

'The truth has been revealed to me through what *you* would call a myth. It's turned out to be quite literal.' Then I leaned closer and whispered, 'I have it here, right here in my briefcase: the *proof* of your "divine purpose".'

'Well, you certainly brought it to the right place!' He laughed and held up his hands. 'Okay, I believe you.'

'For Christ's sake!' I turned away. 'I just wanted to see how you'd react.'

'I think I know what you're getting at, Martin.'

'Do you?'

His expression changed to one of concern. 'Anna said you haven't been feeling very well lately. She was here the other day and we had a little chat. She mentioned that you were seeing a psychiatrist. You know, Martin, it can happen to anyone. You won't believe this, but I had to get *my* head straightened out once. I was confused – I mean about what I *really believe.* But I found out that when it comes right down to it there's only one thing we *can* believe.'

'Anna doesn't know a thing about it. I haven't told her anything. The people who say I'm sick are lying. They've been controlling my mind, trying to make me serve their own evil purposes. It's a conspiracy ... to destroy the world. They want something that I have. All I want is sanctuary. Not for myself, you understand. It's for ...'

Suddenly I realized there was no point in continuing.

'Sanctuary?'

'Forget it.'

'I'm afraid we live in rather confusing times, Martin,' the priest said gently. 'The world seems a desperate place right now. I know what you mean when you say you need sanctuary. We *all* do. Try to really understand what's going on out there and, well – as a friend of mine once said – let no one underestimate the *reasonableness* of going crazy.'

'Don't give me that shit, Father. I understand perfectly well what's going on out there. We all know what's coming down, *Father*, we just can't face the fact that it really *is* going to happen. And soon. All the prophecies are coming true.'

'Only in God can we hope to find true understanding.'

'But don't you see, I'm the only one who can *do* anything about it. Anna should be here by now. I'm going to see if she's outside.'

'Wait a little longer. She'll be here soon. Let's kneel and pray together.'

Something in the tone of his voice made me uneasy 'Why are you trying to keep me here?'

'O Lord' he slid forward onto his knees – 'in the darkness of the world's hatred, greed and prejudice, help us to keep alight the flame of love . . .'

His voice echoed sonorously around the bare walls of the chapel.

'Did Anna put you up to this? You were looking for me out there, weren't you? She must have called you – right after I spoke with her.'

I stood up and, stepping across the heels of his sneakers, started toward the door.

'Yes, your wife called me,' the priest said; 'she asked me to say a prayer for you. She loves you very much, Martin.'

SEVENTEEN

She was standing on the steps with her back to the church, gazing out across the park in the direction of Grant's Tomb. I watched her for a moment through the revolving door. At first I thought she was looking to see if I was sitting there on one of the benches. But then she turned, hanging her head, stamping her feet against the cold, and I realized that she was just waiting.

Why didn't she come into the church?

As I put my hand out to push open the door, she started around and our eyes met through the smeared glass. By the look she gave me I knew at once that something was wrong. It was a look of true compassion – a sad, brimming little smile that said it all.

Then across the street I saw the ambulance, a long gray Mercedes without windows, double-parked. The doors opened and two men got out.

Ignoring Anna's faint cry, I turned and ran back to the front desk. I asked the startled-looking receptionist if there was another way out of the church. She just stared at me. Behind her I could see the priest striding along the passage that led from the chapel, his boyish face set like a mask.

Off to the right at the back of the nave, a group of schoolchildren and their teachers were piling into one of the two tower elevators. The other was out of order.

'A ticket for the bell chamber,' I said quickly.

The receptionist froze. Without waiting, I slapped a quarter down on the desk in front of her and made a dash for the elevator, squeezing in behind the last of the children.

As the doors closed, I heard Anna shout, 'Wait, Martin! Wait! It's not what you think.'

*

A fat middle-aged woman in a bright yellow parka stood at the back of the crowded elevator, reading from a pamphlet:

'"The Rockefeller Memorial Carillon occupies the bell chamber at the top of the Riverside Church tower, which rises 392 feet above street level. The elevator goes as far as the twentieth floor, where there is an interesting bell exhibit and antique practice clavier. From there a stairway leads up to the bell chamber and observation platform. There are 147 steps to the top ..."'

She paused and looked up with a long-suffering expression.

'Now, I'm trying to tell you children about the bells. Won't you *please* listen?'

The children, who looked young enough to be in the third grade, continued laughing and talking among themselves. The elevator climbed slowly, making no stops. We were packed in like sardines. With some difficulty I turned around and faced the doors so that my back was to the crowd. Transferring the briefcase to my left hand, I reached inside my coat and undid the clasp that attached the chain to the ring on my belt.

'"The carillon was a gift to the Riverside Church by the late John D. Rockefeller, Jr, in memory of his mother. It contains 74 bells weighing a total of over 100 tons. The Bourdon, which strikes the hours, weighs twenty tons and is the largest and heaviest tuned carillon bell in the world ..."'

After taking a moment to find the right key, I unlocked the briefcase. Holding it close to my chest, I cracked it open a few inches and felt inside for the crystal. As my hand closed over its cold-ribbed surface, a little girl with very black skin and narrow catlike eyes suddenly wormed her way in front of me. She watched intently as I drew the crystal out of the briefcase, slipped it under my shirt and pushed it down inside a pocket of my coveralls.

'What you got, Mister?' she whispered. I shook my head and held a finger to my lips. Then I snapped the briefcase shut and wrapped the loose end of the chain around my fist. The little girl began to back away.

'"Inside the bell chamber there are two rooms, the Machine Room and the Clavier Cabin. The Machine Room contains equipment for automatic operation. The larger bells are equipped with an electro-pneumatic 'assist' to sound swinging peals before worship services and on special occasions. During daylight hours the carillon automatically plays the 'Parsifal Quarters' arranged from the 'Holy Grail' motif in Wagner's opera Parsifal ..." You two at the back, will you stop that *at once*!'

The elevator shuddered and came to a halt.

'Now, there's no need to rush. Let the other people get off first.'

The steel doors slid open, and with loud happy shrieks the children rushed forward. I crossed the hallway ahead of them, looking quickly to right and left. The exhibition room, a light and airy space extending the width of the tower, was deserted. The children, ignoring the polished exhibits around the walls, made straight for a big leather sofa in the corner, piled onto it, and as though it were a trampoline, bounced up and down on the worn cushions. The woman in the yellow parka, who was bringing up the rear, still reading aloud from her pamphlet, yelled at them to get off the church furniture, to show some respect.

Following a sign that said TO THE CARILLON CONSOLE AND OBSERVATION PLATFORM, I walked around to the back of the elevator shaft, where a narrow winding stairway led the remaining hundred forty-seven steps to the top of the tower.

A typed notice pinned to the door marked OFFICE OF THE CARIL- LONEUR announced that the next recital would begin at 1.30. It was past that now, and the bells were silent. From the exhibition room below I could hear the boisterous cries of the school outing. There was no sound coming from inside the carilloneur's office. I tried the door; it was locked.

A couple of flights up, climbing around to the west side of the tower, I found a window on a level with the stairs and looked down. A long way below I was surprised to see the two men still standing in front of the toy-sized ambulance. Somerville must have given them instructions to wait. Then I noticed a row of police cars parked a few blocks south on Riverside Drive, and I realized that they probably had the whole place sealed off by now. He could afford to take his time.

At the top of the stairs, I came to a narrow metal door. It opened outward into a high, windswept chamber filled with machinery – a sighing, clanking labyrinth of pipes and girders that reminded me of a ship's engine room. Rusting iron steps rose, zigzagging, three stories to the roof. Walkways fenced in with green meshed wire crossed the tower at different levels. On a platform overhead I could see the clavier cabin, the hub of the carillon, spoked with wires and wheels, springs, ropes and pulleys that ran out in all directions to operate the bells. There were bells everywhere. Suspended from a framework of steel crossbeams, they were arranged in series according to size, the smallest nearest the roof, growing larger like the blossoms of a gigantic iron hyacinth as they descended through several octaves to the massive bass row, which squatted only a few feet above the chamber floor.

It was bitterly cold up there. In place of windows, latticed embrasures stood open to the sky to let the sound of the bells ring out over the city. The air rushed through from every side, and the tower seemed to rock gently in the wind. At that height the feeling of being exposed to the elements was unnerving. My head swam with vertigo as I reached for the handrail and started to climb.

I stopped on the console deck and looked quickly around, then crossed to the other side of the platform and glanced through the windows of the clavier cabin. There was a man inside sitting at the carillon keyboard with his back turned, reading some sheet music. He was in shirt sleeves and smoking a pipe. Over the thumb and index finger of each hand he wore a protective leather covering – presumably for striking the wooden levers of the keyboard. His small, elderly feet, encased in white sneakers, dangled high over the pedals. There was an electric fire on the wall of the cabin, a couple of framed photographs and a brass clock: I felt I was looking in at someone's home. But the carilloneur wasn't aware he was being observed.

There wasn't much time. My only chance now was to find a place to hide the crystal. They would never put me away until they had it safely in their possession. Maybe they wouldn't think of searching the clavier cabin. I knocked on the glass. The old man turned a page of music, but didn't look up. I knocked again, a little harder.

A voice close behind me said, 'He can't hear you, Martin. I'm afraid Father Ignatius is as deaf as a post.'

I swung around.

It was Somerville, alone, coming down the stairs that led from the roof. The wind tugged at his clothes, making him seem taller and thinner than he was. He looked like a shadow moving down the wall of the tower.

'I thought I might find you up here,' he said casually, as he turned on the bottom step and advanced slowly toward me, smiling, holding out his hands as if to show me that he meant no harm.

I started to back away. 'Don't come any closer. Don't even look at me. I don't want you anywhere near me.'

'Martin, I'm not going to *hurt* you. I just want to talk.'

'Keep away from me, Somerville. I'm warning you.' I moved to the rail, holding up the briefcase in my chain-wrapped fist so that it covered my head like a shield.

'Let's compromise, Martin. You stay where you are and I'll stand over here. We can talk like this at least until the recital begins.'

Avoiding his eyes, I glanced sideways at him. He had taken up a position on the rail farther along the platform, and was leaning over, looking down into the carillon.

He said, 'They're rather beautiful things, bells, don't you agree? Something about the shape that's so satisfying. And that wonderfully evocative sound, "The mellow lin-lan-lone of evening bells." They have an interesting history. Did you know that in the Middle Ages people believed the vibrations of a great bell had the power to drive out demons? They used to use bells to treat the insane. In those days, of course, there was no such thing as "mental illness". People were simply said to be possessed by the Devil.

'As an exorcism, they would tie up the unfortunate person inside a large church bell and leave him there for several days while it was continuously tolled. Lin-lan-lone ... More often than not, the vibrations burst the eardrums and the patient died – which was a cure of sorts, I suppose.'

He laughed.

I looked at him out of the corner of my eye. 'Stay where you are!' I noticed that while we'd been talking he'd edged his way along the rail.

Somerville smiled and shook his head. 'I haven't moved.'

'I suppose now you're going to tell me that things have improved since the Middle Ages, that treatment of the mentally ill has become a little more sophisticated? Where's Anna?'

'She's down below, waiting for you. When you're ready we'll go down and join her.'

'I'm afraid I'm not going down.' I turned suddenly and shouted at him. 'Stay where you are! Don't come a step closer!'

He laughed. 'I really haven't moved. You must be imagining things. Look here, we can do this two ways. Either you come –'

'I know what you want,' I said, and unclipped the other end of the chain from the handle of the briefcase.

'All I want is to help you, Martin. Believe me. Before it's too late. Last night you tried to kill your wife. Doesn't she deserve to be protected? Come down, for Anna's sake. Trust me, Martin. There's nothing to worry about. It'll be like taking a long vacation. And you *need* a rest. You really do need to relax. Just relax . . .'

There was a scent of almonds in the air. I looked up and Somerville was standing at my side. His expression was apologetic, his gray eyes full of kindly understanding. For a moment I thought that I'd made a mistake, that I'd been mistaken about him all along. He reached out a smooth, hairless hand.

I hit him in the face with my mailed fist. He staggered back and fell against the side of the clavier cabin. I saw the blood spurt from his lip and felt momentarily reassured. Then I drew the empty briefcase back and flung it over the handrail as far as I could out into the carillon. It struck a steel girder, slithered off the skirt of a bell, then clattered down to the floor of the chamber.

'If you want the pendant, go fetch it!' I shouted, and started to run. At the top of the stairs I looked back and saw Somerville slowly picking himself up, wiping his bloodied mouth on the back of his hand. At that moment a tremendous peal of bells rang out, followed by another and another and another until the whole tower was filled with jangling thunder.

Father Ignatius had begun his recital.

EIGHTEEN

Just as I reached the bass platform, the door to the bell chamber burst open and a group of schoolchildren came crowding through. They pushed by me with their hands over their ears, shouting and laughing. Immediately behind them a second stream of children flowed up the narrow stone stairway from the exhibition room. I could see the fat woman in the yellow parka heaving her way up, herding more kids before her; I could hear her yelling at the stragglers. There was no room for me to pass. Looking up, I could see the soles of Somerville's shoes through the slatted walkway overhead. He'd almost reached the last flight of iron steps. Why hadn't I hit him harder?

I vaulted a low gate marked NO ADMITTANCE and ran down a broad girder that led between the massive bass bells into the middle of the carillon. As soon as I thought I was out of sight of the platform, I stopped and, using one of the bells for cover, crouched down and looked back underneath its rim.

Somerville was standing on the platform now, surrounded by children. Only the lower half of his body was visible, but it was clear from their faces that he was talking to them. One of them came to the rail and pointed in my direction. It was the little cat-eyed black girl who'd watched my movements so closely in the elevator. She was chattering excitedly, though I couldn't hear what she was saying against that chaos of bells.

Somerville's legs scissored rapidly away from the group. He stopped for a moment by the door to the stairs, as if he were considering going down to get help. Then he seemed to change his mind. With surprising agility he climbed the gate and, ignoring the briefcase, which lay where it had fallen a few feet from the edge of the platform, came along the girder toward me. I saw him draw a small silver object from his coat pocket.

It was a hypodermic syringe.

I should have killed him while I had the chance.

There was no other way out. I glanced up at the nearest cross-beam overhead. Too high for me to reach. Inside the bells, all the way up to the roof, I could see the iron clappers, painted red and white, striking at random as the wires from the clavier cabin jerked their release. Here, at the center of the carillon, the noise was much louder. I jumped down onto the chamber floor and ran across to the second row of basses. Stepping over another girder, parallel to the one Somerville was standing on, I ducked down out of sight. My only hope now was to work my way back to the platform where the children were. He wouldn't start anything if there was a risk of someone else getting hurt.

As I edged my way around the back of the bells, I saw that Somerville had crossed to the second girder ahead of me and was standing there, blocking the path. I looked around in desperation. Off to his right, set apart from the other bells and closer to the wall of the tower, rose the massive dome of the Bourdon. A little way beyond it, an embrasure without a lattice gave a picture-postcard view of the Hudson. I could see the taloned wings of a gargoyle hunched over the top of the window, and in the distance the faint blue outline of the George Washington Bridge. For a moment I considered trying to climb out and pull myself up on the stonework to the observation platform above. But the thought of it made my head spin.

A swinging peal rang down through the bass octave, so loud I had to clap both hands over my ears. I saw Somerville do the same, clutching the silver needle to the side of his head. Breaking cover, I ran out from behind the bass bells, hurled myself down in front of the Bourdon and scrambled underneath.

Inside the barrel of the bell, I climbed up onto one of the two steel struts that raised its twenty tons a few feet off the chamber floor. Protected now from all sides by a six-inch mantle of cast iron, I was confident there was no way Somerville could get at me – unless he tried to follow. As I got my breath back, feeling inside my coveralls to make sure the crystal was still there, and unharmed, I kept my eyes on the bell's flared mouth, which described a wide circle of light around my feet.

I didn't have long to wait. He came in under the far side of the Bourdon, hoping to catch me off my guard, but his shadow gave him away. The moment I saw his head and shoulders appear under the rim, I sprang down on top of his crouched back and knocked him to the ground. As we rolled over, I got one hand to the wrist that held the syringe; the other, with the chain still wrapped around it, found his throat.

Somerville was stronger than I'd expected, but he tired quickly, and I managed to force his hand back against the steel strut until he gave a sharp cry and the hypodermic dropped to the floor. I kicked it away, and it slithered outside the bell's perimeter. Then, getting to my feet, I pulled his head up and held it flat against the inside of the bell.

At that moment there was a small pneumatic hiss immediately above me. Looking up, I saw the enormous iron bulb of the clapper tremble for an instant before it came crashing down against the sound bow of the Bourdon, not a foot from Somerville's head.

The air seemed to explode all around us. I saw Somerville's mouth open. He was screaming, but I heard no sound come out.

As the vibrations subsided, I noticed a thin trickle of blood oozing from his ear. I relaxed my grip on his throat, and he sank forwards onto hands and knees.

'Is this how it's done?' I shouted at him. 'Is this how you drive out the demon?'

He didn't answer. I pulled him up again by the lapels of his coat and dragged him back against the rim of the bell, this time bringing his head into line with the trajectory of the clapper.

'Surely you know this piece of music? How long do you think you have, Somerville, before Father Ignatius plays that note again?'

He began to struggle. I held him fast.

'For God's sake, Martin ...' There was a look of sheer terror in his eyes. 'You don't know what you're doing.'

'And if he doesn't play it, we'll just stay here till the clock strikes the hour. At the most, I'd say you had about three minutes to live. Now tell me – who *are* you? How did you find me?'

'Martin, don't – don't do it. You're sick; you need help.' He brought his hands up and tugged feebly at my wrist in an attempt to loosen the grip on his throat. 'I can't *breathe*.'

'How did you find me?' The veins stood out on Somerville's temples, and the sweat ran down the hollows of his cheeks as he stared ahead of him, transfixed by the iron clapper poised a couple of feet in front of his face.

'I didn't *find* you, Martin. You came to me. For God's sake . . .'

Just then, the music reached a crescendo and the bells began to ring out a series of descending arpeggios, ending successively lower down the scale. I watched Somerville's glistening face as he listened for the final note. There was an abrupt flourish, a pause – and then, finishing on a high resonant chime, the carillon fell silent.

'The recital's over.' I smiled at him. 'What time is it?'

Somerville raised a trembling hand as if to show me his watch, but instead lunged forward and quickly reached inside the pocket of my coveralls. As his hand touched the crystal, I felt a tremendous surge of energy flow through his body. He tried to draw it out, but it wouldn't come. I still had both my hands around his neck. I could feel the loose skin of his throat tighten as he wrenched his head away from the sound bow. He was fighting for his life now, and for a moment I thought he was going to break free.

But I was the stronger now.

From somewhere above us came again that small pneumatic hiss. I closed my eyes, and holding Somerville's head against the iron, waited the eternity it took for the clapper to strike home.

NINETEEN

After it was all over, I stripped off my suit and shirt, wiped my hands on the sleeves, then crawled out from under the Bourdon. The bell chamber was deserted. No one had seen what happened. The school party had gone up to the observation platform on the roof. The ambulance men and police must still be down below, waiting for Somerville's signal – I'd found a beeper attached to his belt, but I guess he never got the chance to use it. I retrieved my briefcase and stuffed my blood-spattered clothes inside it along with the hypodermic and the crystal. The coveralls I'd been wearing under my suit were clean. Then I walked back along the bass platform and made my way down the spiral staircase to the elevators.

The only elevator that worked was already there, waiting. I realized it might be a trap, but I had no choice – there wasn't time for the stairs. I took the elevator down to the third floor, the doors opened and I stepped out into a brightly lit corridor. Fighting the urge to run, I walked quickly through a complex of administrative offices until I reached the east wing of the building. I remembered hearing the fat woman in the yellow parka telling the children about a fallout shelter in the basement. In peacetime, she said, it served as an underground car park.

It was too late now to look for somewhere to hide the crystal. I followed the yellow-and-black signs down the fire stairs and out into the darkened shelter.

At the back of the parking lot I found a white Dodge van with the keys in the dash. I climbed in and started it up. Keeping Somerville's hypodermic on the seat beside me in case I needed a weapon, I drove up the exit ramp, slowed and waved casually to the attendant in the booth. He didn't even look up from his paper. A moment later I was out on the street. I swung north onto Claremont Avenue. In the rearview mirror I could see a police car parked outside the Union Theological Seminary, but for as long as I remained in sight it never left the curb.

On Broadway I turned south and drove directly to Somerville's house, letting myself in with the keys I'd removed from his pockets. I rushed upstairs to get my file from his study and pick up the committal papers that were lying on Penelope's desk. I knew I was pushing my luck now, but I needed the evidence. While I was up there, the phone started ringing. Someone answered it right away – probably the service, but it gave me a bad scare. There was no time to waste. Soon every patrol car in the city would have the license-plate number of the white van, and a description of the driver.

I left it illegally parked on Ninety-sixth Street, took a cab down-town, withdrew some cash from the bank and walked to the Port Authority Bus Terminal, where I bought a ticket on the first bus out. It was going to Atlanta. From there I made my way west – Interstate 40 to Flagstaff, Arizona – then headed up north toward Oregon, where the safe places are.

Since I remain an outlaw, a so-called 'fugitive from justice', I can't afford to give too many details about what happened after that. There was naturally a great uproar over Somerville's death. A nationwide APB was put out for my arrest – news coverage of the story was extensive – and for several weeks I had to keep on the move, roughing it and living in constant fear that someone would recognize me from a photograph and turn me in.

Now that the fuss has begun to die down, I can spend more time in the small towns I pass through. Sometimes, if I like a place, I'll even stay a week or two. Yet I have no desire to settle down anywhere and rejoin the world. Eventually I hope to find some place, in the desert or the mountains, where I can be sure the crystal will come to no harm – where I can keep watch.

I know now that I'll never make them see I didn't kill Somerville, that he *can't* be killed, and that even if he could, there would always be another to take his place. I didn't kill Somerville, I *prevailed* over him.

But I believe the day will come when I can go out of the wilder-ness, and on that day I shall tell the truth, I will tell my story, and men will follow me.

He just wanted a decent book to read ...

Not too much to ask, is it? It was in 1935 when Allen Lane, Managing Director of Bodley Head Publishers, stood on a platform at Exeter railway station looking for something good to read on his journey back to London. His choice was limited to popular magazines and poor-quality paperbacks – the same choice faced every day by the vast majority of readers, few of whom could afford hardbacks. Lane's disappointment and subsequent anger at the range of books generally available led him to found a company – and change the world.

'We believed in the existence in this country of a vast reading public for intelligent books at a low price, and staked everything on it'
Sir Allen Lane, 1902–1970, founder of Penguin Books

The quality paperback had arrived – and not just in bookshops. Lane was adamant that his Penguins should appear in chain stores and tobacconists, and should cost no more than a packet of cigarettes.

Reading habits (and cigarette prices) have changed since 1935, but Penguin still believes in publishing the best books for everybody to enjoy. We still believe that good design costs no more than bad design, and we still believe that quality books published passionately and responsibly make the world a better place.

So wherever you see the little bird – whether it's on a piece of prize-winning literary fiction or a celebrity autobiography, political tour de force or historical masterpiece, a serial-killer thriller, reference book, world classic or a piece of pure escapism – you can bet that it represents the very best that the genre has to offer.

Whatever you like to read – trust Penguin.